This one's for the girls.

A NOVEL BY GINGER SCOTT

Be Wild...
and love the
Reckless!

♡
Ginger Scott

Prologue

The caramel aroma that scented the air was thick. The smells of the Annual Wilson Orchard Apple Fest always began to permeate the streets the night before. Thin lines of smoke trailed from windows and front porches down residential streets of Woodstock, awakening the noses and stirring hungry bellies one at a time until they found the Harper residence.

This was going to be Owen Harper's first year at the festival. His dad took off special from his job at the warehouse just so he could take his middle son to the hometown tradition where the town's best bakers lined up their pies made of the fruits from Old Man Wilson's trees.

Owen liked the pies. He always ate them when his parents or grandparents brought them home. But what he really wanted to do was go on the Ferris wheel. His older brother James had been to the festival twice. James was ten, and he'd always been tall, so he could pass the height requirement easily and ride alone. But Owen was not yet five, so he would need a chaperone. His mother worked long hours, and his father rarely got a weekend off. But today...today was an exception. And today, Owen Harper would ride the Ferris wheel and look out over the town until he could see the roof of his house.

He promised to bring his younger brother Andrew to the festival one day too. He'd be old enough to walk to the festival on his own then, and tall enough to serve as his brother's chaperone—and together they'd both feel like they could fly.

Owen's dad talked to himself a lot. It wasn't anything unusual to Owen. He'd often watched his father have arguments within his own mind, his lips muttering fragments of words over his cereal. He learned to ignore the nonsensical tirades his dad would have with someone who seemed to be invisible while he drove his son to school. And the long hours on the porch at night, when his dad would stare off at nothing for hours at a time—those were routine, too. Owen loved those nights the best, because he would get to lie in the hammock, and sometimes he'd wake there in the morning.

Bill Harper was talking to himself a lot today. And everyone was staring. But Owen didn't understand why. Nothing was unusual.

His father paid their admission, and his son breathed in deeply, his lungs so full of the caramel, cinnamon, and apple fragrances that he was sure he could actually taste them.

His father's hand was rough from working heavy machines for hours every day, and when he pulled his son's hand into his, his skin felt scratchy. Owen didn't care. His own fingernails were chewed away and his palms were dirty from his morning hunt for worms in his mother's garden. He squeezed his father's hand tightly and let his grin stretch the freckles on his cheeks as he took in the sounds of popcorn popping, kids screaming on the roller coaster and carnival workers yelling out from all directions to win prizes.

Everything about today was perfect—just as Owen had dreamt it would be.

Bill Harper pulled his son up to the ticket booth, and stood him next to a hand-painted post. Owen stood tall, stretching out a little and lifting his heels up just enough that the woman checking his height wouldn't notice he was cheating. He didn't want anything to go wrong, and this would be just a little bit of insurance. In the end, he didn't have a reason to worry. He was forty-four inches—two inches taller than the requirement. Still too short to ride alone, but tall enough to ride. And that was all that mattered.

As his dad handed the tickets to the man wearing overalls and working the controls for the Ferris wheel, Owen noticed the people in line behind him staring again. His dad was talking off to the side, arguing with himself over something. But it was nothing unusual. His dad did this—often. Sometimes Owen did it too, because he wanted to see what it felt like.

Their brows were all pinched, and when one woman pulled her two girls in close to her body, away from him and his father, it made Owen angry. He sneered and actually let out a faint growl, which only made the woman hold on more tightly to her girls, who looked like they were about the same age as Owen. Their blond hair was pulled up on either side in pigtails. They

2

wore matching dresses—pink—and they looked afraid. He had scared them, and eventually they left the line.

Owen was pleased.

He forgot all about the angry and frightened faces as soon as his carriage lifted from the platform and he and his father climbed higher in the air. The wind was colder up there, and everything about the day smelled like Halloween. It was morning, so the lights weren't on for any of the festival rides, but it didn't matter to Owen. The earth looked magical from up above.

While their cart was paused at the top, Owen twisted in his seat, counting rows of trees and buildings until he was sure he had the right road in his view. He counted chimneys to seven. And then he was sure he found it. He turned back around when the wheels started to spin again, satisfied that he could now check off the box in his mind—the one to see his house from up above.

He wanted to show his father. But Bill Harper was talking to himself. His son had learned it was better not to interrupt. He'd wait. His turn to talk would come eventually.

It always did.

After four more pauses, every carriage on the wheel was full, and the ride began its first full circle, the speed faster than Owen had expected. It was a little scary, and he wanted to hold his father's hand, but Bill Harper was still talking, his hands flying in front of him in various directions while he argued with someone—the person Owen could never see.

The air was cold when the wheel hit its top speed, so the young boy pulled the zipper up on his jacket with one hand, his other hand gripping the bar in front of him tightly. As he leaned forward, he noticed the woman with the two blond girls standing below, and he thought about spitting. He didn't, but he chuckled to himself when he pictured it.

His dad would think that was funny. He liked things like that. Bill Harper was very much a boy—he liked dirt, and messes, and swear words and beer. Owen wanted to grow up to be just like him.

By the third pass of the wheel, Owen was no longer nervous, and he loosened his grip on the bar in front of him. He wasn't brave enough yet to stretch his arms out, but he could close his eyes. With his head tilted toward the sky, he smiled big and shut his eyes tightly, letting the crisp air sting his face. With each pass along the ground, he heard the laughing and yelling of more people entering the festival, and the closer his cart climbed to the sky, the fainter those sounds became, until they started up again.

This was going to be the best memory of his life. He knew it.

His car paused at the very top while the riders on the other end of the wheel exited their carts. His ride was over. It was perfect.

When his father reached around and unclipped the latch, Owen didn't flinch. His dad worked with machines all day. He had worked with them for years. He knew what he was doing. He didn't make a sound when his father stood up, reaching for the long support beam above them. He held on tight when the cart swung forward. His father didn't tell him to, he just knew he was supposed to. He wouldn't want Owen to fall out.

It wasn't until his father took his first step out onto the beam below that Owen knew something was wrong. And then he saw the face of the woman below. He heard one of the little girls scream. Owen's world shifted, and everything began happening in slow motion. He slid his body to the place where his father had just been sitting, he reached his tiny hand—the one scuffed with dirt and scratched from trees—out to grip his father's leg, hoping he could just reach the denim of his jeans...reach anything. He reached, and reached, and reached. But no matter what, Owen was too small, his arm not yet long enough.

He tried to scream, but no sound would escape his mouth. His lungs felt flat. His stomach felt sick. This was no longer going to be his favorite day.

His father's boots gripped the beam, and his large hands held on to the large steel bar above him. He was moving slowly down, closer to the center of the Ferris wheel. He was moving down, and that was the only thing that made Owen feel okay.

The words of the carnival worker were a blur. He heard the man who ran the ride speaking over a loudspeaker, but he couldn't quite make out what he was saying.

Owen turned behind him to see if someone was coming to help, but that cart was empty. The one below him was full, and he could see a man with two kids sitting still, watching Owen's father climb out into the center of the wheel, his hands letting go every so often to point while he yelled.

Bill Harper was yelling. He was yelling at someone who was invisible, someone who couldn't be heard yelling back. He was pointing at him, shoving him, laughing wildly, and then crying.

Then he took a step, and Bill Harper fell to the earth.

In the end, all anyone could seem to talk about was how sad it was that Carolyn Potter's apple pie went to waste that year.

Owen never went to the festival again.

And he'd make damn sure his baby brother never went either.

13 Years Later

Chapter 1

"Kensington! Come downstairs! Your sandwich is ready!"

We've been in the suburbs—no, *the country!*—for less than six hours, and already my mom has morphed into some form of June Cleaver. I half expect to walk down the steps and see her in one of those poufy A-line dresses with a pretty bow cinched about her waist.

She's been walking on eggshells with me ever since we handed over the keys to our old home. I didn't want to move here. Nothing about this move is about me though. And that's why my mom is playing up the *nice.* Not that she isn't normally nice. Normally, she isn't really there at all. Mom's the head nurse practitioner at a major hospital in Chicago. Dad's a conductor and a music professor in Milwaukee. He was just promoted to the head of the department. So we moved here...to the middle. Woodstock—exactly halfway between the two. "An ideal and convenient location," everyone said.

Convenient.

Far.

Lonely.

My two best girlfriends are starting their first day of senior year at Bryce Academy today. My old school. In the city. I wanted to stay. Mom didn't like me taking the train on my own, though. So I'll have to live vicariously through the pictures and texts they send. This morning's was a shot of Gaby frowning by my old locker. Morgan tried to get her face in the shot too, but all I caught was her ear. She was terrible at taking selfies. I miss them. But there's some strange comfort in visual proof that they miss me too.

It's hot here in the summer—hotter than in the city. There are more bugs, and the grass is itchy. It's green everywhere, and I'm not really used to that either. The houses all seem...*old.* Everyone has a front porch, and driveways that stretch into these enormous garages that sometimes aren't even attached to the houses at all. That's going to suck when it snows.

"Kensington!" Mom yells again, her voice less bubbly than before. The edge in her tone makes my lip tick up into a faint smile; I prefer her being real.

"I'm coming!" I yell, sending a quick heart image message to my two friends, then shoving my phone into my back pocket. I pause at the stairs to look out over the vast emptiness that is my new home. Our things are trickling in, but everything seems swallowed up by this house. It's not like the brownstone we lived in just south of Wrigley. Everything there was tight, and cramped, but it all had its place. Everything was at home. *I* was at home.

And now I'm here.

"Put the piano in the dining room...yes...about there. Perfect. Thank you," my mom says, quickly removing the sheets and pads from my piano. I think she thinks unveiling it quickly will somehow make me happy, like she's just pulled a bouquet or chocolates out of a hat.

"Where are we supposed to eat?" I ask, looking at my piano as it sits squarely under the dated, brass chandelier of our new dining room—like the world's cheapest spotlight. I had a practice room before, in our old house. Nothing fancy, just a door that I could close anytime I wanted.

I miss that door.

"We have a breakfast bar in the kitchen. It's fine. It looks nice there, doesn't it?" she asks without really asking. She walks back to the kitchen, her half-eaten sandwich dangling from her hand.

I think my piano looks stupid there. I think it looks stupid anywhere but in its home back in Chicago. But this isn't really about what I think, so I keep my mouth shut and follow my mom's footsteps into the kitchen where a ham sandwich sits alone on a gigantic white plate. The wastefulness amuses me, and I lift my sandwich, brush away the single crumb, and put the perfectly clean plate in the dishwasher.

"Thanks," I say, holding it up and taking a bite. Mom purses her lips, but she goes back to her lunch in front of her computer at the counter.

My mom finishes her sandwich quickly and without much conversation, then begins carrying boxes from the garage to various rooms around the house. Everything has a label: TOWELS, DISHES, CLEANING SUPPLIES, MOVIES, and KENSI for the few boxes that go to my room. I haven't been called Kensi or Kens out loud in years. I miss that too.

The kitchen has more boxes than I do; most of my things are still in the back of the Honda. My music books were already here and waiting for us when we unlocked the doors this morning. Dad brought them on his way to the office, afraid they'd get misplaced or damaged during the move. I could never say this to him, but there are only a few pages in that box that I really care about—the ones with notes I wrote, for me, for my ears and heart to hear.

I've been playing the piano since I was about three. My grandmother left my mother her old piano when she died, and I somehow knew what to do with it the moment the movers left it in our home. I couldn't reach the pedals, and my fingers barely spread far enough to strike a chord, but I could hear something and instantly mimic the sound. Music came to me before most of my words, and my father was quick to nurture my gift.

Dad plays brass instruments, so he always sought out the help of others to instruct me. My first music teacher was no longer able to teach me after a year, and I outgrew the next by the time I was ten. I've been studying with Chen ever since. He's a music composition professor at the University of Chicago and has scored many of the independent shows that play in the theaters downtown. My father hired him to give me private lessons, to challenge me and make it impossible for the best programs in the country to ignore me and "my gift." But what my father doesn't know is that when Chen comes over—while he's not at home—we play jazz.

Now that we're out of the city, I'll only be able to see Chen once a month, unless I take the train into Chicago on my own. My dad expects me to step up my independent playing. He even went as far as to make sure my extra periods at school were all time in the music room.

I think of everything I miss because of this move, my afternoon jazz with Chen is what I lament the most. It's been replaced by a gilded light fixture and a soaring ceiling that will make my playing echo out into the streets. It will be impossible to run away from the sounds my fingers will be forced to make. But I will practice, and I'll play the Bachs and the Mozarts and the Beethovens—those seemingly impossible songs that have become habits for my hands. I'll practice because that's what my father expects, and if I meet his expectations, he'll support my decision to study in New York or...or Paris or London or Rome. Anywhere...but here.

And then, I'll be free.

Unable to avoid reality any longer, I finally give in and venture to the driveway and the open hatch in the back of the Honda where most of my belongings still rest in taped-up cardboard boxes. My clothes are all stuffed into pillowcases; the wrinkles will have to be dealt with later.

With the last box wedged between my hip and the bumper, I reach up to slam the hatch closed again. The dark pair of eyes staring at me from the other side of the car make me jump—effectively dropping my boxes to the ground, spilling clothes and books and random trinkets from my girlfriends.

On instinct, I bend down to gather everything back into my arms, expecting help with my now disorganized load. Instead, I hear the steady drumming of a basketball along the pavement, and when I bend down just a little lower, I see his gray Converse slide slowly away from me, up our driveway toward the garage.

"Unbelievable," I whisper to myself as I stand with only half of my things, relenting the fact that I'm now going to have to make two trips. My red sweater is barely clinging to my grip, one sleeve dragging along the ground as I cross the driveway to my backdoor. My new neighbor keeps his back to me the entire time, his focus on the slow dribble of his ball. I give him a good long stare as I push my ass into the door a few times, my free fingers fumbling for the handle, desperate to get it open.

"Thanks for helping," I whisper again, following it up with the word *asshole* in my head.

Suddenly, his dark eyes are on mine, and I would swear he heard me with the smug smirk that creeps into one cheek. The ball never stops moving. His hand never stops moving. He's operating completely independent of the hypnosis he's attempting to put me under—the soft squint to his eyes somehow making them more ominous. I'm not quite sure he isn't evil. And I'm also not quite sure that this hypnosis isn't working.

A gift, the door behind me unhinges and I stumble backward inside, somehow catching my balance so I don't make a complete ass out of myself in front of mister darkness.

I race upstairs quickly, tossing my pile of things on my bed without care, hurrying to the window to orient myself with exactly what my view is in relationship to the driveway. With one push of the curtain, I know.

His eyes are right back to me, almost as if he were expecting me to look—expecting me to find him. The damned smirk on his face is still there, and my heart is thumping away at my stomach, not so much from flutters...as panic. The ball is still in motion, and I can't help but beg myself to remember the sight of him, so I can think about it later and decide if he's really as scary as my instincts tell me he is.

His white T-shirt V-necks, and the sleeves hug his biceps. He's wearing long black basketball shorts, and his hair is short, but long enough on top for the strands to twist in various directions. From a distance, he's a really good-looking guy. But I have a feeling—and a fear—that it's his eyes that hold the power. From fifteen feet up and fifty feet away, they literally smolder. If I weren't such a social pariah, I would march back down the stairs and introduce myself. I'd ask him why he's dribbling a ball in my driveway, using the hoop bolted to the eave of *our* garage. But my feet are stuck to the carpet of my new bedroom, and my hands are burning from the roughness of the curtains my hand is now squeezing.

When I think I can't handle much more, his lip twitches, and then he blows me a kiss and turns around to shoot the ball into the hoop.

What. The. Hell. Was. That?

I let go of my grip on the curtain and fall to my knees, wishing there was some way I could erase the last five minutes of my life. Instead, I slide so my back is against the window's wall, so I can't see him, only hear the rhythmic thump of the basketball for the next twenty minutes.

When I feel safe enough to look again, I crawl to my knees and peel the curtain fabric back an inch. The hoop is quiet. The driveway is quiet. Now is my chance.

Racing to the driveway, I scoop up the remaining things that I left there before and close the hatch to the car. I don't glance at his house, and I don't dwell long enough to know anything for certain. But I am positive that the front door was open—the inside of the house barely hidden behind a thin porch screen.

And I'm pretty sure my mystery neighbor from hell was standing there...watching.

Chapter 2

Yesterday was registration. I missed it. Too busy with the move for my mom to find the time to drive the two point five miles to Woodstock South. I don't have a car. I barely have a license, so borrowing a car without one of my parents in the passenger seat is out of the picture too. And two point five miles—while not far with wheels—is a hell of a long way by foot.

So I begin Woodstock South High School today—completely and utterly lost.

Dad dropped me off on his way to Milwaukee. It was early enough that I was able to get the printout of my schedule from the front office and find my way to the music room. My first two periods are music—the first one with the band as a whole, and the second one is independent study. This is the only part my father made sure of. The rest, me getting into honors English and math, was all my doing, all the result of my persistent emailing to my guidance counselor to ensure I was not trapped in a public school classroom with burnouts.

This is the first year I've gone to school without a uniform. I know most girls my age would love the rebellion of this, the freedom to choose, to find a *look* all their own.

I miss my uniform.

Uniforms are easy. No decisions to make. Instead, I spent the first half hour of my morning switching from jeans to leggings and back to jeans again. It's fall in Illinois, the leaves are changing, and the winds come and go.

I'm glad I settled on the jeans now as I stand outside the band room door, my knuckles pink and tender from rapping on it repeatedly, hoping someone will let me inside.

"You in, Harper?" I hear a male's voice behind me, rounding the corner. I'm unable to stop myself from turning to see who it is. Soon I'm looking right into the eyes of my mysterious neighbor, the one I named *Demon Spawn* last night as I worked myself up over how cocky and rude he was in the driveway. His lip ticks up, and his eyes squint when he notices me, but he looks away fast.

"You know it! Let me just...make an appearance," he says, pounding his knuckles with the first guy to speak. The group of four guys passes me, and the demon never glances my way again. Once they're a few steps away from entering the main hall doors, I hear them erupt in laughter, drawing my eyes to them again, expecting them to all be looking at me—teasing the new girl.

But they're not. They disappear behind the doors seconds later, and finally the band room door opens and I slip inside.

"Oh my god, how long have you been waiting out here? I'm so sorry; we never hear the door in the morning. It's too loud in here," says a girl with reddish blond hair piled into a bun on top of her head. She's wearing tight black jeans and a black hoodie, and her gloves are missing their fingers. She almost looks tough, except her face is dotted with freckles and her breath smells like strawberry from the giant wad of gum she's popping through her smile.

"Not long. It's okay," I lie. I was out there knocking for a solid five minutes, but this girl seems nice.

"Oh, good. Here, come on in. I'll introduce you to Mr. Brody," she says, waving me forward. I drop my backpack next to the others that are piled by the door. The room is full of noise—saxophones, trombones, flutes—everyone tuning.

"I'm Willow, by the way," she says, reaching out her hand. I shake it and notice how cold her fingertips feel compared to the knitted part of her hand still covered by a glove.

"Nice to meet you. I'm Kensington," I start, but pause, struck instantly by the realization that as much as I don't want to be here, it is a new beginning. And new beginnings do have their perks. "But people call me Kensi."

"Kensi...cool! I like that!" she says, her enthusiasm maybe a little obnoxious. I like her anyway.

"Mr. Brody, I found Kenny," she says, already blowing my new identity, as I trail behind her into a small office to the side of the main band room. A small man stands at my introduction. He's maybe four or five inches shorter than I am, and his glasses are propped on top of his head, which barely has any hair. He's eating a donut, so he finds a tissue on his desk and rests the half-eaten treat on it before dusting his hands for crumbs along his gray pants.

"Kensington Worth, yes. Glad you found the room!" he says, his glasses falling right into place on his nose.

"People call her Kenny," Willow interjects for me. She's assertive, oddly so. I like her a little more, and I'm starting to hope she'll be my friend. I could use a dash of assertive.

"Actually, it's *Kensi,*" I correct.

"Ohhhh, yeah. Sorry, Kensi," Willow says, her face embarrassed at her slip.

"Well, all-righty then. Kensi it is," Mr. Brody says, popping the full other half of his donut in his mouth as he ushers us back into the main room. "So, Kensi...what's your instrument?"

I'm puzzled by his question. This should have been settled. I play the piano. My dad made sure everyone in this entire school system knew I played the piano. And he made sure everyone knew they were to accommodate my need to play, whenever he demanded.

"Piano?" It comes out unsure.

"Right, right. I know that. I mean for band, for marching. You can't really march with a piano." I heard him, but inside I was hoping maybe there was a way I could rewind—reverse myself right back outside the door, back home, back through my boxes, and back to the city.

Marching.

What the hell was I going to do?

"I...I don't know. I don't really *play* anything else. And I don't...march," I say, looking around the room as the hundred or so students begin to file into chairs based on the instruments they play. Yeah...there are no *piano* groups here.

"No problem. We'll make you a pit player," he says, shrugging his head to the left for me to follow him.

"Pit...player?" I ask, but I start to understand the closer we get to the percussion instruments. "Here's a pair of mallets. You'll find your way around the xylophone in no time. You sight read?"

"I do, but..." I start to protest, suddenly aware that he's walking away and mallets are now in my hands.

The xylophone is essentially a piano. The keys are all the same, only you strike them with sticks. I used to love playing on them at my father's office when I was young. But I haven't played one in years.

"Hey, I'm Jess," says one of the guys standing near me. I shake his hand and repeat his name in my head over and over again. *Jess, Jess, Jess. Willow, Willow, Willow.* I know two people here now.

"Hi, I'm Kensi. I guess I'm playing xylophone," I say through a nervous smile.

"Yeah, looks like it," he says, bending over and pulling a harness for a snare drum over his head. "Welcome to the drum line."

"You about ready, babe?" Willow says over my shoulder, causing me to turn and pinch my brow, wondering how I got moved to *babe* so quickly. My question is answered when she brushes by me and pulls Jess's face toward hers and kisses him quickly.

"Sure. Let's get this pep-rally shit over with," Jess says, spinning one of his drumsticks over his head, his eyebrows raised, feigning enthusiasm.

"Pep...rally?" I say, just as Mr. Brody drops a flipbook of music on top of the xylophone. *My* xylophone now, so it would seem.

"Yep, first day of school always starts in the gym. Pep rally. It's our thing," Willow says, pressing a whistle between her lips and blowing hard. "Let's go, peeps. Meet you in the gym in six minutes!"

"She's the drum major. She likes the power trip. Normally she's a flute player. Flutes suck! I get it. And her uniform is pretty hot, so...ya know," Jess says, winking at me. He's a typical drummer—shaved head, double piercings in his ears, chain dangling from his back pocket.

Everyone is packing up, lugging their instruments out the door, and I feel like my chest is caving in on me, as if my rib bones are actually cracking into pieces and stabbing my heart and other internal organs. I glance quickly at the booklet of music in front of me. Fight song, national anthem, a bunch of top-forty tunes. Yeah, it's all pretty simple stuff. If I can sight-read Beethoven, I should be able to read this.

"Jess!" I catch him before he steps through the door. "How...how do I get *this* to the gym?"

He grins at me, then slides his sunglasses on. "You push it," he laughs, then lets the door close behind him.

Fucking drummers.

Right. Push it. Okay, I can do this. I tuck the music book under the first layer of keys and then shove the mallets into my back pocket. I slide the wheels back and forth a few times to make sure they're not locked, take a deep breath, and push what is *so very much not a piano* to the doorway.

I'm the last one in the room, so I fling the door open, hold it with my hip and then back the xylophone out, banging nearly every key on the door jam as I do it. Then it hits me. I don't know where the gym is.

I don't know where the gym is!

There's a natural flow of students walking down a hill, so I follow them. And when I start to see instruments in a few hands, I sigh with relief.

The doors to the gym are within sight. Unfortunately, Demon Spawn and his group of friends are also nearby, almost guarding the door. My inner voice is wishing he won't notice me, but the awkward new student is hoping one of them will help me inside and hold open the door.

Neither wish is granted, and his eyes land squarely on me, his lip doing that twitching thing again that lets me know he sees me. It also lets me know he isn't going to be of any help at all.

I'm lifting the front wheels down a level on the sidewalk and am only a dozen or so yards from the entrance when I look at him again to catch him nod a laugh to his friends—just before he kicks his foot toward me, covering my pathway in gravel.

It doesn't take long for one of the tiny stones to wedge itself into one of the wheels, causing a high-pitched screeching sound and leaving a long, chalk-like skid for the few feet I drag my frozen wheel along the walkway. I stop, bend down, and push the rock out with the back of my mallet, my face burning from the attention. When I stand again, he's looking at me—laughing.

"You're an asshole," I say, which only makes his lip twitch again.

"Hey, sorry, this is hard to haul alone," Willow says, opening up the door and staring down Demon Spawn. "Not every guy at this school is a douchebag. Most of them help a girl out when she needs it."

My demon neighbor slowly raises his hand, holding up a middle finger before blowing her a kiss.

"In your dreams, Owen," she fires back.

Willow grabs the front of my keyboard and helps me guide the xylophone inside, all the way to the far end of the gym where the band is now set up.

"Thanks," I say, and I mean it. So far, this first day has sucked epic proportions.

"No sweat," she says, leaning against the wall next to me.

I recognize the principal from my visit to the office this morning to get my schedule. He taps on a microphone a few times and then begins to say a few announcements, something about busses, student parking, lunch hours—none of this applies to me. Of course, an hour ago, a xylophone didn't apply to me either.

When I look to my right, I notice Demon Spawn, who I guess is *really* named Owen, shuffle along the front of the bleachers until he and his friends are almost next to me. He chuckles lightly when he's near me, then turns to climb to the top of the bleachers. Maybe I imagine hearing his arrogant laugh, but I sort of don't think I do.

"What's his story?" I whisper to Willow.

"Who, Owen?" she asks.

"I guess. That's his name?" I respond.

"Yeah. That's Owen Harper. He's...well...he's a dick. Sorry, hope you're not offended by that word," she says, covering her mouth, like she's trying to be demure. I like Willow. She's direct and funny, and she seems like she's fine with who she is. She reminds me of Gaby and Morgan.

"I'm from the city. I've heard worse," I smile, and she leans into me.

"Cool. Okay, well then…he's a major fucking dick!" she laughs, and I join her.

"Right. I think I already had that much figured out. Rocks kicked at me sorta clinched my hunch, but thanks," I whisper to her, trying not to interrupt the rest of the principal's speech.

Willow shrugs, then kicks off from the wall to stand in front of the band after the principal tells everyone to rise and remove their hats. I note the key that they're playing in, and leave my music tucked away. I know the national anthem, so I won't have to read this one. The fight song is going to be a different story though.

Near the end of the song, I allow myself to glance in Owen's direction, and he and his friends are all standing still with their hats against their chest, respectful of this, at the very least. I don't know why, but for some reason I'm relieved that he's not *that* much of an asshole.

We play two or three more songs before the football team is announced, and I manage to figure out the fight song quickly, playing along. My dad would throw a fit if he knew this is how my first period of music was going. I'm kind of having fun, though, so I don't think I'll tell him.

Willow helped me haul the xylophone back to the band room, and Owen wasn't around to kick any more speed bumps under my legs. In fact, he seemed to disappear entirely after the pep rally this morning.

My second period was blissful, spent alone in one of the music practice rooms. I cheated on my lessons and instead spent the hour playing jazz. My next two classes were less pleasant. Part of being placed in honors math and English meant I could expect homework right out of the gate, which I got—several chapters of reading and a lengthy problem set.

What I didn't expect was to hear the teacher call out "Owen Harper" in both of my classes. Harper—I'm pretty sure that's his last name. That's what that one guy called him when they walked by me early this morning. He didn't strike me as an *honors* kind of anything.

By the time the lunch hour rolls around, my stomach is growling so loudly that I'm sure people near me in the hallway can hear it.

"There you are. How were your morning classes?" Willow asks. She's a junior, so I don't have any classes with her.

"All right, I guess. I have homework already," I say, and she scrunches up her face in disapproval.

"Yeah, me too," she says.

I follow Willow to the cafeteria and mimic everything she does. I grab a tray, shuffle along the counter, and pull the same sandwich, apple, and drink from the coolers that she does. I won't be able to copy her for long; I get a feeling she eats kind of healthy, and I'm going to have to delve into the pizza and fries line one day this week.

We both punch in our numbers for the lunch account and take our trays to a table near the window where Jess is waiting for us along with another couple I recognize from band this morning. Everyone sits—everyone...but me. I'm frozen, locked into where I'm standing, my elbows somehow unable to operate well enough to place the tray on the table in front of me.

On the other side of the glass, Owen Harper is kissing a girl. She seems pretty—her hair a long, dark brown, very different from my wavy blond layers. I try to notice more about her, but I can't take my eyes off the place where his hands are cupped around her face, holding her lips to his with this animalistic sense of ownership. It's almost offensive, but it's also...*something else.*

His right hand slowly slides into her hair, and he tilts her face ever so slightly to one side, giving his mouth a better angle, as his lips grow more aggressive. I'm hypnotized by the power he has over her—over *me.* His lips move over her mouth with a sense of possession, and his grip on her upper lip with his teeth slides away with a slowness that simply oozes sex. I'm blushing—just standing here, a voyeur, and I'm blushing.

I have never been kissed like that. *I have never really been kissed at all.*

He moves down her neck next, his tongue blatantly sliding along the nape then under her jaw. Their friends are all standing nearby, but nobody is looking. I'm stunned no one else is seeing this. His hands are now clutched around her head and body, her shirt twisting up enough to reveal her bare midriff. It's almost a soft porn show in front of the main window for the whole cafeteria to see. Yet, I'm the only one looking.

And then his eyes open, in a purposeful haze, and he looks. Right. At. Me.

My heart stops. My stomach feels sick, and my lip puffs out with the small gasp that escapes me from the shot of adrenaline now coursing through me from getting caught.

Owen never stops kissing. His eyes toy with me for the brief seconds I stand there in shock. He's laughing with those eyes. He's teasing me—as if he knows that I am so far out of my comfort zone that I may pass out from humiliation at any moment. But I don't. I look right back at him. I can't help myself. And his eyes soften, but not in a gentle way. They become sexier, more daring—he's daring me. *Keep watching; go ahead.* That's what his eyes are saying now. The gray color suddenly looks like a storm brewing, and I'm caught in it, no chance for survival.

"Earth to Kens! We're down here. Tell them to get a room!" Willow says, pulling at the edge of my shirt, yanking me down into my seat, away from the danger tempting me on the other side of the window.

"Sorry, that was...huh...I just guess couples never really did that sort of thing at my old school. You know...so...out in the open?" I say, forcing my eyes onto my tray.

"Oh, they're not a couple. Owen just does that sometimes. And girls keep lining up. Like lemmings," says the small girl sitting with us. Her hair is cut into a sharp bob cut, and her eyes are lined in smoky-gray eye shadow. It's a look I wish I could pull off, just once. "I'm Elise, by the way. I play the flute. And this is Ryan. He doesn't play anything, but I like him anyway."

Ryan shrugs and gives a quick smile before turning his attention back to whatever seems to be interesting him on his phone. Elise ribs him with her elbow, and he rolls his eyes and puts his phone down on the table to give me a proper smile before turning back to her. "There, satisfied?" he says.

She looks at him with wide eyes, then turns back to me. "Ryan is my *ex* boyfriend. I just dumped him because he was rude to my new friend Kensi," she says, and Ryan sighs deeply, this time putting his phone back in his pocket and standing with his hand outstretched.

"Sorry, just stressed. I'm waiting to hear about a college thing. And I'm *not* an asshole, despite what she says," Ryan says, tilting his head toward Elise.

I shake both of their hands across the table, and spare a glance back out the window as I do. The make-out session seems to have ended, but Owen is still looking at me. His arm is slung around the girl's shoulders, and his thumb is caressing her bare skin.

"It's because the Harper brothers have wild hearts," Willow says. For some reason, her statement sparks a collective sigh from her friends. "What? You guys know it's true."

"No, Will. None of us know it's true. We just humor you. And you know I hate it when you start talking this mystical crap," Jess says, standing with his empty tray. "Anyone need anything to drink? I'm not sure I can hear the *wild heart* speech one more time."

Willow pulls a pinch of crust from her sandwich and throws it at Jess before he turns to leave. He catches it at his stomach and throws it back, smirking while he does. "All right, I'll be back in about seven minutes. That's how long this usually takes," he says. Willow squints her eyes at him and shakes her head as he leaves.

"Wild hearts?" I ask, bringing her back to the point. I'll admit, I'm curious.

"Willow thinks because she was *there* when it all happened— that she knows, has some sort of inside knowledge on why the Harper boys are so fucked up," Elise says, pulling open a bag of chips. She offers me one, but I shrug it off. I'm too intrigued by this story now to eat.

"There's more than just Owen?" I ask, wondering why the house next door always seems so quiet.

"Yep, there are three. Owen's the middle brother. His older brother James is a real loser—total druggie. And his younger brother Andrew is a freshman. You'll see him around sometimes," Elise says.

My stomach sinks a little knowing that there are more of them living next door to me, and I turn to look out the window again. Owen's attention is finally on his friends, but his arm is still around that girl, his thumb still stroking her arm like he's keeping her on a leash, reminding her that he's here and he'll get back to her later.

"So drugs...is that what makes them *wild*?" I ask.

"Ohhhhh no," Willow says, piling the remnants of her sandwich and the half-eaten apple up on her tray. "That happened later. And I'm pretty sure it's just James that's a druggie. Their problems started a long time ago, though."

Willow scoots forward, glancing once over her shoulder, and I feel like I'm learning some dark secret. With a slightly lowered voice, she starts to explain. "We were five, maybe not quite. And there used to be this carnival that happened every year—the apple fest. Well, I was there with my cousins, because they usually had cool rides and games and stuff. I was in line waiting for my turn to throw the rings at the bottles when my aunt grabbed ahold of my arm and pulled me close to her body. She was trying to shield my eyes, but she was too caught up in everything happening to do a very good job. I saw everything."

"I'm confused. What to you mean? What did you see?" I ask. Willow's storytelling sucks. I'm starting to understand why Jess left. I'd leave too if I already knew how this ended. But I don't; so I'm glued to my seat.

"Well, Owen's dad was Bill Harper. He was sort of known as the town's crazy man. He talked to himself and did a lot of weird things—like posting strange signs in the back of his car telling people to leave him alone. Anyhow, apparently he finally snapped, and when my aunt pulled me away from the games, I looked up at the Ferris wheel, where everyone else was looking, and I saw Bill Harper standing out on one of the steel beams, about a hundred and fifty feet in the air. He was yelling out these crazy things; none of it made sense."

"What does this have to do with Owen?" I ask, my periphery catching a glimpse of my tall, mysterious neighbor still standing outside.

"He was there. He was on the ride, in the cart, when his dad walked out of it, stepped out to the edge, and jumped. He killed himself right there in front of Owen. And the Harper boys have been ruined ever since," she says, and I can't help but hurt a little thinking of Owen as a little boy. I wonder what he was like then. And I wonder if Willow's right—if he would have been different, wouldn't have kicked rocks at me or would have helped me carry my things inside if he hadn't been damaged.

"They're not *ruined*," Ryan finally says. "Owen's a good guy. He just has to trust you; that's all."

"You're just saying that because he's on the basketball team with you. You have to say that because he's so good," Willow says.

"Yeah, he's good. But honestly? He's always been pretty decent to me. Maybe I've just never labeled him though," Ryan says. I take note of the hint of disappointment in his tone over how Willow is talking about Owen, and it makes me wonder where the truth lies.

"He has an arrest record," Willow says, a little defensively.

"Fuck, Will, so do I! Half this school has some sort of something on their record. We drive too fast, we get caught at parties with beer, we steal shit from the convenience store. It's what we do because there's shit-squat to do out here," Ryan says, standing and kissing Elise on the head. "I'm just saying maybe we're all a little fucked up, and the only difference is the world knows Owen's story, because it happened out in the open. The rest of us...we all just keep our shit private."

Elise doesn't add anything to Ryan's speech, but she looks at her boyfriend with a sort of reverence when he speaks. With trays in their hands, they slide from the table together, leaving just Willow and me now to finish the story.

"I guess Ryan's sort of right," she says, slipping her backpack over her shoulders and nudging me to do the same so we're not late for class. "But...I don't know, Kens. That guy? He has some extra crap going on. He lives on the edge, like he doesn't have fear or something. I've heard he's played that game, Russian roulette...you know, where people take turns holding a gun up to their heads with only one bullet inside? He does that at parties. I don't think that's normal, do you?"

I shake my head *no* when she asks. No, that's not normal. And I think I knew the first time I looked into his eyes that there was nothing normal about Owen Harper. But what scares me is I had this flash of an idea—a fleeting thought—that there was something special about him, too.

When I dump my trash and stack my tray, I hold the door for Willow to walk through. I sneak one final look to the courtyard outside. Owen's hand has finally dropped from the girl's arm, and he and a group of five other guys and girls are walking away—away from the school completely.

He's wearing gray jeans, black Doc Martens, and a tight black, long-sleeved shirt that fits his frame perfectly. From a distance, he's a shadow. I don't know about the *wild* theory. But Owen Harper is definitely dark.

And he sleeps thirty feet away from me.

Chapter 3

Why did he bother to show up at all? Why did he leave after lunch? Why did he miss his classes on the first day of school?

Who did that?

I can't quit thinking about what Willow said. Ditching classes, three at least as far as I could tell from his absence during roll call in science, and flaunting his make-out sessions aren't exactly things I would consider *wild.* But that last thing she said—about playing roulette with a loaded gun—I couldn't seem to wrap my mind around that. It frightened me, and it made me dread going home, being *near* someone who could do that.

Mom was working the late shift at the hospital, and Dad wouldn't be home until late in the evening, so I was going to experience my first ride on the country-bumpkin bus. It's really more suburban than that, but compared to the city, where transportation options are waiting around every corner, this feels like I'm waiting for the tractor pull to swing by to give me a lift.

Willow's car slows at the curb next to me, and her honk makes me jump. "Hey, what are you doing?"

She asks a lot of obvious questions.

"Well, maybe my powers of deductive reasoning are flawed, but I was assuming that this was the place where one waited to take the bus home. You see, there's this *sign* here," I say, tapping my fingertips on the metal sign that reads BUS STOP. "Then, there was this gathering of students all in some sort of line-type formation. So I thought..."

"Wow, you're a smart-ass," she says, reaching up on her visor and pulling a pair of sunglasses down to push them on her face. "Good thing I like smart-asses. Wanna ride?"

I wasn't really looking forward to what was shaping up to be a pretty packed bus, so I shrug on the outside and open the passenger door. Inside, I do a dorky happy dance over the fact that I have a friend...with a car...who is willing to take me home. Now, just to convince her to pick me up in the mornings.

"So, where do you live?" she asks, and my mind jumps forward to thoughts of my neighbor.

"About six blocks that way, right off of Eighty-seventh and Canterbury," I say, waiting for her to realize where I live—*who* I live by—but she doesn't seem to put it together. She turns her radio up and starts singing along with one of the hit songs on the pop station. That seems to be the most popular station around here. Not a lot of alt-rock listeners, it seems. That's okay, though—I'm sort of good with all music. Habit of my passion, I suppose.

"So, how do you like Woodstock, so far?" Willow asks. I look around at the brick and stone houses, the rows of trees and colorful leaves dusting the streets. Honestly, it's beautiful here. But it's still not the city, and I don't know how to explain that to someone.

"It's nice here," I say, inciting a quick laugh from my new friend. "What? I mean it. It's nice."

"Right—*nice,*" she says. "You mean...*boring.*"

"Oh, no. I mean, well...yeah. Maybe a little boring. But that's okay. I'm not really into crazy parties and nightlife. It's just, in the city there's always something going on, all the time. I guess I got kind of used to the noise. At night, it just gets so quiet here. That's...that's a little strange," I explain, pointing to the street to make sure Willow makes the turn.

The conversation is about to make a shift, because I can tell by the look on her face that she realizes who my neighbor is now.

"Well it looks like you can kiss that quiet goodbye," she says, nodding forward to Owen's driveway. He's climbing into a beat-up old pick-up, and the girl from earlier is sitting next to him, riding in the middle of the cab between Owen and another guy. He peels out of the driveway, his tires leaving a tuft of smoke and the smell of burnt rubber in the air. The girl screams something as they speed by us, Owen never once glancing our way.

"Yeah..." I start. I unbuckle my seat and pull my bag to my lap from the car floor. "That's sort of why I had those questions. I haven't really officially met him yet, I mean...other than the rock kicking thing. He's just kind of quiet...and, I don't know, mysterious maybe?"

"Kens, trust me on this one. Owen Harper isn't quiet. You just haven't given him a reason to be loud yet. That's probably a good thing," she says. "Just keep your eyes open, and watch out for James. He's the one you need to worry about. That boy's nothing but trouble."

"Great. Nothing like living next door to *trouble*," I say with a deep breath. "Hey, thanks for the ride."

"Sure, I'll be here at six-thirty or so to give you a ride in the morning. Be ready, though. I hate being late," she says, reaching over to turn the radio back up to DEFCON levels. I can barely hear her singing along with the music as she backs out of my driveway and heads for the corner.

The Harper driveway parallels ours, and I spend a few minutes looking at the dark black lines Owen left in his wake. There are fainter ones surrounding it, which means he must peel out often.

Typical boy.

The house is empty—every room is mine alone until at least midnight. I spend the first hour munching on peanut butter cereal and watching people reveal the real father of their baby on one of those talk shows. It's an embarrassing obsession of mine, but watching shows like this is my greatest relaxation. There's something about the circus of absurdity—I find it calming. Helps me put all of the drama I think I have in perspective.

My reading and math homework is a breeze compared to my nightly assignments from Bryce. I feel like I'm learning things I was taught last year at the Academy, and if I were a better student, one who was more driven by academia, I might care that I'm not being challenged. But as long as I get to play the piano every day, I really don't care that my math and science and literature are simple. There's nothing wrong with easy. And I think I've earned easy. Besides, I know all my parents will ask about is music anyhow.

The sun sets around six, and unlike in the city, things actually get dark here. I almost find it charming—the soft rustling sound of the dried leaves being blown along the porch and driveway is strangely comforting.

I leave the front door open, the porch screen closed to let in the chilled air. It's making the house cold, but I like the cold. It justifies pulling on my sweatpants and long-sleeved shirt. If I knew how to light the fire, I'd do that, too. Summer is leaving, making room for fall. I spend a few minutes dumping a pack of powdered cocoa into hot water, then stirring, and I blow on my cup as I walk to the piano. I take a sip too soon, and the liquid burns the tip of my tongue.

Once I set my cup down on the piano bench next to me, I pull out my sheet music from my boxes. There's something that just isn't right, and I've been dying to play through these lines— alone, without the critical ear of my father nearby to offer his opinion, or rather to point out that I should be perfecting my classics training instead of spending time doing the part I actually love.

My eyes closed, I let my fingers find their home. It's natural. It always is, the way the polished slivers of black and white feel slick to my touch.

I crack an eyelid open and relent a smirk at my strange surroundings. This is not where I want to be, not where I want to play, so I close the eye again and pretend I am back in my practice room, my door closed and my sounds for nobody's ears but mine. The rest just happens—fingers flying, pounding, stopping abruptly, and shifting from soft to quiet.

I like the change in music—to move from smooth to staccato, sometimes no transition at all. My father hates it, so I save these moments for nights like this. And before I know it, I fall into my routine, the blues rhythms coming through, taking over. My eyes open because this sound—the sound of my heart—has made me feel at home.

Without warning, though, my bliss is interrupted.

Thud.

Thud.

Thud.

The sound is constant, halted only by the loud clanking of a ball shanking off of the metal hoop outside. The shadows of the trees are sharp and dark against my curtains, and I can tell someone has turned the driveway floodlights on. *My* floodlights. The ones attached to *my* home. Where the basketball hoop is also located.

After what feels like a full minute of deep breathing, I find a fraction of my calmness from before and let my fingers glide back into their position. With my eyes closed, I do my best to tune out the continual barrage of noise taking over outside, and I almost get back into my groove, when the *thud* from before ricochets off of the side of my house.

"Oh, come on!" I shout, standing quickly from my bench and spilling the hot chocolate onto the floor. "Damn it!"

Changing direction, I head into the kitchen first and grab the towel folded over the cabinet under the sink and race back to the spilled drink, doing my best to soak it up from the wood floor.

Thud. Thud. Thud.

Maybe it's the sound—the fact that it still continues—or maybe it's the fact that I'm now on my knees cleaning up my spilled drink, my little night of happiness suddenly ruined.

Maybe it's him.

Something pushes me, just enough, and I toss the towel back into the kitchen and pull my hoodie tight around my body, flinging the screen door open in front of me and leaping from the porch stairs. By the time I round the front of the house and start my way up the driveway along the side, I'm full of adrenaline, not even affected by the sting of the cold, and I ride the wave of bravery right into Owen Harper's face.

"Uhhhhh, do you mind?" I say, grabbing the ball quickly and clutching it to my body, both arms wrapped around it tightly like I'm hugging a teddy bear.

Owen stares at the ground where the ball was bouncing just seconds before, his posture frozen and his face almost surprised. With a tiny jerk, he tilts his head up until his focus is on the ball in my arms, his gaze never quite making it all the way to my eyes.

"I never mind. Can I have my ball back now?" he says, the devil's smirk creeping slowly on one side of his lips until the smallest dimple forms.

Asshole.

When he reaches his hand toward me, I shuffle backward quickly, squeezing the ball even tighter, and for a flash second, something happens to his eyes—they grow dark.

"Careful," he says, his smirk curling slightly, like a fisherman's hook waiting to catch me.

I've spent three years going to one of Chicago's most elite private schools, which left me with some pretty solid experience when it came to navigating high school factions. I avoided the rich kids, and they avoided me right back, so that one was easy. I was friendly to the pot smokers, because those kids threw the best parties, but not friendly enough that I was ever guilty by association. I led among my circle—popular with the music students, crossing over to mingle with the drama crowd and the artists.

Owen—he didn't fit any of those boxes. But I'd force him in one if I had to. I've already lost my practice room, my sanctuary. He wouldn't take away my quiet moments alone with my piano too.

I match the dare in his eyes, take one step back, and drop the ball down to my foot. My kick is swift and purposeful, and despite my lack of any athletic ability at all, the ball flies down the street, into the darkness, the only proof of its existence the sound of its bounce growing fainter with every few feet.

"You're in my driveway. Get your own hoop," I say, folding my arms up in an act of defiance. Only then do I realize how hard my heart is pounding. I don't know if it's the adrenaline still working its way through my arms and chest, or if I'm scared.

Owen's gaze is still over my shoulder, out into the street where I sent his ball. He's slow and resolute with every movement, and the longer it takes him to speak the more aware I am of what I've done.

I woke the tiger.

His soft chuckle isn't friendly at all. Neither is his movement—the way he leans forward and spits on the ground, like a man does just after he's thrown a punch. But Owen doesn't make a move toward me, and he doesn't say a word. He only backs away slowly, raising his hand as he nears his front steps, small puffs of fog coming from his mouth and nose—his breath like a dragon's.

I should walk away. I know I should walk away. If I walk away now, he has no power over me. But I. Can't. Move.

With every step up his porch, his arm raises higher, until finally, at his door, he's pointing at me. He's pointing, and he's smirking. And then he pulls the trigger before winking and blowing the imaginary smoke from his finger.

With the slam of his door closed behind him, I fall to the ground.

Chapter 4

Sleep isn't coming. I have been in my bed all night with the lights off, but my curtains open. I sent messages to Morgan and Gaby earlier in the evening, thanking them for the pictures they sent from the first few days at Bryce. I felt so connected to them still, and it broke my heart to see everyone in those images smiling, living—without me.

I did my best to fill them in on my mystery neighbor. Morgan summed him up quickly, texting that he was a "loser," but Gaby seemed to think there was something else to him. She always understands me, and I knew she'd have a different take on things. Of course, she asked if he was hot; she always asks if the guy is hot. But she also asked if he looked sad, or just angry, trying to get at what it was I found so threatening—and appealing. I didn't have to tell her I was attracted to him, which meant I didn't have to admit it to myself. I didn't have to tell her because she already knew. She always knows.

When my phone buzzes, vibrating my pillow, I smile, and my mood lifts for the first time in days. It's late—almost two in the morning. Gaby's been working on her winter ensemble performance, and it's been keeping her at the school studio all night for weeks. She got permission to use the practice rooms and the recording equipment over the summer, when she began writing the arrangements. I admired her balls for even asking the dean, but of course he said yes. Everyone says yes to her. They say yes because she has a fierce determination that comes through in everything she does, and people can't help but want to nurture it, to love it.

Despite how exhausted I knew she must be, she still called.

"Hey," I answer, fighting through my own yawn.

"Sorry, did I wake you?" she asks. "We texted an hour ago, so I thought you might still be awake." She's fighting through her own yawn now, too.

"I'm up. It's not a sleeping kind of night," I admit.

"I had a feeling," she says. She could always sense when something was wrong. It was her gift, her duty as my best friend.

And hearing her voice now makes me cry, but I keep my tears silent, because I like hearing Gaby happy.

"This isn't about the mystery neighbor, is it?" she asks, her question a formality. Gaby knows why I'm really sad. I'm homesick—desperate for anything familiar. And she's my one thing—like a dash of medicine—that can make my new life survivable.

"No, it isn't," I say, breathing a heavy sigh and flipping through the pictures I have on my phone, on my Facebook page, and in the box I pulled out from under my bed. These pictures are both blessings and curses. I cherish them because they remind me that my life before was real. But they also remind me it's gone.

"Does it help that I miss you just as much as you miss me?" she asks.

"A little," I say, laughing, my heart slightly lighter than it was five minutes ago. "Okay, a lot."

"Good, well I miss you more. So that should help with that non-sleeping thing," she says, unable to stave off the yawn that trails at the end. "Wanna talk about how sucky this is?"

It's sweet she even asks. It's sweet, because she's heard me gripe and complain non-stop for weeks about this move and how unfair it is. She's helped me try and decipher why it's so important that we live closer to Wisconsin, why my dad always wins the decision-making game in our family. There's nothing new to say, though. And I know she's exhausted. So tonight I let her off the hook.

"Nah, I think I'll just hang up and dream sweetly over the fact that you miss me more. That should do for tonight," I say, and I swear I can hear her smile.

"Okay. I'll send more pictures tomorrow. And maybe snap a shot of mystery neighbor for me," she chuckles.

"Yeah, uh...no. I'm not coming near him. I'm afraid you'll have to stick with your imagination," I say.

When she says "Goodbye," and hangs up, I let one more tear fall.

I carry feeling pitiful right through sunrise, which is partly to blame for my insomnia. The rest was the strange sensation that

Owen Harper was lying on his bed, across our driveways and lawns, staring right back at me.

"Honey, take your breakfast to go. You'll be late for the bus," Mom says, folding the toasted Pop Tarts up in a napkin and handing them to me.

"Actually, I have a ride," I say, sliding into one of the stools at the breakfast bar and breaking one of the pastries in half. The goo that oozes out the side is hot, and it burns my fingertips. "Damn!"

"Careful," my mom says. Such a harmless word—one she's said to me a million times, a million more as a nurse.

But hearing it this morning throws me back into a nightmare, and all I can hear in my head is Owen's voice—the way he said "Careful," and the sinister, barely-there grin that glowed as he walked away.

"Ken...did you hear me?" Mom is waving in front of me now.

"Oh, no...sorry, burned my hand a little," I say, not feeling the burn at all anymore, at least not the one on my hand.

"Who is giving you a ride?" She has her hand on one hip, as if she's concerned about me with someone she doesn't know. I've been walking to school on my own in the city for three years, but a ride from a *very* harmless girl at my new high school is really giving her cause for worry?

"Oh...I made a friend," I say, smiling as I take a bite. This will make her happy, because this will help abide some of the guilt she feels for moving me out here. "Her name's Willow. She's in band. Drum major, actually."

"Drum major, eh?" Mom says, holding her hand out for my napkin, clearly irritated at the crumbs I'm spilling all over the floor. "The band marches out here, huh? Your father is going to HATE that." She flashes her eyes wide when she says the word *hate*.

"So let's not tell him. He's never home on Friday nights," I say, holding my mom's sightline while she considers this. It's true; my father will hate it. He's a purist, thinks I should be practicing orchestra and classical and piano—nothing but technical-music-skills work, twenty-four-seven. But it's also true that he is *never* home on Friday nights. Friday *and* Saturday, to be more accurate. Those are performance nights, and the full orchestra doesn't leave the building until well after midnight. My dad is rarely home before two or three in the morning, and sometimes he stays there on Friday nights, like he did last night. He's been putting in long hours setting up his new office.

"Depends," Mom says, pausing at the garbage can before throwing my napkin away. She chews at the inside of her cheek for a minute, and then she flips her gaze to me. "Do I get to come watch?"

The giggle escapes my mouth quickly, and I slide over and give her a hug, playing the role of good daughter—something we both need a little of. "Yes, you can come watch. But no going overboard."

"So, I can't become a booster or anything like that?" she teases.

"Oh god, no. You can come to one, two shows tops," I say, holding out a hand for her to shake on our deal, knowing that's all her schedule would allow her to attend anyhow.

"Two, with an option for a third—especially if you're playing for homecoming and riding on one of those float things," she says, and I laugh. My mom grew up in rural Illinois, and Bryce never had anything like she had in high school. She grew up with football games and bonfires. Instead, my old school was all about performance, with fall and winter and spring showcases. My mom's been regaling me with tales of life at a normal, public high school for the last three years.

"Fine," I say, giving her hand a firm shake. "If there is ever a float involved, you can be there."

Willow's honking outside ends our conversation, and my mom waves goodbye, grabbing her ringing cellphone and tucking it in the crook of her neck while she grabs a pile of magazines to head upstairs to nap before her next shift.

The music blaring from Willow's car is just as loud as it was yesterday when she drove away, and as I climb in, I spare a glance to the Harper house and note that Owen's truck isn't in the driveway.

"Think he'll bother to attend any classes today?" I ask, my stomach twisted because I know how many of those classes are with me.

"Hard to say. That boy...he does what he wants," she says, backing out of my driveway. "Nobody questions him."

No, I suppose they don't. Why would they?

His truck is parked near the exit. I spot it the second we pull into the parking lot, but after a quick scan around us, I don't see him anywhere.

"You're looking for him," Willow says, her voice startling me a little. She's standing at my passenger door, holding it open for me. I didn't even hear her exit.

"He just...I don't know. He makes me nervous." My explanation is met with an intense stare, and Willow drops her brow then quirks an eyebrow up at me. "We had an incident," I confess.

"As in what? You bumped into his truck? Accidentally opened a piece of his mail?" she says, holding the door wide for me as I climb out and sling my bag over my shoulder.

"As in I drop-kicked his basketball out into the darkness of night because he was making too much noise," I say, wincing now that I realize just how bold I was, and how stupid it sounds out loud.

"Oh my god, you went all *cranky old neighbor* on him?" she pauses, then her face gives in to laughter. I hit her arm, willing her to stop before Jess gets close enough to hear.

"You have a cranky old neighbor?" Jess asks, putting his arm around Willow and kissing the side of her neck.

"Oh, she has a cranky neighbor all right. But he ain't old," Willow teases, and I shove her again. "She lives next door to the Harpers."

"Ha. You're fucking kidding me, right?" Jess asks, leaning forward to check my facial expression for confirmation.

"Afraid not. And I doubt I'll be going over there for a cup of sugar anytime soon," I say. As we round the corner of the building, I notice a few boys all wearing beanie caps and hoodies sitting on a set of picnic tables down the hill. They're smoking—blatantly smoking on campus—and one of them turns around to catch me staring, and smirks as he grinds his shoe over his cigarette butt on the walkway. He nods in my direction, and the guy sitting next to him turns around.

Owen turns around.

His eyes lock on mine fast, and even without words I can hear everything he's thinking—I see my entire evening replay in the reflection of his eyes, the smallest twitch sending the corner of his lip up, and shivers travel down my spine.

One of his friends distracts him, and for once, I'm aware enough to take advantage, slipping into the music room before he can look back. But that look on his face stays with me, follows me for the rest of the hour, and I think it may also be there tonight, in my dreams.

My father would find my entire first period of school to be a tremendous waste of time. Today's first half hour was spent on the school's fight song—something that sounds pretty elementary, and the same every single time we play it. The second half of class was spent learning how to snap to attention on Willow's direction. It was all so military; so very…unmusical.

So purposeless.

So…fun.

My first two days of band practice have been a break for me, a breather from the constant pounding of my fingers up and down the keys. I've lived my entire life with the constant drive to move my hands faster, make things louder, create fuller chords and stretch my fingers so far that they actually ache at the end of the day. But in here, in this room, with these new friends—*could I call them that yet?*—there was absolutely no pressure.

The second hour was mine, and I relished every second that ticked by, making up for my failed night of playing at home. I brought my music book with me, and spent the time working on that one line of notes, leaving the room almost happy with it.

I'm still humming the passage on my way to English, enjoying this little personal celebration of satisfaction, when my happiness gives way rapidly to tension, the kind that drowns.

It's as if Owen was waiting for me to come, his feet perched up on the back corner of the only other open desk in the room. It was my seat yesterday, near the front, and surrounded by other students—other students who clearly moved out of the way for Owen Harper.

I take my last deep breath at the door and promise myself to not be intimidated, at least not on the outside.

"Excuse me," I say, dropping my heavy backpack to the ground next to my seat and resting my eyes on his gray Converse. I will myself not to look at him, and it's harder than I thought it would be. The challenge only grows the longer I stand there and wait for him to move his feet, finally realizing he has no intention of doing so.

I haven't made any friends in this class yet. Willow and Jess are a year younger, and Elise is only in science with me. It seems academically, I'm destined to be paired with Owen.

"Wow, so it's true what they say about you," I say, pushing at the sole of his right shoe with the tip of my finger. It slides a few inches to the right along my desktop, but he quickly flexes and puts up resistance.

"Your little band geek friends been telling you stories, Ken Doll?" he says, and his voice has that same edge it did last night. It's raspy, and tired—as if he doesn't sleep at all. But it's also deep, and I'll admit, it's a little tempting, like something you know you shouldn't like, but crave hearing again.

"It's Kensington, because you and I...we aren't friends. And yes, they've shared a few important facts with me," I say, catching the teacher walking in from the corner of my eye. I give Owen's foot a hard shove, and his weight is finally knocked off balance.

I do my best to ignore him throughout the rest of the class, focusing on the reading questions and discussion points for *Death of a Salesman*. But I feel him behind me the entire time, the small hairs on the back of my neck standing to attention, anticipating his breath—his breath that never comes.

When the bell finally rings, I drop my pen flat on my paper and note how white my knuckles are from my grip. I shove my things back in my bag and close my eyes before standing to leave, every bit of me expecting Owen to be waiting right behind me to continue our face-off.

But he's gone—the only trace is the trailing fabric of his black hoodie wrapped around his waist as the door swings closed behind him.

The pattern repeats in math, Owen's feet back on the only open desk in the room, my desk. And like a fool, I do the same thing and expect a different result.

"Excuse me," I say, like an echo from an hour before.

"You're excused," he smirks, clicking the top of his pen and chewing on the clip part while his eyes dance over me slowly.

The math teacher is less punctual, the bell ringing without much fanfare as students continue to talk to one another, text their friends, and keep their headphones pushed in their ears. Owen continues to stare.

"Whatever," I say, shoving my back hard into his feet as I sit down in my desk.

After two or three minutes, he finally gives in, letting his feet slide away until they're finally under his desk behind me. I catch the tips of his shoes with my glance downward for confirmation.

The principal walks in a minute or two after, and everyone finally slides into their seats, the chatter subsiding.

"Okay, ladies and gentlemen. I'm afraid you're stuck with me for today. Mrs. Carrol had an emergency, and she's not going to make it in today. So pull out your last assignment and turn to the next set of problems in your book," he says. We all obey, even Owen, who I notice has a full page of math problems noted on his pad.

"Eyes forward there, Kensington. No cheating," he says, careful to say my full name slowly—condescendingly. It pisses me off.

"Oh, don't you know? You and I have different assignments. You see, I work out of the calculus book, not the book with pictures of apples asking you how many nickels Peggy spent at the grocery store," I say back quickly, some strange sensation also working down my arm. I think...I think I actually want to punch someone.

A deep chuckle vibrates in Owen's chest, and I force my glance away from him, back in my lap and at my paper on my desk. I force my focus on the next twenty problems, completing them with time to spare, so I continue to the next set until the bell rings.

Just as before, Owen is gone when I turn around. And just like the day before, he's making out with the same dark-haired girl outside the window when I slide my lunch tray on the table.

Today, though, I ignore him. Or at least, I pretend to. I won't give him the satisfaction. Owen Harper may get his way with everything in this school and town and life. But he won't get his way with me.

"Looks like he's sticking with Kiera this week, huh?" Elise says to Willow as she drops her tray down to join us at our table.

"Yeah, it's rare for the flavor of the week to last an actual week," Willow responds. I assume they're talking about Owen, so I don't even ask.

Jess takes over the conversation when he joins us, talking about some concert coming to Chicago in a few weeks, some band they all seem excited about. I've never heard of Phantom Ant, but when Elise urges me to go with them, I shrug and nod *yes*. I've been to concerts in the city before. Granted, most of them have been classical, but I don't think my parents will have a problem with me going.

I'm doing my best to remember the names of songs they're saying so I can look them up later when the tapping on the window behind me becomes impossible to ignore.

"Uh, Kens?" Willow says, gesturing over my shoulder.

I know I shouldn't, but I turn around anyway, and I give Owen my full, undivided attention. His friends have already left, and he's slowly walking backward, showing me his middle finger and smiling with that faint half-grin I've seen far too often over the last three days.

I don't know what makes me do it. In fact, I don't know why I am the way I am with Owen. I've been careful and timid and obedient my entire life, my only mission to please everyone— please my father, Chen, my mother, my friends, my teachers. Please, please, please, please, please. That's all I do. And all it's done for me is land me in Woodstock, away from my friends and the senior year I was expecting to have. I'm not pleasing Owen Harper, too. So I stand with my tray and raise my arm slowly by my side, my eyes zeroed in on his until I'm pointing at him. I close one eye and cock my head slightly to the right, like I'm making sure I have him in my sights—and then I pull the trigger.

"Jesus H Christ, Kensi! What's wrong with you?" Willow asks. She pulls my arm back down, but I keep my eyes on Owen, staring into his gray-blue eyes—eyes that look like a wolf's. "What are you doing?"

"I'm starting a war, Willow," I say, my heart speeding up and my breath growing more ragged as reality catches up with me.

I'm starting a war with a guy who doesn't lose—a guy who doesn't play by the rules.

A guy who scares me, and who knows where I sleep at night.

Chapter 5

Each day happens exactly the same. Owen sits behind me, lounging his feet on my desk until I make him move. He makes out with the dark-haired girl named Kiera—practically putting on a show for me at lunch—then he taps on the window and sends me off with a message. One day it was a kiss to the glass, the other, he threw a dollar on the ground. I went outside when he walked away and put it in my pocket, and when I got home, I pinned it to my wall.

Despite the stories and rumors, Owen Harper didn't scare me. Everything he did was predictable; all show with no real threat, and nothing I couldn't easily ignore. I had my circle of friends, and I wasn't interested in winning a popularity contest, so I was fine not being a part of Owen Harper's *cool crowd.*

I'd endured bigger threats than he could offer—threats my father dealt out any time I talked about the idea of maybe not going to college at all, maybe studying jazz or just performing on the road, period. He was quick to poison those dreams, stopping short of disowning me. I was more than welcome to walk my own path in life; I'd just have to pay for it all myself, and not expect to live under his roof ever again.

What hurts more is how my mom always supports him. I'm not the same naïve girl I was a few years ago. I understand the economic dynamics of my family now, and I know my mom earns at least twice my father's salary. But he has this hold on her, and she puts him on a pedestal. My father, Dean Worth, is a talented musician, and when he commands the orchestra, it's impossible not to feel prideful watching him work. But my mother has let that pride take all of the power—and somehow, power over me, and my life, was bargained away with it.

The first football game was at a school only a town or two over, so the bus trip was just long enough to be an adventure. Our team lost, but the band sounded good, so I celebrated with Willow, Elise, and Jess afterward at the ice cream parlor in the old part of town.

Normal teenagers would want to keep the party going, to stay out with their friends until the sun threatens to rise. But I know there's an empty house waiting for me at home, and I'm desperate to touch my piano. What I want and reality, though, are two very different dimensions. I know something is off the second we turn the corner to my street.

There are cars packed in both my and Owen's driveway, many with lights on, pointed directly at the hoop anchored to my garage. There are about a dozen guys all playing ball and crushing beer cans right below my bedroom window, *my bedroom window* that I can see plainly through the thin veil of curtains thanks to the flooding lights.

"You wanted war," Willow says, shaking her head at the scene.

"Yeah…" I say, grabbing my heavy bag and pulling it over my shoulder as I step out of her car. "I guess I did."

"You want me to stay? Come in for a while?" She's asking to be nice, but I can tell she doesn't really want to be a part of whatever the hell this is that I started.

"No, it's all right. I'm just going to put some music on and go to bed. Really, let them do whatever out here. I don't care," I lie.

I wait at the front door until Willow pulls away, then push my key in and quickly shut the door behind me.

"What are you doing?" I whisper to myself, letting my bag, coat, scarf and sweatshirt all fall into one pile by the front door. I pull my boots from my feet and slide along the wood floor in my socks toward the kitchen, stroking my hand along the smoothness of the piano top as I pass it. I could still play, but for some reason, playing while there's practically a party happening on the other side of the wall is far less appealing. It's not so much their disruption and the noise as it is my fear of them hearing me—of them stopping and listening. Maybe a fear of them mocking me and taking away something that's *mine*.

I grab a Coke from the fridge and climb the steps, careful not to turn on my light. I don't need to give them a reason to look up. On all fours, I crawl to the window and lean my back against the side of my bed, cracking the tab on my soda.

Someone's radio is blaring rap music. Not the radio-edited version, but the kind with full swearwords and demeaning lyrics. Kiera is out there, sitting on the hood of Owen's truck, and she's taking long drags from a joint, her head swaying side-to-side, not even remotely in sync with the beat. She's ridiculous, and watching her gives me a thrill for about five minutes.

Owen doesn't seem to be aware of her at all, which she doesn't seem to care about because I'm pretty sure she's high off her ass. He's busy playing basketball. It's barely in the fifties outside, but he's not wearing a shirt. There's a white T-shirt tucked into the back of his black jeans, hanging from the waistband like a rag, and his chest is dripping with sweat. They must have been playing all night.

Sliding against the wall, I let my head come to rest on the frame of the window, my hand tucked under my chin, and I watch. Owen is so focused out there playing this game of pick-up ball—this game that doesn't matter anywhere but in his head. At one point, he's arguing a call, shoving his friend in the chest and threatening him. They're both tall, but Owen's more muscular, his frame that of someone who looks as if he's been in a street fight or two.

Their language gets more vulgar as the hour goes on, as more beer cans get crushed into a pile in my driveway. I wouldn't be able to sleep through this even if I wanted to. I know if my father were home, he'd have the police here to haul everyone away. No one is older than eighteen out there, and I've seen at least three cases of beer go down, as well as two or three joints.

It's one in the morning, and I hear one of the guys call out for the last game. Everyone pulls money from their wallets, handing it to Kiera, who stuffs it in her bra, and they pass the ball to Owen for the final game. He's dribbling it, each bounce slower than the first as he points to guys and splits them up on a team, then he throws the ball to someone and jogs over to his truck, pulling a ringing phone from inside the cab.

There's something about the way he's pacing—the way his hand is on his neck and his eyes are down at his feet—something is wrong. For him to be agitated, it must be *really* wrong, like as in a kind of wrong I can't even fathom.

47

"Yo, O! We doin' this or what?" one of the guys yells out at him. Owen raises a hand, crouching down and pushing the phone more tightly to his ear. "O! Come on, man. Are you pussying out because you're out two hunny?"

Two hunny…as in two hundred dollars? Owen stands up from his crouch, the phone still pressed to his ear, and he stares long and hard at the guy giving him a hard time. He doesn't say anything to his friend—if that guy is even a friend—but something is communicated between them just from one look.

"Yeah, whatever man. We gotta go anyhow. Hey, Chris, grab my shit and let's get out of here," the guy yells over his shoulder.

Within minutes, Owen's driveway is empty, and soon he's racing down his front porch, dressed in a dark button-down shirt and a pair of gray jeans. His hair is wet; he must have raced through a shower. His keys jingle in his hands as he jogs to his truck and climbs inside, his engine roaring and his tires squealing from their rest.

It's almost two, and my father will be pulling into the driveway any moment. He said he'd be home tonight, and I'm not so sure I want him to see the mess our neighbor left behind. I walk down the stairs to the kitchen and grab a large trash bag, pausing at the back door to gaze out at the shadows cast over my driveway by the bright floodlight. The ground is strewn with trash, piles of lazily crushed beer cans, and cigarette and pot butts. I can't let my dad see this, and not because I care about Owen Harper getting in trouble, but because I don't want to hear my father's lecture about drugs, drinking, being out late—being a real teenager in general.

When I finally push through the back door, I'm too late, though, the headlights are sending new shadows over the drive as my dad pulls in. I'm already standing in the middle of the mess, so I bend down and start putting cans in the bag, my brain working fast at answers for the questions I know will come.

"Kensington?" So very many of our conversations begin with my name. And it's never Kensi or Kens. It hasn't been anything less than formal since the day I started playing the piano.

"Hey, how was the show?" I ask, buying myself time.

"Performance. Concert. Not *show*. This isn't Broadway," my dad says.

"Sorry, I meant concert," I say, careful not to roll my eyes.

"It was good. We're still having some trouble with the cellos. The replacements aren't nearly as good," he says, his voice growing fainter as he paces out into the middle of the mess. I'm done distracting now. "Kensington, what…is this?"

The funny thing is I know my father knows that this mess isn't my fault. I don't do anything wrong, and I've never been in any *real* trouble. I've been scolded, chastised for dreaming, for playing jazz during a practice session, for skipping a lesson, for not getting a scale just right, but serious trouble—like the kind you get from surmising the state of my driveway—that doesn't mesh with me, and my father knows this.

"Yeah, well…" I say, looking over at the dark Harper house. "Our new neighbors…they kind of like to party? Well, or…at least one of them does."

"I see that," my dad says, kicking one of the crushed cans over into the Harper lawn. "But why am *I* dealing with the leftovers?"

"I don't really know. I think it's the basketball hoop," I say, looking over my dad's head at the rusted hoop and rotting wood backboard hung above our garage.

"I see," my dad says, his hand rubbing the beard on his chin as he steps closer to the front of our garage. "This neighbor…the one that likes the hoop—is it a *he?*"

"Yeah," I say, my voice a little hesitant, causing my dad to turn and look at me. "I mean, girls don't really do *this.*"

"No…they don't, do they?" my father responds, turning back to face the hoop. Almost a full minute passes, and I begin cleaning up the mess until I'm distracted by the sound of our garage door opening. My father slides out a ladder, and then goes to a stack of boxes in the back of the garage, searching through three of them before finding what looks like a ratchet set.

He brings the slender toolbox out to the driveway and picks out three or four sizes, then climbs to the top of the ladder, reaching up to loosen the bolts on the basketball hoop.

He's taking it down. I think I knew he would, and I know deep down that's why I told him—why I said everything just as I said it. It was all a delicate game of chess that I mastered for this very moment. Only I didn't expect to feel nervous that Owen would come home suddenly. Worried that we would be caught.

And I certainly didn't expect to feel regret.

That's the emotion tripping me up most. Regret—is that even an emotion? Or is it just a result? I'm not sure, but I know my stomach is sick with it as my father finds the perfect fit, his arm pulling one side of the hoop loose from the backboard while he goes to work on the last bolt, the ache in my stomach traveling to my chest when the rusted ring finally falls to the ground. My dad steps from the ladder, folds it back up and puts it in its place along the garage wall. Then he picks up the hoop, carries it to the end of our driveway and throws it on top of the morning's trash. In the morning, the garbage truck will haul it away forever.

"Pick up the rest of this mess," he says, not bothering to look my way, instead pulling his phone from his pocket to answer a call—probably from my mother—the back door slamming to a close behind him.

It takes me nearly an hour to gather the rest of the debris in our driveway, and I pick up the can my father kicked onto the Harper lawn, the bottoms of my sweatpants getting soaked from the frosty dew covering their long grass. It looks like it hasn't been mowed in weeks, though it will be dead and covered in snow soon, so I suppose there's no reason.

Our lawn is small—most of our front yard made of small plants, wood bark, and bricked walkway. The rest is just a long driveway—Owen's basketball court.

The air is growing frostier, and my breath comes out in a thick fog as I drag the heavy bag of trash to our can near the street. I flip the lid over and hoist the bag up, stopping it right on the edge, pausing to look at the large metal ring weighing down everything inside. The paint is worn from most of it, and at least two of the bolts look to be stripped. It's trash, and it has no business hanging on my house. No one in our family will ever throw a ball through it.

But Owen will. He did. And he will again.

Only, now he won't.

"Damn it!" I yell, my voice echoing in the emptiness of our quiet neighborhood street. I kick the bottom of the large, black, plastic canister, then I pull the bag from the edge and drop it to the ground. I have to stand on one of the can wheels to reach the hoop inside, and its brackets make it heavy and hard to bring back over the edge, but I manage to. I slide it down the side of the can, leaning it against the can while I throw my trash inside and shut the lid.

Holding my breath, I take a few steps closer to my house, looking to see if my father is still inside, still talking to my mom on the phone, but the lights are all off. It's quiet, and I'm pretty sure he's gone to bed. The metal is heavy, but I'm able to loop my arms inside the hoop and carry it to the garage that my father left open. I put his tools away first, knowing he probably won't need them again for quite some time, if ever. He isn't really *handy*; he's more the type of man who likes to be prepared. Then, I slide the hoop behind the stack of boxes to keep it safe.

I'm saving it. I just saved Owen Harper's basketball hoop. *No*...I saved my hoop, at my new home—the hoop Owen Harper uses, at my new home. And I have no idea why he uses it, why he steps foot night after night on my driveway, below my window. I have no clue why he pushes my buttons, or why I let him.

I saved his hoop, and I don't really know why I did it. But I had to.

Goddamn it. I had to.

Chapter 6

I spend the rest of my weekend practicing until my mom gets home, going into quiet mode when she needs to catch up on sleep. When she wakes on Sunday, we find the box labeled BLANKETS and make a large bowl of popcorn, settling in for a binge on home improvement shows. My mom has these fantasies of home construction...not necessarily building a home from scratch, but taking a sledgehammer to something—something like a wall.

She would be good at it. I could even see her having her own show—*Home Surgery with Karen Worth.* She did a lot of painting in our row home in the city. She'd change entire rooms on her week off, even if they didn't need new paint. She always said she was addicted to change, but I kind of think change terrifies her, and making those small changes, the superficial kinds, was her way of being brave.

"We should make a fire," my mom says. "Your dad said he got some wood during the week. Go check on the side of the house."

I haven't been outside once this weekend, not since the clean up. Owen's truck came home sometime after I fell asleep Saturday morning, and it hasn't moved from its spot. I would have heard him.

Slipping my feet into my warm boots, I wrap my scarf around my neck twice and push through the front door, letting the screen slam behind me. I follow the small woodchip path along the side of the house, along the driveway, noting Owen's tires still at rest at the end of their skid marks.

My neck is still craned to the side when I hear the sound. He's standing right in front of my mom's car, his ball dropping every few seconds to the pavement, then bouncing back up into his hands. I could run, but he'd hear me, so I keep my eyes down at my feet as I walk past him to the wood stacked in the corner.

"You really had to take the fucking hoop down?" he asks. He bounces the ball two more times while I look at the pile of wood, deciding I can carry two logs at once.

"It didn't do it," I say, not lying. My inside voice begging my outside voice to tell him I saved it. *I saved your hoop. It's here. I promise.* I don't know why I care so much.

"Right," he says, throwing the ball against our garage door, making it ring out loudly. "Like hell you didn't."

Grunting to myself, I shift the wood in my arms so I can hold it tightly to my chest, and I walk back around the corner of the house until I can see him. His eyes are different now. They're...sad. But they're angry, too. And it's the shades of angry that won't let me trust him.

"Really," I say, coming to a stop a few feet away from him. "Like hell I didn't. It was my dad. You kind of left a *mess*, and my dad doesn't put up with bullshit."

There's stillness in the air after I tell him this, and I'm caught in it, my eyes unable to move away from his. He's chewing at the inside of his cheek. His brow falls a little, and there's a shift in his eyes, the sadness making room for the danger that usually lives there.

Willing myself to walk away, I let my weight shift, and I bring my lips into a tight smile and begin to turn on my heels.

"So who does your dad talk to late at night, out here in the driveway?" he asks, suddenly interested in my family.

"Uh...my mom. She works a lot of overnights. And my dad gets home late," I say, realizing I have yet to see Owen's mom— or *anyone* else in the Harper house.

"Right, that's what I thought," he says, and I turn with a shrug, really missing the warmth and easiness from just a few minutes ago inside. "But I meant the other times."

Something about what he says—the way he says it—slams into my chest, and I halt, hugging the heavy wood even tighter, bits of the bark cutting into the palms of my hand.

"You know..." he continues, my back still to him. "Who does he talk to out here while your mom is asleep in bed? Those times."

The tear surprises me, and my hands are full, so there's no way I can stop it, so I let it slide down my face into the threads of yarn in my scarf.

"I bet it's whoever drives that blue BMW I see parked here when I come home for lunch. I bet that's who it is. Whoever...*she* is," he says, every word purposely hurtful. I hear his feet shuffle toward his ball, and soon, it hits the ground again, only this time it's dropped and discarded, rolling by my feet until it stops at the tire of my mother's car. He's casting one more stone, just to let me know who's in charge. And for the first time since I've met Owen Harper, I'm willing to relent—he's in charge. And his words just broke my tiny shred of happiness like a thin sheet of glass.

My arms ache from flexing with the weight of the wood, so I force my feet to climb the steps inside, and I busy myself with the fire, sparing a quick trip to the restroom to wash my hands, and wash my face of any trace of that one solitary tear.

By the time I come out of the bathroom, my mom has the fire roaring, and she's holding out a mug for me, her smile innocent.

She doesn't know. She can't know.

Owen's words—his hurtful, despicable, mean, purposeful words—are all I can hear through the next two hours of pointless television. I sit there next to my mom and feign our world is fine. If I could only shut off the sounds echoing in my head, I could maybe find a way to forget, to chalk this up to just some cruel prank.

But I can't.

When my mom busies herself with housework, I turn to my piano, pulling out the books of sheet music I'm supposed to be memorizing—only now, it's not just a thing I'm not interested in. Now it's a thing I want to fight against doing with all I have. I open those pages and I see his face—my father's face. I play those notes and I hear his voice, his expectations and condemnations for the music *I* like.

Playing from these books has quickly become a thing that represents something ugly. Something I realize I haven't felt love for in a year, maybe more. Something disappointing. My father.

With a smooth stroke, I take my finger and push the loose sheets of music and the book behind them from the ledge to the floor, leaning to the side to see them slide in various directions. A mess—a beautiful, classical, fake mess.

My hands do as they wish, sliding into place, running smoothly over keys until notes blend into one another, sliding from one note to the next sloppily, while sad-sounding blues chords fill the giant dining room and foyer of my house.

My house. This fake house. This place *he* made me move.

I pound harder, playing runs, pausing to breathe and look out the window. Owen's truck is framed perfectly by the picture window in our living room, the taillight like that of a lighthouse, guiding me to truth.

I play what I want to play, even when my mother warns me that my father will be home soon. I keep going, the sounds only those *I* want to hear, and when his car idles to a stop in our driveway—I play louder.

I play him right through the front door, and I hold my head up high, daring him while he walks closer to me, the stern look on his face no longer holding the value it once did. There's no threat here any more. And I couldn't give a shit if he's disappointed in me now.

"You know I don't like that crap," he says, pushing the lid forward, threatening to close it on my fingers. But I anticipate this, and I stop it as I stand to my feet, letting my fingers tap out one last faint pattern that I know my father will hate.

"Have you practiced your showcase? Or did you just spend the entire day wasting time?" he asks, walking back to the front door to kick off his shoes, loosen his tie, and drop his briefcase full of music—full of *his* music. Probably full of his lies, too.

"Who is she?" I ask, my voice loud enough that my mom hears. I hear her hear, the sounds in the kitchen coming to an abrupt stop.

"Who is she, Dad?" I ask again, my voice wavering with the tears I'm fighting to keep inside. I won't be weak for this. He won't face me, and the longer it takes him to speak, the more I start to feel everything.

"Who is she!" I yell, grabbing the last music book lying on my piano and throwing it at him.

My father turns to face me slowly, and the more his face comes into view, the more I see just how broken everything is— my life, my mom's life, our family—we're broken.

"Dean?" my mom's voice questions from behind me. She walks up to him slowly, her hands clutching a towel from the kitchen. With each step she gets closer, the more honest my father's face becomes, the more the puzzle comes into view.

This house, the move—all of it—it's because of *him*, because he was unfaithful. Because he did something my mom couldn't live with, at least, not in our old house, in my *old* life. She couldn't live with the memories from where we were.

My mom slaps my father so hard that his face jerks harshly to the side, and the bruise is almost immediate. Then she hits him again. And again. My father stands perfectly still, taking every hit.

"You son of a bitch!" she yells. "You promised. You promised that it was done. We'd move here, away from the school, away from *her*. It was over, and we'd start over. I would try to forget, and you would never see her again."

School.

Her.

Blue BMW.

Her!

There are key words that ring through my anger. I think I knew the moment Owen opened this wound. But I just couldn't believe my nightmare was *that* horrifying. I didn't want to believe it.

"Dad?" I whisper behind my mother, everything coming into focus, everything hurting me from all sides all at once. My mother turns to me slowly, her hand covering her mouth, her entire body shaking when she realizes what I've put together.

"Ohhhhhh...." I start to cry hard when I see her, when my nightmare is confirmed. Shaking my head, I rush around them both up the stairs to my room, slamming the door behind me, and logging into my computer to sift through my Facebook posts until I get to it—and it's all right there, staring me in the face.

There I am, standing next to my best friend, Gaby, in front of her 18th birthday present—a brand new, blue BMW. It's this picture, the one my father took, and it's the way Gaby is looking back at him, through the lens.

How could I have been so blind to it all?

I hear Owen's tailgate slam, and I rush to my window to watch him round his truck, his keys in his hand, his step quick and determined. I don't have much time.

I grab my wallet from my nightstand, and push it and my phone into my back pockets before stuffing my feet into my wool boots and throwing a white hoodie over my body. My parents are screaming at each other as I come down the stairs, and I realize my mom has broken a few dishes at my father's feet.

"I'm going out," I say, but really only for her benefit.

"Like hell you are, young lady!" my father yells, his step gaining ground on me as I head down the porch steps.

"You can go to fucking hell!" I scream over my shoulder, my legs picking up into a run as I hear Owen's engine turn over. He's slowly rolling from the driveway when I slam my fist on his hood, positioning myself in his path. My dad is still undeterred, walking right at me, and I'm so ruined that I don't care if Owen runs me over.

"Kensington, you don't understand. And it's a Sunday night. You need to get your ass back in this house," my dad yells. Powerless. He has become powerless. And when I look at him, and he looks back at me, he knows I know it. He knows I know it all.

And he knows I'm not coming back inside that house—not while *he's* in it.

"Get your hand off of my fucking truck!" Owen yells, his head leaning out his window and his arm heavy on his horn.

I rush to the side and pull his passenger door open, climbing in and buckling up, locking the door to keep the other side out.

"Oh, fuck no! Ass out of my car! You heard your dad. Get back in your own goddamned house," he seethes.

My breathing is hard from anger, and I don't know if my body needs to cry or scream. "This is your fault. You started this. *You* pushed over the first goddamned domino! So you get to take me out of here. I don't care where, but I swear to God, Owen, if you don't make those tires squeal in about four seconds—I'm going to shove you out of the way and drive away from this place myself!"

Owen spends the first three seconds trying to decide how serious I am, and when I pound my fist on his dashboard, he decides his life is easier if I stay in the truck. "Fuck!" he yells, shifting into gear and pealing away, his back tires fishtailing in the street and the smell of burnt rubber filling the cab. "I don't need this...this...this family-drama shit, all right? We're driving around the block a few times, and then you're going home."

"No," I say, my jaw tight, my teeth clenched.

"Ooooohhhhh yes we are," he chuckles, and I pound his dashboard again.

"No!" I say forcefully, the tears starting to fill the bottom of my eyes now. "No, no, no, no, no!"

I keep repeating the word, keep pounding my palm against Owen's dash, until his hand finally catches mine, holding it down flat while we sit at a stoplight near the outskirts of the historic downtown.

"All right, I got it. *No.* Just...easy on the truck," he says, his palms rough against my skin. I stare at his hand touching mine, my mind trying to make sense of the way it looks. My perfect fingers, my skilled, trained, long and powerful fingers look like weak flowers, wilting flowers, underneath the weight of his large hands.

"I hate you," I let go from my lips in a whisper.

"Yeah, well...you and everybody else," he says, pressing his foot back on the gas as the light turns green.

Owen drives through the heart of town, then turns down a two-lane highway where we drive for minutes in silence. My passenger window feels cold against my cheek, and the regular in-and-out reflection of the streetlights on the window glass keep me from drifting into crying. I just wait for the next reflection to come, counting in my head to see how long it takes. I count, until we run out of streetlights, and then I hold my breath and try not to think about my best friend sleeping with my father—and ruining my life.

"Where are we going," I say, my voice hoarse. Owen remains silent, and I start to ask again, but then realize I don't care where we're going. I'm just glad we're gone.

There's a rustling sound as he reaches into a pocket on the front of the bench seat, then he tosses two strips of licorice on my lap.

"Hungry? Chicks eat when they're upset, right? Isn't that like a thing?" he says, glancing at me and ripping a bite from the red licorice. I hate red licorice.

"I don't think that's a thing," I say quietly, setting my strips of candy on the dashboard closer to him.

It's quiet for several more minutes until we hit a small convenience store parking lot. There are a few other cars parked out here, and I recognize most of the other people from school. I'm suddenly wishing I jumped into a stranger's car to run away.

"Stay in the car. I don't need anyone asking questions," he says, his voice practically an order.

Owen parks next to another old pick-up truck, and I notice Kiera sitting in it. I wonder if they're still together, or whatever it is they are. Kiera's eyes are on Owen as he steps in front of the truck to talk to another guy, the both of them leaning against the front of his truck. This guy looks a lot like Owen, only his face isn't as handsome. He's hard looking, and he doesn't seem to smile. Not that Owen smiles. The only time I've seen Owen smile was when he was teasing me—and when he delivered the news that ruined my world.

I notice the other guy pull out a pack of cigarettes and offer one to Owen, but he shakes his head. I'm glad he doesn't take it, and I wonder if that means he doesn't smoke. I hope he doesn't smoke.

I don't know why I hope he doesn't smoke.

Owen pulls his phone from his pocket when it rings, and he starts pacing in the middle of the parking lot while he answers the call, his feet kicking at a few rocks and his other hand rubbing the back of his neck. When he gets off the phone, he holds his thumb up to the guy he was talking to and smiles—a real smile—then jogs back to his truck.

He slams the door to a close and buckles his seatbelt, and I test mine to make sure it's tight, somehow hoping that will keep me safe wherever it is we're going. Owen doesn't share our plans; he just pops the truck into drive quickly, the wheels kicking up gravel as we fishtail back onto the highway and head back the way we came.

"Where are we going?" I ask finally. Owen glances up at the rearview mirror, then leans his head out the window slightly and adjusts the mirror on his door. The wind coming in is cold, and I fold my arms tightly around my body, trying to fight the chill.

"Party," he says, a smirk on his lips as he notices something in his mirror.

"Party? But it's...Sunday. We have school tomorrow," I say, and Owen looks at me finally, then laughs. No other response.

Seconds later, the truck with his friend and Kiera race by us, the guy's motor growling so loudly that it almost pops as he speeds by us, dust kicking up in Owen's headlights as his friend passes him and moves back to our lane.

There's no pause in Owen's reaction. His right hand grips his steering wheel and he rolls his window up with his left, and the moment it's closed, he punches the gas with a force that sends my back hard against the seat. My hands grip my seatbelt by instinct, holding onto it to make sure it's tight—to make sure I stay in this vehicle.

"Owen, slow down," I say, my heart starting to make my body shake with its beating.

Owen hears nothing, and he starts rocking forward and back with his eyes intent on the truck in front of us, like laser beams locked on the taillights leading our way.

"Owen," I say, this time a little louder.

The grin on his face is maniacal. It's actually maniacal—I've never seen that expression on someone before. We inch closer and closer to the truck in front of us, and Kiera leans over, draping her arm on the back of the seat in the other truck, her eyes on Owen, her mouth twisted into a tempting smile, urging him to do it, to be dangerous.

There's a fast jerk to the truck as he veers to the other lane, and I hear his friend's truck rev a little faster at the threat of being beaten. Owen leans forward and pushes his pedal to the floor, and after a few seconds, we're dead even with the other truck.

"Owen!" I yell, but he can't hear me. He's somewhere else. His hand is pounding on the steering wheel, and I look at his lips and notice them moving, speaking quietly. "Come on, baby. Come on," he's saying, over and over.

His friend is laughing, his head tilted back, and Kiera is clapping. Everyone here is having fun. This is fun. This is what they do for fun. And I want to throw up. In fact, I might throw up.

"Owen, you're scaring me," I say, my voice coming out in a shrill. But he presses forward.

I have no idea where his other friends are. There were at least three other cars in that parking lot. But no one is near us—not in this race. We move about a quarter length ahead of the other truck, nowhere near enough to pass, and as we top a hill, I notice the lights coming at us in the distance.

"Owen!" I scream, my hands grabbing at the side and front of the seat now. Anything to brace myself. Anything to survive whatever is going to happen.

"Come on, baby. Come on," he's still whispering.

We're racing, our engine fighting to be just a little stronger than the other guy's, and the lights are coming closer to us. The other car is just over this hill, and we're either going to veer off the road, or we're going to die.

I don't want to die.

I don't want to die.

"Owen! Please stop! Owen! The car...that car! Stopppppppppp!" I scream. I'm grabbing his arm, trying to get him to change course, and he punches the gas with one last thrust, and our truck slides past his friend's, only a second before the car coming at us head-on rounds the top of the hill and honks at us—the sound of the horn blaring and lasting for several seconds in the night air.

"Yeahhhhhh baby! Wooooooooooo!" Owen is shouting. He rolls his window down and holds his hand out the window, giving his friend the middle finger, and his friend reciprocates.

"Owen!" I yell, my body plastered to the vinyl seat, my heart stopped now from my near-death experience.

"Did that scare you?" he asks, his voice an odd kind of calm. Unable to speak, I merely nod *yes* to him, my arms still clutched to anything I can grasp, and my body no longer cold, sweat dripping down my back and arms.

"I told you to get out of the truck. You should have listened," he says, his focus more calm now, his eyes back on the road.

A large farmhouse comes into focus, and we pull into the gravel driveway, followed soon after by his friend with the other truck. We sit in the truck cab, waiting for everyone to arrive, and there's an awkward silence. Owen's arm is resting on the window, and he's pulled a bag of sunflower seeds from the front seat pocket. I watch as he spits the shells out the window meticulously, one at a time, like he's aiming for some goal I can't see.

I may as well be invisible. He hasn't looked my direction once, and I'm too afraid to confront him—afraid of what he'll do next. His friends finally pull into the lot around us, and Owen steps out when they do. I notice Kiera kiss the other guy, and I wonder how someone could jump from one boy to another so quickly. I also wonder how Owen can be so flippant about it—his friend is kissing the girl whose lips were on his only two days ago, and he looks as if he couldn't care less.

I don't want to be here. But I don't want to be home, either, so when Owen shrugs over his shoulder for me to join them, I slide from the seat and close the door behind me. Everyone walks to the house, and Owen isn't waiting for me. I linger behind; the temptation to walk back to the truck—to hide there for as long as the night lasts—is strong. I feel foolish suddenly, the adrenaline from what just happened catching up to me, and my body quivers with a rush of tears that I quickly squash with the sleeves of my sweatshirt. When I look up again, Owen is waiting for me at the door.

"You almost killed us!" I yell, stopping in my tracks.

"But I didn't," he says, holding the door open and waiting for me to follow him inside, where everyone else has gone. He waits, his eyes rested on mine for several long seconds, and I notice them shift. In the truck, there was a determination in them, like a warrior—the kind you send in for the toughest kill because you know they won't feel any of it. It was like nothing else existed.

But for these few seconds, they soften, and he's actually looking at me. And he looks afraid.

"I'm sorry I scared you," he says, his teeth biting the tip of his tongue as if he wants to say more, but he stops himself. His eyes stay on mine, and my body freezes, my mind not sure what to say. I'm empty. I have nothing—feel nothing. I nod at him, and shuffle my feet closer and step through the door. My back brushes against his chest as I pass him through the small space, and I can't help but notice how warm he feels. Maybe I'm just cold.

"Don't do it again," I whisper, glancing sideways at the nearness of him. I won't look at his eyes; I'm not sure how they'll look, and if I'm going to follow him inside, I need to feel safe— the way his eyes felt seconds ago. Instead, I focus on his chin, and neck and the way his dark shirt hugs his chest. His lip ticks, finding its comfortable place back into that sinister smile, but he doesn't respond, so I step inside.

The house is dark, and I follow Owen to a large, sunken living room where everyone is sitting in front of a television that's barely audible. A joint is already being passed around the room, as is a bottle of clear liquor. I have no idea what it is, but I know the moment it makes its way to me, it's going to start a conversation, because I don't drink. And Owen Harper, he's not the boy who's going to pressure me into something.

"Ahhhh, new girl. Yeah, new girl needs to drink," says the guy from the truck race. He holds the bottle out in front of me, but I nod *no* and shrug it away. "Fuck, O. You brought *this prude* to hang out? What the fuck is wrong with you?"

He takes a big swig from the bottle and runs his sleeve along his mouth when he's done, then hands the bottle to Kiera. She's lightly laughing at my expense, but I don't care.

"I don't drink," I say, standing my ground early. "I like my brain cells."

Kiera spits out a little of the drink at my response, and her *new* boyfriend starts to laugh loudly.

"Dude, O! Seriously, are you like…fucking with us with this chick or something?" he says, his speech already sloppy, proving my point.

"I didn't *bring* anybody. She hijacked my fucking truck and wouldn't get out," Owen says, letting his long body flop into a beanbag across the living room from me, his legs stretched out and a small golden drink in his hands.

"Good thing I did. I'll drive your ass home," I say, letting my eyes zero in on him as he raises his glass to his lips. He holds it there as he leans forward, resting his elbows on his knees, his eyes mocking me.

"Nobody drives my truck. And we're not leaving for hours, so I'll be fine," he says, brow raised before tilting the glass back and letting the amber liquid flow down his throat. He keeps his stare on me as he sets the glass down and settles into his seat.

"We'll see about that," I say.

"Yeah, we'll fucking see about a lot of things," he says, pulling his arms behind his neck and leaning sideways as he stares at me for several long, uncomfortable seconds.

His friend from the truck reaches for Kiera's hand, lifting her to stand, and the two of them leave their seat on the sofa and walk up the stairs. The casualness of it all feels so sad—maybe even a little gross—and I can't help the face I make in reaction to it.

"You have a problem with House hooking up with Kiera?" Owen says, bringing my attention back to him.

"His name is *House?*" I ask, keeping the focus on the easier topic.

"Matt House. We've been friends since kindergarten. I call him House. He calls me Harper. Whatever. And you clearly have issues with people having sex," he says.

"I don't give a shit *who* has sex," I say fast, my response not really a lie. I don't care who does what, but that doesn't mean I understand how little importance people place on something like sex. My face is red; I know because I can feel my cheeks tingling. But the darkness shrouds me.

"You're a virgin," Owen says, his lips taking their time with that word. My cheeks burn stronger, and for the first time, I feel flustered from the embarrassment.

"So." That's all I can think to say. At first, I consider adding more, defending myself, but the more time that passes, the happier I am with that response. I won't make apologies for not being easy.

"Your daddy would be so proud of you, proud of his little girl keeping her snatch all sewn up, waiting for her *prince charming*," Owen says, the cruel look glimmering in his eyes and curling his lips.

His words make me want to cry, and I can feel the pressure building, the water wanting to spill down my cheeks, but I won't let him have this. I breathe long and slow, and I hold his gaze, meeting his challenge, until I know I can speak without my voice wavering.

"Nobody likes you. They all think you're crazy. They feel bad for me, because I have to live next to you," I say back. I'm expecting Owen to wince, to feel my words on some level, but he only leans forward and lets his grin stretch larger across his face.

"Then why, little miss sunshine, are you here?" he asks, resting his chin in the palm of his hand. The two other couples here with us have all left the living room for the kitchen, where they're playing some drinking game. Owen and I are alone, and nobody is interested in our war of words. That means no one will hear the details of my broken life.

"I'm here because you took what was left of my barely-decent life and ripped it to goddamned shreds," I say to him, waiting for him to argue and say he didn't.

"What, the little bit about the affair? I was right, wasn't I? Your dad...he's stepping out on your mom. Who is she? Someone...*younger*?" He's seen Gaby at the house. I can tell he knows it's a younger woman by the way he's looking at me, luring me and taunting me. But he doesn't know *how* young. And I don't plan on giving him anything else he can use to hurt me.

"Why do you play basketball in my driveway?" I ask, taking control of the conversation. Owen keeps his eyes on me, his tongue teasing at the edge of his lips as he decides whether or not he's going to let me.

"The Stratfords used to live there. They sold the house to you. They always let me use the hoop, because we don't really have a place for one. I didn't think you'd be assholes and take it down," he says, and I feel a small pang in my side because Owen actually looks sad. He also looks less like the hardened eighteen-year-old and more like a lost little boy.

"Well, like I said. I didn't take it down. My dad did. And it turns out not only does he have a low tolerance for bullshit, but he's a royal fucking asshole, too," I say, finally letting my eyes move from Owen's face to the front pocket on my sweatshirt. I push my hands inside and focus on the tattered strings from the hoodie lying along the front. I'm startled when Owen is standing in front of me, a small drink in his hand. "I told you, I don't drink."

"Yeah, and I bet a week ago you thought your dad was the greatest man alive," he says, moving the small shot glass closer to me.

I take it in my hand and look at it, smelling the edge of the glass and feeling surprised that the odor isn't strong. It's only a small shot, and I won't drink any more—just this one. The urge to do something wrong—something against my grain—is suddenly overwhelming. I lift the glass to my lips, pausing before I drink to look into Owen's eyes. When I do, they're glowing again, and that same feeling of connection is there—the one from the driveway, the one from when he apologized for scaring me on the highway.

I tilt the glass back, and cough the second the burn hits the back of my throat. Owen chuckles softly, then hands me a bottle of water, and when he takes the glass away, I notice his fingertips tickle against mine, pausing as if they're surprised by our touch.

"Just so you know," I say, waiting for him to look at me to finish the rest, "I never thought my dad was the greatest man alive."

He holds my sightline and his mouth sits in a comfortable, flat line as he steps backward until he's at his beanbag again, and he lowers himself to sit.

"Just so you know," he says, holding a newly filled shot glass in his hand, holding it steady in front of his face, but pausing when it's raised between my gaze and his. I sense he's reading me, but I don't know why. "I always thought my dad was..."

He drinks fast, and his eyes close as he holds the burning sensation in. After a few seconds, he opens his eyes again, and the look, the pained, lost boy, is there now.

"I always thought he was the greatest man alive. All the way until he wasn't," Owen says, and my gut twists with a hurt I've never felt before. Sympathy. That's what I feel for Owen Harper.

Just then, I realize, he's not really wild at all. He's heartbroken. And maybe I don't hate him as much as I thought I did.

Chapter 7

Owen didn't talk for the rest of the night. We spent several more hours at that house—the one I found out later belonged to some girl named Sasha. Her family farms, but they have a large staff that really runs most of the business. Sasha is home alone often—alone with Owen and his friends and their...recreational habits.

We didn't talk during the ride home, but Owen drove slowly. I think he did it for me. The ride home felt...different. I didn't fear Owen. I hated him for telling me what he told me. I also hated my father. And Owen missed his. As the sun rose, I spent the miles we drove trying to find a way to make those thoughts match up in my head—find a way to make Owen's pain hurt just a little less. And then I became consumed with the realization that I was caring a little too much about Owen and his feelings.

I'm starting to recognize the town, the trees of my street are familiar, and the closer we get to my house—and Owen's—the more my stomach hurts. I sit up on the edge of the truck seat and push my hands under my legs, worried about what will be waiting for me in my driveway.

My phone doesn't have any messages on it, and I'm grateful for that. My mom let me run away, probably because she needed to be alone too. What worries me is where my father is—and if he's home.

Home. Such a farce. This is nobody's home, and now I hope like hell my mom kicked my dad out of it.

"You're worried about your old man. Worried he's there, huh?" Owen asks, his tone on the verge of caring, as if he's really interested, as if he isn't loving every second of my suffering. I won't look at him, only glancing at his profile, but I notice the tilt of his face toward me. It's just enough to let me know he's looking at me, and it makes me uncomfortable, so I pull my arms around my chest. This is the first time I've heard his voice in hours. He had two or three more shots, long ago, but still I should have driven the truck. I don't like that I let him drive.

Maybe I'm still afraid to confront him.

"Yep," I respond to him, nodding as I let my head slide to the side, my cheek pressed on the passenger window. I let my breath fog it up, blurring out my view, like I'm erasing the parts I don't like outside.

"His car's gone," Owen says, making my heart slow instantly.

"Good," I say, pausing with my lips open, my breath fogging the glass once again, this time making the cloud on the window thicker. "I think that's good. That's...good, isn't it?"

I look at him when I ask this, something pulling me to him, forcing me to look at him. When I'm confronted with his calmness, the serene look on his face, a renewed fire grows in my belly, and it makes me angry again—angry with Owen, angry that he was the one to tell me, angrier that he took pleasure in it. He's barely pushing his shifter in park when I shove him hard against his door.

"You...asshole!" I yell, shoving him again, then leaning back against my door, on the other end of the bench seat. He's staring into my eyes, emotionless, completely unaffected by my outburst. My hands are cold from his poor heating system, and they sting when I slap him with them again, my palms coming to a thud against the layers of clothing covering his body, but I push at him anyway, shoving hard. I want to hurt him.

"You...goddamned...fucking asshole!" I scream, so loudly that I'm sure if anyone were awake and outside, they would hear me.

I shove again, and Owen sits there, bracing himself for the impact, but not stopping me. He doesn't stop me—he doesn't say a word. I hit him a few more times, knowing I'm not hurting him, that I'm not strong enough to come close to hurting him, but I do it anyway. I go until I feel foolish, then I get out of his truck and slam the door closed behind me.

The crunch of the wood chips between our driveways is loud under my feet. I walk quickly, never bothering to turn to face Owen, to see if he's following me, looking at me or stepping out of his truck. I march up the front steps of my house, holding my hand on the knob and breathing deeply. When it's unlocked, my heart breaks a little knowing I'm going to have to face whatever life is left inside.

My mother is sitting at the table when I walk in, my father's belongings strewn around the first floor in piles. Everything looks just as I thought it would, but it doesn't make me sad. What makes me sad is the fact that I'm not sad at all to see traces of my father's disappearance. It's just the opposite—I feel nothing.

"Your dad is at a hotel. He won't be coming back. Not...not for a while," she says, her voice showing how tired she is, how hurt she is.

I don't answer, but I nod just enough for her to recognize a response, then I continue up the stairs to my room, the one that looks nothing like my room at all. I stand in the doorway for a few minutes, surveying my things, mostly still in boxes, and I note the time on my clock—almost six. Willow will be here in thirty minutes, and I know I would never be able to wake up if I actually fell asleep, so I grab my pillow and blanket from my bed, and curl up by my window to wait for the alarm to start my next miserable day.

Owen's room is lit, and every now and then, I notice shadows crossing it. There's another car in his driveway, an older sedan. I wonder if that's his mom's?

From my view, I can see all the way through his door, and he passes his room a few times, like he's pacing out in the hallway, until he finally closes his door shut behind him. He pulls his sweatshirt and the T-shirt that was underneath over his head, and I watch the entire thing, letting myself admit that he's attractive. He's more than attractive. His skin is this warm color that's almost golden, his stomach toned, his arms strong...and I let myself imagine how they would feel holding me.

No one has ever held me. Not a boy, anyhow. I've danced with boys, held hands, kissed—but not *really.*

Owen pulls his phone from his pocket, texting someone before putting it down on a small night table near the wall by the window. Reaching up, he shuts off the lamp that's illuminating his room, and just like that, he disappears.

And I admit to myself that I miss him.

"You look like total shit," Willow says as I climb into her car, wearing a change of clothes, but yesterday's hair.

"I feel like shit," I say.

"Yeah? Oh, hey...uh...if you're going to vomit? You need to tell me. I need to know because I'm, like...one of those sympathetic vomiters. I'm serious—if you throw up, I'll throw up. And then we'll both be throwing up...in my car. Yeah, maybe you should stay home?" She's talking so fast that it makes my head hurt. I only drank the one drink, but it was enough to leave me feeling not quite right.

"I'm not sick. I'm just tired. It was a long night," I say, noticing Owen's window is still dark, his truck still in it's place—right where we left it.

My mom was awake still, her body frozen to the same chair it was in when I got home an hour before. I have a feeling she'll be there when I get home.

"Homework?" Willow asks, her car skidding over the curb as she backs out of my driveway.

"Uh...yeah...a lot of homework," I lie. I like Willow, but not enough to relive my nightmare, at least not yet.

School is easy, and I'm grateful for that. Owen misses our morning classes, and his crew is noticeably missing from the window show I've gotten accustomed to during lunch.

The afternoon passes in a blur. Owen never shows up, and nobody looks for him. It's strange how nobody asks why he's missing, and I feel like I'm literally watching him slip through the cracks of the education system.

There's a project assignment in science, and I make plans to start it right away, gathering the requirement sheets and supplies from the classroom before meeting Willow in the parking lot—Owen's truck still nowhere to be found. Elise and Ryan are in Willow's back seat, and I notice how much Ryan reminds me of Owen. Not so much in the face, but his body—his long legs folded to fit in the tightness of Willow's car, his strong arm draped behind Elise, his eyes dark, clothing dark, his hat pulled low.

I'm thinking about Owen. I'm looking at Ryan, and I'm thinking about Owen, and I'm so aware that I'm doing it that I'm ashamed. But I keep thinking about him. He's a distraction—he's also the reason I need a distraction. And he doesn't have to know I think about him.

"How come Owen misses so much school?" I ask, hoping Ryan will give me a little piece to the puzzle. Willow's gaze falls on me fast, and I realize how jarring my question is. "I just saw him last night, in front of his house," I say, my words coming out rushed and nervous. "And I know he's fine, or not sick or whatever. It was weird he wasn't here. That's all."

I'm overly-justifying my question, and Willow knows it too. She keeps her eyes on me a little longer, until the light flicks to green and she pulls away from our school. Her questions are lining up in her mind, and I know they're coming. I just hope I can avoid them a little longer—until I know how to answer them.

"Owen's grades are fine. That's all that matters. He's never ineligible for basketball; he doesn't miss practice, and his grades are good," Ryan says, following up his explanation with a harsh sigh. He's defensive over Owen, and I sort of wish I had someone like Ryan to be defensive over me. "Seriously, Kensi. Don't believe half of the shit you hear. It pisses me off—how people talk about him? He's a good guy."

Willow lets out a rush of air with a laugh at Ryan's words, and he kicks his leg forward into the back of her seat.

"You hush. You're not qualified to be impartial," Ryan says, and something about the way he says it makes me turn my gaze to Willow.

"Like hell I'm not," she says, her face suddenly less...perky.

"What does that mean?" I ask.

"Willow went out with Owen, freshman year. She's still mad about him breaking up with her," Ryan says, and everything inside of me feels heavy. I'm jealous. *I'm jealous!*

"One..." Willow starts, her eyes on Ryan in the rearview mirror, "I did *not* go out with him. We hooked up, at a party, for like...an hour. And two, I am over him. I just don't agree with the way he used me, then ignored me. And I don't like the way he continues to do that to girls, over and over again. It's...it's demeaning."

It is demeaning. I can't argue with her there. But…it seems to me that at this point girls know what they're in for with him. I've been here for a few weeks, and I have him figured out.

"Whatever," Ryan says, turning his interest to the window, to Owen's house outside. "He's a good guy, that's all I'm saying. Don't date him if you don't like the way he treats girls. But don't judge him. He'd never hurt anyone."

A small laugh escapes my throat, and I cover it up quickly with a cough. Ryan notices, and our eyes meet. I shake his gaze off and turn my attention to the door, to my house, to my crappy life inside.

"Thanks for the ride. I'll see ya in the morning?" I say, holding the door open and noticing Ryan still studying me.

"Yeah, I'll be here a little earlier. We have extra rehearsals in the morning, okay?" Willow says, and I nod, closing the door behind me and blocking out Ryan's stare.

I'm not sure what I expected when I stepped inside, but it wasn't this. Our house—the one I left this morning—is completely void of my father. The only remnant of him the memories I have trapped in the music boxes stashed in the corner…and my piano. The house smells of Pine-Sol, and my mom is listening to music loudly in the kitchen, her hands covered in rubber gloves.

"I thought you were working?" I ask, scaring her a little with my voice.

"Oh! Sorry, didn't hear you come in. Uh…yeah, work. Seems I'm a little upset, and I might have had a little bit of an issue inserting a catheter? So, I'm taking a week of personal time. The chief sort of insisted," she says, running her arm along her nose. Her eyes are red, and I can tell she's been crying.

"So, you're…cleaning?" I ask, holding up a bag of trash tied and propped in the corner.

"Seems so," she says, going back to scrubbing. "I'm getting rid of…things. Anything we don't need, it's in boxes in the garage."

She didn't say it, but I know she means she's getting rid of my father, of *his* things. She's being a little manic, and when I look around the house, I'm a little frightened by how much she's done in the six or seven hours I've been gone.

"Okay, well...do you want to keep going? Or, I don't know...can I help? I have a project to work on, but it's not due for a while," I say, setting my backpack on the counter and my project supplies down next to it. My mom feels lost, and I'm right there with her.

"There's a lot of trash. There's more on the side of the house. Maybe see what you can fit in the can?" she asks, already back to scrubbing the sink. I notice she's thrown my father's food away, the packets of tuna he likes all bagged up neatly—ready for the trash.

"I can handle trash," I say, watching her wipe her brow with her sleeve, watching her pretend. I pick up the small bag of food and garbage and leave through the back door, ready to pretend right along with her.

I notice the bags stacked along the wall when I step outside, and I recognize my father's dress shoes peaking out of the top of one of them.

"That's a lot of nice stuff. Your mom throwing it all away?" Owen asks. I close my eyes, my back still to him.

"Guess so," I respond.

"You should sell it," he says, and I hear his steps moving away from me. I turn and notice he's taking out a bag of trash too.

I drag our garbage and the first bag of my father's things to our can, which is sitting right next to the Harpers'.

"You take out the trash," I say, not sure why I'm surprised seeing him do such a simple thing. But I am. I'm amazed.

"Yep," he says, flinging his bag into his container and closing the lid. I notice how empty it sounds, and I look over my shoulder at the dozen bags waiting for me.

"Hey," I start, but stop instantly, biting my lip to give myself time to think. I almost asked him for a favor, and I don't think I want to do that.

"If I can have those shoes, you can dump your crap in our trashcan," he says, finishing my thought—almost.

"Really?" I'm flummoxed. He's being nice. Or, I think he's being nice. "And...the shoes?"

He gestures to the bags, to the one on top with my father's dress shoes.

74

"Oh," I say, feeling a little strange about the thought of Owen wearing my father's shoes. "I...I guess?"

"It's for my grandpa. He needs a new pair," Owen says, somehow becoming a little more human with this revelation. He has a grandpa. I don't know why that strikes me as strange, also.

"Sure, then. That's fine," I say, walking over to grab some of the bags. I pull the shoes out of the first and turn to hand them to Owen, surprised when he's close to me. He's so near me, and his eyes aren't dark. They're bright. He looks...happy. "Does your grandpa live close?"

I hand him the shoes, and for a few seconds, we're both holding them. Owen is looking at the shoes. *I'm* looking at Owen's hands and remembering how he stopped me from beating up the dashboard of his truck. I'm remembering how big his hands were—how they covered mine completely, how they were rough, yet warm and soft all the same.

"He lives in a nursing home, just on the other side of town. That was his truck," he says, nodding over his shoulder.

I don't know Owen's grandfather, but I'm suddenly happy he's getting my father's shoes. I like Owen's truck, and I rationalize that I probably would like his grandpa, too. Maybe a better man will wear those shoes.

"Here, let me help you get these in. I think we can fit them all in both cans," he says, setting the shoes down and picking up three bags at once, lifting them easily and stuffing them in my already-overflowing can. He's pushing with his arms, and I have a flash memory of how they looked when I watched him pull his shirt from his body early this morning.

"You missed school today," I say, waiting to see how he responds. He doesn't, much, only offering a shrug. "You miss a lot?"

"I get good grades. But I have to work, and sometimes I just can't do both things at once," he says, walking back to the side of my house for more bags. I lift one for every three he takes, and in two more trips, we have all traces of my father neatly stowed in the giant green trashcans by the curb.

"Where do you work?" I ask, trying not to overanalyze how civil our conversation is right now.

Owen presses down one more time on the top of my can, then pulls the black hat from his head, running his fingers through his dark hair, smoothing the long strands back so they sit neatly under his hat again.

"It's just some job. Look, thanks for the shoes, but I've gotta go," he says, suddenly short and on the verge of rude.

He pulls his keys from his pocket and heads toward his truck, tossing the shoes in the passenger seat and leaving me behind—feeling stupid for even asking questions about him.

I still watch him pull away, though. I don't even disguise it. And strangely, things feel more right talking with Owen than they do with Willow, or Elise, or Ryan. Owen may be my best friend here in Woodstock, and *that* is pathetic.

I step back inside the house, and the warmth feels good. The air is a constant chill now, and I know real winter is coming. In the city, the buildings hid the snow and grayness of the sky. Everything always felt alive, even when the cold was biting. But you can see it coming out here. The leaves have all fallen, and the trees are sticks. The gray of the clouds, the color of winter is consuming—and it's all around.

My piano looks like the sky. I just don't want to play it.

My mother is still cleaning. She's moved upstairs, working on my bathroom or hers; I can't tell. Our house isn't dirty, but I get what she's doing. She's erasing my father. Unfortunately, I can't drag a thousand-pound piano into the driveway, otherwise I'd erase him, too.

My scarf and beanie are still lying on the sofa near the front door, so I grab them and bundle myself up before heading back outside. My feet carry me to the garage, and I lift the heavy door, having to jump to get it up all the way. I walk to the back, to the boxes of tools that my mom will have a much better chance of using.

There's the hoop. Its rust has left a mark on the wall behind it, and I know it's heavy. I remember from dragging it here in the first place. I move the boxes out of the way first, knocking one over and spilling bolts and drill bits in a thousand different directions. Once I sweep them into a pile, I pour them back in the box, not caring how disorganized I'm leaving it. My dad would hate that, and doing it brings a smile to my face.

Gripping the rim of the hoop with both hands, I drag it back out of the garage, and it scrapes along the pavement, leaving an orange mark behind. That makes me smile, too.

I unfold the ladder and place it under the spot on the eave of the house where the hoop hung only a few days before. The bolts are still there, and if I can just manage to get the hoop to the top of the ladder, I can slide it against the garage until I can lock it in place.

"Honey, careful up there," my mom says, her voice igniting a rapid fire in my chest. I wait for her to question what I'm doing, but she doesn't. She's too lost in her own world to care about this. "I'm running to the store. I'll pick up some things for dinner. Need anything?"

"No, I'm good. Thanks!" I yell, thinking to myself about that word—*need.* A week ago, I needed to move back to the city, needed time alone to play my music...how I wanted to. I needed my friends—the ones I used to trust. But now, all I need to do is get this hoop up on the goddamned garage.

I grunt the entire time, and the metal rim scratches my arm through my sweatshirt in a few places, but after at least twenty minutes, I manage to get the hoop back up on the brackets—the weight of it no longer depending on my strength. It takes several more minutes to find the drill in the garage, but when I do, I'm able to lock the bolts down tight, and I push up on the rim to check that it's stable.

After putting the tools and ladder away, I walk backward, shutting the garage door with a tired leap, and admiring my work. It's almost as if it was never gone. I hope the boy who uses it at night comes back.

The car makes a skidding sound as it pulls up our driveway. I turn around expecting my mom, expecting to help her haul in a few bags of groceries. But I'm met with the dimmed headlights of a blue BMW—freezing me instantly.

She looks so different when she steps out of the car. She seems...*older*...and like a stranger. Her blond hair rings around her face, the curls perfect, and I can tell she spent a lot of time on her appearance. She wanted to look her best for me, for this...whatever *this* is. Ambush, I am guessing.

"Kensington," she says, my full name floating from her breath, soft and airy, like she's trying to seduce me.

"Go home, Gaby," I say, brushing the dirt from my hands and sleeves, my belly quivering with nerves that my mother is going to pull in the driveway behind her and have to see this.

"I just want to talk," she says, her hands stretched out, like she's helpless.

"You could have called. Go home, Gaby. My mom will be home any minute, and she doesn't need to see you here. I don't need to see you here," I say, moving toward my house, toward my door.

"Kens," she says, saying my name the way my new friends do. She hasn't called me Kens since we were little, and she no longer has the right to.

"Gaby, you cannot be serious! Coming here? Right now? I mean, are you serious about this?" I can feel my temper boiling, and I notice Owen's truck pull up behind her, which only makes my nerves fire away more. I don't want him to see this. I don't want to be here. I want to disappear!

"Please, Kens..." she starts, and I interrupt.

"Don't talk to me like that! Don't say my name like that! Like we're...what? Friends? Jesus, Gaby! You slept with my father!" I scream, and I notice another guy standing next to Owen, both of them near the front of the truck, watching me—watching *this*.

"I didn't mean to. It just happened. I fell in love with him, Kensington. I love Dean. And I tried not to, but your dad, he loves me too. We didn't mean to hurt you, hurt your mom." She's saying so much. She's saying *too* much, and I notice Owen ushering whoever is with him toward the house—away from my embarrassing display—and I'm grateful.

The distraction lets Gaby get closer without me realizing, though, and soon her hand is touching my arm, and I recoil quickly.

"Don't you fucking touch me. You...you!" I push her as I let go of myself, let myself feel the rage. "You were my best friend, and you betrayed me. You betrayed my MOM! We took care of you, let you stay in our house. My god! What were you doing in my house? Uhhhhhhggggg! You called him *Dean*! Like he's your boyfriend! Oh...my god!"

"It wasn't like that, Kens. I promise," she starts, but I hold my hands up, then I shove her back on her feet. I move her, and she lets me, until she's at her opened car door.

"Just...go, Gaby. Please...just go," I say, my head shaking, and the tears filling up the corners of my eyes. Gaby's face is a reflection of mine, but I have no sympathy for her. I want her to feel the pain of a million needles—I want her heart to ache and her breath to choke her. I want her to cry and never stop. And I want my mom to feel better. I want to move back to the city, away from this place. But I can't even do that, because that's where Gaby is, where *Dean* is.

She climbs back in the car and slowly moves away. I break, reaching down and filling my hands with small rocks from the side of the yard. "I hate you!" I scream, my voice cracking from the force, and I let the rocks fly at the front of her car, pelting it and leaving small marks behind. I reach down for another handful, and cock my arm, ready to throw.

"Don't," Owen says, his hand wrapped around my small wrist, locking me up, unable to move. I snap to his eyes, and they're no longer void of feeling like they were this morning. There's sympathy in them, and that's the only reason I let my muscles relax. "It won't make you feel better. Let her go."

The stones fall from my fingers, and I bring my hands up to my head, scratching into my hairline with frustration as I pace. "What will?" I ask, and he quirks an eyebrow up. "Make me feel better. What will make me feel better?"

"Nothing," he says, and his answer comes so fast that it makes me sad. I'm sad because I get the sense that Owen is right, and he's speaking from experience.

"I'm. So. Angry," I say between deep breaths, letting my guard down a little more, but tensing when I realize that the guy who was in the truck with him is still here, standing a few feet away. Owen follows my gaze, the corner of his lip raising slightly, then lowering fast.

"That's my brother, Andrew," he says, and the younger version of him nods once in response, stepping forward and reaching out his hand. His manners feel so natural, and strange, given how much he looks like his older brother.

"I'm Kensi," I say, shaking his hand.

"I know," he says, smiling enough to show his teeth. Owen gives him a sharp look, and he scrunches his shoulders up defensively. "What? I know her name. So what?"

Owen keeps his disapproving look on his brother for a few more seconds, and I can sense a silent exchange happening between them.

"You ever hit someone?" Owen asks, making a sharp turn in the conversation, his eyes back on mine. They're still bright, and...gorgeous. But there's also a challenge lingering in them, this flare I see every now and then, when he's confronting me, taunting me—pushing me.

"No," I say back, my response clipped and short on purpose. He doesn't like it when I talk to him this way. I can tell because he stutters on his feet a little, like he's not used to someone being so blunt with him.

"Hit me," he says, and now I'm the one falling on my feet.

"Are you nuts?" I ask, and his brother chuckles behind him.

"Haven't you heard, Kensi? We're all fucking nuts. Harper boys are all fucked up in the head," Andrew says. Owen is quick with his reach, grabbing the sleeve of his shirt and jerking him slightly. Andrew continues to laugh lightly, but he straightens up fast and starts to kick at the driveway, moving toward the truck and away from Owen and me.

"I'm being serious. Hit me. You need to feel something," Owen says, stepping a little closer—a little *too* close—to me.

"Owen, I don't want to hit you," I say, letting out a long breath and feeling my arms tingle in fear at the thought of doing something so...so...violent.

"Yes you do," he says, taking another step, his chest now completely blocking my view of his brother.

"No, I don't," I say, shoving him off balance. He steps back quickly with one foot and looks down to his feet, his lip curling on the corner into that smile again, and soon his feet are back where they were, his eyes wide and intensely looking at my face.

"You sure about that?" he asks, moving an inch or two closer, close enough that I notice the scent of his shampoo, his cologne, and the way I remember the inside of his truck smelling.

"What are you, in fight club or something?" I tease, trying to bring lightness to the most awkward and heavy conversation I've ever had with a boy.

"Something like that," he says, stepping nearer. "Go on, Ken Doll. Hit me. You want to, and it will feel *soooooo good.*"

He's so close that I feel the tickle of his breath now. His brother is still close enough that I know he's watching him lure me, and I wonder how normal this behavior is. His right hand reaches to my shoulder, pulling a wave of my hair into his fingers, and he twists it slowly, his eyes moving from his hands to my lips and back again.

"Come on, Ken Doll. Hit me," he says, practically a whisper. He brings his mouth lower to my neck, his hand pulling the wave of hair back until it falls from his fingers completely.

He reaches in again, sweeping a pile of my hair out of his way, his eyes daring mine, that wicked look growing stronger until I can no longer see them, his mouth and nose lost under my chin, his lips almost touching me. I haven't breathed since he started this game.

"Are you...afraid? I won't hit you back. I don't do that," he says softly against my ear, my body now covered in shivers, but my legs holding strong, fighting against the pounding in my chest. "Or...would you rather I kiss you? Maybe that would be better, help you...forget. I bet you've never been kissed before. Virgin. Ken Doll, *my little virgin.*"

With swift force, I bend my elbow and bring my fist into Owen's lower stomach—close enough to his crotch to make him question everything he thinks he knows about me, to make him second guess his assumption that I'm weak. I'm lost, but I'm not weak. When he starts coughing, backing away from me with his arms wrapped around his stomach, he starts to laugh, and I begin to think that Owen Harper might actually be crazy.

"Thata girl," he says, standing with his hands along his back, bending forward and back, trying to work out the damage I did to him. "You feel better?"

"I feel like you're an asshole," I say, igniting a new round of laughter from Andrew.

"You're right about that, Kensi. My brother's a real asshole," he says, coming closer so he can mock his brother. "Dude, she laid you out. You a'right, man? Swallow a nut?"

Owen pushes his brother back a few steps, then coughs a few more times. "I'm fine, douchebag," he says, then brings his focus back to me. "Let me ask you again. Do you feel better?"

His smile is gone, his mouth tight, in a flat line. His eyes penetrating me completely, and I keep my focus on him as I consider this, think about his words, and ask myself with my inner voice: Do I feel better? Absolutely not.

"No," I say quickly, my eyes drifting to his chin, to his neck, and then his chest. What felt better was having him close, smelling him, thinking he might actually put his lips on mine, that he might touch me. Thinking he might actually *want* me in a way that I've never been wanted is what felt good—more than good.

But hitting him only made me feel bad.

I don't hate Owen Harper. But I want him. Unlike I've ever wanted anyone. And while that takes away the ugly I feel about my father, it also scares the ever-loving crap out of me.

Chapter 8

Owen came to school for the rest of the week, and his routine was back to the same—his feet up on my desk, his make-out sessions on display at lunch, this time with a new girl I didn't recognize. His friend he called House started nodding to me in the hall, and by the end of the week, I was nodding back. Owen was still making me the focus of his attention, but it felt less cruel now.

"I've never actually seen him flirt with anyone before," Willow says, throwing a French fry at my plate, drawing my attention from the window where Owen is backing away, nodding his chin at me with a slight acknowledgement and an even slighter grin.

"What, that? Please. He's not flirting. He just helped me out with some crap at my house this weekend, and we talked a little. But he's still an ass. Just less of an ass," I say, trying to convince Willow, but clearly doing a very poor job as she smiles at me like she knows all of my secrets.

"Right, he's an ass. Or...is he dreamy? Which one is it?" she teases, and I pick up her fry and throw it back in her lap.

"He's an ass," I say, standing with my tray and pulling my bag over my shoulder.

"Okay. But, I'm not stupid, you know. I can tell you like him," she says, throwing her trash on top of mine, then passing me to hold open the lunchroom door for me to follow.

I don't answer her, because I don't want to lie. I do like him. I've been dreaming about him, and when I don't dream about him, I pray to dream about him. I wait by my window, hoping to hear the sound of his ball bouncing in my driveway. He hasn't been out there since I've put the hoop back up, though. Most nights, I lay quiet and listen for his truck to leave or pull into the driveway. I wish I had a car, so I could follow him to his work— so I knew where he was when I don't see him.

We get to the spot in the hallway where our paths divide, and Willow tugs on my sleeve, stopping me before I'm about to say goodbye.

"It's okay to like him, you know. I meant what I said the other day. You know, in front of Ryan? I kissed him, like two and a half years ago, at a party. It was *nooooo* big deal. And I love Jess. I don't have a *thing* for Owen Harper. Yes, *I* think he's a jerk. But..." she pauses, looking down and stepping closer to me. "But I don't have to like him. And if you do, I will still like you. And maybe you'll make me think more of Owen, just because you're so awesome."

She smiles when she's done and tugs at my sleeve one more time, a nonverbal queue asking for my acceptance and understanding.

"Okay," I say, sucking in my bottom lip with the weight of everything that small *okay* admits to. Willow doesn't judge, and she doesn't make it more than it is. She just nods and tells me she'll meet me in the parking lot so we can go grab a bite to eat before the football game tonight.

Owen is waiting for me in science class, his feet on my chair this time rather than my tabletop. His hands are folded behind his head, and my heart is literally smacking into my chest bones, rattling my insides to the point that I actually feel dizzy. I'm sure it's in my head, but I swear he heard me say "okay" too.

"This is a record for you, isn't it?" I say, pushing his heavy Converse-covered feet from my seat before sitting down and pulling out my notebook. I can hear Owen leaning forward, and I know his face is close to the back of my head, but I will myself to face my desk and not turn around.

"What's a record?" he asks.

"You've been here every day this week. Seriously, they should give you an award. At least a certificate," I say, not feeling as proud as I usually do when I take digs at him.

"Didn't have to work this week," he says. I can hear him lean back in his seat. "Got fired."

I turn around when he says that, wanting to evaluate the look on his face, make sure he's being *real*. His eyes meet mine the second I lean over the back of my chair, and there's a heavy seriousness to them.

"I'm sorry. That...sucks," I say.

"Yeah, it does," he says, bending forward to pull a pencil from the side of his backpack. He slides a notebook out and flips through the pages, and I can't help but notice that his paper is filled with notes, and his handwriting is actually decent.

"Well, at least now you have time for school," I say, moving my gaze from his hands to his eyes and back again; the intensity of the way he looks at me makes it hard to stare at him long.

"Ha, I guess. I'm getting a new job, though. Have to. We've got bills," he says, and I feel like one more page of his story has turned for me to read. Owen Harper is responsible, more than any teenager should be.

"What about your mom? Or...does she live with you? I'm sorry. I just...honestly, I've only ever seen you and your brother," I say, not wanting to admit how much I know about his personal life, not wanting to give credence to the rumors.

"My mom works nights. She's a security guard at an impound lot. She's taking online classes to be a medical tech, so she usually studies while she's sitting in the booth. Her job pays shit, and with gramps in the nursing home..." he looks up at our teacher as he walks in, then taps his pencil a few times on his notebook and nods forward.

We're dissecting next week—baby sharks. We spent the hour looking at slides of the various parts we'll be required to identify. I didn't write down a single thing. All I could do was listen to the sound of Owen's pencil scratching paper behind me, the sounds of his breath, of his feet sliding along the floor, of the noise his hands make when they scratch at the stubble on his chin and his knuckles crack.

It was a two-minute conversation, but I feel like I know more about Owen Harper than anyone else in this entire school. And all I want to do is learn more.

When the bell rings, I gather my things quickly and turn to face Owen, hoping he'll pick up where things left off. But he's already gone—vanished.

I spend my last hour in health class doing the same thing I did in science—piecing together sections of Owen's life. I never see his brother Andrew at school, and I have yet to meet James, the one everyone says is *real* trouble. Owen seems to always be alone.

Alone.

When the bell rings, I pack up and pull my phone from my pocket to text my mom and let her know I'll be staying at school and grabbing dinner with Willow. I worry about her eating on her own, spending the night by herself. My mom and I have fallen into a routine the last few days—homework, dinner, and a movie. I think that routine is distracting her from my father. He tried to call last night, and my mom turned her phone off. I hope she's strong enough to do the same when I'm not there watching.

"Hey, so Jess wants burgers. You good with burgers?" Willow asks as she slips her arm through mine while we exit the main hallway out onto the front lawn of the school.

"Sounds good. I'm hungry," I say, my voice trailing off when I notice Owen sitting on the tailgate of his truck, parked next to Willow's car. He's waiting for me, and Willow sees him, too.

"Unless, of course…you'd like to maybe have dinner with someone else?" she teases.

"Stop," I whisper harshly, my face burning. I've never been a fan of being teased about boys. It was something Gaby always did to me. One of many thoughtless things my so-called best friend did to disregard my feelings it seems.

"He's waiting to talk to you. He's never here after school, Kens. There's a reason he's here," she says, and my stomach flutters with the same sensation I get when I'm climbing up in a rollercoaster. I think this is thrill.

As we get closer, Owen swings his long legs outward and stands up, closing the tailgate behind him and leaning his arm over it, his head covered in a dark gray beanie, and the ends of his hair sticking out a little on the front and sides.

"Hey," he says, looking up at me quickly, then back down at his feet. He leans out from the edge of the truck with his arm still holding it while he stretches his long body. He looks nervous and uncomfortable, and it's giving me hope about the reason he's here…waiting for me. I hate that it's giving me hope. I know what that means.

"Hey," I say back, looking to Willow for help, a life raft—anything!

"Wow, well that was deep you two," she says, and my eyes grow wide with embarrassment. Owen laughs lightly and pushes his hands into the pockets of his black jeans before stepping closer to me. Willow glances at me before unlocking her car and tossing her bag inside. Jess is walking up, which now has my heart racing even faster, pulsing harder, and my mouth has forgotten how to work.

"I guess you probably already have a ride, huh?" Owen says, cocking his head to the side to look at me with one eyebrow raised.

"Yeah, uh...I have to be at the game tonight. Band," I say, sucking in my lip and cursing band for the first time.

"Right...right," Owen says, nodding and taking a small step back. "I forgot you do that. That's cool. Just thought I'd see if you needed a ride home, but yeah...so, I'll see ya later."

He pulls his keys from his pocket and tosses them slightly before grabbing them in the air and turning on his heels. I want to jump in the other side of his truck, run away with him, go home with him, go anywhere with him. Hell, I want to sit in the truck and wait while he fills out job applications and does whatever else it is he does when he's gone.

"Hey, Kens?" Willow asks, her arm over the top of her car while she looks at me. Owen pauses at the sound of her voice. "You know, Jess and I were thinking we'd just go grab dinner at his house, since it's so close. We don't have to be back here until six, in case...you know...you wanna do something else?"

My lips actually hurt from the force of wanting to smile, but I keep it hidden, pushing my lips tight and only letting the corners of my mouth curl.

"Could you bring me back here? By six?" I ask Owen, hoping he simply says *yes*, that he doesn't bail on this completely.

"Yeah, that's cool. I've got time. I have to pick up Andrew, so..." his voice fades away, and his attention moves to the cab of his truck. I secretly love that he's so unsure of his words with me. This is different from teasing. This is different from being cruel. And I like it.

"We'll see you at six, Kens," Willow says with a wink. Jess is already in the car with her, looking over his shoulder at Owen and me, and I'm sure she's filling him in on everything she thinks this is about. That's probably for the best, because Willow might understand what's happening better than me.

"You ready?" Owen asks, from the other side of his truck. I didn't really expect him to open my door or anything, but he seems so uncomfortable being alone with me now.

"Oh, uh...yeah. Should I just throw my stuff in the back of the truck then?" I ask. Owen shrugs a nod, so I lift my heavy bag to the back of his truck, securing it between the metal side and a tire, then climb into the cab with him. His truck looks different in the daylight, but it still brings back memories of the last time I was in here with him, when I swore at him and slapped him like a girl. I feel a little ashamed, because I can tell he's remembering that, too.

"So, where's Andrew?" I ask, wanting to start a safe conversation—*any* conversation.

"He's at the community college. He splits his time between here and there, usually doesn't get done until after our school lets out," Owen says, his lips forming a prideful smile. "Andrew's sort of smart."

"Wow, so he's like, what? Taking college classes?" I ask. We had a program like this at Bryce, but the professors came to our school.

"Yeah, he has eight credits or something like that. English and algebra, I think? If he passes with an *A*, he gets full credit toward his diploma. It's free, so I made sure when he was selected he took advantage of it," Owen says, his eyes on the road as we pull away from the school—the opposite direction of everyone else.

"That's amazing. You must be proud of him," I say, knowing he is by the way he talks about his brother.

"Yeah, well...one of us should get a college degree," he says. I can't tell if he's being humble or bitter.

"What about you? Where are you going?" I ask.

"Depends," he says, glancing up at the rearview mirror, then beyond his shoulder, his eyes grazing over me as he does. "I'd like to play ball somewhere. But then...who's gonna pay the bills?"

Owen doesn't add anything after this, and I don't know what to ask, so I reach forward and twist the knob on his old stereo to listen to some music. Nothing comes in very well, the classic rock station sounding the best; I leave the dial there. A few minutes later, we pull up at the front of the community college, and Andrew waves from a bench.

"You're going to need to scoot to the middle," Owen says, looking at the small space next to him, the one with the hump in the middle of the floor.

I unbuckle my belt and slide there, bending my knees in front of me and looking for the seatbelt straps.

"There's no belt here. Sorry...I'll be careful, though. I'll keep you safe," he says, his eyes flashing to mine for a beat before moving back to the steering wheel. I notice the hard swallow in his throat.

"Door's locked," Andrew says, his voice muffled from outside. He's pulling on the handle, but nothing's happening. I start to reach over to pull the lock at the top, but Owen puts his hand on my arm, stopping me.

"I got it. It's broken," he says, careful not to look at me while he leans across my body. I practically suck myself to the seat, holding my breath the entire time his body is stretched across my lap. I can see the bare skin on his side as he reaches over, his shirt pulling from his jeans, and I notice the gray band of his boxers.

I'm noticing things I've never noticed about boys before.

When he straightens up again behind the wheel, he turns his focus to his side window, almost as if he's trying to pretend I'm not here, that my leg isn't touching his. All I can feel is his leg— and when he moves it from the gas to the brake and back again—I take pleasure in the movement.

"Hey, Kens," Andrew says, startling me back to the present.

"Hey. Hope it's okay I tagged along," I say, wondering why Andrew called me *Kens*, if he knew I'd like it, and if Owen was the one to tell him so.

"Oh, it's okay," he says, leaning forward to look at his brother. I'm uncomfortable by his suggestion, and I can tell it's making Owen angry by the way he starts jerking the wheel and driving a bit rougher.

"Kensington has to be back at school for band at six, so I'm going to drop you off at home, we'll eat, and then I'll bring her back," Owen says, suddenly acting formal, like a parent.

"We should go to the game," Andrew adds, still leaning forward with the same grin. I keep my face forward, my eyes focusing on a small chip in Owen's windshield.

"I don't go to football games," Owen says, stopping quickly at a light. His change in speed makes me slide forward a little in my seat, so I flex my legs against the floor to hold myself back.

"You said you'd be careful," I say, interrupting his pissing match with his brother.

"Sorry," he says, taking off again a little slower.

"Well, maybe I want to go. Can I go? I'll hang out near the band, by Kens," Andrew says, smiling at me. I'm not sure if he actually wants to go, or if he's trying to goad his brother—but both thoughts make me smile in return.

"Don't call her Kens, Andrew. You don't know if she likes it," Owen says, jerking the wheel hard again while he turns right to head down our street.

"You know that's not true, asshole. You're the one who told me," his brother says, clearing up that small sliver of doubt I had left that I had an effect on Owen Harper.

We fly into Owen's driveway, but his truck skids to a stop. I feel my legs weaken in their fight to hold me in place, and I shut my eyes tightly and bring my arms up to brace myself. Owen's hold on me is fast as his arm quickly covers my chest, and I grab hold of it on instinct.

A rollercoaster ride.

When my adrenaline rush begins to fade, I loosen my grip and look down at the dark knitted fabric of his shirt and how its contrasts with the paleness of my small fingers.

His arm is warm.

"I'm so sorry," he says, his voice more of a whisper, just for me.

90

"I'm okay," I say, sparing a look at his face. The pain in his eyes is evident, and even though he scared me, I want to erase his guilt. "Really. Owen...I'm okay."

I squeeze his arm one more time, letting my hands feel how strong his muscles are, feel the heat of his skin, sense the beat of his pulse in his veins.

"That's not what I'm sorry about," he says, his voice cracking a little this time.

When I turn to face the open door Andrew left on the other side, Owen's apology becomes achingly clear. My father's car is in our driveway, and he's standing at our back door, practically lying against it, pounding and begging for my mom to answer.

"Fucking hell," I say, the thrill I felt from that small touch of Owen's arm replaced with feelings of regret, anger, betrayal, and dread.

I slide from the seat and move closer to my driveway, my father still unaware I'm behind him. He's slurring—badly—and within a few more steps I can smell why.

"Dad, you need to leave. I'm calling you a cab," I say, pulling my phone from my back pocket.

"Like hell I do. This is my house, and that bitch is going to let me inside," my father says. Hearing him say those words—*that word*—about my mom makes my arms begin to itch, wanting to swing and hurt something or someone.

"Dad, this is all because of you. You're drunk, and you're being mean. You need to leave!" I yell, stopping when my dad finds his footing and stumbles a few steps in my direction.

"You..." he says, pointing over my shoulder. I turn and see Owen near my side, only a few steps behind me. "You're that kid next door. You're a disruption, and you need to stay the FUCK away from my daughter!"

"Dad! Stop it!" I say, sliding to the right a step as if I can protect Owen—as if Owen needs my protection.

"Sir, I think you've had too much to drink tonight. You really should listen to your daughter. If you don't want a cab, I'll take you somewhere—anywhere," Owen says. I turn to look at him as I feel his hand flatten against my back, and when I do, my dad yanks at my shoulder, sending me to the ground.

"You punk-ass little shit! She has worked too hard for you to screw it all up. If anyone is leaving, it's you...right now!" My father hoists his sloppy arm forward, hitting Owen in the eye, and Owen stumbles back a step, but rights himself quickly. When my dad moves toward him again, I get up and run to my front door to get my mom.

"Mr. Worth, you need to stop. I don't want to hurt you, but I'm not going to let you assault me..." I hear Owen say as I race through my door to find my mom sitting at the bottom of the stairs, crying.

"You have to call the police, Mom. Now! Dad's hurting our neighbor," I say, trying to snap my mom out of this strange trance she seems to be in.

"It's been an hour. He's been out there for an hour. I don't know how to make him leave," she sobs, raising her hand to cover her mouth and mute the sound of her wails.

When I hear the sound of a punch being thrown, I pull my phone from my back pocket and dial 911.

"What's your emergency?" the operator asks.

"There's an assault happening outside, in my driveway. Hurry, fast, please!" I move to the window and see Owen straddling my dad on the ground, trying to hold his arms still, but my dad is fighting. He's fighting so hard. Andrew is moving back inside his house on Owen's urging.

"Ma'am, I am going to need your address..."

I pull a bill from the front counter and read off our address that I have yet to memorize—then sprint back outside to Owen. He looks up when he hears my footsteps, and my father takes advantage of the distraction, punching him hard in the same eye again.

"Mother fuck!" Owen says, wincing, and leaning his face against his shoulder, pushing down on my father's flailing arms again, this time with more strength.

"The police are coming. They'll be here any minute. I'm so sorry, Owen. I'm..." I let out a short cry—mortified that this is my life, that Owen is watching this. The boy who minutes ago had my heart racing is now straddling my dad in a pile of dust, trying to keep him from hurting my mother more than he already has.

92

"Don't," Owen says, his eyes on me again, his right one already blue and puffy—because of me. "Don't you dare apologize."

I nod, then pull my left arm around myself, squeezing in an attempt to stop the rush of nerves and fear coursing through me. The lights flash in the distance, and soon, I can hear the sirens.

"They're here," I say to the operator, pushing my phone back in my pocket without ending the call, just in case. Two cop cars pull in quickly, and two of the police officers rush to Owen, pulling him away from my dad and pushing him flat along the ground.

"Do not try to fight us!" one of them yells, while the other pulls Owen's arms together behind his back, binding them with a thick plastic tie.

"No! He was helping! Don't hurt him!" I start to protest, but they dismiss me and go to work on my dad, sitting him upright and pulling his arms behind his back as well, though with less force than they used against Owen.

"Oh my god, Owen. Your eye!" I say, moving closer to him.

"Miss," one of the officers says, holding his arm out and barring me from taking one more step in Owen's direction. I look across the lawn and see Andrew standing at the doorway, and he's shaking his head at me, telling me to leave it alone.

"I'm fine, Kens. I'll be okay. Go check on your mom," Owen says, his voice a strange calm. He spits to the side, and it's bloody, which only makes me want to get to him more. "Kens...go!"

My mom. He's right. She'll know what to do. Only, just seconds ago, she was practically a statue—frozen in her depression inside my house. I rush inside and she's moved to the window, standing there swaying, holding the blinds open with her fist.

"I need you, Mom! You have to come out. You have to explain that Owen didn't do any of this," I say, but she doesn't move, and her feet keep rocking. "Mom!"

This time I yank on her arm, and she turns to look at me, her face shaking a little, like I just woke her up. "Mom! Come!"

"Right, yes…okay," she says, looking around the house for a few seconds, like she's missing something. She finally grabs her wallet, and I follow her back outside.

"Ma'am, can you explain what happened here tonight?" the first officer asks. I notice the tag on his uniform reads Blakely.

"My husband…he…he was drinking. We're…separated," my mom says, her words coming out in a stutter as she watches the police officers push my dad's head down as they load him into the back of one of the cars.

"Are you hurt, ma'am?" Blakely asks, and my mom quickly shakes her head *no.*

"The boy—" she says, looking to me and then out to Owen who is being jerked to a stand by Blakely's partner, "he was only helping. Please, he was just protecting my daughter."

Blakely stops his pen on his notepad and looks up at my mom when she says this, then to me, before looking back over his shoulder at Owen who is slowly being led to the other car. "That boy? The one right there?" he asks, motioning to Owen with his pen.

"Yes," my mom says, her eyes fighting against the need to cry.

"I'm afraid we're still going to need to talk to him," he says, nodding his head to his partner to continue.

"Can't you talk to him here? Or just call him or whatever? I mean…he saved me!" I sound like a pathetic little girl, and my stomach is overcome with this sinking feeling that they're not going to listen to me, that they're going to take Owen away, and it will be my fault.

"Miss, if you're lying, you're going to be in a heap of trouble. That kid right there—he's not worth lying for, you understand?" Blakely says, but all I can see is the door closing on Owen behind him, and Owen going peacefully—willingly.

"I understand," I say, my eyes moving back to Blakely. "I'm not lying."

He holds my attention for a few long seconds, the sound of his pen clicking open and shut like a bomb ticking away in my ears. "Mosely, let him go," he says, pushing the button on the radio pinned to his collar.

"You sure about that?" I hear his partner respond.

94

"Seems so," Blakely says, and within seconds, his partner is stepping back out of the vehicle and opening the door for Owen. I don't breathe until his hands are free. When the car holding my father pulls away, I move closer to him, letting my mom finish her talk with the police officers.

"Come on, you need ice," I say, pulling at the sleeve of his shirt, urging him to follow me inside.

Owen's quiet as we walk up my porch and through the main living room, but he pauses at my piano. I backpedal a few steps, and nod toward the kitchen, and he catches up.

"Let me see," I say, placing my hands on both of his shoulders, gently guiding him to one of our stools. I step closer, until my body is practically between his long, outstretched legs, and I move my hands to his chin, tilting it upward so I can see how bad his bruising is in the light.

"That's going to be really bad. God, Owen...I'm so sorry," I say, but he quiets me fast.

"Shhhhhh," he says, his head tilting back down and his eyes on me. His hair is super messy, the beanie he was wearing lost somewhere in the scuffle with my dad.

"I'm so embarrassed," I say, closing my eyes and letting my head fall forward. I want to cry, but I'm so drained; I can't even do that.

"Don't be. Not with me. Not over this," he says, his hand slowly sweeping a strand of my hair away from my face. His gesture sends a short wave of shivers down my neck and arms, and I hate my father for ruining this moment. I want to enjoy it, but I can't.

I turn to the freezer and fill a small plastic bag with a few ice cubes, then wrap it in a dishtowel. "It's the best we have. Don't get a lot of shiners in our house," I chuckle. My joke is stupid, but Owen smiles at it anyway.

"Thanks," he says, taking it from me, his hand covering mine completely when he does. God how I want him to hold my hand.

I move to the stool next to him and prop my elbows up on the counter, digging my hands into my scalp and massaging my head, like this situation is something I could somehow erase, only keeping the good parts.

Our silence doesn't last long, and Blakely comes in to sit in the third stool to take down our version of the story. Owen lets me do most of the talking, and I notice they don't write down anything he says anyway. Seems the Harper-brother rumors have even tainted the local law enforcement's opinion of him.

By the time the police leave, it's time for Owen to drive me back to school, and the trip back feels shorter...or maybe it doesn't feel long enough.

"Thanks for the ride," I say, laughing slightly when I realize how simplified that sounds. "And saving my mom. And me. And for beating my father's ass." My laughing picks up a little more, but it's a nervous laugh, so I suck it in and try to hold myself together.

"Mind if I tell people my brother James did this?" he says, pointing to the now puffy cheek just below his bruised eye socket. "If people know an old man did this, that won't be good for me."

He doesn't laugh at first, so I just nod yes, and start to say I understand.

"Kens," he says. "I'm kidding. I just meant I won't tell anyone. And Andrew won't either."

"Oh," I say, biting my lip and smiling briefly before sliding a step or two away from his truck.

"I'll see you later. I've got some things, okay?" he says, his brow pinching while he looks down to his lap, the light from his phone illuminating the cab of the truck.

"You shouldn't text and drive," I say, causing a whisper of a laugh to leave his lips, and a smile to creep up the side closest to me.

"I wouldn't do anything dangerous," he says, winking and tossing the phone into the empty seat beside him. His tires kick up gravel as he pulls away, and I wait at the front of the school until his taillights are so far away that I can no longer tell if they're his.

Chapter 9

I woke up instantly. That sound—it was better than an alarm. That sound was the one noise my subconscious had been on the lookout for—the one thing my ears have been begging to hear.

The bouncing was methodical, and then the clanging of the metal against the eave of the garage was undeniable.

I speed from my room—dressed in only sweatpants and an extra-large thermal shirt— stuff my feet into my boots and race down through the front door and down the porch stairs. My expectations are stunted the second I see a guy, not quite as tall and not nearly as muscular as Owen, tossing a ball up at the hoop—and missing. Repeatedly.

Andrew.

"Oh, damn. I'm sorry. That's...that's probably loud, huh?" he says, looking at his watch and then to me, realizing I'm in whatever I slept in.

"Yeah, it's...it's okay, though. It's eight. I should be up anyways," I say, pulling my arms close from the chill, also trying to bluff the disappointment no doubt painted all over my face.

"You put the hoop back up?" he asks.

That means he knows it was down.

"Yeah, my dad...he was the one who took it down the first time. I felt bad," I say, but I don't know how to finish, so I leave it at that.

Andrew bounces the ball a few more times, then turns to take another shot, this time the ball ricocheting off the eave of the house, missing all traces of the rim and backboard. "I suck at hoops," he says, his sideways grin matching his brother's. I step closer and pick up the ball. Bending my elbows, I push the ball as hard as I can toward the hoop, and it falls about two feet short, clanging off of the metal of the garage door.

"Me, too," I laugh.

Andrew kicks the ball up gently a few times until he gets it back in his hands. "Soccer," he smirks. "I always played soccer."

"Ah," I say, holding out my fingers and wiggling them. "Piano. I always played the piano."

He nods with a quick smile before looking down, an awkward silence settling over both of us. I shiver once, a breeze rustling the newest bronze and yellow leaves in our driveway.

"He likes you," Andrew says, his words like a blanket of warmth, instantly heating my entire body. My eyes are wide, but I keep my gaze at the ground, away from his.

"Ha," I let out a quick, sharp laugh.

"No, really. He hasn't flat-out said it, but he won't tell me he doesn't," he says, and the chill creeps along my skin again.

"That's nice of you to say, Andrew. But I'm pretty sure your brother would have been happier if this house sat here empty," I say, kicking at the ground, and moving my hands to the inside of the sleeves of my shirt.

"Maybe at first. But not now," he says, tossing the ball in the air a few times, then catching it and setting his sightline on me. "He's heard you play. And he says you don't anymore. Just...he noticed. And he's always leaving his window open and shit, even though it's cold as hell. He listens for you."

I chew at my bottom lip, every muscle in my mouth working to keep myself from smiling.

"Where is he?" I ask, pretending to just now notice his truck is gone. I noticed the instant I recognized Andrew was the one out here. I think I actually *felt* that Owen was gone.

"At work," he says, shrugging and walking backward on his heels, moving to his house.

"I thought he got fired?" I'm suddenly a little suspicious.

"He did. Got a new job, though, at the strip mall. He takes out trash and power washes the sidewalks and crap," he says.

"How's...his eye?" I'm embarrassed to ask this, embarrassed because I know everything Andrew witnessed. And the fact that he has yet to bring any of my drama up means he truly is a good person.

"I didn't get to see him. I'm sure he's fine, though. O can take a punch, trust me," he says with a chuckle, turning to face the steps to his house before pausing and looking at me over his shoulder. "Hey, don't tell him I told you, okay? You know...that he likes you? He'll beat my ass so fucking hard for that."

98

Andrew laughs when he asks, but I don't think he's kidding either. I cross my heart and chuckle, as if this is all a joke anyhow. But there's also that little part of me that is revving from the faster heartbeat in my chest—the part of me that likes that Owen listens for me. And that part of me wants to play the piano for the first time in days, with the hope that he'll hear it.

It's the first full day my mom's been back at work since everything in our lives changed. I've been thinking, though, how my mom's life changed months before mine. She's been pretending to be fine for a while now, but I don't know how she could have been. And as mad as I am at her for pretending, I keep forgiving her every time I feel the urge to be angry.

I have so many questions. I wonder if it all started on Gaby's birthday at the start of summer, when she spent the weekend at our house. She's always been close with my father—the two of them sharing a love of classical music that makes me roll my eyes. My father constantly compared me to her, wishing I had the same appreciation and respect for his work that she does. He loved her compositions—they were classical, not jazz. Or maybe they were just hers, and that's why he loved them. I wonder if that's how they connected? Was it those times my father helped her at the school, helped her with arrangements?

I wonder if all of those nights he was working late, and Gaby was spending late hours at Bryce, if they weren't really together—somewhere else entirely. I'm pretty sure I know the answer to this one, but maybe, just maybe, *every* word from my best friend's lips wasn't a lie.

I wonder if he waited until she was eighteen. Not that it makes it any better, but...

I've been at the piano for an hour. I keep flexing my fingers, popping knuckles, and running the palms of my hands along the wood above the keys. I can't seem to do much else. Every time I lower my hands to play, I hear my father's voice, looming in my mind, telling me jazz is a waste of time, and that my showcase is garbage—won't be good enough.

"You should probably lock this at night." Owen's voice startles me. I kick away from the piano, knocking over the bench beneath me as I struggle to get to my feet. My back is on the floor quickly, my feet kicking in my fight to stand again.

"Shit, you scared me!" My heart is thumping so loudly, I can hardly hear him talking as he closes my front door behind him and walks closer to me, a bag or something in his hand.

"Here," he says, reaching for my hand, helping me to my feet. His grasp on my wrist is for a purpose, and he lets go quickly, but I still look at that spot he touched on my skin, rubbing my own hand around it, like I'm trying to recover from a burn.

Owen sets my bench upright again, then slides onto the end of the seat, looking over the keys, and the pages spread out on the ledger.

"I'm sorry, you...were practicing?" He's starting to stand; I don't want him to leave. I move closer to the piano, resting my hand along the top, trying to make him more comfortable—and maybe blocking his exit just a little.

"No...I mean, I was thinking about it, but...I'm just not feeling it," I say, watching his finger trace the small layer of dust that's formed along the top of the ledge where my music books sit. He stares at the line he's drawn along the wood for a few seconds before breathing in deeply and pulling the small plastic bag to his lap.

"My mom's out—at work. Andrew's out, too. And I was going to make some grilled cheese for dinner, but then," he says, pausing to pull out a brick of cheddar cheese from the grocery bag and setting it on the bench next to him, "I realized I don't have any bread."

He looks up at me with a sideways grin that's unlike any face I've ever seen him make. There's no taunting to it, no motive or front. And with this one look, everything that's always been so hard and scary about being near him fades away.

"I have bread," I say, motioning for him to follow me to our kitchen. He trails closely behind me, and lightly kicks a box that's taken up a sort of permanent residence next to our kitchen island before he pulls himself into the stool at the counter and sets down his block of cheese.

"You've been here for what...a month?" he asks, looking around at the few boxes still remaining in the kitchen. Some of them have been repacked, and are getting donated or shipped tomorrow.

"Some of this stuff...it's my dad's," I say, my back to him so I can't see his face. It's easier to say the hard things this way.

"Oh," is all he says.

"Hit me with the cheese," I say when I turn around, and he makes that same silly smile again—it's almost...*playful.* He picks up the cheese and tosses it to me, but my fingers fumble the reception, and it slides through my hands, arms, knocks off my knee, and skids along the floor.

"Good thing it's wrapped," he teases.

"Shut up," I sass back, picking it up and squinting at him, like I'm daring him to cross me. He makes the same face back, but it's overly exaggerated, and dare I say *goofy*; it makes me laugh.

Owen is making me laugh. And it feels....

If there is one skill I have in the kitchen, it is making grilled-cheese sandwiches. The secret is not to be stingy with the butter, and I lather our bread well so that way by the time I slide the sandwiches from the pan, both sides are golden brown.

"Here, you can have the one with more cheese," I say, sliding a plate over to him. He picks up his sandwich and inspects it, raising an eyebrow at me before putting the bread almost in his mouth and stopping.

"How do I know you're not poisoning me?" he asks.

"You don't. You're just going to have to trust me," I smile, then take a bite of my sandwich, letting the crunch drag on slowly while I close my eyes and let my lips hum an *mmmmmm* sound.

"Right, trust you," he says, his expression soft and his eyes cautious while he considers me. I was joking about our sandwiches, but I get the feeling Owen is now on a different subject. He's making this heavier than I meant it to be, but I like that he's having such heavy thoughts. I don't think trust is something Owen has done in a long time, and it's a belief I fear lately I may be at risk of losing.

Owen finally gives in, and within five bites, maybe six, his sandwich is gone.

"Look, you're alive," I tease as I take his plate and rinse it in the sink.

"So it seems," he says, patting his chest, then gripping over his heart and making the most ridiculous croaking noise.

"You're so obnoxious," I say, reaching over to him and pushing on the arm that's resting along the counter as he sits. Before my hand slips away, he grabs it with his. It's an action I don't think he meant to do—a move he didn't calculate—and everything feels awkward. Both of us are giggling nervously for a few seconds, our fingers sort of tangled and unsure, until he finally grips my hand tightly, squeezes it once, then pushes it away.

I'm thankful for the bread that's still out on the counter, grateful that I have this distraction to busy myself with now. I twist the bag closed and turn to face our pantry, taking a deep breath and staring intently at the knuckles of my hand, the ones that were just embraced by the roughness and warmth of Owen's. When I turn back to face him, he's no longer sitting, but instead is standing by the kitchen window with his back to me, his hand by his side and his fingers flexing and contracting.

Our touch. He felt it, too.

"Thanks, by the way," he says.

I watch him for a few seconds before responding. "It's just a grilled cheese. I mean, I know mine are, like, practically the best in the Midwest, but...oh all right, yes, you're welcome," I joke. I'm joking because I'm uncomfortable. And I'm uncomfortable because all I can think about is the way his hand just felt wrapped around mine—the way he squeezed and paused, and the way he's still trying to cope with the feeling of it on his own hand.

"I meant the hoop," he says, finally turning and looking at me. His eyes are more serious now, and there's that hint of darkness to them. "Thanks for the hoop. You didn't have to put it back up. I can just shoot at the school."

"I wanted you to play here," I admit, a little too quickly. Owen's lip twitches in response. I train my eyes back on the counter, running the dish towel along the perfectly clean surface, then tucking it in one of the cabinet doors, smoothing out wrinkles and anything else I can think of doing that will keep me from making eye contact with Owen after what I just said.

"We should play," he says. I give in and look up. He's shoving his hands into the front pocket of his dark gray hoodie, his feet sliding closer to the back door. "Come on. Game of HORSE."

"Game of...what?" I ask.

Owen stops at the door, his hand on the knob. "HORSE. You know? I shoot and if I make it, you have to shoot from the same spot and make it. HORSE? You never played HORSE?"

"Never even heard of it," I say. "And that doesn't sound like a game I'd be any good at. You said I shoot and make it, but that...that doesn't happen when I play basketball."

His lips slide into the same sweet grin he wore when he first entered my house, then he gestures over his shoulder and opens the door. "Fine, we'll play PIG instead," he says.

"You're just making shit up now," I say, grabbing the zip jacket from the stool in the kitchen and pushing my arms inside. Owen laughs as we shut the door, and he doesn't stop until we're standing directly under the hoop, his ball in his hands.

"I'm not *making shit up*," he says. "You earn letters when you miss shots. You play PIG to make the game shorter. We'll practice with PIG."

"This sounds...pretty stupid," I say, my brow pinched.

"It's not. It's fun. I promise. Here, you take the ball and go first," he says, pushing the ball into my arms. I'm instantly mortified, because I know he's going to see me shoot and miss—horribly. It was one thing to miss a shot in front of his brother. Andrew sucked as badly as I do. But Owen is good. I've watched him play, with guys taller than him. And he's going to laugh his ass off when he sees me attempt to make a shot.

"Is there a shorter word?" I ask, looking at the ball in my hands and then up at the hoop. Owen laughs lightly.

"No, PIG's as short as it gets. Don't worry; you'll be fine. Go on, take your shot," he says, stepping back a few paces and blowing into his hands to warm them.

I am going to miss. There's no doubt about it in my mind. My only question to answer is how badly do I want to miss? I feel like it would look less awful if at least I attempted a farther shot, so I cross the driveway to a crack that runs down the middle, lining myself up a good eight or nine feet away from the hoop. I prop the ball into my hands, practically balancing it in my fingertips in front of my chest, then with a deep breath, I heave it forward, coming nowhere near the hoop and sending it off a jagged brick on the garage wall, bouncing down the driveway and into the street.

Yep. Mortified.

Owen's hands have stopped moving in front of his face. He's frozen, looking at the space where the ball trailed by him, his eyebrows slightly raised.

"I told you I wouldn't be good at this game!" I say, honestly a little upset. I'm more upset that I'm upset over something so trivial, but I'm embarrassed, and the longer it takes Owen to talk, the worse I feel.

"That wasn't *bad*," he starts, looking out to the roadway where the ball has come to a rest in the gutter. "It wasn't *good*. But it wasn't bad. Here, hang on."

Owen jogs down the driveway to the ball in the road, his long legs moving him quickly. I like watching him move.

I like watching him move!

He dribbles the ball as he jogs back toward me, and a few times, he raises his eyes to look at me, but never for long.

"Okay, so first, hold the ball in front of you—like this," he says, forming my hands around the ball, moving my stiff fingers clumsily into place. I'm more focused on everywhere he's touching me to even understand what he's doing or saying. "Next, take a few steps closer. You need to start somewhere small."

Small. Right. Small. I swallow while he stands behind me and puts his hands on my elbows, pushing me forward, closer to the hoop. His breath is on my neck. There's a ball in my hand, the air is cold, and all I can think about is the fact that when Owen breathes, a light fog comes out, and it passes by my ear and cheek and I want to taste it.

"This isn't going to work," I say, once I realize how far away I still am from the hoop. He's going to make me try, and I'm embarrassed all over again.

"Yes it will. Boy, are you like this with your piano teachers?" he asks, leaning to the side to look me in the eye. Damn. He's really close to me.

"I'm good at the piano. I don't have to be like this with them," I say, somehow keeping my head about me.

"You probably weren't always good, though," he says, his gaze shifting from my eyes to my mouth just long enough for me to notice and flush everywhere. I look at his mouth to reciprocate, and when I look back up, I realize he's watching the movement of my eyes closely. *Shit. He knows I'm looking at his mouth!*

"Actually," I say, swallowing, because damn, my throat is suddenly so dry. "I was...always good? I'm sort of...gifted."

Now I feel really lame. Really, super, fucking, horribly, awful, terribly lame. Lame, lame, lame, lame, lame!

"Yeah, well I'm gifted in this. So trust me; trust that I can teach you," he says. There's that word again.

Trust.

I refocus on the hoop, and I listen to everything he says, bending my elbows, practicing the motion three or four times, lining my aim up with the small square behind the hoop. Then the time comes for me to follow through.

"Come on, Kens. You got this," he says, taking two or three steps back.

Kens. He calls me Kens, and it feels so natural. Like he's always called me Kens. I like it when he says my name. I like how it sounds.

I like Owen Harper.

I bend my knees, close my eyes once, then train all of my focus on the hoop above my head. With a silent countdown, I heave everything forward and upward again, and the ball leaves my hands in the right direction. I don't make the shot. But I come close. The ball actually hits the board, then swirls along the rim before falling away.

"I hit it!" I say, turning to face him with my palms pressed on my cheeks. "Holy smokes! I actually hit it!"

Owen smiles and shakes his head lightly. "You don't actually get any points for hitting it, but yes, you showed improvement," he says, kicking the ball up into his hands and dribbling it a few times.

"Pshaw, says you! Did you see that?" I say, pointing up and spinning around once before reaching for the ball. "I hit it. That's a *P*. I get a *P* for PIG."

Owen's hand is rubbing on his neck, and he's laughing silently, but he gives in eventually, and bounces the ball to me to try again.

"Sure. Whatever you want, Kens. You get a *P*. Good job," he says, the world's greatest smile stretched on his lips. It's my new favorite smile. An entirely new one that I kind of think might just be for me and me alone. I like it, almost as much as I like him.

We shoot the ball a few more times, and Owen lets me continue to make up rules as we go. I know that's not how the game is really played, but I like how he laughs when I joke and celebrate my near shots. I actually make one before we're done, and Owen lifts me in his arms when I do, swinging me around once, but discarding me swiftly. It leaves me with the strangest feeling, as if holding me for too long would hurt him somehow.

"Did I win?" I ask at the end, and he just grins and nods *yes*, his eyebrows high to show his sarcasm. The sounds of the night fade back into focus, and Owen's breath fogs the air between us. I breathe out once, just to see if my breath can catch his.

"I should head in. I've got work early in the morning," he says, his ball tucked under one arm, his other hand stuffed in his jeans pocket. He looks unsure of himself, and I can't help but hope that it has a little to do with me.

"Yeah. I should get some sleep too. I'm studying all day tomorrow for the dissection quiz," I say, and Owen shuts his eyes tightly when I mention our test. "You forgot, didn't you?"

"Yeah," he says, sighing. "I think I'll be okay, though. I got most of it down."

"If you want..." I start, then stop myself, biting the inside of my cheek to give myself a second or two to think. Maybe I'm just trying to talk myself out of taking a risk. And maybe I shouldn't listen to that voice any more. "I can help you," I say again, my voice fast and sharp, getting his attention before he heads inside. "You know, study? When you get home from work. I could maybe just run you through my flashcards or something. Only...only if you think you need to."

Ryan said Owen was smart. He probably doesn't need to study. And now I look desperate, like I'm flirting. And I want to somehow breathe in fast, suck in all of the words I spoke before he can hear them.

"That would be awesome," he says, surprising me. "What's your number? I'll just call you when I get home."

Call me. Owen Harper wants to call me. On my phone. From his phone. He's typing my name with his long thumbs, his hat low over his eyes, but not so low that I can't see the thickness of his lashes and the way they move along the letters of my name. He hands the phone to me to type in my number, and I manage to find enough feeling in my fingers to take it from him without dropping it. I type in my number, and before I pass it back, I notice he's written KENS, and it makes me smile.

"Cool," he says, pushing the phone back in his pocket and backing up a few paces to his door. "So...thanks. Yeah, and...well...call you tomorrow?"

He actually stumbles a little when he hits the first step of his porch, but I pretend not to notice. I walk back to my door, click off the driveway lights, and move inside. The house is warm, and I didn't realize how cold I was until now. I notice Owen's cheese still on my counter, so I put it in the fridge before locking the back door and turning out the lights. I lock up front, and glance briefly at the piano I *almost* play before moving upstairs for bed.

I leave my window closed while I change into a pair of sweatpants and my favorite long-sleeved thermal, then I open the curtains and shut off the light, sliding my back against the edge of my mattress for my nightly ritual of waiting for Owen to shut his light off, too.

He rarely closes his curtains. The first few times, I felt embarrassed over what I saw, his bare chest, his boxers, his skin when he would change from his pants and shirt. I never saw *too* much, but it was more than I was used to seeing. I've always been a prude. Not because of any religious belief or self-promise to be a virgin until I met the right guy—intimacy just scared me. Dating intimidated me at Bryce, probably because most of the boys there were dropped off in Escalades and Audis and Teslas. They all seemed so entitled, and I didn't trust any of them—ever.

Trust. I trust Owen.

When my phone vibrates, my body jolts with adrenaline, my stomach trained to feel sick at seeing Gaby's name. She's sent me several texts, and I've deleted every single one. Morgan has tried to call, too, and honestly, I know she is probably on my side with everything. Her messages relayed how shocked she was over what went on between Gaby and my father. But I haven't been able to call Morgan back either. I'm just not ready to talk about it with anyone, and I know that's *all* Morgan is going to want to talk about.

My thumb grazes over the END CALL button on instinct, but I pause when I realize the number on the screen isn't one I recognize. I look at Owen's window, and his light is now off, and I think maybe—just...*maybe?*

"Hello?" I answer, my thumbnail flying to the edge of my teeth, a bad habit to calm my nerves that I've been doing for as long as I can remember.

"Hey," Owen says, his voice breathy and timid. "Sorry. I probably scared you again."

"No, no!" I respond quickly, and probably a little too excitedly. "I just didn't recognize the number, and most of my calls lately have been from unwelcomed callers."

"Ah, yeah. I get that," he says, and I can actually hear him settle into his covers. He's in bed. I'm talking to him, and he's lying down, probably without a shirt on. My thumbnail flies right back to the place between my teeth.

"Did you...need something?" I ask, sliding down a little lower by the window, low enough to gaze through it and attempt to see Owen in the darkness.

"Well, I'm having trouble sleeping. It's weird. I don't know if you ever get this feeling, but...I feel like somebody's watching me," he says, and I sink completely to the floor, my hand fast to cover my face.

Oh god!

Oh god, oh god, oh god!

"Kensi?" he asks, and I swallow hard.

"Uh huh?" I say, my voice nowhere near as loud as it was seconds ago.

"Look up," he says, and I squeeze my eyes shut tightly, pushing myself up on my elbows until I can see through my window to his. Owen's waving at me, a faint light over his face while he lies with his arms folded around his pillow, his hand pressing his phone to his ear.

"Oh, hey. Yeah...so...hi," I say, scrunching my hand like a two-year-old waves. "So...your bed. It's like...right there, huh?"

Oh god, oh god, oh god.

"Yep," he says, and even though he's far away, I can tell what smile he's wearing. It's the teasing one—the one that used to torture me when he was being mean, or when I *thought* he was being mean. Now, it's just one of Owen's many smiles—and I like this one, too, even though my stomach sinks with embarrassment over the cause.

"It's okay," he whispers, and I slide back along my bed, bringing my knees into my chest.

"What is?" I ask, the rush of heartbeats drumming in my head, drowning me.

"I look at you, too," he says, and now my heart is rushing for an entirely different reason.

Oh my god, oh my god....

"Kens? Relax," he says, and I notice his light flips off. I don't know if he did that to make it easier on me, but somehow, it does. I'm braver without having to face him.

"I'm sorry. I'm...pretty embarrassed," I admit, crawling on my knees first, then lifting myself onto my bed, sliding my feet under my heavy comforter, then pulling it over my head because all I want to do is hide.

"I really called because I can't sleep," he says, completely bypassing my embarrassment. I could kiss him for that.

Kiss him.

Now I'm thinking about kissing him—not that I haven't thought about that before, but now I'm really imagining it, and it makes me want to pull my blankets in closer, press the phone tighter against my ear so I can feel every vibration of his voice.

"Wanna talk? Until you get tired?" I ask, now more awake than I've ever been.

"Sure. I mean, yeah...I guess," he says, and I like that he's flustered now, too. "It's always weird, when Andrew's gone, and the house is empty. It's just sort of lonely."

"I know whatcha mean," I say, thinking about most of my nights—both in the city and out here. My parents were always working, and from the age it became socially acceptable, maybe about twelve or thirteen, my parents frequently left me alone at night. I've grown used to it, but I've never *liked* it.

"I'm sorry about the phone calls. From...from *her*," he says, and I can tell he's treading lightly at bringing up Gaby.

"It's okay. She'll stop calling soon. Or not. Either way," I say, not really believing the indifference I'm trying to portray, but I try to sell it; I try to sell it hard.

"Yeah, probably," he says, and there's a pause in everything. The house is quiet, and the moon is shrouded by clouds, so the night is darker than normal. It feels like the world is hushed, listening to our conversation. "For the record, what she did? Your friend..." he pauses, waiting to see if it's okay to say more. "That was pretty shitty."

Shitty. Yeah, it was shitty. It also might have been illegal—could probably be constituted as rape in some ways—was morally and ethically flawed, and is going to scar me for life.

Yeah, it was shitty.

"Thanks," is all I say in response. I'm not ready to deal beyond that yet. "How's Andrew?" I ask, desperate to return the focus on Owen.

"He's good. Thanks. My brother likes you, you know? I think he thinks you're cute," he says, and I blush even though I know he's just trying to be funny.

"That's what he said about you," I say, unable to stop the words before I speak them. I start chewing on my nails the instant I realize what I've done, and I hold my breath, waiting for Owen to hang up. But he doesn't. He doesn't respond either. He just lets the silence play out for a really long and uncomfortable amount of time. I think he's torturing me, but I also think just maybe...he's smiling.

110

"So how was your first day of work?" I ask, leaning over the edge of my bed and peaking out the window one more time, on the off chance that he's looking at me, too. All I see is the blackness filling his window, but I smile softly, in case he's hiding in the shadow.

"It was good, I guess. It's a job, and I don't have to deal with people a lot, so that's sort of a bonus. And I make, like, fifty more cents an hour," he says.

"Do you ever resent it? Having to work so much?" I tread carefully; I've learned when Owen doesn't want to have a conversation, he doesn't, and sometimes his end of it is abrupt.

"Nah," he says, yawning a little. "It helps my family, and it doesn't really get in the way of the important things."

"Like what?" I ask, quickly.

Owen chuckles softly into the phone. "Wow, you're like one of those hard-hitting reporters. Right in there with the next question," he says.

"Sorry," I say in a whisper, my face burning again with that familiar sting of embarrassment.

"It's okay. I haven't really *shared* with someone in a while, that's all. Most my friends either already know my deal or they don't care," he says, and I focus on that one phrase—*his deal.* I want to know his deal; I want to know all about Owen Harper and his life and his past and those rumors. I want his story.

"You don't have to…share? If you don't feel up to it, or if it's personal or…whatever," I say, my hand back in place between my lips. I won't have any fingernails left in the morning.

"Well, you already know I play basketball. And it's stupid, but that's one of those important things. I'm good at it. You know how you said you're gifted? Well, I guess it's my gift, if gifts work like that. I lose myself in it, and I like that I get to be aggressive," he says. I think back to when I watched Owen play in the driveway, how masculine every movement he made was. Aggressive seemed to be in his nature even then.

"Well, clearly, I wouldn't know much about basketball," I say, inciting a raspy laugh from Owen. "But, I would believe that you're good…or gifted. You're fun to watch."

I pull my blanket up over my chin after this, knowing how gushing and flirtatious every word from my mouth sounds. I don't regret them, though. I don't regret a single second of my night so far.

"Thanks," Owen says, and my smile kicks in, my cover now hiding more of my blushing face.

"Does your older brother help out with bills too?" I ask. When Owen's answer doesn't come right away, I close my eyes, wishing I could take my question back, my gut sinking, knowing I asked one question too many.

"James," Owen starts, but then his long pause continues.

"It's...it's okay, I'm getting too personal," I say, grasping at hope that Owen won't hang up, that he'll call me again.

"James is a junkie," he says. There are a million reactions I could have had, but what I didn't expect is how much I want to hug Owen right now. Nothing about his small description of his brother sounded sad or affected or heartbroken, but somehow through it all, I know Owen is. I can just sense it.

"I'm sorry, Owen," I say, careful to say his name—to take care of it and respect it. If he doesn't share with people often, then I'm guessing very few people really know about James.

"Thanks. But it's okay. It is what it is. My mom kicked him out a year ago. He started using meth, and getting into some really hard shit. She didn't want Andrew exposed to that. I didn't either. But he still calls me. You know...when he needs something," he says, a certain amount of disappointment in his tone.

"Like...money? Or drugs?" I say, now sitting up in bed.

"Not really money. But I've bailed him out once or twice. And I got him off the hook with a dealer he owed some serious money to. It's usually a problem when James calls," he sighs.

"But you answer," I say, my words practically filling in the blank space left at the end of his.

"Every. Time," he says.

"When was the last time you saw him?" I ask, hoping, for selfish reasons, that it's been a while. Willow said James was the one to stay away from, and now I'm not sure I want him a house away from me.

"The other night. He didn't come here. But he was fucked up out of his head, and he was in a bad place, with some bad people. I had to leave in the middle of a basketball game to go haul his ass back to his apartment," he says, and I close my eyes, remembering that night I watched him get a call in the middle of playing basketball. I remember how angry he was, how fast he drove away, and how vicious his eyes were when he got back.

"That isn't fair to you," I say, my arms pulling my pillow in close to my chest, my mind imagining Owen's heart beating through it, wishing it were him I was holding.

"Nope," he says.

I hold my pillow for several long seconds, letting my face slide against the coolness of the pillowcase. Ryan is so right about Owen; people don't have him pegged right at all. And as much as I want to tell everyone that, I also want to keep it to myself—keep Owen to myself.

"So, you were thinking about practicing tonight...when I walked in?" Owen finally says, cutting through the silence. I think I may have been drifting off to sleep with him in my fantasy.

"Oh, yeah. I was...sort of, " I say, squeezing my eyes tightly, trying to force a little more awake time from them. "I can't seem to figure out what to play. It probably doesn't make sense to you. But, it's just that I was sort of on this directive, had all of these goals, and they all centered around the things my father wanted me to play. And now that he's out of the picture..."

"Those aren't your goals anymore," Owen finishes for me.

"I don't think they ever really were," I say. I know they weren't, but admitting this out loud, saying it without someone on the other end protesting—it feels nice.

"Do you still like playing?" he asks.

"Yes, of course I do," I say. "But not any of the things *he* would want me to play." Saying that feels good too, and it makes me stretch and move my fingers in anticipation.

"So play for *you*. Tomorrow. Play for Kensington. I'd like to hear you. I mean...if that's something you're okay with. Someone listening to you play?" The nervous, fumbling Owen who's unsure of his words seems rare, but he makes my heart race.

"I could do that. I mean, unless it's not cool for Owen Harper to be hanging out with a band geek," I joke, my palms actually sweating. I can't tell if I'm excited at the thought of playing for Owen or terrified.

"I'll make an exception," he says, his laugh even raspier than before, and his voice saturated with sleepiness.

"Well look at that," I say.

"What?" he asks.

"You're finally tired," I smile, satisfied, as if I actually did something to help Owen find sleep. His effect on me was just the opposite, and now all I want to do is tiptoe downstairs and play my piano.

"Yeah, I think you're right. Hey, thanks," he says.

"For what?" I ask.

"I'm not really sure. But I know I should say it anyway," he says, one final yawn escaping his throat.

"Good night, Owen Harper," I say, loving every syllable of his name on my tongue. Owen drifts off before he can say another word, and I leave my phone on for a few more minutes just to listen to him breathe.

He isn't scary at all.

Chapter 10

Owen must have worked all day Sunday because I never saw him again. And I looked—constantly. My mom seems to have found a way to put on her performance face at work, but at home, she's simply...manic. When I woke for school this morning, she had started ripping out pipes from under the sink, and all of the cabinet doors were down. She said something about finally getting her hands into something, making it her own.

If it keeps her from crying on the foot of the stairs, I guess tearing apart our house is a good alternative.

Willow's horn blaring outside saves me from having to help with my mom's latest plumbing emergency, so I yell that I'm leaving, grab my backpack, and rush out the door. Being in band means we always have to get to school early, and though the first few weeks had me grumbling from waking up before the sun, this morning, I'm practically skipping. I'm skipping because Owen's truck is in the driveway, which means he's probably going to school today.

"Wow, look who's all happy this morning," Willow says, snapping the gum in her mouth twice and chomping loudly while she analyzes me and my happiness.

"Had a good weekend," I say, meaning it. True, Friday night was a nightmare, but my short-lived basketball career made up for the unwanted visit from my father and from Gaby the week before.

"Uh huh," Willow says, pulling a thermos from her center console and loudly sipping on what smells like coffee. "So, Owen dropped you off for the game Friday night. You, uh...see him again?"

The blush that radiates all over my face is fast and unexpected, and I know I wouldn't be able to lie now even if I wanted to.

"That's a yes," she says, and her smile is genuine, but there's still a shade of disappointment there, too.

"You sure it's okay, that it doesn't bother you if I'm friends with Owen?" I ask, wondering if Willow was being totally honest about her feelings and being over him.

"Kens, I cross my heart. Just promise me you'll be careful. I know it's been three years since I hooked up with him, and he's probably grown up a lot, but still...just be careful," she says, repeating that word again.

I'm always careful; it's why I did exactly as my father said for most of my life—played things carefully, classical...*perfect*. I hold up my hand in what I think is the scout's honor sign and smile a promise to Willow, but I never say it. And as much as I probably should be careful, I kind of want to be reckless.

We pull into the school lot and park right next to Jess. There are no reserved spots, but everyone sort of has their place. We always park at the bottom of the hill, right by the exit. Jess is swinging his feet, clutching a paper in his hand while he sits on the trunk of his car. He looks like an actual kid in a candy store, his smile large and his cheeks red from the morning air. The vision has Willow and me giggling.

"Who wants Carolyn Potter's famous apple pie?" Jess asks, waving the piece of paper over his head. Whatever is printed on it seems to have Willow in a state of thrill, joy, or frenzy. It's hard to tell amid the dancing and jumping she's doing as she takes the paper from Jess's hands.

"Holy shit! It's back!" she says, pounding on the hood of Elise's car as she pulls into the lot next to our cars.

"What the hell, Will? Let me put it in park before you start going all *morning-person* on me," Elise says, dragging her heavy backpack and flute case from the back seat and finally shutting the door behind her. "Okay, what's got you all...*this way?*" Elise waves her hand in Willow's direction, her face twisted with an annoyance I can truly appreciate. Willow is shot out of a cannon in the mornings, but Elise is more my speed—slow to wake, in need of caffeine, and not much for public happy-dancing at six in the morning.

"I think this will change your mind," Willow says, handing the flyer to Elise. I watch her eyes graze over the words, and the more she reads, the more her lips curve until she's smiling so big she's actually showing teeth.

"No. Way!" she says, shoving the paper into my hands. "We're going, right? We're all totally going. Oh my god, this week cannot end fast enough!"

I straighten the heavy pack on my back and read over the flyer now in my possession.

WILSON ORCHARD APPLE FEST

"Is this that thing? That story you guys told me about?" I ask, my focus solely on the part of that story that had to do with Owen—and how this one event changed his life forever. This festival is like the moment he told me my dad was spending time with another woman, and I can't imagine reliving that moment again—*ever!*

I wonder if Owen's seen a flyer like this one?

"Yes! That's it! Oh my god, Kens. You have to come with us," Willow says, looping her arm in mine as we trek up the hill to the music room. She's only focusing on the festive part, completely missing my point.

"I don't know. I'm not really into carnival games and things like that," I say, still thinking about Owen. I want to find him before he finds out, to take him away until the festival is over and done—so he can never know it came back again in the first place.

"It's not just the games and the rides. Kens, oh my god, the freaking apple pies! You have to come, just for a little while. At least go and eat with us?" Willow is actually making a pouty face, her bottom lip jutted out, and her eyes practically watering with sadness.

"It is a lot of fun," Elise adds, nudging me with her arm as we walk through the band-room door. She starts to walk backward to face me. "Ryan will want to go, so we'll all be there. And he never likes to stay at things long, so we can totally take you home early if you want to leave. Come with us?"

Elise isn't full-on begging; that's not her style. But I can tell she really wants me to join them, and I get the sense this is a meaningful thing for my new group of friends—a part of their past they want to share with me. I need friends, good friends that don't lie to me. So I nod *yes,* and Willow practically squeals in my ear with excitement.

Mr. Brody makes a few attempts to play through some of our songs, but band rehearsals are ultimately cut short, the entire class seemingly abuzz with news that the apple fest is back. And when Mr. Brody announces that the band will actually be playing in a mini parade down the orchard road to open the festival on Saturday morning, you would think we were invited to star in the half-time show for the Super Bowl. Everyone was so excited.

With the band performing, I no longer have an excuse to miss—at least not the opening of the festival—so I resolve myself to the fact that I'm going to at least get a really good slice of pie out of this deal, and then I hold my breath and wait for my next class. I pray somehow word of the festival hasn't made it to him yet.

I'm not sure whether it's good news or bad news that Owen missed our morning classes. I'm hoping it was because of work, or something else non-festival related. When I see him climb up to sit on top of one of the outside tables at lunch, I feel the weight rise from my chest.

I position myself so I can glance at him from my periphery out the window while we eat lunch, and my body flushes the few times I catch his gaze on me. Every time I look his direction, he seems to be smiling. I also notice that, unlike other days during the lunch hour, there doesn't seem to be a girl in his arms, no one entertaining his lips, grinding on his lap, or kissing at his neck. And that makes me happy, too.

"Owen Harper alert," Willow says, her eyebrows raised as she stares at me from the other side of the table. I turn to the side and realize Owen is no longer on his table outside, and his friends have all left as well. I somehow missed them leaving, but Willow has spotted him again—right behind me.

"Hey, Kens," he says, his voice sounding calm and comfortable as he seduces me right here in front of my friends. I've become addicted to his voice, so much so that I even considered calling to listen to his voicemail once or twice—fear that he might pick up the only thing stopping me, as silly as that sounds. I swivel in my seat and peer up at him, and my response comes out more like a croak.

"Hey, Owen," I squeak. My palms are sweating, and I'm pretty sure my arms and back are as well. In fact, everything about me feels like it's on fire, never mind the gray skies and cold front threatening to bring a massive chill outside the window. Right now, in my body, it's summer in the desert.

I glance around the table and notice all of my friends suddenly only interested in their trays and food, but their faces are all smirking, and it makes me blush even harder.

"Hey, O. What's up, man?" Ryan says, the last to slide into his seat. Thank god for Ryan, the only one acting normal. "Conditioning starts next week. You coming?"

"You know it. I might miss a few; I've got work. But coach already knows," Owen says, tapping his fist into Ryan's as he sits down next to Elise.

"Good. Oh, hell man, what happened to your eye?" Ryan asks, pointing to the spot on his own face that mirrors the deep blue bruise left on Owen's cheek. It's the last remnant of his run-in with my father, and the very conversation playing out at our lunch table right now has my throat closing and my stomach threatening sickness.

"Oh, you know. Just messin' around with House and the boys, pick up games and shit. Some guy didn't like a call, elbowed me," Owen says with a shrug. He never looks my direction, but as he sits in the seat across from me, I feel his foot slide up next to mine and tap it twice. He lied for me, just like he promised he would.

"Dude, some guys just can't keep their cool on the court. I hate that shit. I don't know why you play those pick-up games anyways," Ryan says, leaning over and kissing Elise on the cheek. She looks up for a brief second, but she puts her head back down quickly, almost like the rest of my friends have some secret pact to give me pretend privacy when Owen comes to the table. Truthfully, it's only making me feel weirder.

"So, Kens. Was wondering," Owen starts, looking around the table at the tops of everyone's heads. He shakes his and pinches his brow at how strange my friends are all being. I kind of want to die.

"I have to work Friday, but I thought maybe, if you're not busy, I could repay you for that grilled cheese emergency this weekend? My mom's going to be home, and she'd like to meet your mom, if she's off Saturday night," Owen says, his eyes focusing solely on his knuckles, which he's cracking nervously, over and over. His foot under the table is now tapping quickly with nerves, and it's starting to make the entire table shake a little.

"Uh, Saturday?" I repeat his question, my mind searching for a way to make Saturday happen twice—one version I can live through with Owen and his mom, and the other where I can go to the festival and perform with the band. I'm about to lie, about to pretend there is nothing else I have to do on Saturday so I can make Owen's leg stop shaking and so I can spend Saturday night with him, meet his mom, when Jess decides now would be a good time to quit looking at his lap and insert himself back into my reality.

"You can't, Kensi. We've got the apple fest," Jess says, and everyone stops breathing simultaneously. He couldn't say I had *a thing*, a *band assignment*, a *performance*, something...*anything*...with them—no, Jess had to go and be specific, painfully specific.

I flash my gaze back to Owen, and now he's the one looking at the top of the table, his hands no longer wringing, his foot no longer jiggling. His face is just pure emptiness—as if he's just had the wind knocked out of him—and the way his lip is hanging open and quivering with the struggle to breathe lets me know that this is the first he's heard of the apple fest. It lets me know that Willow wasn't exaggerating her story about Owen and that day. I know it because the look of absolute pain that's fallen over him, taken over his body completely, isn't one that could come from anything but tragic loss. And Owen's experienced the deepest tragedy of all.

"I'm...I'm sorry. I just found out," I say, reaching toward him, but not quickly enough. He's shoved his hands in his pockets and is already standing and sliding away from me.

120

"Nah, it's all right. Next time, maybe. Hey…I won't be in class this afternoon, so maybe just hit me up with whatever I missed?" he says, his eyes still low—low and sad. So unbelievably sad.

"Yeah. Sure, I'll just send you a text later," I say, keeping my focus on his face, the voice inside me begging him to look up, begging him to be okay. I feel like I'm holding the paddles to his chest, shouting "clear!" and counting over and over while I watch his life drift away. With his back against the door, Owen finally lifts his chin, and that same ice and hardness that was there the first time he looked at me is back, and he doesn't bother to smile as he turns to leave.

"I'm not hungry," I say, standing with my full tray and rushing to the trash. I follow Owen's footsteps to the doorway, but after I dump my food and step onto the walkway outside, I'm only there in time to see his truck speed around the corner of the lot, out onto the roadway, the motor revving like it does when he races—when he runs away.

"Kens, I'm so sorry," Willow says, her hand on my back feels like a knife.

"Just…don't," I say, jerking away. It's not her fault, and I know that. But I don't want to hear empty apologies. They won't make me feel better. "It's okay. I just didn't want him to find out…like that. I'm just worried about him, that's all."

I turn to her and shrug, taking in a deep breath and exhaling slowly, trying to keep the mist in my eyes from forming full tears.

"You just didn't want him to find out at all," she says. I close my eyes and nod slowly. "It's a small town, Kens. By dinnertime, everyone is going to know. That flyer I showed you this morning? There will be one on every tree in town, every business window, and probably everyone's front door. He was bound to find out. And he'll be okay."

I let out a breathy laugh, my gaze falling to Willow's feet first before shifting up to her eyes. "Owen is so far from okay, Willow," I say, my chest crumbling with my admission, with hearing me talk aloud about Owen—the Owen I think I know— to someone else.

"You can't hold him together," she says, stepping an inch or two closer to me. She stops before she's close enough to touch my hand. I think she can sense how fragile my spirit is right now—how volatile my emotions are—so she doesn't say another word. Instead she goes back into the cafeteria to join our table of friends, where I'm sure they'll analyze everything that just went down.

Ryan will stand up for Owen though. And I'm thankful for that.

As promised, Owen skipped classes for the rest of the day. He missed the following day as well. I texted him both nights, giving him the basic points he missed and due dates for assignments. But I didn't hear back from him. And his house was dark both nights, his truck never once appearing in the driveway.

I never saw Andrew, but I'm sure Owen stopped in for his brother, somehow getting him to school and bringing him home. But I have no proof. The hoop has been silent out front too. In fact, I wouldn't be shocked if Ryan told me that Owen packed up after our last conversation and skipped town. I think part of me was trying to convince myself of that lie. But now I'm confronted with an entirely different truth—the truth where Owen is back outside on the lunch tables with his friends, and another girl is sitting on his lap, his tongue on her ear.

"I told you he'd be okay," Willow says, and even though she's trying to couch it like she's trying to make me feel better—what she's really doing is saying "I told you so" about Owen being *Owen* and going back to his cruel and hurtful ways.

"Looks like it," I say, not giving her—or Owen—the satisfaction of looking up from my lunch.

I eat slowly, and I turn my profile to the side, keeping Owen just in my sight's reach, but I deny myself every temptation of looking his direction. I know he wants me to see him. I know that's why he's out there, making this spectacle just for me. And I know he's doing it because something else hurts.

But fuck him. I have no role in what happened to him years ago. And he's not going to use it as an excuse for being an asshole.

Jess is talking about the parade Saturday, and Elise keeps switching the conversation to the rides she's seen coming into town. I'm not sure about hooking myself into something that arrives by truck in the middle of the night, and is disassembled minutes after the carnival closes, but I remain rapt in Elise's conversation, pretending I'll ride anything and everything she wants.

Every now and then, I glance next to her, to Ryan, and he's chewing on the end of his straw, listening to his girlfriend talk, but looking from me to Owen and back again. I follow my friends from the table, dumping my trash and pulling my backpack over my shoulder, when Ryan stops me last at the door before we leave.

"I know he makes it hard, Kensi. But that guy out there...that's not really him. O's better than that," Ryan says, and I want to believe him. But I also know that men lie, and break promises, and destroy friendships and marriages—and right now that's the only rationale I can think about.

"Sure he is, Ryan. Sure he is," I say, patting him on the arm as I muscle past him and let the door close behind me.

Elise distracts me during science. I'm careful to avoid any one-on-one time with Owen during dissections—immediately pairing myself with Elise, who is still obsessively talking about the festival. I've never been, and already I hate this festival and what it's done to my routine. It's like it's taken over my friends' bodies and minds, too. But I'm grateful for Elise's constant conversation though, and it makes the forty minutes of class fly by.

My next class isn't going to be so easy. When I enter our English class, Owen is sitting in his seat right behind mine, his smirk in its familiar place.

"Saved your seat for you," he says, barely looking up. Like I believe he hasn't orchestrated everything he's about to do and say.

"Whatever," I respond; glad I don't have to push his feet off my chair. I don't like hot and cold. My dad was always hot and cold, probably because he never really wanted to be there in the first place.

"Wow, someone's moody," he says. I know what he's doing. He's shifting everything he's feeling to me; he's making me the bad guy, because he can't be mad at an entire town—at everyone in Woodstock—for being excited about an event that to him means nothing but nightmares and the stirring up of old gossip and rumors. Thing is, though, that's also not very fair to me.

"Someone else is an asshole, so *touché*," I say, not even bothering to fully turn around in my seat to acknowledge him. He hates that, because he wants more of a reaction. He wants that push and pull. I hate that I'm goading him as much as I am. I wish I could just keep my mouth shut.

"Awwww, are you...jealous, Kensington?" His lips are at my neck, and his breath is making the tiny hairs on my skin stand to attention. I hate that he called me by my full name, hate that he's trying to hurt me. But mostly I hate that *yes*, I'm jealous of some stupid *girl of the moment* he was just locking lips with at lunch.

I can still feel him there, close enough that I know if I jerked my elbow back hard and fast, I would give him a matching bruise on the other eye. But I fight my newfound instinct for violence, and instead do something far worse.

Turning in my seat, I put both of my palms flat on Owen's desk and face him, his eyes piercing mine with their coolness. "I'm very sorry, Owen," I say, and he leans back, folding his arms, his face painted with smugness as he waits for me to take his bait, to go ahead and embarrass myself. No, Owen—not today.

"Did you hear me?" I ask, keeping my voice low, keeping this a conversation for our ears alone. He merely quirks his brow in acknowledgement, but it's enough. "I know that this apple fest— or whatever the hell this event is—is painful for you. And I know that you're worried your dad is all people are going to talk about. And some of them probably will. And those people, Owen? Those people fucking suck. But I'm just trying to make new friends at a school I never wanted to come to. At a school I'm at because guess what? My dad fucked my life up too. And my new friends asked me to go to a carnival and eat some pie that's apparently, like, the greatest goddamned pie on the planet. They want me to stay out late, and ride some questionable rides I probably won't even really like. And you know what? You, your family, your dad—they haven't brought it up once. Not. Once. So I'm going to go with them, try to make a good memory, and then I'm going to come home and fall in my bed from exhaustion. I hope I can bring myself to look out my window once before I shut my eyes, but I'm not so sure I care for the view anymore."

Owen's face didn't flinch a single time, and his expression never changed. But I kept my eyes trained on his, looking deep into them, and I think maybe—just maybe—I saw a little crack or two underneath.

I turn back to face the front, pull my notepad from my book bag and spend the next hour ignoring Owen's breathing. When the bell rings, *I'm* the first to leave, and I don't give him another glance.

Chapter 11

I am destined never to sleep in again. It's five in the morning, and Willow is knocking at my door and texting my phone at the same time. I hurry downstairs, and let her in while I finish getting ready.

"Crap, it's cold out there," she says, shutting the door quickly behind her and pulling her other glove from her hand to breathe on her palms to thaw them out.

"Seems like a weird time for apples," I say, rummaging around the downstairs for my other boot. The house is in disarray, my mom's remodeling now spreading to the railings for the stairs and the now knocked-down wall that divides the formal dining room—also known as my dusty piano room—from the kitchen.

"Yeah, but the apples are at their best now, right before winter hits. That's why they always want people to pick the trees bare," Willow says. "Wow, you've got a lot going on in here," she adds, taking careful steps toward the kitchen.

"Yeah, my mom's sort of gone nuts with this remodeling thing," I say, tossing a box of paint tarps out of my way during my search. "Sorry, I'll just be a second. I can't find my boot. And I need to grab my jacket."

"Your dad at work?" Her question is completely innocuous, and a few weeks ago, I would have just answered, "Yes," without a second thought. But it paralyzes me now, and all I can do is stand in front of her with one boot in my hands, looking around the torn-up shreds of my house—proof that my mom is going through some sort of breakdown.

"My mom kicked him out," I say, nodding and looking around at every little thing left in our house. The only items even remotely my father is the piano that Willow is now leaning on.

"Oh," she says, and I can tell she's not sure where to go from here.

"It's sort of new, and I don't quite know how to talk about it yet. Or...do I talk about it? Maybe I do," I say, my eyes catching a tuft of gray fur in the corner, under a box. My boot!

"I get it," Willow says. "My parents are divorced. They split up four years ago. It got ugly, but it's better now."

"My dad cheated," I say. "I'm not sure it's going to get better."

"Mine too," she says, tapping out a few short notes on the piano. "But eventually my mom met someone else too, and now they sort of get along."

"Yeah, well, my dad had an affair with my best friend, so…" I don't know what makes me just come out and say it like that, but it feels good to say.

"Fuuuuuuuck," Willow says, her eyebrows stretched up into her hairline and her hands gripping the front of the piano bench.

"Yeah, that's sort of the reaction I had," I say, trying to make light of it, as if this will ever be something I can make light of. When she taps out a simple melody on my piano again, it stirs something in me, and I move to sit next to her and splay my fingers out over the keys, pressing down hard to form a minor chord, letting it echo in the empty house.

"I only ever get to hear you play the xylophone. You still practice the piano a lot?" Willow asks, and I press down on the minor chord one more time, this time slowly, so the notes aren't as loud.

"I haven't practiced in a few weeks. It was sort of always that thing my dad made me do, and now…" I say, changing one note and playing the chord again.

"Do you hate it now? The piano?" she asks, trying to match the chord I just played. When she presses her hands down, something's off, so I move one of her fingers and she does it again, this time getting it right.

"No," I breathe, running my hands over the smoothness of the keys, searching for that comfortable place where they feel home. "I don't hate it. I love it. But I hate my dad, so I feel like maybe I should hate this too."

My eyes closed, I let my fingers feel for a few more seconds, and then I slowly let them take over, playing softly at first, but growing stronger and more forceful with every single note—until I'm practically pounding out rhythms, my arms flexed and my fingers typing up and down the keys quickly, running the length of my instrument until I stop abruptly in the middle of the song.

"Well, damn," Willow says, and I pull my hands back into my lap, curling my fingers, perhaps a little from shame for giving in and playing something my father would have liked. "What was that?"

"Rachmaninoff," I say. "And I'm never playing it again."

Willow doesn't question me or ask me to play something else, and she never asks about my father's affair. My awful admission though has somehow made us closer, and I'm actually looking forward to the parade and a night with my new friends.

The parking lot at the school is mostly empty, everyone's car parked along the curb closest to the band room. We're one of the last people to arrive, and I feel bad because I know it's my fault we're late. Willow doesn't seem to care, though; she steps out and walks a few lengths to Jess's car, a small blue hatchback that he's filling with drums and drum carriers.

"Ahhhh there she is," he says when I slide next to Willow.

"Uh...yeah. *Ta da*...here I am," I smile, not quite sure why he's so happy to see me.

"So here's the thing," Jess starts, and I take a small step back on instinct. "You can't really march with a xylophone, and Joe's out of town for the weekend so we're going to need someone to fill in on bass drum...how do you feel about playing bass?"

"I've never played drums in my entire life," I say, shrugging. Before I can get my hands in my pockets, though, Jess is lifting a huge drum harness over my head. "Wait...did you hear me? No, not happening."

"Yeah, actually, this is totally happening," he says, resting the heavy metal over my shoulders and handing me two large mallets. "Lean forward and lock into the drum."

"Jess, I don't know how to do any of this," I start to protest, but Willow is smirking behind him. She just heard me fly through one of the hardest pieces of classical composition—from memory—and the small quirk in her lip is her way of challenging me. I let out a heavy sigh, my breath blowing the stray strands of hair in front of my face. "Fine. Just tape the music to the drum."

"Done," Jess says, his mouth making a clicking sound when he winks at me. "Thanks, Kens. You'll be great."

I lift the heavy drum holster back over my shoulders and set it next to Jess's car. "Bet this would totally piss your old man off," Willow whispers in my ear. I smile at the drum, and then laugh lightly, my head tilting back. She's right. Dean Worth would hate the very idea of this.

"Jess?" I holler out to him, catching him before he's out of range. "Think I can get some bigger mallets?"

I swing one of them around, twirling it in my fingers for emphasis, and Jess's body shirks with his laugh as he shakes his head. "I'll see, Kens. For you? Anything," he shouts.

I keep the mallets with me, and even though Jess wasn't able to find any others, I manage to pound the drum loudly with the padded ones he's given me. For a full mile, our small high school band winds down the dirt road through the orchard, families with strollers and dads with toddlers sitting on their shoulders lining either side. We play the school's fight song seven times, and the crowd around us claps along the entire way.

As much as my father would hate this, my mom would love it, and I'm starting to feel guilty that I didn't tell her about it. She's working all night, but I think she would have taken the night off for a crack at a little campy high school fun with me.

By the time we march to the entrance, the families watching the parade have dispersed, and everyone's crowded around an old barn-turned-ticket booth. I feel my shoulders relax the second Jess lifts the drum harness away from me.

"Not bad for a piano nerd," he says.

"Thanks," I say, hugging myself so I can rub the sore spots on either of my shoulders. "You could probably talk me into doing that again sometime. You know...in a pinch."

"You totally liked it," Jess teases, and I smile because yes...*yes I did*. Reaching across me for Willow's hand, Jess pulls her into his body, hugging her and leaving his arm slung over her shoulder while we walk to the end of the ticket-booth line.

Despite the complete lack of order, we buzz through the line quickly. At the main gate, we hand our tickets to an old man in overalls, who stuffs them into a dented coffee can. The simplicity of the entire thing amuses me, especially when I turn over my shoulder and watch the man trade his full can for an empty one, handing it to a little girl who takes it back up to the ticket booth to recycle the tickets again.

"We have to wait for Ryan," Elise says, waving us over to join her at a small picnic table near the front of the festival. Until today, I went along with the hype for this event, not really understanding the strange adoration every other person seemed to have for it. But even I can't deny the power of the smell being carried through the trees that surround us. It's not apples, but something entirely...*better*. There's a sweetness and a smokiness as well, and it makes my mouth water, craving the crunch of what in my mind must be the world's most amazing crust and the tartness and sugary goo of apple-pie perfection.

"I told you," Willow whispers in my ear, putting her arm around my shoulder and lying her head on my arm. I breathe it in again, and I swear I can almost taste it. "Best. Pie. Ever."

"I need to have some of that, and soon," I say, leaning my head to the side slowly until it rests on hers. For the first time since I left the city, since I said goodbye to Morgan and Gaby, I feel like I have a real friend.

"Hey...Kens?" The way Elise says my name gets my attention fast, so I lift my head and stand from the bench, brushing the dust and leaves that have fallen onto the table away from my sweater and leggings. She nods her head over my shoulder, and her lip pulls up on one side, a faint smile that makes my belly fill with butterflies and hope.

Turning slowly, I scan the crowd as my eyes pan along the various booths for games and treats, until I see three very out-of-place figures pacing near the front entrance. Owen looks terrified. To anyone else, he probably looks frustrated or irritated—his usual intimidating stance as his feet shuffle in the dirt, his thumb impulsively sliding over the screen of his phone like he's texting or waiting for an important call. But I've learned the subtleties of Owen Harper, and right now, he's nervous—he's afraid of being judged.

I start to move closer to them, but before I get there, Ryan walks up behind them and gestures in our direction. Andrew sees me first, and he smiles and holds up his hand in hello. Owen's eyes don't find me right away, but as he gets closer, his gaze finds mine, and his pace slows down to almost a complete stop. His chest is moving in an out like a panic attack—his brother, House, and Ryan all passing him, leaving him behind. When he's finally close enough for me to truly see the look in his eyes, I can tell he's in hell.

He's come to hell, on purpose—and I think he did that for me.

Willow nudges my shoulder, looking over at Owen, who is dressed in black, from the black cap pulled low to shadow his eyes to the dark jeans and black shoes. He's hiding, but I see him. "He looks like he wants to run," she says.

"That's because he does," I breathe, before pulling my arms around my body tight, covering my hands with my sleeves as I step closer to my lost friend—*friend*.

We meet in the middle, and it seems so appropriate.

"So, did you come for me? Or was it the pie?" I tease, kicking my boot into his Converse. Initiating this touch makes my stomach drop with nerves.

Owen laughs once, breathing in through his nose, a puff of fog escaping with his breath. "It's...it's really good pie," he says, his head cocked to one side, lip curled and one eye squinted while he waits for me to buy his line. He's here for me. And my heart hurts with happiness.

"That's what everyone says, but...I don't know. I've had good pie before," I say, urging us back in the direction of our friends.

"Well, it's been a while," he says, a distinct pause as he looks out at the festival, the lights flashing and families milling around about us. "But I'm pretty sure I'm remembering right, and you're going to be eating your words."

"Yeah, well I'd rather be eating pie," I say, folding my arms, my hip slouched to one side in our playful standoff.

"You want me to buy you pie?" he asks, and something about this simple surrender, this sweet offer from a boy to a girl, has my chest swelling with hope.

"Yeah...I'd like to eat pie with you, Owen Harper," I say, biting the edge of my bottom lip to hold my soft grin in place, to keep the full-on smile from creeping too far. It's my first foray into blatant, forward flirting, and my hands are numb with nerves. I'm pretty sure my mouth no longer works, but the way my stupid little sentence makes Owen's cheeks flush makes my courage worth the effort it took to muster it.

Owen and I trail behind the rest of our group, Andrew and House peeling away to step in line for some ride that looks like it's sole purpose is to induce brain damage and vomiting by the way it flips people around over and over again. Willow keeps glancing over her shoulder; I get the sense she's checking up on me to make sure Owen isn't upsetting me.

We all stop at the largest food booth in the center of the festival grounds, and Owen orders for me, asking a man with a grizzly beard and biker tattoos wrapped around both arms and neck for two slices of "mama's best."

"He's not Mama, right?" I ask, and Owen chuckles.

"No," he says, still laughing a little when the biker man hands him two plates slathered with caramel and large chunks of apple and crust. I follow Owen over to a picnic table, sliding in across from him. "It's Carolyn Potter's recipe, but she died a few years ago. Those are her boys. They look rough, but they're not really. That one?" Owen nods in the direction of a more heavy-set blonde guy who also has a beard and his own impressive set of tattoos.

"Yeah?" I acknowledge, pulling my plate in front of me and smelling the aroma steaming from it.

"He's Santa," Owen says, pushing his fork in and lifting up a hefty bite of pie. "Not like...the *real* Santa. I mean he plays Santa. Every year, at the hospital."

I take a moment to admire the man he pointed out, watching closely as he laughs with his brothers, all of them large and weathered, but wearing smiles that are infectious. *Santa* looks like he's picked up his mother's duties, and at one point, he's actually whistling as he peels a ringlet of skin away from an apple.

"Do you know them well?" I ask, stopping to take my first bite of pie. The second it hits my tongue, I concede, my eyes flipping to Owen's while the flakiness of the crust disintegrates into a perfect buttery blend in my mouth, the caramel coating the crunch of the apple, and the tartness coming through at the end. "Holy shit!"

Owen laughs so hard he has to cover his mouth with his arm, his mouth still full from his bite, he's coughing from almost choking. "I told you. It really is good pie," he says, and I like the way his eyes look right now. This moment. *This* is the Owen Harper I like the very best. "And yeah, I know them pretty well. House's mom is married to the cashier; his name's Dale. And my dad…"

Owen stops there. He's pretending to chew his bite while he looks out at the festival crowd, his thumb rubbing over the handle of his fork. After several long seconds, he brings his eyes back to mine, taps his fork a few times on his plate while his teeth hold the edge of his tongue, almost as if he's deciding how much of himself is safe to reveal. "My dad used to help out at the hospital with him…on the holidays. I remember a little, but I was four or five, so it's all sort of fuzzy, ya know?"

"Yeah, I know fuzzy," I say, thinking about my youth, before my life became all about the piano and concertos and following in my father's footsteps. Owen looks away again, and I can tell he's trying to remember more, feel more—bring his past in line with the present. I study him while he's not looking at me. His eyelashes are long and dark, and his jaw is squared, like a man's. My last boyfriend, if you could call him that, had soft skin, a voice that wasn't fully settled in and he watched cartoons in the afternoons. Jacob was privileged, and drove his father's Infiniti to school every day. But looking at Owen now and holding him up against what I remember of Jacob, I realize just how far away from becoming a man he was.

"Why do people think you're so much trouble?" I blurt out, and Owen laughs through his last bite, holding his hand over his mouth so he doesn't lose it.

"Kens, I mean…*all this?*" he says, waving his hand from the top of his head down to his legs, all the while still chewing and mumbling through his words. "I'm pretty high maintenance."

He reserves his serious face while I stare at him, and eventually I pick up the edge of my crust and throw it at him.

"Hey, that's like a felony, you know—wasting perfectly good crust! Shame on you, pie privileges revoked," he says, stealing my plate away.

"You can have it. Ugggg, I'm so full," I say, hand rubbing my stomach.

Owen doesn't even hesitate, shrugging and piling the remnants of my pie into his mouth in two bites—then carefully dragging his fork over the surface to make sure he's captured every single crumb. It makes him seem like a little boy, and frankly, it melts my heart.

He stands when he's done, carrying both of our plates to the trash, and I take advantage of this moment to admire his body, how tall he is, how broad his shoulders are, how warm everything about him looks. A part of me is aching to touch him.

"Seriously, what's the story behind your story?" I ask again, trying to keep myself focused, hoping I'm not pushing too hard. Owen reaches behind his head, pulling his hood over his hat and zipping the front of his jacket closed while he stuffs his hands inside the pockets. He does this when he's uncomfortable, and I've seen him do it before, but this time his smile doesn't leave his face.

"Yo, Ryan," he says, leading me over to the next table, where the rest of my friends are still finishing their slices. "So Kens wants to know why people think I'm an asshole."

"Hey!" I shout, slapping my hand against his arm. "I did not say that!"

"No, not directly. But, let's face it, Kens. People don't call me trouble; they call me an asshole," he says, his lips pressed together in a tight smile, his shoulders raised.

"I'll tell you why he's an asshole," Ryan says, surprising me since he's always the first to defend Owen to me. "He's an asshole..." he continues, standing and pushing his empty plate in Owen's chest, "because he's a ball hog who doesn't like to pass. Hey, ball hog, go take my shot and throw my plate in the trash, would ya?"

Owen blows a kiss at Ryan, who does it right back, and the two of them laugh, but Owen throws Ryan's plate away anyway.

There's a genuine respect between them both, like Owen has with House. I wonder why they aren't closer.

"I could give her a few reasons if you'd like," Willow says, standing to throw her garbage away next.

"Oh, I'm sure she's heard everything you've got to say," Owen says, reaching out and taking Willow's plate from her as well. His gesture surprises her, and I notice her brow pinched as she follows him with her gaze while he does her this small, but in many ways enormous, favor.

"Uh...thanks," she says, and he blows her a kiss next. "And there he is."

"You don't hate me. You hate the me I was when I was fourteen," Owen says, challenging her. Willow pauses at the end of the table, keeping her eyes on him, her eyes squinting while she considers what he said, and she finally sucks in her bottom lip and nods once before responding.

"Okay. Clean slate. But..." she says, coming closer to him, just close enough that I can hear her whisper at his back, "don't give me a *new* reason to hate you, okay heartbreaker?"

Owen's laugh is fast and soft, and more of an acceptance of her warning. He never says anything out loud, and Willow pats his back—with a little extra muscle—while she passes behind him.

"Rides!" Elise finally chants, standing next to Jess, grabbing his trash and practically leaping from the table. "I have waited," she starts, pausing to count on her fingers, "like *way* too many years to get my ass on that rollercoaster. Ryan Barstow, I hope you've got an iron stomach, cuz we're riding that thing a dozen times."

"Yeaaaaah, I got something you can ride," House says, stepping up behind us and grabbing his crotch, literally taking the conversation to the playground.

"Don't do that shit," Ryan says, poking his finger hard in House's chest, then grabbing Elise's hand and kissing the top of it before pulling her into his arm at the side as they walk away. She doesn't seem offended, and she's quick to shrug House's statement off, but I'm a little bothered by it. I'm not sure how I would handle him talking to me like that—well at all, and I wonder what Owen would think.

With a single comment, House has managed to send everyone in various directions; the only people left with him now are Owen, Andrew, and me. I'm starting to understand why Ryan and Owen don't hang out often. I'm pretty sure it's House.

"Dude," Owen says, wincing at his friend.

"Oh, don't give me that shit. You know I only have one level. I don't tone it down for no one," House says, shrugging his shoulders in his giant hoodie, then pulling it up over his head. He's embarrassed, whether he wants to admit it or not.

"I need some cash," Andrew says, holding his hand in front of Owen's chest, twitching the ends of his fingertips, like he's scratching an itch.

"Then I guess you need a job," Owen says, his hands still lodged in his pockets.

"Yeah, I'd get one of those, but I have this super overbearing brother who makes me take double high school, so I'm not really sure when I'll find the time…" Andrew trails off because Owen holds a twenty out for him in the middle of his speech.

"Yeah, yeah. Good point. Just go to college. Now take my money; it's all I'm good for," he teases, and Andrew winks at him once and pats his shoulder before jogging over to some carnival game with House.

And for the first time tonight, Owen and I are completely alone. A group of kids run by waving tickets, and a mom rushes behind Owen with a pile of napkins held fast to her son's bloody nose. There's activity everywhere, yet it feels like Owen and I exist in a bubble.

"I got busted with a gun," Owen says, and his statement is so out-of-the-blue, it makes me shake my head. I'm trying to find the context.

"What?" I finally ask.

"You asked why people think I'm trouble," he says. "That's when it started. I was in sixth grade, and I brought my big brother's gun to school."

"Oh," I say, my chest growing tighter with worry about rumors I fear Owen is about to confirm.

"There was this big kid, his name was Hunter, and his dad was on the town council or something like that. Anyway, Hunter made my life a living hell. He told everyone…" Owen looks away, taking a deep breath, so I reach over and tug on his sleeve to bring him back to me. When he turns, his face tilts to the side, and his lips form a perfectly straight line, not a smile, but not a frown. They are complete nothingness.

"About your dad?" I finish for him.

Owen nods, looking down at his feet. "He would follow me home with his friends, yelling shit like 'your daddy was a crazy man' and 'when are you going to go crazy?'"

"That's not very nice," I say, and inside my head I paint a mental picture where I punch this Hunter kid. Owen smiles at my response.

"Yeah, well, one day I brought James's gun to school, and I told Hunter about it and said I was going to shut him up," Owen says, his eyes drifting into that dark place as he remembers. His confession is scaring me, but I hold my ground and keep the worry away from my face.

"I didn't mean it. I was just *acting* tough. And I didn't know any better. My grandpa practically raised us, and he wasn't very well most of my life. And my mom, she was working, even back then. But Hunter ran to his dad, who called the cops, busted my locker open, and the next thing I know my mom was piecing together every penny in our savings account to bail my ass out of juvie."

"Wow…I gotta be honest. I was expecting you to tell me it was all lies," I say, unable to stop my upper body from convulsing in a shiver as the breeze picks up, dropping the air another ten degrees. Without pause, Owen unzips his jacket and drapes it over my shoulders, still careful not to let his hands touch my skin.

"Thank you," I smile, pulling the sleeves over my arms and wrapping myself with the fabric still carrying the warmth from his body. I imagine for the briefest moment that instead of his jacket, I'm in his arms.

"You want me to be honest?" Owen says, and there's a glimmer in his eyes that worries me, making me wonder, but I nod anyhow, giving a slight tip of my chin, then I wrap my arms and Owen's hoodie around me even tighter. "If there's a rumor you've heard about me..." he says, his head tilting down ever so slightly to make sure my eyes are met by his, "it's probably true."

"You held a gun to your head?" My question is a whisper, my inner voice pleading for him to tell me *everything except that.* Everything. Except that.

Owen stands his ground, his head still tilted so our eyes are locked, and he never flinches. Not. Once.

I wipe the tear away quickly, but not before he sees it, and his mouth falls with his spirit.

"Why?" I ask.

Owen shrugs at first, looking beyond my shoulder. When I turn, I notice our friends are walking toward us, Elise excitedly leading the way. When I turn back, I catch Owen's intense gaze waiting for me.

"I don't really smoke. And if you've ever noticed, I don't do drugs. I never once take that shit my friends pass around. I drink. Yeah, I do drink, but that's it. The rest? The rest are all risks I control. I like to feel that edge, to know where it is," he says, a fire flashing in his eyes.

"But what happens when you lose?" I ask, and his fire fades quickly, and suddenly he's back here with me.

"Then I'll know I'm just like him," he says, and my chest completely slams closed, my heart exploding all at once.

"Ryan's sick. I made him go on the big drop too many times," Elise says, and I breathe in a sharp, quick breath—trying to erase, or at the very least bury, everything I just heard.

"Oh, poor guy. You guys done then?" I ask, trying to ignore the look Willow is giving me over the fact that I'm smothering myself in Owen's jacket. I'm far deeper than she realizes.

"Elise wants to ride the big wheel, then we can go..." Ryan stops himself, looking at his friend and realizing his major slip. Everyone is hit with discomfort simultaneously, and no one wants to be the next to speak.

"It's okay. Really," Owen says, being brave. Perhaps just taking a risk. "I'm here, and that was hard enough. It's just a stupid Ferris wheel."

"Right, it's way different, too," Willow says, but Jess leans into her shoulder hard, stopping her from making this worse. "I just meant...from when we were kids...shit. I'm sorry Owen. Hey, I'm just going to go buy my ticket."

"And I'm going to go with her and make sure she keeps her mouth shut," Jess says as Willow elbows him while they leave. Elise and Ryan follow them, and Ryan mouths a "sorry" as they pass; Owen shrugs it off.

"My brother always wanted to ride this thing," he says, looking up at the flashing lights, the spinning buckets, the massive height.

"I could take him...if you want?" I say, and Owen drops his chin, his eyes softening at the sight of me.

"Take me on what? The wheel? Oh heck yeah, I'm in!" Andrew says as he strides up behind me. I follow him to the ticket line, and he's talking about how one of the games he was trying to win is fixed, something about the bottle tops being too large for the ring.

His voice is muffled in my ears because I'm desperately trying to keep my attention on Owen. When we step up to the window, I make my request for two tickets, ready to pay for Andrew's, but Owen's hand reaches over my shoulder, and he slides a ten through the small slot in the window.

"Make it four," he says. "You can ride with House," he says to Andrew.

"Oh, it's okay. Really, I can just wait on the ground with you. We'll eat more pie," I stammer, trying to give him an out as the woman in the booth takes his money and slides four passes into his hand.

"You couldn't possibly want more pie," he smiles, handing House and Andrew their passes, his eyes having a silent conversation with his brother and friend. "Guys, really...it's just a ride."

Andrew nods and moves to the line for the ride, but House sticks with Owen for a little longer, his eyes telling a different story. "I'm fine," Owen says, he grits through his teeth, his voice almost threatening toward his friend.

"Sure you are, man. But if you suddenly decide you're not, you tap out, got it?" House says, holding up his fist, waiting for Owen to accept. Owen just pushes it away finally, his motion harsh and abrupt as he turns and leaves his friend standing with me while he joins his brother in line.

I walk to join them slowly, and before House and I get too close, I ask: "What is tapping out?"

"It's our safety plan. When we race, there's always a point where we have each other's backs—where it's safe to admit we've had enough. We bail on whatever the situation is, back off the gas, pull over and calm down," House says.

"You ever need the safety plan?" I ask, and he nods *yes.*

"Has he?" I know the answer as soon as I ask, but it's confirmed when House sucks in his bottom lip and raises his brow.

The ride before us goes quickly, and Owen is handing the carnival worker our pair of tickets before I'm ready. Instinctually, I look around us, expecting to see a crowd gather, to see people whispering in horror, amazed at what Owen is about to do. But nobody cares. My friends are all up in cars on the other side of the wheel, their view of this completely obstructed. They have no idea how brave Owen's about to be— and I'm terrified that he's not really being brave at all, that he's only being *wild*, as Willow would say.

"Locked and ready," the carnie man yells, signaling something to the ride operator. With a jerk, we stream upward about twenty feet, halting fast and our gondola swinging back and forth while we wait for the bucket below us to load more riders.

Owen's brow is already beading with sweat, and he pulls his hat from his head and runs his long sleeve over his face, his dark eyes blinking fast.

"We don't have to do this," I say, but he interrupts me.

"Yes. Yes, we do," he says, and suddenly, his hand finds mine. His grip on my fingers is hard, but the way we lock together is almost familiar—right. Owen tugs on the fabric of his left sleeve with his teeth, chewing on the ribbed edge for a few seconds before grasping it with his thumb and holding it to his closed lips, his eyes darting from the safety latch to the pivot wheel to the line of people still waiting to load. With every new thing he notices, his grip on my hand gets tighter, and when we swing up even higher, his breath falters.

"I'm going to ask him to stop the ride. Owen, we're getting off," I say.

"No!" he says, closing his eyes and squeezing them, tucking his chin into his chest, then shaking his head *no.* "No," he whispers. "Please, Kensi. Help me through this."

Without pause, I pull Owen's right hand into my lap, and I cover it even more with my other fingers. His leg starts to bounce, and the rhythm is making the cart swing a little too much, so I lift his hand again, this time bringing it to my chest so I can hold it to me closely.

"Close your eyes, and I'll tell you when they're done loading, when you can just look out at the city, okay?" I say.

"Okay," he whispers, doing as I say.

"One more round, and that's it...almost there...loading. Latching. Waving. Okay," I say, still clutching his hand in mine, his fingers fretting and fighting to find more of my hand to grip any time I threaten to loosen my hold.

"Are we moving? Kensi, I can't tell. Are we moving?" he asks, his voice soft and vulnerable.

"Not yet. Soon, Owen. We'll be moving soon," I say, locking my eyes on his closed lids, watching them twitch with panic.

His breathing starts to stutter even more, and I begin to open my lips to beg him to let me make them stop one more time— when his eyes open, his soul looking right into mine. Then the sky begins to move behind him. I keep his gaze, doing my best not to interrupt, to blink, and I let my mouth form a faint smile. "We're moving," I say, his hand still held to my chest, my heart no doubt pounding against our grasp on one another.

"Owen, you can look out now, look at the town and the stars," I say, glancing over his shoulder as the lights from the festival fade and refocus with every pass we make. Owen keeps his eyes on me, never blinking. But I know he's seeing something. I know he's safe, that he doesn't need to "tap out," because he's smiling, and his eyes are showing traces of something new, like the life of a child lost years ago.

It's joy.

As the ride slows, we pause at the top, still frozen in our pose, our hands tethered to the point where I can no longer feel beyond my first knuckles. But Owen's smile remains, and his breathing starts to even out, his chest rising and falling at a normal pace. I spare a look away as my friends exit below us, and I notice Willow point up to our cart as she reaches her arms around Jess and squeezes him.

"I think they're proud of you," I say, gesturing to the group waiting for us about thirty feet below. Owen doesn't look, and he doesn't break our trance. But he does finally speak.

"You are the most beautiful girl I've ever seen," he says, and all at once, I fall for Owen Harper.

Chapter 12

Beautiful.

Owen Harper called me beautiful. And then just as quickly, he was gone. I squeezed his hand tightly while the ride slowly brought us down to the ground to exit. We walked down the long, metal exit ramp, where Willow was waiting for me, her eyes full of questions, and when I turned back to find Owen again—he had disappeared.

Gone.

He does that. Just...goes.

His truck was nowhere to be found when Willow brought me home. His room was empty for the entire night. And he's been away all day.

That's why I practically race down the stairs at the sound of the basketball, and I'm not even disappointed when it's only Andrew and House shooting the ball. They might be able to tell me something...*anything!*

Of course, my boldness stops stone cold as soon as House opens his mouth. "Ken Doll! Looking to *hold hands* with your boyfriend while you both eat cookies and drink milk and watch cartoons?" He's saying everything in this overly-childish teasing voice, and I hate that it's embarrassing me.

"Dude, don't be a dick!" Andrew says, throwing the ball hard into House's chest. I like Andrew more and more.

"What? You saw those two acting all junior high and shit last night. Don't pretend like you weren't making fun of them as much as I was," House says, throwing the ball back at Andrew twice as hard, ricocheting it off his less-coordinated hands. Andrew scrambles to pick the ball back up and looks up at me sheepishly, guilty for enjoying a laugh at my expense. I forgive him because he honestly feels bad. House can eat it, though.

"It's Kensi," I say, looking beyond House's broad body into the open front door and windows of the Harper house, wishing to see someone inside.

"Yeah, I'm not calling you that," he says, spinning the ball on his finger a few times, a cocky smirk smeared across his face. I snatch the ball from his right hand and pull it under my arm. My heart is smacking the insides of my ribs as I realize how ballsy I'm being. I stare him down while he maneuvers a wad of chew in his mouth, spitting obnoxiously, the tobacco staining my driveway. I can't help but revolt when he does it, and I let my disgust show. House isn't any different from the privileged boys in uniform I used to have to deal with at Bryce. Instead of flashing his money around to intimidate me, though, he uses his size and masculinity. I bet it's effective on others, and on girls who probably harbor secret crushes on him.

"Oh, *Kensi.* I'm just messin' with ya," he says, snatching the ball back from me and passing it around his body once or twice, his eyes squinted, waiting for me to react.

"Owen's at work," Andrew says, saving me from *all this.*

"Oh...okay," I say, suddenly feeling awkward, like I no longer have a reason to be outside my house.

"You can hang out with me? I'll show you a good time," House says, sliding his giant arm over my shoulder, the material of his sweatshirt is actually damp with his sweat.

"I'm good...thanks," I say, slinking out of his grip. His laugh is almost demonic as he tosses the ball back to Andrew and pulls his keys from his pocket.

"All right, but you're missin' out," he says, walking to his truck near the curb.

"Am I?" I ask, my heart actually hurting with the anxiety coursing through my chest. House makes me nervous. Owen may think he's harmless, but I'm not convinced.

"You let me know when you're done playing footsies with O, and I'll show you a real man," he says, nodding to Andrew, then stepping up into his truck and roaring his engine loudly.

"He's all talk," Andrew says, bouncing the ball a few times to draw my attention back to him.

"Sure he is," I say back, not believing it for a second. I know House's type, and it's entitled. Money has nothing to do with it. He just needs to know he's not entitled to me.

"You like my brother?" Andrew says, and my throat burns with fear at having to answer that question. I can't look at him, so I keep my attention on House's taillights as he pulls away.

144

"We've become friends," I say, my voice unsteady, unsure, and my mind flashing through the dozens of nights I've waited to see just a glimpse of Owen outside, my palm burning with the memory of the touch of his hand in mine. "Yeah..." I add, my voice even softer now. "I like him."

"He'll be home late tonight. But...he'd like to see you," Andrew says, his foot kicking into mine, teasing me like a little brother should. I nod once and smile at him, and his smile is broad and satisfied.

I head back into my house and tiptoe up the stairs to my mom's bedroom door. Her shift was late, and she's been sleeping most of the morning, so I don't want to wake her, but when I press my ear to the door, I hear her talking on the phone.

"We can talk, sure...but...not now. I'm not ready to talk now. I think I just need time," she says, her half of the conversation piquing my curiosity about the other end of the line. I'm sure she's talking to my father, and I don't like that she's talking to him. I want to cut him out of our existence, to just take a giant eraser to all he was and all he is, and I want to do that for Gaby, too. But then there are those memories, the few good ones of us as a family, home together, on holidays. And maybe we can only let in those small things, but keep everything else out.

I hear the conversation end, so I step quickly to my room, folding my legs up on my bed and pulling my laptop in front of me, acting busy. My Facebook page is still up. I had been looking for pictures of Owen—anything about Owen—but he seems to avoid being online. I found a mention of his name in a town newspaper archive; he was named to the state's all-star basketball team. But that was all.

My exploration started with a hunt for pictures because I wanted to see his face. But soon I started looking for the bad things, arrest records and proof that Owen was also all of those things Willow and Jess and Elise say he is. But those records don't exist online. And even though it's probably just because he's a minor, I still like the fact that I can't find the bad things. I'm ashamed I even started looking for them in the first place.

What I settled on, though, was my folder full of photos of Gaby and me. I've dragged them into the trash a dozen times, but

I keep pulling them back out. As much as I want to erase my father, I don't want to erase Gaby. I only want to erase what she did. God, how I want to erase that.

"So I was thinking of making pasta for dinner. You know, Grandma's sauce? What do you think?" My mom startles me when she comes in my room, and I snap my laptop to a close. Her eyes linger on it, her head tilting, but she doesn't question. It's almost like she knows enough to know she doesn't *want* to know what I'm looking at.

She doesn't. It would kill her to see these photos—reason enough to delete them all the moment she leaves my room.

"Sure. Pasta's good," I say, holding my hands still on the silver top of my computer, my eyes doing their best to bluff happiness. After a few long seconds, my mom turns to leave.

"Hey, Mom?" I ask; she pauses and looks over her shoulder. "Can we have the neighbors over for dinner with us? It's usually just Owen, and his brother. Their mom works nights, and they've just been good...to us..."

My mom knows what I mean—Owen's been good to me, defended me, defended her, stood up to my dad. She smiles softly before she speaks.

"That sounds like a good idea. I'll try to clean up the kitchen some, enough to have guests," she says.

"They won't mind the mess," I say, the double meaning there for both of us. Owen understands life's messy. She nods and smiles once again before leaving, and the second I hear her feet hit the stairs, I open my laptop and delete the visual reminders of my former best friend.

It's the least I can do.

My piano hasn't made a sound for days, minus the moment I played it for Willow. And when I played, it felt like a goodbye. But today...

Today I just feel like I need to touch it. I've been sitting at it for more than an hour, my mom clanking around the kitchen, cleaning and cooking. All I can bare to do is run my hand along the cover over the keys, my finger tracing along the fine lines of the wood grain. Something so beautiful is also so ugly.

"Kens, hun? I think your phone is ringing," my mom shouts from the kitchen. I slide from the bench quickly, not wanting her to see where I'm sitting. I think I'm worried she'll encourage me to play.

"Thanks," I say, passing through the kitchen to the small table in the nook where my jacket and backpack are sitting. My phone is sitting on top, and there's a message notification on the screen. I grab all of my things, and head back upstairs as I listen to the message, recognizing that the number was Owen's and not really wanting to listen to his voice while my mother watches the smile form on my face.

"Hey, uhm. Damn. Kens? I really hate to ask for this," his message begins. I pause it, his concerned voice making me nervous. I hurry the rest of the way to my room, toss my belongings to the ground, and move to my bed to listen to the rest, my eyes peering out my window to the spot where I'm wishing for his truck to appear.

"I'm in trouble. Not like...*real* trouble," he says, and a voice near him adds, "this is pretty serious, son."

"No, it's *not* serious. That's what I'm trying to explain to you," he says, the phone muffled while he talks to someone in the room with him. "Look, Kensi, I need you to come down to the shops I work at, they're on Eighth and Central. I need you to get something out of my truck, but I'm being held for...shit, I'm being held for shoplifting. This dickhead cop won't let me go, even though he's wrong!"

"That's enough; time's up, Harper," the voice bellows in.

"Just come, Kens. My mom's not home, and Andrew can't help. Please." It's that last word, the *please,* that breaks me. He doesn't sound like Owen at all, instead more like the frightened ghost of Owen that I got to see terrified dozens of feet in the air on that Ferris wheel.

My feet are wandering my room, carrying my body that's not even caught up with my mind yet. I don't know what to do, and I barely know what Eighth and Central means. Owen needs me, and I *have* to go.

I have to go.

I grab my boots and the heavier coat hanging on the hook behind my door. The sky has been gray for days, threatening to open up. These early storms, they aren't really snow. But they aren't rain either. The air has been frosty, and the cold has been harsh. I'm used to the city, which while the wind cuts to the bone, the buildings offer you the occasional reprieve, making it livable to move around outside. There's nothing to hide behind out here, even the trees have lost most of their leaves and are mere spindles standing on dead, lifeless ground.

I'm down the stairs quickly, my wallet and phone sandwiched in my hands. I need the keys. My mom doesn't let me drive often, and I've never had a car of my own. There's never been a need.

I have to go.

"Mom?" I ask, my lip trembling that she's going to say *no*. For some reason, the more time that passes, the more worried I am that Owen is in big trouble.

"What, babe?" she asks, her eyes watering from the onion she's chopping. She runs her face along the bicep of her sleeve, then looks up at me, and I try my best to look calm.

"It was Owen. He's at work, had some trouble with his truck," I lie. "He needs me to come get him. It's only a few blocks. I won't be gone long; can I borrow the keys?"

"Oh, poor kid. Here, let me just turn the stove off. I'll come with you," she says, my stomach starting to fill with the drumming beats of my heart, the heaviness of stress weighing me down more.

"No, no," I start, and she pauses, tilting her head in that way, the same way she did before when she caught me looking at pictures of Gaby. The face she makes says she knows, just not everything. "You're in the middle of cooking. And I'm really looking forward to tonight. I don't want to stop you, or to mess any of this up," I say, this time not really a lie. "Let me go. Let me do this. Please."

Please.

I say the same word Owen said, hoping it resonates. Something does, but my mom waits for a few long seconds before nodding her head toward the keys on the counter.

"If the speed limit is thirty, you drive twenty, okay?" she says. I smile and cross my heart, trying to keep it light, inside wishing I was a better driver so I could be there as quickly as House would be.

He called me. He didn't call House.

That thought...it feels....

I'm careful as I buckle myself into the car, tossing my wallet and phone into the passenger seat. I maneuver down the driveway, onto the road and to the end of our block, and then I shut my eyes while I sit at the stop sign, not a single car coming in either direction. Which way is Eighth? Which way?

My gut tells me to turn right, so I do. I'm rewarded by street names that count down from Seventeenth to Sixteenth to Thirteenth and soon Tenth. When I find Eighth, I actually laugh out loud with the kind of glee I didn't think was real.

"I'm coming, Owen," I whisper to myself.

I see the main grocery store near the strip mall in the distance, and despite my mother's best warnings, I punch the gas, skipping part of the curb as I pull into the parking lot, and my tires squeal as I move down the main lane through the mall. I can see the small security vehicle and the squad car parked next to it, the lights flashing like there's an emergency.

I park right next to the cars, grab my things, and rush into the small gift shop where Owen is sitting, his hands cuffed.

"Owen! I'm here. What's..." I pause when I see his dejected face. His hands are pulled tightly behind his body, and everything about him looks tired and defeated.

"Miss," the officer says.

"Kensington," I say to him, my full name. This feels like I should be formal.

"You know this young man?" he asks.

"Yes. We're friends. He's my neighbor," I say, not really sure what the right definition is for our relationship. I want to say whatever makes this better for Owen.

"We were sort of expecting a parent," the officer says, tipping his glasses down and looking at Owen with an intense scowl.

"I told you. My mom is *working.* I don't have anyone else. And I didn't do anything wrong!" Owen says, his temper showing its familiar flare.

"I'm sorry. Could someone explain what's going on? How can I help?" I interrupt, my hands shaking while I move to a small folding chair across from Owen and an older man.

"I'll tell you what happened," the man sitting next to him says, his white hair tufting on either side of his head, his eyes framed with thick black-rimmed glasses. "This young...hooligan...tried to pocket this charm bracelet while he was emptying out the trash! That's what's going on."

The man waves a small, silver bracelet toward Owen, and it jangles while he shakes it to emphasize his opinion. I look to Owen, looking for confirmation that this is false. But there's a part of me that wonders, the part that knows how dangerous Owen can be. This...this would be such a small thing for him—not even a thrill from the crime.

I wait while he shuts his eyes and shakes his head, and I'm not sure what he's feeling. "I told you, I bought it this morning, from the girl who was working here," Owen says, and my chest fills with air, my body washed with relief.

"There, see?" I say, standing, practically demanding and proclaiming him innocent.

"Then where's the receipt, you little piece of shit?" the old man yells, standing and smacking his hand down on the seat he just abandoned. I look to the officer, who stands silently, his pen already armed to take down the guilty report.

"We've done this already. I can't find it. But maybe it's in my truck. Just let me look," Owen says, his voice trailing off because he knows the response he'll get.

"Bullshit, you'll just take off," the old man says.

"Where the FUCK am I gonna go?" Owen yells, his eyes simmering now, the shadow closing in over him. "Fuck! You know who I am! You all know my family! This isn't a big town. You seriously think I'm going to shoplift a bracelet for sixty bucks—then leave my home and go off into the sunset? Where the fuck would I go, man? Use some goddamned logic at least if you're going to judge me without any facts or reasons."

"Let me look," I say, my eyes darting between the officer and the shop owner, neither of them paying attention. "Owen, where are your keys?"

"In the back. This prick took them," he says.

"Don't you call me that," the old man says.

I ignore them all, march to the back where Owen's keys are sitting on a stack of notebooks on an old metal desk. I grab them and walk back through the store. "Hey, you can't take those. Those aren't yours!" the old man yells as I pass him.

"Yeah, well they aren't yours either, you prejudiced asshole!" I say as I storm through the door, the small string of bells dangling from the door handle announcing my exit.

I find Owen's truck quickly, parked near the road, away from the shops, in a spot no customers would want. I unlock his door and scan my eyes over his seat, the only thing there an empty licorice wrapper and the paper from a stick of gum. Owen's sunglasses are on the dashboard, as are a few papers. I leaf through them, noting that one of them is a letter from Bradley University, interest in Owen's basketball intentions. The letter looks yellowed, so I look to find the date—two months old.

I toss the stack of papers back to their spot on the dash and pull open the glove box, finding nothing but his insurance and registration card and an envelope with a few dollar bills inside and some gas receipts. It has to be here. I know it in my heart that he isn't lying.

Stepping away from the truck, I look at the long bench seat through the open door, and I pull my hand to my mouth, my teeth working on my short, already chewed down thumbnail while I think. With a small tilt of my head, I notice something different along the floorboard, deep in a corner along the floor of Owen's driver's side. There's a small speck of pink, and when I step closer, I realize it's paper. Scooting forward on my elbows, I move my body under the steering wheel and lift slightly on the gas pedal, sliding the floor mat back a tiny bit.

MOORE'S GIFT HUT is written in large, bold letters along the top, and a handwritten note details a bracelet, today's date, $58.47, and it's signed by the name *Patricia*. I grasp it in my hand, wrinkling it, but more concerned about somehow dropping it, or a gust of wind carrying it away. I slam Owen's door to a close and run back to the store where the officer now has Owen standing, his palm on his back getting ready to guide him through the door.

"It's here! It's here!" I say, pushing the receipt into the officer's hands. He sets his clipboard down, lets his other hand fall away from Owen, then unwrinkles the pink paper for inspection.

"Sir, is this receipt from your store?" he asks, handing the paper to the old man, who scrambles to push his glasses to the tip of his nose, holding the paper up in the light. I'm looking at an entire stack of similar pages stuck through a pin on his counter, and I turn to Owen and wink. But Owen's face still looks sullen.

"Patricia, yeah she was here this morning. And the numbers all match up," he says, standing and walking over to the counter, pulling a few old receipts out just to make sure the handwriting is to his satisfaction. He's putting on a show, because he's embarrassed; he was wrong.

"All right, looks like things worked out this time, Harper," the officer says, pulling a pocket knife from his pocket and cutting the strip of plastic on the disposable cuffs that were holding Owen hostage. He rubs his wrists and stretches his arms across his chest, then turns to look at the old man across the counter.

"Well...you can't be too careful," the old man begins, his voice stuttering, panicked. He can't believe he was wrong. Owen doesn't say a word, only holding out his hand until the old man realizes what he wants, and hands him the bracelet.

"I've been stolen from a lot this year," the old man continues, trying to explain to me now, but I'm no longer interested in anything he has to say either. I follow Owen out the door, and as we pass my mom's car, I expect him to stop, but he keeps walking. After he's several paces ahead of me, I call his name, but he doesn't turn around. His pace is steady, and his shoulders are low, ashamed.

I jog until I'm caught up with him again, and follow his footsteps until we're at the driver's door for his truck. "Owen, wait!" I say, wanting to say something better, something that would show him I didn't doubt him. But then again, there was a moment where I did. I doubted him, for just a fraction of a second—because of everything I've been told.

"Here," he says, tossing the silver chain, heavy with charms, to me. I catch it in both hands, looking down at it with a pinched brow, confused. "I got that for you."

He leaves quickly, never looking me in the eyes. The light is fading as dusk starts to settle in, so I shuffle my feet back to my car, my fingers rubbing obsessively over the metal trinkets in my hand. I flip the dome light on as soon as I'm buckled in the car, then I open my palm and look at my gift from Owen. I fall apart all at once; each charm is thoughtful, precious—one a note, one a piano, one a pick-up truck, and the last one a Ferris wheel.

I dial Owen three times, each call going right to his voicemail. So I give up, slam the car gear into reverse, and speed away from the shopping center. A few times, I convince myself that I can see Owen's lights, that it's his truck I'm following. But it never is, each time the driver turning the wrong way.

When I pull into my driveway, the car skids over the dip in the gutter, grinding metal along pavement, but the noise is just enough to stop Owen as his foot is about to step up his porch.

I push the gear in park, fly from the door and leave the car running in my driveway—my feet skipping carefully over the rocks and dips from the concrete of my driveway to his front yard. Owen doesn't move, but he doesn't leave. He stands there, his hands limp at his sides, his hat pushed low over his eyes, hiding how pathetic he feels—how vulnerable he is. I ignore it all, my hand grasping my bracelet, my gift, so tightly that the metal is leaving an indentation in my palm.

"I love it," I say, walking swiftly up to him, my breathing coming hard. "My bracelet. Owen...thank you. I love it."

He doesn't say a word, but he glances down at my open palm, his eyes twitching with the motion of my hands as I struggle with the clasp and work to wrap the chain around one wrist with my opposite hand. I hold my arm against my chest, keeping the end of the bracelet in place and finally hook it closed.

"It's beautiful, Owen. This...it's beautiful. Thank you," I say, my eyes glossing over with the want to cry. I stand before him, waiting for him to say something, say *anything.* Instead, he's motionless, and I give up. "I just wanted you to know how much I love it. How thankful I am...I'm sorry, Owen," I say, my smile fading fast, my eyes falling low as I turn and walk back to my house, to a kitchen full of pasta and sauce, enough to feed a real family. Only I'm coming back alone....

"You're beautiful. That...it's just a bracelet. But you..." Owen says, and I stop, my throat catching my emotion at the sound of his voice. It's deep and raspy, just like that first night in his truck. His hand is on my shoulder, my feet stopped and my body shivering.

With slow movements, his feet glide closer, an inch at a time, while his hand sweeps my hair around my neck. He slides his touch down my shoulder and arm until his hand is completely wrapped around my wrist. Lifting my arm slowly, Owen slides the edge of my sleeve with his finger, exposing the bracelet along my pale skin, the weight of the charms sliding up as he brings my hand closer to my shoulder, closer to him.

I can feel him breathe along my neck, and when the warmth of his mouth tickles my fingers, then my wrist, my eyes roll to a close—the feeling unlike anything I've ever experienced before. This is the dream I've had in my bed every night since I've met Owen Harper. Only this isn't a dream at all. It's really happening.

Owen loosens his grip on my wrist, letting go completely—then moving his hand to my jaw, pulling my chin up so I look at the dark, cloud-covered sky. When his lips touch the freezing skin along my neck, my knees grow weak, and I nearly slip to the ground.

With a more forceful grip, Owen reaches into my hair and turns me into him quickly, my breath catching when I realize how close I am to him, how much of him I can smell, feel, touch— taste. Both of his hands rise to my cheeks, his thumbs giving each one a gentle stroke while he looks at me.

No boy has ever touched me like this. No boy has ever given me a gift. And I've never wanted a boy to kiss me more than I do right now—to kiss me like the way they do in the movies, like a grown woman, like the woman I'm so close to becoming.

Every movement he makes is slow and studied, his eyes watching as his hand works in and out of my hair, then runs

154

along my arm again, feeling the bracelet against my skin. When Owen leans into me, I begin to shut my eyes, my lips quivering, ready to meet his, but his mouth keeps moving, finding my neck and ear first, his tongue taking small strokes along the way. I've watched Owen do this, watched him kiss other girls like this. And as much as I also secretly wanted to be in their place, I now know that I don't want to be them at all.

I want to be more.

"Owen, I'm not Kiera," I breathe, his touch halting with my words. His hands never leave their spot, cradling my head, but Owen's mouth leaves my neck, his eyes serious when they come into view, his mouth a tight, straight line. My hands move to grip his elbows, to steady me in my moment of weakness, my legs threatening to betray me and send me to the ground again.

After several long seconds under his scrutiny, under the power of his gaze, he pulls me even closer, shutting his eyes as his mouth comes within a fraction of an inch of mine, his bottom lip grazing my top lip and sending a lighting bolt into the depths of my belly.

His mouth brushes against mine a few more times, each pass leaving me wanting more, forcing my lips to part, my skin to radiate with need, until finally he speaks. "You're right," he says, holding my head to his, our mouths ready, waiting. "You're so much more."

His mouth covers mine fast, his strong lips working my naïve and novice ones quickly into submission. His hands crawl around my head and body until he's pulling me to him so tightly that it becomes hard to breathe, but air—breathing—it's so unnecessary. I follow his lead, copy his every move, and grip him tightly, my fingers exploring the powerful muscles along his back and sides, feeling all of those physical things I've hungered for, until I'm stretching on my toes to reach him just to keep our lips intact.

With one swift action, Owen's hand slides down the small of my back, to my butt, and he lifts me up against him, carrying me while he takes giant strides to his truck, our lips never once breaking their hold on one another. He sets me on the bed of his truck and shifts his hands up the sides of my body, his finger's pausing at my ribs, his hands flexing with indecision. I can tell he wants to touch me, to feel me, and I love that his hands crave the feel of my breasts. The mere thought of him touching me there—in a place where boys who weren't worthy have barely felt me—makes my mouth hungrier, and I put all of the passion I'm feeling into our kiss.

I don't know when the back light clicked on, and I never heard the door, but when I let my eyes slip open, I notice. My wits are with me enough to realize that my mom is probably still watching this from somewhere inside our house. And while a small part of me doesn't care, there's another part that doesn't want to talk about boys and kissing and what's appropriate and what isn't with my mother. Not that I mind talking to my mom, I just don't want to talk about my beating heart with someone whose heart is broken.

"Dinner," I breathe out one word finally—a word that makes no sense to Owen, and barely registers with me. Our lips part, but Owen's hold on my face remains, his forehead resting against mine while he stands in front of my dangling legs, his feet shuffling with what I think might just be excitement and nerves.

"You want...dinner?" he asks, his lip pulling into a smirk on one side, a deep dimple impressing on one cheek.

"My mom. She said I could invite you for dinner. She's...she's been cooking all day. For you...and Andrew," I say, my cheeks finally finding feeling again after the rush of heat that coursed through them.

"Is she trying to poison me?" he jokes, his lips giving mine one small peck while his forehead sways side-to-side against mine in a way that feels natural and familiar.

"No more than I tried with the grilled cheese. You seem to have a very high tolerance," I smile.

"Well, I've had girls try to poison me before. I guess I'm immune," he jokes, and I can't help the way my lips slide into a frown at the mention of girls—*other* girls.

"Yeah, but I'm smarter than them. So I might be able to get the job done," I say, swinging my legs just enough to lightly kick him in the knee.

"First of all, *ouch!* Don't kick the knees. I've had surgery," he says, as he lifts me from the truck, swinging my body around until I'm resting on his driveway, his arms still looped around my body while my hands are clutched against his chest, searching for warmth. "And second of all, you're not just smarter than other girls. You're…"

He doesn't finish his words, instead sucking in his bottom lip, letting his teeth hold it in place while his head falls to mine one last time.

"So are you," I say, letting myself have something I want, say something I mean—something risky and scary.

When Owen's eyes close completely and his smile slowly pulls his lips loose from his teeth, I understand what the rest of that sentence is.

Everything.

Owen Harper is everything.

Chapter 13

"So?" Willow says, her face full of nosey curiosity while she watches me climb into her car.

"So...what?" I respond. I'm not going to make this easy.

"Come on!" she says with a laugh while she backs down my driveway. "You can't text me that you kissed Owen, and then pretend it never happened! You ignored every single follow-up text and my two phone calls after that. You're a bad bomb dropper. No cleanup afterward. Like...at all!"

I giggle, and the sound of happiness coming from my mouth is nice, foreign...but nice. It's a sound I haven't made in a while. "You kissed him. You know what it's like. What's to tell?" I tease, moving my book bag into my lap and pulling my gloves out to slip on my hands.

"Kens, I was fourteen when I kissed him. We were still dancing with bent elbows and rocking back-and-forth in the school gym at that time. I've seen that boy kiss now, and trust me—it's *different!* I want deets," she says.

"Deets?" I say, slowly, one eyebrow cocked in her direction.

"Gahhhhh! Details. Deets! Don't make fun of my hip language, now spill it!" Willow's gum snaps, and I study her for a few seconds while she signals at the light and turns down the street to our school. She's so different from Morgan and Gaby. They both come from money, lots and lots of money. My family was comfortable middle class, sure. But I also used to have to listen to my mom dodge creditors and argue with my dad over bills. Those conversations never happened in my friends' worlds. And while I always found Morgan and Gaby to be more down-to-earth than the rest of our peers at Bryce, that feeling of not being a *real* member of their club was always there—even with Gaby. Willow looks like someone I'm supposed to know, like the friend that perhaps I was always supposed to have.

Like someone I can trust.

"How long have you been with Jess?" I ask, changing the subject, but with a reason.

"Uhhhh, like, more than a year. Why? Is this still about that thing Ryan said? That I'm into Owen? Kens, you know I'm not..." she says, and I interrupt.

"No, no. I know, I was just curious," I say, leaving my gaze on her. I bite at the inside of my mouth, a little nervous to push our friendship. "Have you and Jess....you know?"

I know she knows what I mean. I can tell by the way her eyebrows flare quickly, and the way she adjusts her grip on the steering wheel.

"Uhm, you did only kiss him, right? I mean...was there...more?" she asks, and I correct this quickly.

"Yeah, I mean no. I mean...yes, just a kiss. We just kissed," I say. My armpits are actually sweating, and my chest is pounding, I'm so uncomfortable. I've only ever talked about things like this with Gaby. She had a lot of...*experience,* clearly more than I was aware of, and now she's gone. And I have so many questions. "It's just...I like him, Will. I like him...a lot. I'm pretty sure I've never liked a boy like this. No...I know I haven't. And he's..."

"You're afraid he's going to try to push you too fast?" she asks, and I feel silly just hearing it out loud.

"Oh wow. I'm seriously living an after-school special, huh? Uhhhhhhg!" I say, throwing my face in my hands. I feel a little ridiculous, and presumptuous that I'm even thinking about things like Owen and sex at all. But I am. I'm thinking about it, about a *me* and *Owen,* down the road, when sex might enter into the picture. And when I think of that, I start to think that for him—a guy like Owen—sex is probably already in the picture. And then I replay that thing he said, the night at the party, when he accused me of having a problem with people having sex. I'm such a fucking prude!

"I just like him, Will. I like him a lot, and I've never..." All of my attention goes to my lap, to my fingers that I'm picking at, to my knee bouncing up and down.

"This summer," she says, and I stop breathing, waiting for the rest. "Jess and me, our first time was this summer. I wanted to wait. And really?" She pauses, looking to the left at our school while we wait at the light, Jess's car parked in its usual spot. "I wanted to wait more. I mean…I don't regret it. But I wasn't *really* ready."

"Oh," I say, sucking in my lip hard, not sure what to say next.

"It got better. And we're careful, and we…we're, I don't know, active? Boy, that sounds really fucking clinical, doesn't it? We do it, sometimes? And I'm glad it was Jess, that he was my first," she says, her lips curving into a smile when we see him standing at the curb, waiting for her to pull in. "But you don't have to, you know?"

"But there have been so many. Haven't there? I mean, Owen and girls…" I say as she puts the car in park.

"Probably. But, really, what do I know? Maybe he just makes out and kisses, and that's it," she says, pausing in the quiet of her car for a few seconds before we both break into hysterical laughter. "Yeah, probably not!"

We both laugh hard while we gather our things, but my laughter dies down quickly, my thoughts going right back to that kiss, how it felt, and how different a boy like Owen is from the safety of group dates and school functions I was used to before.

I trail behind Willow and Jess along the walkway, and am about to step into the band room, when I notice someone sitting on the tables nearby. Owen's hands are wrapped around a paper cup steaming with coffee, his fingers poking through black cut-off gloves; a beanie is pulled over his dark hair.

"Kinda early today, aren't you?" I ask, my fingers instinctively moving to my hair, tucking it behind my ear—a nervous tick in his company, and my face is blushing at the sight of him. He looks up, his lips puckered while he blows over the top of the hot liquid in his cup, the steam making small swirls in front of his lips. The way they slide so naturally into a smile erases every tiny worry I let in during my car ride with Willow. The way his face lights up when he sees me—*when he sees me*—that's enough.

Right now, the way he looks right now, is enough.

"It was weird, I had these awful stomach pains, like someone…poisoned me," he teases, his eyebrows lowered while he stares at me, his legs stretching out slowly as he stands.

160

"Damn. You're on to us. My mother and I are black widows, with a trail of high school boys and men buried in yards all over Illinois," I say, finishing my last word just before Owen's arm sweeps me into his chest, the softness of his coat backed by the hardness of his body, every single inch of him warm.

"Kens, trust me, you buried me a long time ago," he says, his lips kissing the top of my head, his arm holding me tight to him. This is where I want to be for the rest of the morning. And I am his just a little more.

"I have to go to band," I groan, and he squeezes one last time before letting me go, the cool air wrapping around me the second his arm leaves my body. "I'm sorry."

"No, it's cool. I figured I'd just come early, see if I could see you," he says, and his cheeks—they actually blush. "I had to drop Andrew off early. He's doing this robotics thing."

"Oh," I say, my smile caught in my teeth, my tummy fluttering. "Will I be seeing you in class today, Mr. Harper?"

"Yes, Miss Worth. I will be attending class this week. In fact, I should be here every day, from now on," he says. "Sort of quit the job that tried to arrest me for paying for something," he says, his eyes gliding down my body, to my wrist, where my gift still circles my arm. I haven't taken it off since he gave it to me, even when my mom raised an eyebrow when I told her it was a gift from Owen.

"Is that going to mess things up for you? I mean, you said you needed the money," I say, worried about him.

"Yeah, we do," he says through a deep breath, cupping the back of my head and kissing my forehead before he begins to slide away from me. "But my mom's taking a break from school, so she's picking up a second job. I don't like it, but she wants me to focus on the rest of my year."

I'm hanging on the open door, Willow just out of view, watching my every move from inside, ready to make fun of me the second I close the door. "So I'll see you in a couple hours," I say, my fingers, my lips, my toes—every part of me tingling just watching Owen's eyes rake over me. His lip quirks on the side, the small dimple, the one I used to think seemed so arrogant, punctuating everything about him that makes me weak. Then he blows me a kiss before pulling his ear buds from his pocket and tucking them into ears and going back to his coffee.

"You...are in trouble, missy," Willow says, her head shaking at me, not quite in disapproval, as I close the door and move to my instrument.

"Yeah, I'm in pretty big trouble," I admit, enjoying every second of it.

We spend our morning band practice marching. Most of my time is spent practicing chords and new sheet music on the xylophone—wheeling it to the field to watch the rest of the band march, wheeling it back when we're done. My shoes are caked with wet, dead grass, so I spend my independent hour—the time I'm supposed to be practicing the piano—digging away the grass and mud. It's an excuse not to play. I don't even pretend it's anything but.

When Owen's feet are waiting on my desk, his pencil eraser pressed in-between his lips, his cocky smile underscoring the intensity of his eyes as they watch me move through the desks between the door and our row, I melt.

I melt.

I melt every time.

I don't bother to move his feet, instead sitting in my seat, resting my arm along the top of his ankle, enjoying the nearness of any part of him. I catch the stares from the others in the class. Most people take us in, dismiss us, and then move on. Others, girls who I've seen in the rotation, whisper and stare a little longer than most. But Owen never moves from our touch, and neither do I.

Every class is the same. And when it's time for lunch, Owen actually waits for me by the classroom door, walking by my side to the cafeteria. Just before I reach to open the door, his pinky grabs mine. I stop to notice, my eyes looking at the way our hands look together, my fingers shaking with nerves, until eventually Owen weaves his entire hand through mine, his grip leaving no doubt that this touch—it's intentional, and it isn't fleeting.

"You wanna skip lunch and head outside to make out in front of Willow and Jess?" I joke, really just a mask for how nervous I

162

still am with him. Owen smiles and laughs once, but then he shakes his head, leans in, and kisses my cheek.

"Nah. I'd rather just *be* with you," he says, his eyes meeting mine, but looking down quickly as he pushes the brim of his hat lower. He's nervous, too.

We both pick out a few small things for lunch, and Owen follows me to the table, my friends all watching him sit next to me, take my tray for me, then open the tab on his soda.

After several long awkward silent seconds, Owen puts his soda back down on the table and wipes his hands along his jeans, drying them from the moisture from the can. He reaches across the table to Jess, his hand out for a shake.

"Hi. I'm Owen," he says, his eyes daring Jess to break, for the table to break and everyone to finally get over whatever it is they all seem to find weird. Jess takes over eventually, smiling back and shaking Owen's hand, laughing at himself.

"Sorry, we're band geeks. We lack social skills," Jess says, and Willow ribs him.

"Speak for yourself," she says.

"Especially this one. She's like *head* band geek, so...*ya know,*" he says, grimacing and earning an even harder jab from Willow.

"Owwwww! Hey," he says, rubbing the spot she poked, looking up as Ryan slides behind him to his seat next to Elise.

"Hey, O. What's up?" Ryan says, his eyes setting on Owen's left arm, which is now around my shoulders, his fingers slowly scratching at my shoulder, possessively. "Ahhhh, never mind," Ryan adds, a quick wink before giving the rest of his attention to his lunch.

"You coming to practice today?" Ryan says, his mouth mumbling through a giant bite of his sandwich.

"Yeah, I should make them all now. Quit the job. Mom's getting a second, at least, for a while," Owen says, and I reach down and slide my hand over his knee, just wanting to let him know I know the depth of it all—how much his mom working, him working, is integral to his family.

"Cool. Hey, you should come watch, Kens," Ryan says, his eyes smirking when he mentions the invitation.

"Oh, no. She'd get bored," Owen says, and I can feel him stiffen next to me.

"No, I wouldn't. I love watching you play," I say, a little too quickly, the admission that I've watched him before, ever at all, falling out in front of everyone.

"You love watching me, huh?" he teases, his mouth slowly taking in a chip, crunching leisurely, while his smile slips back into place.

All I can do is stare back into his eyes, his eyes that are daring me to say anything different, to pretend and lie, and try to convince the rest of the table that I don't watch him. His eyebrows raise, and my face burns from the redness.

"Practice is at four," he says, his head falling to the side, and his look growing more adoring.

I melt. Every time.

"I'll take you home," he says. "And maybe tonight you can have dinner at my house."

"Okay," I say, smiling while my lips hug the straw for my juice drink, my body still burning from everyone's attention.

Willow doesn't ask any questions on our way to class, and after school, she only sends me a quick text, reminding me to *have fun but be careful,* and some picture of a basketball and a heart. She follows it up with a graphic of a condom, which mortifies me—so I spend the next five minutes looking for a picture of a middle finger to send to her.

My mom is working her night shift, so I don't even bother to text her, knowing she won't see it for the next several hours anyhow. I wander the empty halls, looking around for Owen or Ryan or even House, but everyone's gone. I give my backpack one final check, then slide it up over my shoulders and exit the main building.

I can hear the squeak of shoes as I near the gym, and when I open the door, I recognize Owen quickly. I slip through the front hallway to the side entrance and take a seat in one of the bleachers, near the end. A few parents are watching too, one of the dads standing at the front of the bleachers, yelling out things every now and then. It makes me chuckle to myself. It's not so different from my father standing behind me, watching my hands move along the piano keys. He used to shout things too.

Owen hasn't seen me yet, and I'm glad. He's being himself, his confidence something I envy. He's leading the other guys through drills, the ball always a little sharper, more controlled, when it's with him. It's strange to see him like this, dressed in shorts and a T-shirt with the sleeves torn away. His arms are more defined than I thought, probably because the last time I watched him play in my driveway, his shirt was off, and the only thing I could stare at was his stomach and chest.

He has a tight, black brace wrapped around one of his knees, and I remember him telling me he had surgery once. It doesn't seem to bother him as he glides effortlessly up and down the court, stopping on a dime, switching direction, moving the ball from one hand to the next and rolling it off his fingers near the rim. His touch is flawless.

The coach whistles, and all of the guys jog over for a water break. Ryan sees me first, and I smile, lifting my hand and waving close to my body, not wanting to be a distraction. He elbows Owen, and he looks over and winks, but his focus goes right back to his team.

For two hours, Owen runs. He never stops running. His body never once looks tired. I could watch him for hours, days maybe. He's clearly the best on the team, Ryan a close second, and the way he controls everything is mesmerizing. He shouts things, pushes other players in their chests, smacks their asses when they do something right and scolds them when they're wrong. And nobody ever questions him. They all want to please him— even the coach.

It's almost like they're afraid...

When practice is over, Ryan runs out from the locker room first, sitting next to me on the front step of the bleacher while he slips on his other shoes.

"Owen will be right out. He wanted me to tell you," he says, a faint smile on his face. Ryan doesn't show a lot of emotion, but I get the feeling he's rooting for Owen and me.

"Thanks," I say.

He nods once, finishes getting his shoes on, then starts to stand, stopping with his elbows on his knees. "You wanna know why I like Owen so much?" he says, his face slightly in my direction, his eyes looking at me from the side.

I nod.

Ryan looks toward the door, which is still closed, and leaves his focus there as he speaks. "Last year, my little brother tried to kill himself," he says, my breath leaves my body. "He's small. Like, really small—opposite of me in every way. It's not his fault. Something he was born with, just a weird mutation of our genes. The whole family is tall, like me. Jake, he's short. He's in eighth grade, and he's maybe four feet tall. Anyhow, some kids in his grade, they thought it'd be funny to nominate him for the king or whatever they call it at his junior high dance. That's the only reason he went, because he was nominated, and thought he might win something. So he goes, and he ends up winning, and he gets to dance with the prettiest girl, have his picture taken, all that shit."

Ryan turns to me for the rest of his story.

"My brother came home on cloud nine, thinking he was finally accepted. Then the next day, he found out that everyone voted for him to make that girl have to dance with him, because she had broken up with her boyfriend, the popular guy, and they wanted her to pay for it. They plastered her locker with pictures of her and Jake—with things written everywhere that said stuff like 'that's the best you can do now, bitch.' The girl was mortified, and she left school for the day, too embarrassed to stay."

"That's awful! Awful that someone would do that to both of them. Did they make fun of Jake, too?" I ask, my hand pressed to my cheek in disbelief.

"Now see, that's the thing. Nobody ever paid attention to him, said anything to him about it, teased him—nothing. It was almost as if he was invisible, just the tool for the prank. And being invisible...well, I guess that was worse. He came home from school, after a full day of being invisible, and then he swallowed a bottle of pills. My mom called me away from practice, and Owen had to drive me to the hospital."

166

"Owen stayed with me all night, brought my mom a change of clothes from his mom's closet the next day, and when my brother finally got to come home and go back to school, Owen showed up with a few of his friends, hung out on the basketball courts outside the school, made sure nobody said anything about the pills. Then he started taking Jake to school, picking him up with Andrew every morning. He hasn't missed a single day in over a year. Not once. Even when he has to work, and he's running late, and when I know he'd rather give the pretty girl who moved next door a ride. He shows up, at our front door, and my brother loves every fucking second of attention he gives him."

Ryan stands finally, his eyes back on the door, where Owen is finally exiting, talking to the coach, his bag slung over his back, his body dressed in his usual black jeans, black sweatshirt, black shoes—like a superhero in disguise.

"I like Owen so much because that dude has character—more character than any adult I've ever met. And the fact that he can do something like that, for a thirteen-year-old kid he doesn't even know that well, while he's got shit to deal with of his own...he's not what people say he is—but I get the feeling you know that," Ryan says, Owen now within hearing distance of us. Ryan smiles as he nods to Owen, who gives him a suspicious look. "See ya, Kens. I'll say hi to Elise for you."

"Was he hitting on you? Cuz, that shit ain't cool," Owen jokes. I shake my head *no* and stand on my tippy-toes, reaching up to kiss him softly, my entire body tingling with a new feeling for Owen Harper. I'm not sure what it is, but I think it might be pride.

I follow Owen to his truck, toss my bag in the seat between us, and buckle in. When he gets in on his side, he shakes his head and lifts my bag up, tossing it on the floor by my feet. "I love Gramps' truck, but your seat is way too far," he says, patting the seat next to him. I'll have to pull my knees up to my chest because of the hump in the floor, but the ride is short—and the few minutes of discomfort are well worth having Owen inches away.

"House said you were looking for me yesterday?" Owen mentions as he pulls us out of the school's parking lot.

"I was. I...I heard them out front playing basketball, thought it was you," I say, looking down at my knees. I'm not sure why I'm embarrassed, but I am.

"I like that you look for me," he says, leaning into me. I'm tempted to tell him *that's good, because I do it a lot.* But I keep that thought to myself; instead, taking my opportunity to steal glances at him while he drives. It's rare to see him without his head covered; he's always wearing a hat or beanie or his hood from his sweatshirt. I think it's like a blanket to him, gives him comfort. But right now, his hair is tasseled in all different directions, messy from his practice, damp with sweat, and possibly the sexiest thing I've ever seen.

That's the thing with Owen. He's...*sexy!* I've found boys cute before, attractive, and sometimes tall and strong, but never sexy. The thought of Owen running into one of the guys from Bryce makes me giggle—and the small noise I make catches his attention.

"What's funny over there, Ken Doll?" I smack his leg at the use of that nickname. "I'm kidding, kidding! Just wanted to get you back for whatever it is you think is funny about me."

"I don't think you're funny. I was just thinking you were...cute. I think you're cute," I say, keeping it safe, a notch less embarrassing than the truth.

Owen glances at me a few times, biting his lip, his eyes hazed and lowered. He's about to say something back when we pull into his driveway and notice two cars pulled in before him. He pulls the keys out, but holds them in his hand, his eyes on the vehicles in front of us.

"Mom's home," he says, his face oddly unhappy.

"Oh, should I...just go home? Or, is she okay with me coming over? I would love to meet her..." Owen hasn't moved, his posture rigid and his gaze stuck on something out the window. "Owen?"

"Oh, yeah...sorry. You should totally come in. She'd love to meet you. Andrew sort of talked you up, before I could. She'll love you," he says, his smile short of being real. I get the feeling it's masking something.

I pull my bag over my shoulder as I exit the truck and follow Owen up the steps of the front porch. He's about to turn the knob to the front door, when he just leans forward, his forehead resting on it and his sigh the kind that carries the weight of something serious.

"My brother's here, too," he says, and at first I think Andrew. But then I realize—he's talking about James. "I don't know what you're going to get, so just..." Owen rolls his head to the side until his eyes find mine. "Sorry...if this gets weird."

Almost every part of me wants to run, turn on my heels and sprint for the safety of my house. I play tough, and I've walked the line with Owen, but James—what I've imagined about James—scares me. My feet drag when he opens the door, and I consider my moment of hesitation, leaving, running, fleeing...Owen would understand. And then it flashes through my mind all at once—when Owen should have run away from me, when Gaby was confronting me, when my father was in my driveway banging on my door...he stayed.

He stayed.

Owen's house is immaculate. I don't know what I expected, but clean and bright wasn't it. Given that it's mostly Owen and Andrew at home alone, I thought things would be disorganized, maybe a little messy. I expected dark, and masculine.

"O? Is that you?" I hear a voice call from the direction of the kitchen. Owen's house is a mirror of mine, only where I have a piano setting he has an actual dining table.

"It's me, Ma," he yells back, his eyes moving around his house, searching. He's edgy.

"Good! I have a few hours before..." His mother rounds the corner and sees me, her step and speech both stuttering. She's tall, like Owen, and her frame is thin, like a woman who works long hours and never stops to eat. Her dark hair is pulled back into a ponytail, and she's wearing a security uniform, her feet only in socks.

"Mom, this is Kensi. She's our neighbor," Owen says, shrugging at me slightly, I think not wanting to offend me.

"Nice to meet you," I smile, stepping closer to her and reaching out my hand. She rubs both of her palms along her pants, then smiles faintly as she takes my hand in hers.

"Kensi, yes. I've heard about you. So nice to finally meet you. I'm Shannon. Is your family settling in okay?" Her eyes look to Owen for guidance, but he only raises his brows high. There really isn't an easy answer for this one, so I lie.

"Yes, we like it here," I say, leaving words like *parents, father* and *affair* out of the picture.

"I was going to have Kens stay for dinner. She treated me the other night, but I didn't know…" he stops there, letting his eyes speak the rest as they move beyond his mom to the living room where the television is blaring.

"No, please. Please stay, Kensi. We'd love to have you. And I was just ordering a pizza. It's not much, but I don't have a lot of time to cook, so…yes, please—I insist! What do you like? Pepperoni?" His mom is already dialing on her cellphone, her back to me, so I look to Owen, not sure what I should do.

"I can go. Really, it's okay," I whisper to him, and his eyes are telling me it's all right to leave. But then a new voice interrupts everything.

"Haaaaaa, look at you, baby brother. Is this your new girlfriend?" James says, his body filling the entire frame of the doorway between the formal living room and the family area. His hands stretch up to touch the ceiling, causing his shirt to raise and show how thin his stomach is. His hair and eyes are dark like Owen's, and his smile is equally tempting—a trait the Harper boys can use for good or evil at will, it seems. Unlike Owen, though, James seems to lack focus, his eyes wild and everywhere all at once.

"James." Owen's greeting is curt and callus, and I feel as uncomfortable as I knew I would the moment he told me his brother was here. Again, I want to run.

But I don't.

His brother holds Owen's stare, the two of them having a private conversation with their eyes—one I know isn't friendly. Eventually, James shrugs and turns to walk back to the family room and the television he has playing so loudly that the sound is distorting. Owen's mom motions for us to join James in the living room while she moves back into the kitchen, and Owen grabs my hand, stopping me before I take a step.

"You can go home. You don't have to stay here for me. This...this is my life, Kens. And you don't have to be here for this." His hold on my fingers is rough, but purposeful, and he's holding his breath, his nostrils flaring slightly while his pupils dial in on mine, begging me to leave. He thinks he's saving me.

"I'd like to stay," I say quietly, my eyes never flinching or leaving his. I want to run, my stomach sinking when I speak, but I can't leave him. I won't.

Owen swallows, taking a sharp breath in through his nose, then turns his attention back to the next room, his hand still linked with mine as he leads me into an older-looking room with family photos covering the wall. The frames are wooden and tattered, and the pictures of Andrew, Owen, and James seem to span most of their youth—stopping at what I'd guess to be four or five years ago. The back wall is a dark-wood paneling, and the television is propped on top of a coffee table that's pushed against the wall next to the bricked fireplace.

As old and dark as everything in this room seems, it's still clean, and it still feels like a home. James is sitting on a large orange sofa with wooden arms, his legs propped up on another table that's covered in magazines, keys, a wallet, and a gun.

There's a gun.

On the center of the table, an inch away from James's foot, there's a gun. It's black, and slick, and it looks like something a cop should be carrying. My body is reacting, a slow sweat building at the base of my neck, dripping deliberately down my sides, under my arms, my heart thumping wildly.

"Dude, put that away. Mom doesn't need to see that," Owen says, gesturing to the weapon. James studies him for a few seconds, his finger holding the tip of a toothpick that he's chewed into a bend, the other side locked in his mouth, mashed between his back teeth. Owen leans forward, his hand reaching for the gun, about to grab it, when James beats him to it, clutching it, his finger at the trigger. In a blink, the gun is pointed at Owen's neck, his brother standing in front of him, staring him down from inches away, his face threatening.

My breath. Is gone.

I open my mouth to scream, but nothing happens. My pulse is racing, and I'm looking around the room for someone, anyone. We're alone, Owen's mom just a room away.

She's only a room away! I'm trying to move my feet, to do something—anything—but I only end up with my back against the wall.

James's lips curve into a smile, and a slow, insane laugh starts to brew in his chest until it eventually explodes from his mouth. He cocks the gun back, away from Owen, and then tosses it back on the table, as if it were a remote.

"You're sick, and you need to leave," Owen says, his stance never once wavering—the gun having absolutely no effect on him, nor the fact that it was just pointed at his throat.

"Come on," Owen says, grabbing my hand and pulling me back through the house, through his front door, and down his porch steps. My body is shaking by the time we get outside, and I start to cry, cupping my mouth with my hand in an attempt to muffle the sounds.

"Shhhhhh, it's okay," Owen says, pulling me into his chest quickly, his hands wrapping around my head, his lips finding my bare skin along my face, his voice working to soothe me. "He's high. He's always high. And he needs money. That's why he's here. I'm so sorry you had to see that. My mom, she isn't supposed to let him in. But she's weaker than I am. That's why he came now. He knew I was gone."

"Owen, you have to do something. Call the police, something," I say, my suggestion met with a roar of laughter.

"Kens, that's a really good thought. But the cops don't come to my house when I call. They come for other people. The Harpers? They sort of *hope* we kill each other off," he says, and I shake my head in protest the entire time.

"No, they would come. Owen, let them help you," I start, but he pulls me to him tightly again.

"They don't come for things like this. And even if they did..." he says, pulling back to look in my eyes, "there's nothing they could do. He's either going to go away and get help one day, or James is going to die."

"No," I weep, shaking my head.

"Kens, my family's fucked up. I told you. Me? James? Even Andrew? We're all just these time bombs, waiting to see if we turn into our dad. James is just helping it along so he can get to the end faster."

Owen's words hurt. They hurt because I want more for him and Andrew, and they hurt because I know how true they are—I saw it, seconds ago. My chest is tight, and it's becoming harder to breathe.

"Do me a favor," Owen says, his eyes looking up, above my head. I turn to follow his sightline; he's staring at my window. "Go home. Get inside, lock up, and sit by your window."

"No, Owen. Come with me," I say, but he shakes my arm, my hands cupped in his, urging me to listen.

"I'm going to make him leave, Kens. He won't hurt me; I've been here—I've *done* this. And when he's gone, I'll go there," he says, pointing to his window, "and I'll find you."

Every time I shake my head *no*, Owen counters with a *yes*, until finally, I'm walking away from him. I look over my shoulder every few steps, and he doesn't leave his spot until I reach my door.

"Wait for me," he says, and I clutch the strap of my heavy backpack, dragging it inside with me and locking the door behind me immediately. I don't even move it away from the doorway, abandoning it, and racing up my stairs to my window, getting there just in time to see Owen step inside.

I'll wait for you.

I'm waiting for you.

I hold my breath for minutes at a time, my head against the glass of my window, my eyes checking every door and window of the Harper house, waiting for any movement, any sound, or new light or shadows. It stays dark, just as dark as it always is— and nothing happens. Thirty minutes go by, and there isn't a single sound. I text Owen, asking him if he's okay, and I keep my phone close to my chest, waiting for his reply.

Ten more minutes—*nothing.*

Ten more.

Nothing.

My finger hovers over the emergency call button, knowing that if I called—if I said there was trouble at the Harper house—they'd come.

I'm waiting for you, Owen. Please...please come to your window.

The sound of Owen's front door outside scares me, and I bump my head on the glass in my reaction. James is practically jogging down the porch steps, his long strides the same as his brother's, and he pushes his hat low while he swings the door to his small sedan open. Within seconds, he's racing down the road, and my eyes wait for Owen to appear.

When his light flicks on, I let out a small cry from everything I've been holding in, and when he raises the blinds and swings his curtains out of the way completely—I bite my lip and smile. This isn't a flirtatious kind of smile, but rather one of deep relief. Seeing him, after the feeling I got when I saw his brother push a gun in his face, scratches something new inside me, something deep.

I hold my hand up, pressing it to the glass, and Owen sits down in front of his window, leaning forward, resting his head on his hands along the windowsill. We stare at each other like this for minutes, and I rub away the frost on the glass at least twice.

Keeping my eyes on Owen, I slide my phone into my lap, then look down quickly to type him a message.

Want to talk about it?

His response comes a few seconds later.

I think I just want to look at you for a while.

I put my hand back against the glass, this time Owen doing the same, and I stay there, for an hour, looking at him looking at me. And I'm terrified—afraid of what happened tonight, of everything I saw and of the thought that James might come back.

174

And I'm afraid I'm losing myself to danger—the worst kind, the kind that rules your heart.

I'm falling for Owen Harper, and I'm afraid he's going to die.

Chapter 14

The chatter downstairs stirs me awake. My mom's voice is somewhere between normal and a whisper, which can only mean one thing—my father's here.

I'm awake and sitting up in seconds, but I'm not so sure I want to face that much drama this early in the morning. The moon is out, the sun still a half hour from rising. The sky has seemed darker lately, winter bringing a thick layer of darkness that takes over the starts and ends of every day.

My alarm will sound soon, so I push the clock button to at least spare myself the noise of morning DJs that are far too peppy to be real. I grab my jeans, a long-sleeved undershirt and my favorite T-shirt, a black one that reads Mozart Would Have Loved Miles Davis. It's a test day, and I'm feeling unlucky. Actually, I'm feeling unprepared—so I'm going to need all of the superstitious things in my life to align. And clearly, my morning isn't starting off on the right note.

My shower is hot, but the water runs out far too quickly, so I towel dry before my skin has a chance to get cold, drying my hair and scrunching the curl into it. I pull a knit hat over the crown, keeping the little part of my hair that's still wet warm, then I take a deep breath and force myself to go downstairs.

I'm pleasantly surprised when I'm greeted by Owen's back, his feet propped atop the footrest on the stool by the counter, my mom's coffee mug cradled in his hand. Everything pleasant turns to anxiety, though, when my mom makes an obvious detour in the conversation, coughing to announce my entrance into the room.

"Ohhhh, you're up early. Good morning, Kens. You want some bacon? I made some for Owen, and there's some left; it's still warm." She's already putting it on a plate and pushing buttons on the microwave. Owen smiles at me, leans forward, and presses his lips to my cheek while my mom's back is to us.

She made him...bacon?

"Why are you here?" I whisper, my voice quiet but not quiet enough to keep my mom from craning her neck slightly at my question. She's spying.

"I was awake early; Mom left for work, and I couldn't get back to sleep. Didn't want to wake Andrew up yet, so I was waiting on your porch," he says.

"I found him out there," my mom says, topping off Owen's coffee cup—*her* coffee cup, which she gave to him. This is all so....

"Thanks," he nods, taking another drink. The two of them hold each other's eyes, something strange passing between them, but I can't tell if it feels like bad news.

"Have you heard from your brother?" I ask as soon as my mom is out of earshot. Owen only shakes his head *no*.

"I've gotta get Andrew moving," he says, sliding his half-filled mug over to me to finish. I smell it, and can tell it's strong—I drink my coffee with more milk than coffee. I stand to pour it in the sink, then turn to walk Owen to the door, but my mom is already showing him out, thanking him for something.

When she comes back in, she's humming—*humming.*

"What's going on?" I ask, that uneasy feeling too much to ignore.

"Well, I'm dog tired, and I have forty-eight hours off, so I'm planning on napping until about noon, then I'm in for a marathon of HGTV to see if I can turn this kitchen reno into something other than a condemned piece of property," she says, laughing at her mildly funny joke.

"I meant with Owen. What's going on...with Owen?" I ask, and she purses her lips, tilting her head in that way she does when she's trying to buy herself time. My mother has a hard time being anything but honest, and when I think back on it, I realize she tilted her head when she told me we were moving, when she said she was excited about it, and when she told me I'd love my new school just as much as Bryce.

"You know what, never mind. I don't want to know," I decide. If whatever she's keeping to herself is anything like the crap that's unraveled on me over the last six weeks, then I don't want to know; I'm better off not knowing. She can go back to humming.

What's weird though is how quickly she lets me off the hook, how quickly she actually does go back to humming.

I pull my science book out and spend the next twenty minutes cramming for my test, keeping with my theme of only doing lucky things for the rest of the morning. Studying has to be lucky.

Willow's early; I thank my karma for being able to leave the house of weirdness behind. I kick myself though when I realize I'm only getting into a car with a person who's going to interrogate me for the next ten minutes.

"So, how was practice and dinner with the Harpers? You never called, and I was up all night waiting for that phone to buzz, you bitch," Willow says, pushing her glasses tighter to her face with the tip of her finger.

"You're so bad at playing tough," I say, fighting off laughter at the way she said the word *bitch.*

"Am not! Now, don't disrespect me, or I'll cut you, *bitch*," she says, unable to say it with a straight face a second time.

"Yeah, you're one scary-ass mother," I say, my words dripping with sarcasm. "I think it's the rhinestones on the wings of your designer glasses. Yeah, uhm...I'm pretty sure that's it, the mark of a true bad-ass."

"Shut up, my contact ripped, and these are all I have," she says. "Now, how was dinner?"

"We never really made it to dinner," I say, my throat closing at the memory of the night before. I can tell by the look Willow's making that she thinks we detoured from dinner for a different reason—and as nervous as I am about being intimate with Owen, I would have given anything for that to have been the reason we didn't make it to dinner last night.

"Owen's mom was home," I say, clearing her innuendo out of the way quickly. "And James showed up."

"Oh, shit!" she says, giving me her full attention while we wait at the stoplight in front of the school.

"Yeah, it was...well, let's just say those rumors you mentioned seem to be pretty damned accurate," I say, not sure how much about last night I should share. I think I can trust Willow, but still, it isn't really *my* story to tell. I never liked gossip, and Owen's kept my dad's affair to himself.

When Owen's truck is parked in the lot, waiting in the spot next to Willow's usual one, I'm hit with a smothering sense of relief, and I know it's because of how scared I was the night before.

"Well, it looks like you're doing a pretty good job at turning those Owen Harper rumors around," Willow says, her eyebrows lifted above the dark blue rims of her glasses. I suck in my bottom lip, but I let my smile slip through. If I am somehow this exception to the Owen Harper rule, I'm going to appreciate the role, cherish it, and cling to it.

Owen isn't in his truck, but his long legs come into view at the same table he was waiting at the day before. I admit to myself that I was looking for him—I was anticipating him, even before we pulled into the school's parking lot.

I was wishing for him.

"I feel like maybe we were a little rushed this morning," he says, standing and moving toward me, his thumbs looped in his front pockets, his gray jeans hugging his hips, the material gathering at his shoes.

"Why do you always wear your hoodie or a hat or something? Like you're hiding your identity?" I say, pulling the gray and black striped hood away from his messy hair so I can run my fingers through it. It's something I've been dying to do, and Owen watches my face as I let my hands find their way, feeling the soft waves of his hair, gripping the thickness. He lets his face fall to one side, resting on my arm, his unshaven jaw scratchy, but his lips soft and tender when they kiss my skin.

"Well, if I knew you had a thing for hair, I would have ditched the hat a long time ago," he says, half a smirk underscoring his hooded eyes.

"Just your hair," I say, lifting up on my toes to kiss him good morning in a way I couldn't do in front of my mom.

"People used to look at me...*stare* at me. When I was a kid, after my dad..." he says, hand reaching up and running through his hair once before reaching for the hood to put it back in it's place. "I started covering my head to hide. Sounds stupid, but I felt like people saw a little less of me. And habits stick, I guess."

Owen hides. I can't fault that, especially when I have thought so often of hiding myself lately. I reach under his hood once more, running my fingers through the side of his hair and pulling his cheek to me. "I'm okay with being the only one who gets the boy without the hood," I say.

"Ha..." he laughs, but quickly covers his mouth in apology, rubbing his chin and trying to tamper his grin. "Sorry, it was something about the thought of *you under my hood.* For the record, I still think it's funny when people say *balls* too. Guys are all ten-year-olds at their core."

"Clearly," I say, pushing his chest once before I leave. He falls back on his feet, pretending to stumble, but catches his balance quickly and winks at me before turning to walk away.

"See ya in class, Ken Doll," he says, turning around to stick his tongue out once.

"You are such a ten-year-old," I yell. He turns and walks the long way back around the building, and I watch him until he's out of my sight. I love the way he looks.

I've enjoyed the last few mornings of band practice. Apparently, we compete. And apparently, we also win—our trophy case is twice the size of the football team's. It's just in the music room, where nobody can see it.

We've been practicing our show to make it perfect, and I've added a few more instruments to my duties, offering to play the tympani drums and chimes to really sell our closing song. It gives me more things to practice, more things to distract me from my hour of independent study, more things to keep my hands away from the piano—off the keys that haunt me.

Owen's feet are in their rightful place during English, but his head is covered with a hat, his hood pulled completely over it, only his chin visible—that and the wise smirk on his lips.

"Very funny," I say, shoving his feet to the side. His laugh catches quickly, and when the teacher walks in, he's quick to pull his hood down and toss his hat on the floor underneath his desk. It's strange—at school, Owen is always respectful to the teachers.

180

We're discussing illusions from our reading today, talking about whether or not the main character of *Crime and Punishment* is actually good or evil, and how to spot the signs that tell us what to think. Everyone in the class is so quick to condemn Raskolnikov—convicting him without any chatter. I plan on playing devil's advocate. I'd like to think that it's my academic need to think deeper that spurs me to speak up, to interrupt the hanging ceremony everyone's so quick to have. But I kind of think it's more than that.

"But what about his intentions?" I ask, only one or two students really hearing my question over the debate. Mr. Chessman hears too, and soon raises his hand to quiet everyone down.

"Miss Worth, what was your point? I think the class needs to hear this," he says, and I can feel everyone turn to stare at me.

"Uhm," I say, adjusting my posture in my seat, wrapping my fingers around the top of my desk. More than the class's attention, I feel Owen's—my stomach pounding to the rhythm of my heart. "I was just thinking, we're not really considering Raskolnikov's intentions. We're prosecuting him based on the rules, based on laws. But is it really that simple?"

"Interesting," Mr. Chessman says, leaning on his desk and holding his hand to his chin. "Class?"

"It doesn't matter what his intentions were, he murdered someone. The rules are black and white, and he knew them. Case done, piece of cake," says Cal Russell, one of the more outspoken guys in our senior class. Cal won homecoming king, and he's had the same girlfriend for two years—she happened to win queen. It was all *so very* surprising when they won, according to Willow.

"That's a very narrow view," I say, my foot bouncing under my desk, my temper—one of the trait's I inherited from my father—trying to find a way out.

"Is it?" Mr. Chessman asks. "Explain, Miss Worth. I'd like the class to hear your thought process on this. I think this is opening up a great discussion."

Awesome. More talking, which is probably going to lead to more arguing. And I can no longer hear Owen's breathing behind me. His shoe is resting against the foot of my seat, though, so I know he's still here.

"Well," I say, taking a deep breath and thumbing through a few pages of my book. "Yes, you can say it's premeditated, or whatever, because we read those chapters where he *thought* about the crime before committing it. But..."

"But what? You just said it right there, he *thought* about it, and still did it!" Cal says.

"Stop interrupting!" I say, too loudly. Temper winning. "Sorry," I say a little more quietly. "Let me finish. He thought about it, and we got to read his thoughts. We know that he found good reason, he put the options on the scale, to see if the world was a better place with or without his crime, and he concluded, after *much thought,* that yes...the world would be better if he committed this crime."

"Murder. Not a crime, but *murder!"* Cal says.

"Yes, murder—in this case. But, I think as readers we need to think of the larger message," I say, my voice gaining strength. I've read this book a dozen times, and I know my argument well. Cal isn't going to break me. "There's a reason that, despite committing murder, the reader still loves the protagonist. What Dostoyevsky did was paint a portrait of the most heinous crime he could think of, yet open our minds to the possibility that perhaps the criminal isn't so black and white, that maybe we judge without really seeing *everything."*

"How can you *possibly* know the facts, know that he murdered someone, and sit there and defend him?" Cal says, turning his feet to face me in his seat, he's trying to intimidate me, and my heart is pounding faster. I think it's working.

"I'm not defending Raskolnikov, I'm defending the idea that we ignore other facts and judge people based on what we think is convenient," I fire back.

"That's ridiculous," he says, rolling his eyes and moving to turn his attention back to our teacher.

"No...it's not," Owen says, his voice behind me that familiar tone, the one he uses when he reveals things. Just the sound of it breaks me a little and fills me with confidence and pride all at once.

"Mr. Harper? Care to expound?" Mr. Chessman says, his eyebrows raised ever so slightly, his mouth a small smirk. He likes Owen; I can tell.

I hear Owen clear his throat and shift in his seat, so I turn my head to the side, letting my eyes see him from a periphery. His head is down, and he's sucking in his top lip while he thinks.

"What Kensi's saying is that we sum people up based on a small set of facts, and we use those facts and apply them to every action, every case, every word a person says," he says. I tuck my chin low, trying to hide the smile he's building on my face. "And when you're so quick to convict someone, you run the risk of ignoring their innocence."

There's a quiet over the room, and Cal spends a few seconds looking at Owen, hard. His focus shifts to me and then to our teacher, then back to Owen, and it's when he's chewing his bottom lip, sawing on it, his thoughts right on the tip of his tongue, that I know he's going to fire a bullet.

"You mean like the way we all just assume you're a piece of shit because you stole a car, robbed a store at gunpoint, and then held that same gun to your own head later that night just to prove you're nuts just like your old man?"

Cal only has enough time to find his balance and get to his feet before Owen is in front of him, his hand gripping the fabric of his shirt collar, his weight pushing him backward until his body hits the wall with a heavy thud. Owen forces him into the wall twice, just to make sure the air completely clears his lungs, then twists his hand around Cal's shirt, choking him before finally releasing.

Mr. Chessman's hand is on Owen's back within seconds, and Owen lets the crumpled shirt fall back in place along Cal's chest. Before he steps away, he stares long and hard, his nose practically touching Cal's, he's so close. "Exactly," he says, his eyes dark, his breathing ragged—and his fingers flexing, wanting to destroy.

"That's enough, Owen. You know where to go," he says, his head tilted slightly to one side, his expression caught somewhere between pride and disappointment.

"Yeah, I know," Owen says, turning to leave the class. As he passes me, he drags one finger along the length of my desk, brushing my fingertips as he passes. But he never looks down at me. The door swings open wildly, banging into the hallway wall.

"Cal?" Mr. Chessman says, his eyes falling on the smug blonde asshole still straightening his shirt at the front of the classroom.

"What, me? Are you serious? He attacked me!" Cal defends.

"Yes, but you also broke the rules...and what was it you said?" Mr. Chessman's smile shows again. "Ah, yes...they're black and white. Case done. Piece. Of. Cake."

He pushes a pink slip into Cal's chest at his last word, then motions for him to leave the room. Cal grumbles a few swear words as he leaves, and when he reaches my desk, he gives me a look that proves he's already summed me up, too, just by my relationship with Owen. I'm pretty sure I can sleep at night knowing I don't have Cal Russell in my corner. Maybe I'm making my own snap judgments, but I'm pretty sure he's the dark side in this one.

"Well..." Mr. Chessman says, leaning back to sit along the edge of his desk. His arms folded in front of him. "Kensi brings up a very good point, despite the debate we had just a few minutes ago. I'd like you all to think about that as you finish the next three chapters, and come prepared to discuss—*without* fisticuffs—tomorrow."

The bell rings only minutes later, and the rest of the class quickly goes back to their routine, everyone chatting about lunch plans, weekend dates, parties. I wait for the classroom to clear before gathering my things and heading for the door.

"For the record, Miss Worth," Mr. Chessman says, stopping me just before I open the door. "I think you made a *very* valid point."

My breathing suddenly feels easier, and I let my smile respond for me, then open the door and move into the crowded hallway. It's lunch, and I know Willow, Jess, Elise and Ryan will be wondering where I am, but I have to make sure Owen is okay. I dodge backpacks and elbows through the busy hallway until I see the glass door of the principal's office swing open, Owen stepping through, his own pink slip crumpled in his hand, his eyes still dark, angry.

"Are you okay?" I ask, walking up to him, my steps coming quicker. He grabs my hand fast, his grip on my fingers tight, almost painful, and pulls me behind him through the thick crowd in the hall until we reach the back door, near the loading zone for the cafeteria. He pushes down hard, forcing the door open, then pulls my arm, leading me around a corner to a line of recycling bins.

"I'm so sorry..." I start, but Owen's hands find me fast, his fingers wrapping around my shoulders, his force moving me back until I'm flush with the wall, and then his lips crash down on me.

His hands slide from my shoulders to my neck and into my hair, his mouth covering mine as if he needs my air to breathe, and he closes the small distance between us, the warmth and hardness of him pressing into my body, my hands operating on their own instinct, finding his sides and back until I'm clinging to him, grabbing bunches of his black sweatshirt all at once.

Owen's hand moves to his head while he's kissing me, and he tosses his hat to the ground to the side of us, and I let my fingers move to his hair, weaving the strands in and out, letting the softness of them curl around me.

This is the best kiss of my life. Every kiss with Owen has been the best kiss of my life. But this one—it's full of something more. His lips work mine for long seconds, his tongue passing over mine slowly, his teeth dragging over my bottom lip, my top lip, tugging on me and pulling me into him even deeper. I can feel his heartbeat through his shirt, and I let my hands roam over his chest and around his back again, the feel of him exactly as it is every time I dream.

He finally pauses, his mouth still resting on mine, his lips barely parted as they struggle for air. Owen's eyes are closed, and his forehead is resting on mine, his thumbs still gently caressing my cheeks.

"I...," he says, his breath stuttering, his lips quivering, his body relaxing into me. His head falls heavier into mine, and I can actually feel his entire body shaking.

Owen doesn't finish the sentence, instead kissing me again with the same intensity as before. For the entire lunch hour, his lips work mine until they're practically raw; when the bell rings to resume class, he pulls my hands up to his lips, clasped tightly within his, and he kisses them once before pressing them to the side of his face, looking at me with eyes that have cleared, eyes that aren't full of rage and hate.

I'm honest with Elise when she asks where I was.

"Making out with Owen," I say, and she laughs, but it soon fades when she realizes I'm serious. Our conversation is short, cut off by the bell to begin class. I notice Owen isn't in here, that he never came after our last kiss behind the school. He said he'd see me later, and I was too stunned to register or even ask what that meant.

Our teacher passes out our tests, and I notice that she sets one aside and write's Owen's name on it. Despite my lack of studying, I finish mine quickly, somehow pulling mostly correct answers from the depths of my brain.

When the ending bell rings, I don't wait for Elise, my mind still reeling from Owen, his kiss, how I felt—how *he* felt. Then it turns to wondering where he is, wondering if he's okay, to Cal—to the things Cal said.

"You look like an actual ghost," Willow says when I meet her at her car.

"Yeah...I feel like one," I say, my eyes not really able to focus on anything, too busy looking for Owen, for answers. I climb into her passenger seat and buckle up, and I feel her gaze on me as she buckles, then starts her engine. We get to the light at the school exit, where we wait for cars to pass so we can pull out on the road, before I'm able to articulate anything.

"Did Owen really commit an armed robbery?" I ask, and Willow takes a deep breath, never really saying anything, but letting her silence answer for her. "And he stole a car?"

I wait while Willow's brow pinches, her lips pursing in thought. "I only know what I heard, Kens. I...I've never been very close to him. But, yeah...that's what I heard."

186

"And the gun…" I start, and her eyes widen quickly, then just as fast relax again. She's trying to keep her emotions in check, trying to make *this* not a big deal for me.

"Will, did Owen *really* put a loaded gun to his head? Did he really do that?" I ask, my stomach feeling punched, inside and out, at the thought of Owen doing any of those things—mostly the last.

"Again, Kens…I only know what I've heard. I've heard the same things you've heard. But I wasn't there. I don't know for sure. But I bet…" she starts, pausing for a deep breath as we turn down the street to my house. "I bet if you asked him, he'd tell you the truth."

When we pull into my driveway, there's an older-looking Volvo station wagon sitting near the back door of the house, nobody inside.

"Company?" Willow asks.

"I've never seen that car before in my life," I say, my gut feeling sick.

"Want me to, I don't know…wait? Or come in with you? You know, in case it's…" She's worried it's my dad.

"Dean wouldn't drive such a thing," I say, my mouth relishing at calling my father by his given name, forgoing any relationship he has with me.

We both step out of her car and move closer to the Volvo, when my mom and Owen step through the back door of the house, my mom holding a set of keys on her index finger.

"Happy birthday, Kensington. I was thinking maybe we put that license of yours to use," my mom says, and I look to Owen, who's smiling and shrugging behind her, his hands deep in his pockets, his hat turned backward.

"Shut up, it's your birthday?" Willow asks, shoving my shoulder once, kind of hard.

"Not until Saturday," I say, my eyes focused only on Owen's, on the sweetness of them, the love in them.

"On Halloween? That's awesome. Oh my god, we should totally have a party. I mean, like…an appropriate party," Willow says, putting on a fake voice of responsibility for my mom.

"You can all come here. I'm off that day, and I'll make a big dinner. We can carve pumpkins," my mom says, stopping right in front of me and pulling my hand up in hers, transferring the keys. "What do you think, Kens? Sound good?"

I smile and nod. "That sounds great," I say, looking at the small music note key ring in my hand, the lone Volvo key hooked on it. "Thanks, Mom."

I reach for my mom, hugging her tightly, my eyes still finding Owen behind her.

"Thank Owen, too. I couldn't have done this without him," she says, confirming what I'd already figured out on my own. "I didn't want to get ripped off, since I don't know a thing about cars. He went to the dealer with me, made sure everything was working right."

Stepping by my mom, I move closer to Owen, my throat closing up with all of the things I want to say to this boy that I...I love, my god do I love with so much of myself. I'm so afraid of everything, of what people say, of what Cal said, but I also don't care because standing here in front of me, looking at me like he is, I know in my heart that Owen is good.

Owen is *good.*

In front of my mother, in front of my new best friend, I stand on the tips of my toes and kiss him lightly, pulling my face away from his before anyone notices, before anyone sees. And I whisper.

"I see you," I say.

Owen's eyes...they respond.

Chapter 15

I honestly think Gaby is trying to make me hate my own birthday. There's no other reason for her to do what she did.

A Facebook message would have been simple—an email, simpler. A text, something I could easily ignore, delete without reading. What Gaby's done is far more about Gaby than about my birthday. This package—the one I've been sitting on my bed with, staring at, since about seven this morning—is a Trojan horse.

The knock on the door was faint, but I heard it. I was awake, listening for the sound of Owen's truck, waiting for him to be awake too. Instead, the only other person awake at this hour near my home was whoever left this package on my doorstep.

I *know* it was Gaby.

There was no return address, only my name and house number. More than suspicious—it was obvious. Yet, I brought it inside with me anyhow. I tried *not* to open it. But I've never been good at ignoring impulses. The pull—it was just too much. I had to know what was inside.

Digging my nails into the taped sides, I pulled the flap of the cardboard free, then pulled out the layers of tissue paper hiding my gift. I recognized the dress as soon as I saw the blue fabric of the sleeve. I've coveted Gaby's blue Alexander McQueen dress since the day her mother bought it for her. She let me wear it to one of my performances, and it was the one that caught the attention of recruiters from Tisch and Julliard. She never let me borrow it again—and now, part of me thinks she was jealous of the attention I received when I wore it.

Gaby was always in it for our school dances our junior year. And now, sitting here, looking at it resting in crumpled tissue paper—in a non-descript brown box, borrowed from something else—I can't help but wonder if she wore it for my father.

"I'm going to burn you," I say to myself, to the dress, a small smile inching up my lips.

There's a letter in the box—a letter I have no intention of reading. I don't even bother to tear the small seal on the envelope; instead I stuff the letter into the crinkles of the tissue paper surrounding the dress.

The incessant faint knock that's happening at my door again feels different this time, and I welcome being pulled away from Gaby's sad attempt to erase the damage she did to our friendship. I toss the box to the floor, leap to my feet, and patter down the stairs quickly, opening the door to a rush of cool air and faint flakes of snow falling behind Owen.

"Looks like it's a white birthday for you," he says, his hands held behind his back awkwardly. I step up on my toes and kiss his cold lips, then tug him into my house by the collar of his shirt. "So pushy," he teases.

"What's behind your back," I say, pulling on his elbow now.

"Wow, you are like...*all about* the presents, aren't you?" he says, his playful smile curling one end of his mouth as he unwraps his neck from his scarf.

"Maybe," I smirk. "Now, gimme, gimme, gimme!"

I pull the bag from his hand and rush to the kitchen with it, Owen trailing behind me, his feet dragging and his hand running along his chin. "I was kind of hoping you would open it later," he says, his brow pulled in as he looks from me to the front door and back again. "I saw Willow pulling up out front, and now just feels weird..."

He trails off, his shoulders slumped, and his spirit deflated. He's embarrassed, and as much as I'm dying to crack open the bag with his gift, the fact that giving it to me *alone* is important to him means a hell of a lot more.

"Okay, I'll put it in my room. Won't peek; I promise!" I say, crossing my heart and zipping past Owen in my socks, gliding along the floor and up the stairs. When I get to my room, the box with the blue dress immediately confronts me, and its presence pisses me off. I kick it under my bed, and then pull my comforter down on the side, completely hiding it from my view.

The doorbell rings loudly as I set Owen's gift in its rightful spot atop my pillow. I race back downstairs, trying to reach the door before Willow has a chance to push the bell again, but I'm too slow.

190

"Jesus Christ, you're impatient," I say, flinging the door open to a shivering group of four.

"It's cold. My hand slipped," Willow says, somehow still managing to pop a bubble between her lips despite the rapidly dropping temperature on my porch.

"My mom was sleeping in," I explain, before my mother cuts me off and finishes for me.

"She *was.* She's up now," my mom says through an irritated yawn. "Who wants pancakes?"

"Oh, do you have more of that bacon?" Owen says, surprisingly not shy. I'm a little less upset about the bacon-sharing with my mother now that I know their early morning meeting was all about getting me a set of wheels for my birthday.

"You got it. I'll grill up the rest of it," my mom says, winking at Owen. My belly grows warm seeing her accept him so completely.

Willow, Jess, Elise, and Ryan start slipping out of their coats and hats and gloves in my front room, leaving a pile of winter clothing gathered around our front door, and this scene makes me even happier. I love their mess.

"We're still carving pumpkins, right? We *have* to carve pumpkins! I brought my tools and everything," Elise says, and I can't help but quirk an eyebrow at her odd pumpkin fascination.

"It's her favorite holiday. And she's kind of a bad-ass pumpkin carver," Ryan says, shrugging.

"All right then, pumpkins it is!" I say, looking over Elise's shoulder, out the window that is growing frostier by the second.

"Oh, don't worry about that snow. It's not real snow. It's supposed to stop in an hour or two and clear out until next week," Elise says, very insistent that weather does not detour us from our pumpkin mission.

"It's just going to be freezing-ass cold. Awesome time to walk around a field and pick up wet pumpkins," Jess says, rubbing his eyes as he passes me and heads straight for the pot of coffee brewing on the counter. "Can we stop this mid-cycle so I can get a cup now?"

"Seriously? Can't wait the full minute it takes to drip?" Owen says, sliding into the stool next to the counter, pulling me to him so I'm standing between his long legs.

"I'm not pretty without caffeine, yo," Jess says, causing Ryan and Owen to bust out laughing.

"Dude, don't talk like a gangster. You can't pull it off," Ryan says.

"It's the lack of caffeine. It makes me say crazy shit," Jess says, pulling the pot from the machine the moment it stops dripping, filling his cup and blowing forcefully into his mug, working to cool the liquid fast.

"You talk to anyone about this addiction of yours?" Owen says, smirking at Jess as his jittery hands work to tilt the cup up for his first, sloppy gulp.

"Like you should talk about addiction," Jess mumbles, his eyebrows shooting up as soon as he fully realizes the words that left his lips. Owen's arms grow rigid around me, and I know without looking his expression is cold. "I'm sorry man. That was crappy to say. I'm tired and grumpy. Totally uncalled for," Jess says, pulling one hand away from his mug and reaching to shake Owen's hand. Jess's face looks honest and regretful, but I hope Owen can see it too.

While it only takes him a few seconds to accept Jess's apology and shake his hand, those few seconds feel long and ominous. And even after he tells Jess that it's "no big deal," his arms remain tight and his body on guard. I know that it was a *very* big deal, and that one tiny sentence is going to sit on his conscience for most of the morning.

We all devour our breakfast, soaking our pancakes in butter and syrup and stuffing our cheeks until we're all equally sick from the sweetness of the syrup and the richness of bacon. As Elise promised, the small snow flurries have disappeared by the time we're done helping my mom load the dishwasher, and soon we're all pulling on the mountain of winter clothing we left in the pile by the door.

"Make sure you get one for me," my mom says, handing me a hundred dollar bill, urging me to pay for everyone's pumpkin. My father was always stingy with money, never wanting to pay

192

for things with my friends. He wouldn't even buy Gaby and Morgan's museum tickets the times we went in the city. Just one more thing I think about differently now.

"I'm driving," Willow announces as we all pile onto the porch in our heavy boots and coats.

"I'm out. Who's with me?" Owen says, and Ryan is the first to raise his hand, stepping next to his friend.

"Hey!" Willow protests.

"Will, your driving scares the shit out of me in the summer. If I have a second option when there's a chance for snow, I'm taking it," Ryan says back quickly, and I notice Willow shakes her head, a little stunned by his honesty.

"You know you could drive yourself to school in the morning, asshole," she says, her eyes squinting, trying to mask how upset she really is.

"Oh, it doesn't scare me so much that I want to drive my dad's piece-of-shit car. You're still safer than that," he says, and this seems to make her feel better.

"Well all right then," she says, leading the way as we walk down my front steps and toward the street out front. "You know he's not that safe either, though, right?"

"This guy? Hell, he's never had a crash," Ryan says, pointing to Owen, whose hands are buried in his pockets, his hood pulled up over his head and his arms stiff with the wool material of his black overcoat. Owen only rolls his eyes, then pulls his keys from his pockets, urging me to ride with him as well. I go willingly, but for different reasons.

We pile into Owen's truck, and Elise and Jess climb into Willow's car; we head a few miles to the outskirts of town where one of the farmers still has a stand open for fall goods. The pumpkin selection is a little picked over, but we all settle on a few decent-sized ones, and before anyone can protest, I hand the money to the cashier.

"My mom insisted. Part of my birthday present," I say, smiling and enjoying the feeling of treating friends to something—even though it may be trivial.

By the time we get home, my mom has moved a few of the cardboard boxes out to the kitchen floor, where she's cut them open for our carving mess. When I was little, my mom and I used to make a pumpkin for our balcony every year. But that tradition sort of just faded away—forgotten among the other things in life that got in the way. I picked an extra large pumpkin just so she and I could create something together, and when I nod for her to join me, I notice her eyes tear up a little with her smile.

"So, this is gross," Willow says, pulling the lid from her pumpkin, long, gooey strings trailing from the bottom.

"You know there's more inside, right?" Elise says, reaching into hers with both hands, digging her nails in, and scooping a handful of the pumpkin insides onto the cardboard next to Willow.

"Oh my gaaaaaaah," Willow says, bringing her arm completely around her face, smothering her nose. "It smells...so bad."

"You are such a baby," I say, reaching into Willow's pumpkin and pulling out a scoop for her. I let it plop onto the cardboard, splattering some seeds and strings onto Willow's jeans.

"I think I'm out," she says, standing, her nose still buried in her sleeve.

"I'll clean yours for you," I say, and she lifts her arm up long enough to show me her grin and to raise her thumb in approval.

It doesn't take long to understand why Elise likes carving so much. I've managed to create a pretty spooky-looking set of teeth, and Owen's carved his into a series of triangles to form a face—sort of. Elise's pumpkin, however, is straight out of the set for *Sleepy Hollow,* a headless horseman charging forward through thistle with bats and menacing tree roots tangling around him.

"Okay, I officially give up. That is seriously the best pumpkin I have ever seen," I say, laying my knife down on the cardboard and running my messy hands through a towel.

"You should see the one she made last year," Ryan says, standing up and giving up on his pumpkin, which looks about as intricate as mine. "She made a set of four and turned the whole thing into Mount Rushmore."

"You're an artist!" I say.

"Eh. It only works with pumpkins," Elise says, her tongue stuck out on one side of her mouth—her focus still on perfecting her craft.

"It's still art," I say, stepping back and watching her work.

Elise keeps digging and nipping at pieces of pumpkin for the next hour, and eventually, Ryan, Jess, and Owen move outside to play basketball. House shows up with a few other guys, including Andrew, and pretty soon my driveway is serving as home court.

"You like watching him, don't you," Willow says, nudging into me while we sit on the stoop by my back door, sipping hot chocolate. I bite my lip and shrug, relenting to a small smile. It's a fraction of my feelings, because yes, I love watching him. I love how he moves, how masculine he is when he pushes the other guys, when he dominates them on the court. The way the ball transfers from hand to hand is effortless for him, as is his ability to put up a shot from any distance—and have it find the safety of the rusty hoop and net above my garage.

I'm mesmerized by his skill, but more than that, I'm utterly taken with his form. It's barely forty degrees outside, the sky veiled in a thick layer of cloud, but Owen's shirt is off, his chest and abs and arms glistening with sweat. His hat is backward on his head, so he can see, and his jeans sling low on his hips, the red of his boxers like a target for my eyes. The things passing through my mind about him right now make me blush, and I'm almost worried that Willow can hear my thoughts.

"You...love him?" she asks. I think about pretending I don't hear her question at first. But I know she'll only ask me again. I don't answer, but instead shrug and give the same hinted smile I did to her last question. When she breathes in deeply, I know she knows the truth.

I love him.

I want him.

I need him.

I breathe him.

Since the moment my eyes met Owen Harper's, he has owned me, terrified me, consumed me, and I don't even remember the girl I was before him any more.

"Just promise me you'll still be careful. Just...don't let yourself go, not completely. In case you need to come back from him," she says.

With my eyes closed, I nod, knowing that it's already too late.

"Hey," Owen says, his body suddenly in front of me. My eyes start where they shouldn't, and by the time I meet his, his crooked smile threatens to tease me, but he doesn't.

"Hey," I say back, my voice hoarse and raspy.

"So, House and a few of the guys are heading over to Sasha's house, that place I took you for that party?" Owen's shifting the ball back and forth in his hands, nervously. "Anyhow, we can all go, if you want...or not. I mean, whatever."

My stomach sinks, because I can tell Owen wants to leave with his friends, and I can also see how much they don't blend with mine. Ryan is the only connection; the only one among us who seems to move in and out of cliques seamlessly, unaffected. House is leaning on his truck, spitting sunflower seeds into my yard, and Andrew is caught somewhere between both groups, too young to really belong.

"I was kind of planning on hanging out here, passing out candy with everyone, until—" I say, not wanting to say the rest any longer. Not wanting to say I was planning on staying here until everyone left Owen and me alone—not wanting to say how much I just want to be with Owen, and no one else. In a flash, I feel naïve and stupid, and I think of Willow, and her warning.

"No, that's cool. I'll just tell him we're out," he says, his fingers rapping a few times on the ball, his eyes still on me. He's waiting for something, waiting for what? For me to tell him it's okay?

"Why don't you go? Maybe...just come back, if it's not too late. Maybe I'll be up," I say, throwing the *maybe* in there totally passive aggressively, doing a poor job of masking my disappointment.

Willow stands quickly, slipping through the door with the excuse of helping Elise clean up. And for the first time in hours, I'm left alone with Owen, alone while his friends watch us from House's truck along the roadside, his brother and Jess watching from Owen's front porch, and the rest of my friends

196

eavesdropping from inside my house. I'm alone with him, and embarrassed.

The practice conversation happening in my head starts with me telling Owen to just leave, but it always finishes with me begging him to stay. I keep my eyes on my knees, on the toes of his Converse, while I work out my words. I'm interrupted when Owen's hand finds my chin, and I can feel the pressure of his fingers lifting my gaze upward as he kneels down in front of me.

"I don't go without you. And if you don't want to go, we're staying here," he says, his eyes unflinching, his focus completely on me, drowning out the nosey eyes and ears around us.

"Are you sure?" I ask, and he starts to chuckle lightly, leaning forward and kissing the tip of my nose.

"You know what's hot?" he asks, making a turn in our conversation that throws me a little. I shrug and bunch my brow.

"No, Owen. What's...*hot?*" I respond, not sure where this is going.

"When a girl knows exactly what she wants and just asks for it," he says, his eyes daring me. My mouth is dry, and my heart is beating in my stomach. "What do *you* want, Kensi? I will give you anything. You just have to ask."

Elise's giggle slips out, and I know she and Willow are listening on the other side of the door. I also notice Andrew's stare as well as House's just over Owen's shoulder. So many outside forces at play, my head begins to feel dizzy, until Owen's hand pulls my chin back to him again, our faces inches apart, his bare chest within reach, his face like my dreams.

"I want you to stay here...with me," I say, letting myself fall, letting myself trust that Owen will catch me—love me for my honesty.

"Done," he says, his eyes hanging on mine for a few long seconds, his cocky smile tugging at one side of his mouth before he stands and tosses the ball to Andrew across my driveway.

"Sorry, House. I'm out," he says, waving his hand when his friend flips him off and drives away in his truck with the rest of his friends.

"One more game?" Jess asks, dribbling awkwardly as he and Andrew walk up behind Owen. Owen looks at me, and it takes me a few seconds before I realize he's waiting for my approval—not in a rude way, but in a considerate one. I nod back at him and hug my legs tightly to my body.

"Yeah, one more. Then I think we should put some candles on a cake or something," he smirks, watching me the entire time as he falls back on his feet and joins Jess, Ryan, and Andrew for one final game in my driveway.

"Okay, that was hot," Willow whispers after barely opening the back door behind me. She slips out with Elise this time, and they sit on either side of me.

The boys play at least six more games while the three of us watch, taking turns making commentary on their play, mocking Jess's inability to score, and Ryan's pale white skin when he pulls his shirt off. We laugh when Andrew tries to make a layup six times in a row, failing each and every time, until everyone makes a pact not to guard him, just to watch him miss again.

We laugh. Owen laughs.

And suddenly, there's a moment when he's smiling—his eyes find mine, and the connection tugs on me, on my heart. This is the worst and the best year of my life, all at once, yet this single frame, my eyes on his, his mouth curved just right, the perfect smile, the perfect mix of darkness and light—it's winning.

"Yes, Willow," I say, my voice slight.

"Yes, what?" she asks, still laughing at the last play Jess attempted in front of her.

"That question you asked...*yes*," I say, just loud enough for her to hear.

"I know," she sighs. "And I know you won't be careful either. Can't say I blame you." She leans into me slowly, putting enough pressure on my side to embrace me, and not alert Elise. I lean back, and I watch Owen while I draw on Willow's strength, hoping like hell I can survive loving him.

As soon as the sun kisses the horizon, tiny ghosts, superheroes, ninjas, and small princesses fill the streets. Every birthday I've celebrated has been in the city, every Halloween in the city. This day, in the city—it's different. People trick-or-treat in buildings, never leaving their hallways or sometimes floors. When I was little, my mom would walk me down our small

198

street, up the two or three flights for the row homes connected to ours. I visited maybe twelve households, rung twelve doorbells, took home a small pillowcase of candy.

My mom was looking forward to tonight. She went to Costco, bought the big candy bars. And as the night wears on, and less kids ring our doorbell, my mom starts giving out two bars at once. After thirty minutes, and several Snickers of our own, the night seems to be done, and my mom sends Willow, Ryan, Jess, and Elise home with a pack of chocolate bars each.

Owen waits behind, heeding my mom's orders that we stay downstairs, and that he goes home before midnight. When her door closes, Owen sweeps me into his arms, lifting my legs from the ground and kissing me as he carries me to my piano. My friends gave me a few new music books for my birthday, not really knowing about my silent protest against this instrument. That's the beauty of independent study—I can pretend I'm actually still practicing, and there's nobody there to witness and counter my lie.

"So, explain these things to me," Owen says, settling on the bench with me still in his lap. He pulls one of the books over and flips through a few pages.

"Well, this line here," I start, pointing to the top ledger for one of the Mozart books, "is for my right hand. The one on the bottom, with this symbol, is for my left."

"And you can read this?" he says, brow pinched, finger tracing the lines of notes while his other hand trails up and down my back.

"Uh huh," I say.

"Prove it," he says, pulling the book forward and placing it on the music stand for my piano. He's trying so hard to be smooth, and part of me wonders if he also planned this out in a conversation with my mother.

"Ohhhhh nooooo," I chuckle, closing the book and sliding it back along the top of the piano. "I know what you're trying to do."

"What?" he asks, his face an expression totally foreign to him. It's fake, and Owen can't pull off fake. He's clear about everything, and I like that he can't pretend with me. "Yeah...all right. You're right," he says finally, pushing the book a few inches more away from me. "But you haven't played, not really, not since—"

"I know," I answer without him finishing. "I can't explain it, but...I just don't want to anymore."

"But you love this. You love music," he says.

"I did," I say, looking down at my keys, my right hand finding familiar—hating it and loving it all at once.

Owen studies me, his left hand still stroking my back, soothing me—lulling me. "Bullshit," he says.

"Owen, it's not bullshit. The piano, me playing, studying it— that was always my dad's dream for me," I say.

"Bullshit," he says again, his eyes a little darker, challenging.

"Stop it," I say, my tone angrier. "Don't say that."

"Because it's true," he says. "You might associate *this* with your dad, but there's a part of you, a part of your heart, that *loves* your talent. I know it."

"Owen, I know you're just trying to be supportive, or whatever, but please don't. You don't understand," I say, and he runs his right hand over mine, pressing my fingers into the keys slowly until they make a sound, a sound that breaks my heart and fills my chest.

"Yes I do," he whispers into my ear. "I understand, Kens. You know how I know?"

"How?" I ask, a breath in response to him.

"Because I heard you," he says, his eyes boring into me, like he's reaching inside me, rattling my heart back to life. His right hand holds my fingers into the valleys of the pressed keys. "Play for me. None of *this*," he motions to the books spread out on my piano top. "Play what you love, what *you* want to hear. Please, Kens. Just this once, for me, for your birthday."

"Do you know how fucked up it is that you are asking for a present on *my* birthday?" I tease, my heart rapid in my chest, my fingers rigid, not wanting to do this. I'm frightened.

"Not a present," he says, his lips sliding into a smile, a new smile. "A gift."

I roll my eyes, but let them settle on our hands together, mine still resting in their position on the keyboard. Slowly, I slide my hand out from under his and crack my knuckles against my chest. With a deep breath, I nod once to Owen, then move my hands back into a different position—one far away from the usual classics I've been forced to practice. I move them into a loose position, comfortable, barely touching the keys. Eyes closed, I begin to drag them slowly around the middle of the keyboard, my foot pressing the dampening pedal, trying not to play loud enough for my mother to hear. It's pointless, though— the music echoes in the cavern of the tall dining room and front foyer of the house.

Owen's hand stays on my back, his rhythm constant, fingers gliding up and down, until I finally let myself have this small break, allowing my fingers to fly further up the keyboard, breaking rules, changing time, changing speed.

What comes out is completely out of my head, something bluesy, and something that never repeats. I play for maybe a full minute, and somewhere along the way, my mouth curves into a smile, and I don't realize until I open my eyes; Owen is looking back at me. I stop abruptly, my smile collapsing fast.

"What?" I ask, embarrassed, feeling foolish, feeling as though I betrayed myself somehow too, giving in to my protest.

"You're something else, you know that?" he says, his eyes bright, his smile full, and his hand never breaking its soothing touch. "What was that?"

"I don't know," I say, pulling my hands back into my lap, closing them into fists. "I made it up."

"Wow," he says, and when I look at him, he's still smiling.

"Stop it; you're embarrassing me," I say, a small giggle slipping out. I tuck my face into his shoulder.

"All I know is you…you loved that," he says. I look long and hard at the keys, my mouth a faint smile, afraid to give in to Owen's temptation, afraid to admit that I did love it, that I still love music, that I still have this connection to my father.

"Stop thinking it's for him," Owen says, reading my mind. My eyes snap to his. "It never was—your gift? It was never for *him.* So don't go giving it away to him now. He doesn't deserve it."

I lay my head back along his chest, and just breathe. Owen holds me, and we sit still in the silence of the enormous room for almost an hour, my hands never crossing over onto the piano again. I let my eyes take it in, though, mentally playing every sound in my head—my sounds, the songs that were always for me.

Owen is right.

"I never gave you your present," he says finally, snapping me back to the present, bringing me out of the dream I was so happily falling into while resting in his arms. "You think we can make it upstairs?" he asks, nodding up, toward my mother's door, the one that comes before my bedroom.

"You go up first, I'll turn off the lights and lock up," I say, not able to fully look him in the eye. The thought of having Owen in my room, alone with me, has my body feeling alive and warm and electric. I'm also nervous and scared—of being caught, yes, but also of being *that* alone with Owen.

We've never been so alone.

I watch nervously as he glides up the stairs, pulling his shoes off halfway, so he can slip quietly past my mom's room. I wait a few extra seconds, making sure he's in my room, then I lock the back door, walking the length of the house from the back to the front, flipping every light switch off along the way.

I check the front door, bolt it and glance at the clock on the wall. It's already well past midnight, and my mother never once came downstairs. I'm pretty sure she's fallen asleep. She trusts me. And I'm about to take advantage of that—a tinge of guilt squeezing at me from the inside, a tinge that I bury and ignore and replace with anxiety over all the *what ifs* that come along with being alone with Owen.

Holding my breath, I pause at my mom's door, listening for the familiar sounds—the buzz of her humidifier, the dull sound of the low television, the constant stream of infomercials that I know she isn't watching. All signs point to her being asleep, to the risk being minimal, so I continue on into my room. I close the door and turn the light out quickly, surprising Owen.

"Okay, so I know I'm ugly, but really? You have to keep me in the dark, too?" he jokes.

"You're not ugly," I say, reaching to the end of my bed and throwing a pillow at him where he sits. He clutches it in his arms

202

and sets it next to him, on the floor—the space where I usually sit to watch him through the window. I notice his gaze pauses at that window, his smile quirking up. For some reason having him here, knowing I watch him from this room, embarrasses me, so I quickly turn my attention away from that space.

His back rests against the headboard of my bed, his feet stretched out in front of him, the small bag with his gift in his lap. When he pats the space next to him, I swallow loudly, kick off my shoes, and crawl next to him, folding my legs up in front of me. My fidgeting hands and feet create a small barrier between us, a barrier Owen is quick to crash down when he lets his hand graze along the inside of my leg, stopping at my knee.

"Present time?" I ask, my voice a whisper. I'm sure if I speak any louder my mom will crash through the door. I'm not sure what she would do if she caught Owen here. She's not the type to get angry over things like this, and I think a small part of her would be glad to see me do something so typical and teenager. But I also know she wouldn't trust me anymore. And that would make me sad.

Owen holds the bag in his lap for a few seconds, turning it and folding over the top a few times. I can tell whatever is inside is small, but heavy.

"I told you how my grandpa raised us, right?" Owen says finally.

"Yeah," I say back. We're both still whispering, and the fact that Owen is—without me asking him to—fills me with relief.

"He was a fixer," Owen says, and I quirk my head to the side, pinching my brow.

"A...fixer?" I repeat.

"Yeah...I mean that's not like his official title or job or anything. He worked in the warehouse with my dad. That's how my parents met, actually. My dad worked for him," Owen says, his fingers wrestling with the strings on the gift, tucking them in and out of the fold nervously. He doesn't share these stories often, and I don't dare speak or interrupt him.

"When he wasn't working, and even more after he retired, my grandpa did odd jobs for people, fixing things. Not really a handyman, because he didn't go to houses or climb ladders for people. But people brought him things. And sometimes, they'd forget to come back and collect whatever it was he was fixing for them," Owen says, his lips curved into a soft, affectionate smile, his eyes showing nothing but fondness for this memory.

"So..." Owen starts, sliding the bag from his lap onto mine. "This is from my grandpa's collection. He saved a few special things, things that sort of spoke to him. He never really knew why he kept this thing in particular. But then, when I was visiting him at the home the other day, I noticed it again. I've probably stared at this thing for four years, both on the shelf at our house and in his room at the home when we moved him there. It never meant anything...until now. When I asked him if I could give it to you, he lit up. He doesn't light up often anymore."

Owen pauses, his hands folded nervously in his lap, his thumbs tapping one another, his eyes cast down on the gift in my lap. The light through the window is dim, but it's bright enough to see his expression. He's anxious, and maybe also a little happy. I unbend the fold in the top of the bag and untwist the knotted strings, pulling out the crumpled tissue paper from the top. When I reach in, my fingers feel something cold, made of a heavy metal. I pull the object out slowly, holding it in front of my face, resting it on my palm. It stands only a few inches tall, and the shape is similar to a small grandfather's clock, but I know what it is immediately.

My heart knows too, and it kicks—violently.

"My grandpa said the music teacher for the old Woodstock elementary school brought it to him. But then the guy retired and left town, forgetting about it completely. I guess you wind it here," Owen says, his hands gentle along mine as he twists the crank on the back until the small object begins to make the regular ticking sound it's meant for, the sound sweet to my ears. "He said they don't make metronomes like this anymore. One wind lasts about six hours, unless you hold the hand still to make it stop."

"Thank you," I whisper, moving my thumb gently along the sharp edges of the heavy metal. The small object is a dark iron, with small bumps along the edges showing its age. I push my finger against the hand to stop the ticking, then wind it again to listen to it begin, holding it up to my ear to hear the mechanisms move inside. My eyes find Owen's while I listen.

"You like it?" he asks, his bottom lip tucked under his top. I nod *yes*, keeping my eyes locked on his while the ticking sound fills my ear. My chest constricts with an overwhelming love for his gesture, and I stop the ticking once again, placing the metronome back in the tissue paper on the side of my bed, then lean forward on my knees and hold Owen's face in between my hands.

"I love it," I say, the beating inside me so strong it feels as though my gift has been swallowed whole and has begun racing inside my chest. My hands hold still, my eyes on Owens, watching him look over my face, down to my mouth and back to my eyes more than once.

"Happy birthday, Kensington," he whispers, his lips grazing mine as he speaks. His next pass is more forceful, and when I feel his hands slide up my sides and around my back, I give in to my most basic urges, crawling over his lap until I'm straddling him and kissing him as hard as our lips will let us.

His hands slide down my back until they're cupping my butt, the thin cotton of my leggings no match for the heat of his grip. Owen sits tall, and I take his signal and reach down to lift his shirt from his body, pulling the two layers of long-sleeved shirts up and over him, revealing the smooth skin I memorized while watching him play basketball outside. Everything about him is warm—his shoulders, warm, his back, warm—his chest against mine, warm. I can feel him through the fabric of my sweatshirt, but want to feel him more.

Without warning, Owen's hands grip the back of my thighs, lifting me just enough to push me onto my back, and soon he's above me, his knee pushed between my legs, touching me in a place I've never been touched. His kiss is rough and fast, yet somehow not hard enough. When his hands slide my arms up above my head, I let him guide them willingly, his kiss trailing down my neck until his lips stop at the collar of my sweatshirt. His hand trails from my arms, which I leave just as he left them over my head, and the further down my body his hand goes, the less I breathe.

The look in his eyes when his head tilts up to gaze at me is aggressive, almost like an animal, and as much as my hands want to reach down and feel the softness of his hair, I keep them in place, instead watching the dark waves fall into his eyes as he lowers his head again, his hand slowly lifting the bottom of my sweatshirt up my belly.

His lips leave small kisses over my stomach and rib cage as he slowly pulls my shirt up, revealing my skin. His thumb hooks my undershirt next, and soon I'm arching to help him lift both pieces of clothing completely up my body.

I'm terrified that he's seeing me. I'm excited that he's seeing me. My breathing is hard, my lips barely parted as Owen's hand slips the thin pink strap of my bra over my shoulder, kissing my skin where the tension of the strap left a small mark. He does the same on the other side, leaving my bra over my breasts just enough to cover my nipples, which are aching for him to expose them, to feel the cold air of my room.

"You're a virgin, right?" Owen says, his question surprising me, igniting a fire over my face and making me feel sick and fearful and wonderful all at once. His smile is soft, and he's not making fun of me, but I'm somehow ashamed that I don't know what to do, that I'm inexperienced.

"I am. I'm sorry," I say, and he lowers his head with a small laugh. When he lifts to look at me again, he lowers himself, resting the weight of his body on top of mine, the heat of his skin covering me, warming me completely, and all my breasts want is the feeling of his skin against them, no more barriers in between.

"Kens, don't apologize. It makes you beautiful. I just wanted to make sure I didn't make any assumptions, to make sure I treat you...right," he says, his lips kissing me softly, and then gliding down my chin and neck as he raises himself over me again. He pauses when his mouth is right between my breasts, resting his chin on the center clasp of my bra, and he looks up at me, waiting for me to tell him it's okay to move forward.

I nod slightly, biting my lip and closing my eyes, arching my back, wanting to press into him harder. Owen's teeth grip the clasp in the center of my bra, and I don't know if he's torn it open or managed to unhook it, but I feel the lacey material begin to

206

slide open, releasing the tension over my breasts, but keeping my nipples covered. The sensation of his tongue on the curve of my breast drives the arch in my back deeper, causing the material of my bra to completely fall to the sides. The cool rush of air on my nipples leaves them feeling hungrier somehow, and I look down, my eyes meeting Owen's, his sexy smile paused right above one of the peaks. I watch as he leans down, his eyes on mine the entire time, his tongue reaching out and taking a taste of my body, the hardness of my nipple responding with shivers across my skin.

Oh. My. God.

Owen does it again, and the reaction within me is just the same. And when he lets his tongue lave completely over my breast, pulling the pink tip in between both lips, tugging gently with his teeth, I whimper.

"Shhhhhhhh," Owen whispers, blowing cool air over my breasts, which drives me wilder. "You...need to be quiet," he smirks.

He's right. I do. But holy shit do I want to scream and beg and do things that just a minute or two ago I wasn't sure I was ready for. Owen hands me my pillow, and I pull it over my forehead, then over my mouth when his lips find my breasts once again. I let myself have a faint moan, muffled by the cotton and feathers I'm pressing over my mouth, my teeth biting the fabric—until Owen reaches up and removes the pillow, replacing it with his mouth. His lips work mine, his tongue probing deep into my mouth, his teeth grazing my bottom lip, tugging and tasting while his hand cups my breasts. When his thumbs rub over the tips, I can feel the throbbing between my legs grow even stronger, and with every pass, my hips grow bolder, until finally, I roll them into his leg, welcoming the pressure of his thigh and knee.

"You feel that, don't you," Owen whispers in my ear, his leg pushing into me once more.

"Ye....yes..." I stutter, my heartbeat pumping in my stomach, racing with excitement.

"You want me to touch you? There?" Owen asks as he lets his hand run softly down my stomach, down my abdomen, into the center of my legs until I feel his fingers graze over the fabric between my legs.

I nod *yes* quickly, holding my breath. Owen runs his hand over my center again, this time with more pressure, and my center quivers in response. He does this a few more times until I'm unable to control the rolling of my hips, my body wanting more of him. Bringing his hand up my hip, he runs his palm flat against my tummy while his lips kiss me deep and hard. When he pulls his mouth away, he leaves his forehead against mine, taking a long, deep breath through his nose. He's trying to be good, trying to restrain himself—and the good angel on my shoulder is thankful, the bad angel on the other side screaming for him to disobey.

My eyes closed, I run my fingers down his arm until my hand is over his, then I push his fingers lower, until my hand and his both dip under the elastic band of my leggings and panties. Owen's breath comes out fast and hard again, and I can feel the sensation of want in his fingers as they twitch and flex, begging to move faster. Once again, I pull his hand deeper, moving him a fraction of an inch at a time, until I can tell he no longer needs me.

I bring my hand back to his neck, opening my eyes to look into his, and the desire in them is intoxicating—and infectious. I pull him to me, kissing him hard as his hand travels the final inch it needs until his fingers have found my center, his hand plunging forward more, his finger reaching into me, penetrating me in a way that is both painful and amazing all at once. The burn is overcome with my desire the more he does it, until my hips begin to rock once again with the rhythm of his hand.

"So fucking hot," Owen breathes into my ear, his eyes hooded and his smile dark and sexy as he looks over my face. "Tell me what you want."

"Everything," I whimper, my face falling to the side, my hand gripping the corner of the blanket to muffle my sounds as Owen leans down and pulls my nipple into his mouth, sucking it between his teeth to a painful, glorious peak again as his fingers rub over my center, teasing me again and again until plunging back inside. The pressure builds fast, and with every pass of his

208

tongue on my breast and his finger through my core, the risk that I'm going to lose control grows stronger. I feel wet around him, and my hips are no longer able to control themselves, rocking into him, craving him, wanting more than his hand, until I fall over the edge completely.

Owen's other hand cups my mouth, muffling my cries while his eyes watch me, his smile cocky and proud as his right hand continues to work, his finger moving in and out of me until the waves of pleasure become bearable and finally stop. When he pulls his hand out from my pants, he lets his head rest on mine again, and just when I begin to feel embarrassed, he speaks.

"That...was the single sexiest thing I've ever done," he says, running his hand down my stomach and over the sensitive area between my legs again, cupping me hard, gripping me forcefully. "Only for me," he says, looking at me possessively, his hand threatening to push me into orgasm again just by this single touch. I nod *yes*, my lips wanting to smile, but unable to gain control through the trembles I'm still feeling. Owen kisses me again, and I'm grateful for his touch, for the rescue from having to speak.

I'm speechless.

I'm in love.

And I want to do that again.

Chapter 16

Nothing changed, yet everything changed. I caught sight of Owen when I drove myself to band practice Monday morning, and I blushed. I also felt my body warm just from looking at him.

I felt like somehow Willow knew everything that we had done. She didn't say anything, but I read something in her smirk—in the way she looked at me, her eyebrows raised—while she directed the morning practice session.

I was the last one off the field for morning practice, lost in my own happy thoughts. The wheels from the xylophone were catching rocks, squealing as they dragged them over the concrete walkway.

"I'm pretty sure we've done this before, haven't we?" Owen says, his voice lifting me out of my daydream, only to put me in my real-life fantasy. He bends down and dislodges the small pebbles from the wheels of my xylophone and begins pushing it back to the band room for me.

"Thank you," I say, smiling as I look up at him, completely smitten. He kisses the top of my head in response.

"Haaaaaa haaaaa, you a band geek now, Harper?" some guy bellows, his laugh that obnoxious kind that makes him sound drunk even though he's completely sober. I think he's sober?

"Fuck off, Cruz," Owen says, staring intensely at his friend, who backs down quickly. Owen is tall, and his body is broad, his muscles cut, but he's not the biggest guy in our school. Yet, when he gives a certain look, one with warning, it's unbelievably effective. His friend walks over with his hand out, reaching for Owen's, and Owen makes him wait a few long, painful seconds before he reaches back, slapping hands and pulling the other guy in to bump chests.

"This your chick?" the guy asks, nodding to me, his eyes flirtatious. I should probably be offended by being claimed and called someone's *chick*, yet hearing it, and seeing Owen's chest lift in response, makes me feel proud of being possessed—by him.

"This is Kensi, and yes, she's *my chick*," Owen repeats.

"Ahhh right. I feel ya, brother. Kensi, nice to meet you. You coming to our game tonight? You've gotta come see your man in action; he's got skills," Cruz says. I look to Owen as he puts his hands in his pockets and shrugs, forever modest. But he smiles, a smile that makes me think of last night, of his lips on me, his hands on me, and I blush right in front of his friend.

"What time? I'd like to go," I say, looking up at Owen again.

"We play at six," he says, his smile sliding into a pleased look that lets me know he's happy I'm going.

"Sweet. Party at Sasha's after," Cruz says, slapping hands with Owen once more before turning to walk back to the group of guys waiting by the outside stairwell.

Owen starts pushing my instrument again, and I trail behind, now thinking about everything *after* Owen's game—about going to that house again, about the things I saw other couples do there. Not just the sex, but the drugs and drinking. I also can't help but remember how I felt the last time I was there—afraid and angry.

"We can just go home after the game, you know?" Owen says, pausing when we reach the band-room door.

"I know," I say, my lip lodged between my teeth. I never say I don't want to go, because there's a part of me that wants to feel that rush again, of being somewhere that feels dangerous, and somewhere *alone* with Owen.

He sighs deeply and smiles with tight lips, pulling me into his chest, the softness of his black hoodie like heaven against my cheek. I want to do nothing else but stay here for the rest of the day.

Unfortunately, my reality slams into us—Willow opens the door, knocking into my xylophone and ending my hug-fest with Owen, my boyfriend. My. Boyfriend. Owen. I'm his *chick*. I let the silly grin and butterflies in my belly carry me through the rest of the morning, and I even let myself touch the piano a little during my independent study. I wouldn't really call it playing, but it's more than I've done in weeks.

In English, Owen's feet are in their rightful place on my chair again. I reach down and squeeze his ankles, threatening to trap them before he slides them away and I sit in my chair. His breath surprises me when I feel it against my neck, his hand sliding my hair out of the way so he can drop a quick round of tiny kisses on my neck and ear. His desk is propped forward on its front legs just so he can reach me.

He backs away when he hears Mr. Chessman coming, pulling his pencil to his lips, chewing on the eraser, his other hand flipping the edges of his book. We're wrapping up our discussion of *Crime and Punishment* today. Owen's been anxious about it ever since the heated debate that sent him out of our classroom.

"Owen, can you join me in the hall, for just a minute?" Mr. Chessman's voice surprises us both. Owen looks him in the eyes for a few solid seconds, like he's trying to read his mind, before leaning forward and dropping the pencil from his lips.

I watch them both walk from the room, the door swinging open and closed behind them, then I turn my attention to Cal. His smug smile pisses me off, and he nods toward the door, saying something under his breath to the girl sitting next to him, who only giggles. I hate him for judging Owen.

When Owen and Mr. Chessman return to class, there's a long awkward silence, the class watching Owen—waiting for him to pack his things, to leave, or to have some type of reaction. But he doesn't. He simply leans forward again, picking up his pencil, and flipping his book open to the final few chapters, pressing his thumb down the seam to hold his book open.

Disappointed, most of the class turns back to the front, giving their focus over to our teacher. But I notice Owen's hand, the one with the pencil, flexing and twisting and tapping the lead, letting the sharp point leave a red mark on the tip of his thumb. His face is low, his hair pushed forward, and I can tell this is one of those times, one of those moments when Owen wishes he could hide.

I should turn around, give him his privacy, let him cool from whatever it is Mr. Chessman told him. But I can't seem to make my arms, my legs, my shoulders work; I can't leave him. Then, his gaze flicks up, and his eyes find mine, and there's something at work behind them.

Owen looks scared.

I manage to catch him as he rushes out of the classroom, but when I ask him what's wrong, he only bites his lip and tells me "Nothing, really."

But Owen is gone for the rest of the day, missing lunch, missing math, and not there again for science. I slip my phone from my pocket before the final bell of the day and send him another text, only to watch it go unanswered just like my previous six attempts.

I'm racing out to my car when Ryan meets me in the parking lot, and I can tell by the face he's wearing he has news about Owen.

"Hey, Kens. Owen just called, wanted me to come find you, tell you not to worry," Ryan says, his hands waving, his long legs making up quick distance until he's standing at my car with me. "He'll be back for our game, too. He said you should just wait here."

"Where is he? What happened, Ryan?" I ask, having no intention of *not* driving right to Owen—wherever he is. I open the passenger door and toss my backpack inside then move to the driver's side, Ryan following me.

"It's James. He...he came home," Ryan says, his head leaning to one side, expecting me to understand. But I don't.

"He...came...home?" I repeat.

Ryan takes a small step back, letting his bag slide down his arm to the ground next to him. He pulls his hat from his head and runs his other hand through his hair, scratching at his head, his eyes squinting when he looks back at me.

"He does this sometimes. Or, at least, he's done this before. Something must have scared him, or he's broke, or...whatever. He goes a few days without getting high, and then he starts to feel the hell of withdrawals, and then he comes home," Ryan says, his arms slung heavily at his sides, his thumbs looped in his pockets.

"Why doesn't Owen's mom kick him out? Or take him to rehab?" I ask, opening my door and moving one foot inside.

"They can't afford rehab, Kens, come on," he says, and I wince because he's right, I should know better. "And James may be a drug addict, but he's still her son. She loves him."

213

"Is that where Owen is? Right now? Is he at home?" I ask, and I don't have to wait for his answer, because I know that's where he is.

I leave Ryan with his lips parted, ready to speak, and squeal my tires backing away from my parking spot. I hear the whistle from the teacher on parking-lot duty, but I ignore it, maneuvering my way to the front of the exit line, turning right on a red light, into a rush of traffic.

Somehow sparing my car any new dings or dents, I weave through dirt alongside the road until I get to a street that I know goes to my house. I pull up, and immediately I see Owen's truck, and the car I now know belongs to James. But I also see something else.

My father's car is at the end of the driveway, far enough forward to make room for my car— like he's planning on staying here a while. I slow, quietly turning into my driveway, positioning my car near the edge, out of the way so my father can exit. And, near my own escape—I leave my hand on the keys, not sure I should commit to turning the engine off.

On one side, I have Owen's house, and as I roll down my window and listen, everything seems quiet—as it *always* is. There's silence surrounding my house, too, even though my mom's car is also in the driveway. Both of my parents are in that house. Together.

Waiting for me, I can only presume.

I didn't text my mom that I was planning to stay for Owen's game. I thought she would be gone, and I assumed she wouldn't care. But clearly, her ambush screams otherwise.

The *divorce conversation* was bound to come. At eighteen, I hardly feel I need things explained to me. Given the circumstances, I can't see any other end for this game. The moment my father's face shifted when I asked him about the affair, asked him about some other woman—the first thing that flowed through my head was this very conversation my parents are sitting in there waiting to have. That's actually what sickened me most in that first few minutes. How quickly things changed though when Gaby also became a part of this story. It put things

214

into perspective, made *this* conversation not only unnecessary, but a joke.

I'm not having this talk today. And I'm a little disappointed in my mom for trying to force it on me.

With ease, I push my car door closed, latching it enough to make the dome light flicker off, then I jog to Owen's front porch, and I tap my key ring on his front door, wanting to keep everything quiet. When nobody answers after my second attempt, I try my hand on the doorknob, and when it twists, I push lightly, letting myself inside.

"Hello?" I call out, the downstairs lights dim, only a lamp on in a corner by a reading chair. The living room is dark as is the kitchen, but there's a glow from the rooms upstairs. "Hello? Owen?" I say loudly, my voice directed up the stairs. I hear footsteps coming down the wooden floors of the hallway, and soon I see Andrew's sock-covered feet.

"Hey, Kens," he whispers, gliding down the steps quickly and meeting me on the bottom. "You here for O?"

"Yeah," I whisper back, taking his lead. "He left school, and he has a game today. I...I was worried."

Andrew smiles, his hands hanging in the front pocket of his hoodie, his hair disheveled, like he's been sleeping. "I came home sick today," he says, running his hand a few times through his hair when he notices me looking at it, his smile reflecting his youth. "My mom came to get me, because she didn't want to bother Owen. But when we got home..."

Andrew turns to look over his shoulder, back up the stairs, and Owen is standing at the top, his eyes on mine, his face showing a look of disappointment. "Andrew, go back to bed," he says, sighing. He takes a few steps, and meets Andrew in the middle of the stairs.

"See ya later, Kens," Andrew says, a small wave over his shoulder. Owen keeps his back to me, pointing to his brother's door down the hall, and he watches until his brother is back inside, the door closed, before turning back to face me.

"Kens, what are you doing here?" His sigh is heavy, and he looks like he's been mugged, a small bruise forming on one cheek.

"Owen, what happened?" I say, reaching to touch it. He jerks back, moving up and away from me.

"It's nothing. I'm fine," he says, his eyes rolling a little with his temper. "Didn't Ryan find you? I'm coming back for the game. I was just going to meet you at the gym."

"He found me. He said..." I'm interrupted by the sound of open wailing—heavy cries filled with swear words and a few nonsensical things.

"Owen!" James finally yells, his voice broken, sounding nothing like the intimidating figure from before.

"Just...stay here," Owen says forcefully, his hand held up to my face as he turns quickly and takes the steps two at a time, rushing down the hallway to where I'm assuming his brother is.

At first, I do as he asks, letting my hands grip either side of the banister, my body swaying back and forth with indecision—to go up or down. I hear the sound of scuffling at first, then something heavy knocked to the floor, followed by the sound of running water. It's as if my feet carried me on their own volition, and somehow I find myself standing in front of the bathroom. Owen is kneeling, his body leaning over the bathtub, steam coming from the blast of running hot water, and he's soaking towels. He doesn't notice me until he shuts the water off, and begins to twist one of the towels, wringing it of excess water.

"Kens, I told you to wait there!" he yells, his face angry and his eyes stern. He's trying to use his aggression to dominate me, as I've seen him do to others.

"How can I help?" I ask, taking a step into the bathroom, then stopping dead in my tracks when I realize James is lying naked around the corner, his head resting on the side of the toilet, vomit...everywhere. I cover my mouth and nose, both to hide my shock and to stifle the smell. Owen was trying to keep this from me, but it's becoming apparent that he's also trying to keep it from everyone—leaving no one there for Owen.

James begins weeping the instant he sees me, his eyes not able to focus on me entirely, the puffiness almost swelling them shut. Owen slides back against the side of the tub, his hands dropping the wet towel on the floor, his long legs stretching out as he flips his hat from his head, tossing it out into the hall.

216

"Shit!" he yells, pushing his head forward into his hands, his fingers digging roughly into his hair, wrapping through strands and pulling until he finally releases and lets his head fall back against the edge of the tub. When he rolls it to the side slightly, his eyes catch mine again, and his strength is gone. Owen isn't falling apart; he was never together.

"Let me help," I say softly, my lips quivering with nervous energy, my mind putting the pieces together while everything before comes into focus. I have options, I have help—and it's going to be painful. But Owen can't do this...whatever *this* is...on his own. Not if he still wants to live his life.

"Where's his room?" I ask.

Owen nods to the right and looks in a direction toward the end of the hall. I move closer to him and lift the wet towel from the floor, then pull my sweatshirt collar up over my nose and mouth, hiding the gagging I can't help but do underneath. I reach for Owen, and he looks at my hand, his eyes blinking slowly. Everything in his expression shows his acceptance of the fact that he has run out of options, that he isn't as strong as he pretends. His eyelids quiver as they close, Owen fighting not to feel the gravity of what is happening any more than he has to. He takes my hand finally, and lifts himself to stand with me, grabbing the towel from my hands and going to work cleaning up the mess from his brother's frail, pale, and thin body.

He tosses it back into the hot water of the bathtub then turns to me. "I'll deal with all of this shit later. Just...help me get him in his room," he says, and I nod.

I won't leave you, Owen.

We each take an arm, and James works to bring his legs under his body, his frame swaying awkwardly, his balance nonexistent. He probably weighs less than I do, his tall body is so thin, but his length makes it hard to direct him and move him the few feet it takes to get him to his room. He slips on the floor three times, each time fighting to grip our arms on the way down, his own swinging wildly. This must be how Owen got that bruise.

Once we get him to his bed, he grips the sheets and claws his way to the middle before finally letting his weak muscles give way to the coolness of the bed, his lips parted and dry. He looks half alive, and he's shivering uncontrollably.

"Make it stop," he says, the dull look on his face slowly melding into sorrow, then torture. Tears stream from his eyes, his nose running into the edge of the pillow, his head never making it to the top of the bed. "Owen, please. Make this stop! I can't, I can't, I can't, I can't..."

He keeps screaming, his hands clutching the fabric beneath him, fists grabbing blankets and pulling them to his chest. Owen fights to cover his body, the entire time James working against him, his arms jutting, his legs kicking.

Then Owen makes it all stop. He kicks his shoes from his feet and climbs into the bed next to his brother, pulling his flailing body into his arms, onto his lap and holding him to his chest, his arms flexing and working so very hard. At first, James pushes from him, fighting to get back to the bed, pulling and asking for the floor, to go outside, to get to his car. Every time he fights, Owen just pulls him to his chest harder, his chin resting on his brother's head. Owen's eyes find mine, locking on me. It feels as if I'm his anchor.

"You can do this, James. This is the hard part. You can do this; I've got you," Owen says, over and over, until his brother's body grows tired, and he starts to stare off into space—not asleep, but no longer fighting against him.

"I need you to call Ryan; I'm going to miss my game," Owen says to me, his eyes full of regret, shame, disappointment—so many familiar emotions.

"What about your mom?" I ask. This isn't fair, and Owen shouldn't have to give up something for this.

It isn't fair.

"She had to work. She'll lose her job if she doesn't show up. She's...she's called in for this before. Last time was *the last time,* according to her boss," Owen says, his eyes starting to show his exhaustion.

"Owen..." I say, my head falling to the side, not wanting to see him lose so much, to hurt so much. His brother's pain is killing him.

218

"He's in withdrawal. If I leave him, he's just going to do something worse. I...can't..." Owen doesn't finish his words; instead, swallowing hard, fighting to keep the water I see building in his eyes from falling, to make the redness in his eyes go away. He wants to stay strong, to stay hard, to stay *dark.*

"I'll be right back," I say, looking at him long enough for him to believe that I will be right back. But I don't go to his room, to his phone. I don't call Ryan. Instead, I leave his house and walk into my own hell, to my parents who are sitting in my kitchen at opposite ends of the counter, not speaking, but waiting for me. They've been waiting long enough when I step in the house, the first words from my father's mouth are asking what's taken me so long, followed by accusations that my mother doesn't know how to take care of me. Within seconds, they're bickering with one another, not looking at me at all, and if it were any other moment, I would turn around and leave.

But I can't. I can't, because I need my mom. She is the only person who can help Owen.

"Stop it!" I yell, my hands held above my head, waving to get their attention. When they both snap their gazes to me, I drop my hands to my head. "I'm eighteen. I had a birthday...which *you* didn't acknowledge," I say sternly, pointing to my father who opens his mouth to rebut my accusation, but I keep talking, cutting him off before he can begin a single word. "You don't have any right to say *anything* about me, to me, on my behalf! You gave that all up the moment you fucked my best friend, you piece of shit. You don't get to be my father ever again, and when I think about it, you never really were."

There's a feeling of power that comes over me the longer I talk, the words I'm saying freeing, my voice growing calmer, stronger. There is so much I want to say to this man; so much I want to say to my mom, too, for even letting him in the house. But Owen needs me. Those things are going to have to wait.

"Mom," I speak to her, holding my hand up to my father's face, my gesture cruel and insolent, but I don't give a fuck, because Owen needs me. "I need you. It's personal, and I don't want to talk about this in front of *him.*"

I hold her gaze, watching her mind process what she's able to read in mine. Please, Mom. Just this once, stand up to him. Don't let him charm you; make him leave.

"Kens, can we just talk first, then when your dad goes back to his hotel, you and I can talk about anything, whatever you need?" she's trying to make us both happy. That's no longer possible, though—we both don't get to be happy.

"No," I say. Nothing more. I won't talk about Owen in front of him, and I won't sit here and listen to them try to talk about me, their marriage, fake apologies, my dad's rights or wishes for me, his role in my life. I'm not having that conversation—not ever.

"Dean…" my mom sighs, her head leaning to the side, her eyes falling on him. She's exhausted, and I can tell he's probably been here for hours, wearing her down.

"Karen, have you forgotten who the parents are in this house? My god…" my dad says, kicking away from the counter, his stool crashing to the floor with his temper. "Are you pregnant? Did that little thug next door knock you up? That's what this is, isn't it? Jesus, Karen!"

I don't answer. My father couldn't be more off-base, and it takes every breath in my body to stand here and keep my eyes on my mom, not to acknowledge him at all. But he just isn't worth it.

"Dean, I think you need to leave," she says, standing and putting her hand slowly along his shoulder. My dad shrugs her off, his brow low and hard, shirking her touch. "Dean, it's time to go."

"A goddamned mess. You…both of you! You did this to yourself!" My father points his finger back at me as he leaves, his face glowing red, his anger radiating.

When the door slams shut behind him, I turn back to my mom, her eyes wide and staring at the door, her face flushed. She stumbles on her feet, her balance failing her, and then grips behind her for her stool, looking for anything to save her. I wait as long as I can, but time is moving, and Owen needs me.

"Mom, I need your help," I say. She shakes her head, rubbing her temples before nodding a few times and bringing her eyes to me. "It's Owen…"

220

I can see her face flash with panic, worry that my father's guess was right.

"I'm not *pregnant!*" I blurt out, relief washing over her quickly. "But Owen needs you. It's his brother, James. He came home, and he's..." I don't know how to say this in a way that doesn't shed more negative light on the Harper family. I don't know what my mom has heard, and I don't want to contribute to those terrible rumors, but damn if so many of them aren't true.

"James is an addict, Mom. He's detoxing, and Owen's mom has to work, so Owen's at home, by himself, trying to take care of James. He doesn't want Andrew to see any of it, and it's killing him. Mom...oh god, Mom, it's so bad," I fall apart a little, remembering everything I just saw, knowing how hard it is on Owen. I place my palms flat on the counter and breathe deeply, closing my eyes, finding my strength. "Mom, Owen has a game tonight. It's all he's got, and he has nobody to help him. Can you just, I don't know...come take a look? I don't know what to do, Mom. Please...help."

My mom stares at me for long seconds, the air around us quiet and cold. I can't tell if she's judging Owen and his family, or if she's just disappointed in me, that this is the person I've decided to connect with, the one I've decided to love. And I wonder if she knows I love him? She finally stands, silently, and holds a finger up, leaving the kitchen and moving to the stairs. She climbs them and disappears into her bedroom for a few minutes before coming down with a small bag.

"Let's go," she says, everything about her shifting into professional. This is the person I need right now, but I know this person is only here because my mother loves me.

I lead her out the door, across our driveways, and into Owen's house. It's quiet when we enter, and I'm glad that James isn't making noise. I'm hopeful that he's fallen asleep, but I doubt that's the case.

When we get to the top of the stairs, I hold my hand up, wanting to go in first. My mom stands against the wall, and I look into the room, Owen still cradling his big brother, both of their eyes glazing over, staring into nothingness—each for different reasons.

"Did you get Ryan?" Owen asks, his focus coming back quickly. His arms looking tired.

"No," I say, and his posture deflates immediately. "But I got help. Please, don't be mad. She can help."

His eyes look terrified, and when my mom comes around the corner, Owen actually looks sick with embarrassment. My mom doesn't let him feel it for long, though, moving quickly into her medical-care mode.

"How long?" she asks, and Owen cocks his head, his forehead creasing with his confusion, his desperation and all of the hurt. "How long has he been detoxing?"

"Oh...uh, maybe a day or two? He was here a few days ago, and I gave him money. I just..." Owen swallows, the guilt swallowing him back. "I just wanted him to leave. But it wasn't a lot, and I don't think he bought much."

"Heroin?" my mom asks, Owen nodding as she rolls James's listless arm in her hands. "Looks like he's been getting high for a while."

My mom sees a lot of junkies. Her hospital is in the middle of Chicago, and she used to take a lot of rounds in emergency. Since she's been a practitioner, though, she's seen less, her work more with regular appointments. But addicts come in all shapes and sizes, and she still sees them, at least once a week.

"Can you get to a pharmacy?" she asks, and Owen rubs his fists on his eyes, nodding *yes* and breathing regularly for the first time since I've seen him this afternoon.

"Here, this is for buprenorphine, it will help him through the worst of it," my mom says, tearing a page from her script book and handing it to Owen. He reaches slowly, their hands touching as she passes this gift on to him. When his hand begins to tremble, she brings her other hand up and holds on tightly, squeezing.

"What is she giving you, O? Owen? What did that woman give you?" his brother's face is pushed deep into his pillow, his body barely covered with the sweat-soaked blanket, but he's trying to move. His strength has waned so much that the only thing he seems to be able to control is his neck and mouth. "Owen!"

222

Owen looks from my mother then to me, finally moving along the floor to kneel in front of James, pressing his hand firmly on his back, like a weighted blanket, his brother's shivers stopping temporarily under his touch. "I'm going to get you medicine. She's giving you medicine that's going to make you feel better. You need to let me go, James. I'll be right back," Owen says, standing slowly.

James's eyes follow every movement as the three of us move out of the room. When we're in the hallway, Owen turns quickly and wraps his arms around my mom, surprising both her and me. She looks at me over his shoulder and brings her hands slowly up his back to embrace him, holding him to her and telling him it will be all right. But I can tell in her eyes that she doesn't believe it.

She's lying.

I wait with my mother in the hallway as Owen leaves, and then when the door closes we both slide down the wall, our legs falling in front of us, on opposite sides, and we look *into* each other.

The light seeping in through the windows is growing dimmer with every passing minute, and more than twenty pass before either of us says a word, my mom the first to break.

"I'm sorry, Kensington," she says, barely a whisper.

"You have nothing to be sorry for," I say back.

"I do. I'm weak," she says, her eyes blinking slowly, her lips parted and waiting to find the courage to say the rest. "He wants to work through it."

My heart is on fire, burning with flames that have engulfed my chest. But this is not the place to yell, to rile up the broken man, Owen's suffering brother, in the room next door. So instead, I stare at her, waiting for her, daring her to finish, to tell me the rest. *Say it!* I'm screaming inside.

"Don't," I finally say back, my voice louder than it should be, so I hold my breath after, listening to the door, hoping James hasn't found the strength to move.

"He's all I know," she says back, her eyes drifting down to the knots in the wood floors, to the glue holding the planks together.

I can't sit here, and I can't understand how this woman who is so brave, so strong, can be so pathetic. Even the thought that my mother is pathetic stings my soul, and it breaks my heart. I stand as the tear finds the corner of my eye and I wipe it quickly with my sleeve, not wanting her to see. All of this—she says all of *this*—and still, I don't want to hurt her with my reactions.

"Learn something else," I whisper. "If he's all you know, learn something else." I can't look at her when I speak, so I move to the top of the stairs and climb down a few to sit in the middle and wait for Owen to return home.

My mother's phone rings, and I can tell it's the pharmacy. She recites several numbers, giving her consent as a nurse practitioner, then responding *yes* to a few questions before hanging up. We don't speak again, for the next twenty minutes, and when Owen joins us again, our interactions are forced and rehearsed.

"I'm sorry it took so long. They don't really trust my family at the pharmacist's," Owen says, his lip curled up on one side, his attempt at a joke. I smile back, to comfort him.

My mom helps coax James into taking the pill, assuring him that it will make him feel better. Within seconds, he looks utterly passed out.

"He's going to sleep for days. He'll wake up here and there, but not a lot. And..." my mom pulls her top lip into her mouth, pausing, "he's probably going to mess himself. You'll want to change the bed every morning and night. I can come back when your mom is home, explain things to her."

"Can he be left alone?" Owen asks, looking down at his hands that are folded in front of him. I can see the guilt taking hold of him.

"Don't think that's selfish...to want to take care of *your* things. It's not. You're allowed to put yourself first," my mom says, the irony of her words to Owen striking me—making me snicker to myself. I cough and do my best to cover up my slip, but she notices anyhow, her eyes sending me apology after apology.

"Andrew is here. But...I don't want this to be his problem. If I have to miss my game..." Owen starts.

224

"I'll stay. I'll stay until your mom comes home," my mom says. Owen shakes his head *no*, but my mom insists. "I've dealt with far worse. Go...go to your game. Take Andrew. I will stay."

"Andrew's sick. He's probably asleep," Owen says, his body wavering between staying and going.

"Go," my mom says, this time sternly. Owen nods and looks to me, and I nod in response. I take his hand as we walk down the stairs, and I never look back at my mom.

Our ride back to the school is silent, but Owen's hand is in mine the entire time, his thumb wearing a line over my knuckles with the constant rubbing. We get to the school with little time before his game, and when Owen finally looks at his phone, he sees dozens of missed calls from Ryan and House.

I walk with him quickly to the gym, kissing him once hard and fast on the mouth when we reach the locker room entrance, then I move into the gym and take my place in a top corner of the bleachers, hoping that Elise doesn't notice and join me.

I want to be alone.

When I don't see her, I finally let myself relax, my muscles aching from how hard they worked to keep my body moving for the last two hours.

Owen must feel worse than this. I can't imagine. His eye doesn't look good, the bruise turning blue. No one seems to question Owen having a bruise on his face, though. I wonder how many times people assumed his bruises were from a fight when it was really from restraining James.

Through it all, his play—it's flawless. This is Owen's court, and this is the one place he can go and be master—everyone looking to him, every decision his. He commands the court, running effortlessly, his legs never showing fatigue. The way he passes, the way he sees the game, several seconds before his team, before his opponents. He would mock me for making this comparison, but I swear he plays chess out there.

Even when he's not the one scoring, he's the *reason* our team scores. At one point, a guy on the other team pushes him, backing his body into Owen, dribbling into him, trying to dominate him. But less than a second later, the ball is in Owen's hands, and he's breaking to the other end, finding House who takes his pass and slams the ball.

The Owen out here is different from any other Owen I know; yet all of those Owens are still in there. I see them. There's a moment—at halftime—when he's drinking from a water bottle, House's elbow leaning on him, and he spits some of the water out in laughter.

My mom gave him this—a small break from the chaos and nightmare at home.

It makes me forgive her weakness for the moment.

Owen is pulled from the game with five minutes left, the coach opting to sub in other players, thanks to our sizeable lead. And as much as Owen is still invested in the game, this rest—his body being idle—lets the bad start to creep in again.

I wait at the bottom of the bleachers for Owen to walk out, and one-by-one everyone leaves, until there's only me, a few students I don't recognize, and a man in a blue-and-white sweater, an expensive-looking briefcase at his side.

Owen finally exits the locker room, the exhaustion hitting him, his body dragging as he slides his feet to me, his bag with his uniform slung over one shoulder, his hair still wet from his shower. The closer he gets to me, the faster his steps come, and I'm starting to wonder if I'm going to need to catch him when he reaches me.

"Owen Harper?" the sweater man says, stepping out from the edge of the bleachers. Owen shakes his head quickly, his guard up instantly.

"Yes?" Owen says, stepping to the other side of me, pulling me in to him close, his squeeze tight.

"I'm Lon Mathison. We haven't met officially, but I've sent you a few letters," he says, reaching his hand out to Owen. Unlike other times, when Owen hesitates, he doesn't here. Though his body next to me is rigid, and frozen, his arm manages to work, moving out toward our new acquaintance, shaking his hand.

"Right, yes...nice to meet you. Were you...I'm sorry, here for the game tonight? I didn't know you were coming," Owen stammers, looking to me and back to Lon, his brow wrinkled.

"I'm heading to Wisconsin, actually. A few appointments, but I figured…you know, Woodstock was sort of on my way," Lon says, his voice coming out in a singsong way, his head bobbing from side-to-side. "You really handled that team from Union tonight. The Kellis brothers are supposed to be pretty good defenders. Didn't seem to slow you down though, did it?"

Owen blushes from the compliment, pursing his lips in a tight smile. It's the same face he makes anytime someone compliments his play. It's more than humble; it's almost like he's afraid to admit to being good, afraid if he acknowledges it, his talent will disappear.

Or maybe he's afraid people will notice.

"Well, I plan to send a few more letters. So, maybe just hang on to this," Lon says, flipping open his wallet and handing Owen a card. I glance quickly, reading "DePaul University" before Owen slides it into his back pocket.

"Right, well…thanks for coming out," Owen shrugs, his hand back in mine, his thumb tapping over mine, his anxiety absolutely boiling.

Lon nods once, then looks to me, but doesn't bother with introductions. He's out the door and pulling away in his car by the time we exit the building. We make it all the way to Owen's truck without him bringing it up.

"So…DePaul, huh?" I say, trying to get something out of him.

"Yep," he says, his answer short and clipped. Great, I'm getting *this* Owen again. I stare at him, waiting for him to break, to share more. Instead, he stops hard at the light, then turns to me. "Look, Kens. I don't want to talk about it. That guy, he's all dreams and opportunity and shit. And I'm just not feelin' it."

He reaches his hand over to my arm, holding it tightly, his eyes penetrating me.

"That's nothing on you. I just need to get myself ready to go back into war. Please understand," he says, my stomach falling to the floor of his truck, my heart stopping and my mouth watering with dread. I force it all—all of those feelings—down deep, hiding them from him, and I pull my lips in tight, hoping that somehow a smile is produced, and I nod.

"Okay," I say, cupping my hand over his.

His phone buzzes and he pulls it from his pocket, tossing it to me as the light turns to green. "It's a text, from House. Read it to me?" he asks, and I open it and recite House's words.

"You and your chick in for Sasha's? Nick scored some PBR," I read aloud.

"Pabst," Owen says, noticing my eyebrow rise at *PBR*.

"Ah," I say, opening the reply, my thumbs ready to type.

"Just type back 'James.' He'll know what it means," he says, and I do what he asks. Seconds later, House replies:

Sorry bro.

I put Owen's phone away, and grab his hand again, and I hold it until we get home. His mom's car is back in the driveway, and the lights are on in my house. We both have places to go, places with *things* that need to be tended to—things we both would rather ignore. But all I want to do is sit here, in his truck, in the dark driveway under the thin fingers of winter branches of the giant trees in our yards. Owen seems to want the same, because we both remain motionless for minutes, never breathing a word, until the first tiny, white flake hits the glass of his windshield.

"Look," he says. "It's snowing."

Owen's eyes close, and his face is washed in pain. I kiss him and let him go inside, then walk to my own cage, locking the door behind me, dragging my feet past my mother who is asleep on the couch, a book in her lap. I kick off half of my clothes, leaving only my underwear and giant sweatshirt for warmth, then I pull my blanket from my bed and curl up by my window, watching the snow cascade down as I wait for Owen to come to bed.

He never does. And eventually, I succumb to sleep.

Chapter 17

My dad is at the house again this morning. He was staying at a hotel in Milwaukee before, but he moved to a bed and breakfast in the center of town. This all feels so weird, like he's...*visiting.*

An unwelcomed visitor.

The first few days this week, I asked my mom what was happening. She said he was just coming over for coffee and breakfast before work, making an effort to be friendly—assuring me that was it. I stayed in my room the entire time. I refuse to acknowledge him. I know he leaves when she does for work, though. I asked Owen to make sure of it for me, and he did, once or twice, driving back by my house while I was at band. My dad's car was always gone.

I heard him pull into the driveway this morning, watched him walk up to the backdoor with a box of donuts in his arms. My father never bought donuts. Not once. Not even when I was a little girl and had slumber parties.

Willow is coming over, helping me pick out something nice to wear for the dance after the final football game. I'm going with her and Jess and Elise. Owen and Ryan both don't want to go. Ryan, because he just doesn't like dances, and Owen because he doesn't seem to like much of anything lately.

His brother has been with him for five days, and yesterday, I saw James come outside. He was wearing a pink pair of sweatpants and a large gray T-shirt, his mom's clothing I think. He rushed to his car, dug around in the backseat, then swore a few times before going back inside.

He looked terrible.

I quit asking Owen about it. His answers are always short, resentful. I don't blame him. I hate his brother for doing this to him, for doing this to his family. Owen's mom was able to fix her schedule at work, and for the last two days, she's been able to be home with James when nobody else is. It's not a permanent thing. I don't know how long it takes someone to get off of heroin, but I'm guessing three days is kind of fast.

When I hear Willow's car skid over the dip in the driveway, I call her.

"Hey, lemme guess, you heard me bust my axle on your stupid driveway," she says, her engine cutting off both over the phone and out my window.

"If you were a cat, that sound would basically be the bell around your neck," I joke.

"Yeah, yeah," she says, her voice muffled as she stuffs her phone in the crook of her neck. I hear the door slam closed in the background.

"So, when you ring the doorbell, I'm not coming down," I say.

"Another fine morning with good ol' Dad, I see," Willow says.

"Yes. And don't get a crush on him," I say quickly. "I like you, and I don't want to make another voodoo doll of a former friend."

"First of all, *gross*! Your dad is okay looking, for fifty, but he's not my bag," she says. "And second, voodoo dolls?"

"No comment," I say back, kicking the cutout photo of Gaby I made the other night under my bed. I poked my red pen through the eyes to make her look like the devil. It made me feel better for about five minutes.

"Okay, hanging up, about to ring the doorbell. See you in a sec," Willow says, ending our call. I crack my door open just enough to hear the drone of the conversation happening downstairs. My father is talking about his latest set, some new cellist playing in their symphony. My mom is pretending to be interested. She's always pretended to be interested. I can envision it, her head propped on her hand, the nodding and the *ohs* and *uh huhs*. I never really stopped to pay attention before, but I'm more aware now, my perspective...different.

I bet he's sleeping with the cellist.

The doorbell rings, and I can hear snippets of my mom's conversation with Willow, when I notice the shadow of two people climbing the stairs, I leap from my door to my bed, crossing my legs and grabbing the closest magazine available. It's the most cliché move possible.

"Thanks, Mrs. Ward," Willow says, her eyes wide at me in apology that she led my mom up here with her. My mom's not the enemy. She's just disappointing.

"Thanks, Mom. You can go now," I say, my tone clipped. I'm being a bitch. I've been one for five days—ever since I found out my father was trying to woo my mother, and she admitted that she was considering it.

My mom lingers at the doorway, her eyes glaring at me. She looks pissed, but her resolve dissipates quickly the longer she stands there. Because *I'm* right.

"Your dad brought donuts..." she starts.

"Not hungry," I say, flipping pages on the dog magazine, pretending to be immersed in the cute puppy faces on the pages. It's something we got free in the mail, from a shelter. If I had access to my father's checking account, I'd send in a donation for ten thousand dollars.

"Right, well..." she says, but I look up at her, my eyes snapping to hers, challenging her. Well *what*? Well, I should really come talk to him and think about forgiving him for the unforgivable, because he brought donuts and that proves he's a good person? I don't know what she's expecting, or what he is for that matter. But I've come to terms with the idea that my father is only my father genetically from now on.

My mom closes the door finally, discouraged.

"So that was awkward," Willow says, flopping on the bed next to me, her arms and legs out in all directions, her reddish-blonde hair loose and wild.

"Sorry," I say.

"I get it," she says, rolling on her side, turning to prop her head on her elbow. "My parents are divorced, too. I have to take turns picking sides. Or at least...I used to. I quit caring about offending one of them, and honestly, now that I don't make it a big deal, they don't seem to use me as a weapon against one another."

I nod in agreement, but stand quickly from the bed, moving to my closet, changing the subject. Divorce doesn't seem to be a topic being discussed by my parents, and I don't want to draw comparisons with Willow. I'd give anything for my mom to tell me she's talking to a lawyer.

"So, how formal is this thing?" I ask, flipping through the things in my closet. I don't have a lot of in-between clothing. Dances at Bryce were always *extremely* formal.

"Just wear leggings and a cute sweater or a dress or something like that. It's cold as hell outside, and it's going to snow all night," she says, moving next to me and flipping through a few things on hangers. She pulls out a long gray sweater and tosses it on my bed. "That works. Wear your Uggs, and I'll help you put your hair up. You'll be cute."

I sigh heavily as I sit down next to the sweater, pulling it onto my lap. "You know, I'm totally okay *not* going," I say, but Willow cuts me off.

"Stop it. Jess doesn't really dance a lot, and I like going. You're coming to dance with Elise and me. It'll be fun," she says, tossing my boots from the box on my closet floor.

"Fine," I huff, but I smile when she turns, softening my tone. I'm actually happy she wants me there. I just wish Owen was up for coming, too. He hasn't been himself lately...or maybe he has. Maybe that's what has me feeling this way; I'm worried that the Owen I had was brief, and he's gone back to dark.

I decide to wear my outfit to school for the day, opting to ride with Willow instead of driving myself. I question that decision every time she slides the wheels several inches into the intersection with each stop. We don't have early-morning practices any longer now that the football season is coming to an end. Our state competition is next weekend, so we spend every band class practicing the music, no longer worrying about marching and formations. Thank God, because it's so cold outside. I don't march, and only end up standing on the sidelines watching my breath create fog circles in front of me.

Willow helps me twist and pin my hair up over my head before the end of class, and I manage not to ruin it during my independent study. I let my hands play a few classical pieces today. I wanted to see how it felt.

232

It felt…like nothing. But it didn't hurt, either. It didn't make me angry. And it didn't make me think of my dad. But then I let myself play *my* music, and I feel that all over my body.

That's the difference.

With five minutes left before class ending, I do something that I've never done before—I excuse myself to the bathroom, to touch up makeup, to make sure I look good. I want Owen to notice me.

This is apparently where Kiera and her friends go during second period. The smell of stale smoke is in the air, and I know they flushed something the second they heard me walk in. The scent is sweet, yet pungent—probably marijuana. I smile at Kiera, acknowledging that she and I share something in common. I guess we're acquaintances in some sick, twisted way. She smiles back, but never talks to me directly.

She's sitting on the edge of one of the sinks, her legs propped up on the next one over. There's a run in her black tights, and she's dabbing nail polish on the end, trying to stop it from growing.

I'm even more awkward touching up makeup in front of her, and her friends. I can feel them watching me even though they're pretending I'm invisible. It's like being in a room with ghosts.

"You going to the dance?" one of her friends asks her.

"Fuck no! Sasha's having a party; I'll be there," she says, her eyes flitting to my reflection in the mirror quickly before moving back to the run on her leg. I watch as her friend moves closer to her and whispers something in her ear, something that leaves them both laughing and covering their mouths.

Her friend comes toward me after a few minutes, and I work to pack up my things calmly, pretending I've finished whatever I was doing. I'm mentally forcing myself to slow down, not to look nervous. The girl smiles at me in the mirror—then pulls her purse straps from her shoulder, dropping her heavy bag on the edge of the sink. She pulls out a bottle of pills and pours two small white ones in her hand, reaching her other hand down to cup water from the sink and swallowing the water and pills down quickly.

She leaves her gaze on me, her smile never changing, never growing or shrinking. It's just there—like a dare. Her eyes are just the same—taunting, bait. She's waiting for me to flinch, to be offended or question what she's doing. But I don't. A lot of the girls at Bryce did drugs in the bathroom, usually expensive designer ones. What she's just done isn't shocking to me. What's making me uncomfortable is the amount of lips in this room that have kissed my boyfriend.

I smile back at her reflection, amused internally over how hard she's working to intimidate me, her gaze staying on me, her brow lowering. I pull my things together slowly, and then I take the extra step of pulling a towel from the holder and wiping the few drops I've left behind on the sink. Nobody breathes a word when I leave. But the second the door closes, the room behind me erupts with laughter.

I shake my head and roll my eyes. But I also stand still, letting my back slump against the wall around the corner, letting my breath leave my chest in one long exhale, some of my confidence slipping away with it. Their laughter...it still feels bad. I can convince myself of a lot of things, but I think we all want people to like us—like us, or let us be invisible. Right now, I think I'd be happy to have left that room unnoticed.

The bell rings seconds later. I pull my backpack over my body and make my way to class, blending quickly with the backpacks, hats and chatter, shedding everything that made me feel as if I stood out—not in a good way—seconds ago. I step into our English class where Owen's feet are on my chair—waiting for me. My mouth can't help but smile seeing them there. As quiet as he's been, these small gestures are still there. I'm grateful for them.

They let me breathe again.

"Missed you this morning," I say as I slide into my seat, my hip cozying up next to his ankles, my body wanting any kind of touch. Owen's eyes stay on me as he leans forward, sliding the hood from his head. His feet finally fall to the floor.

He tilts his desk as he leans far enough forward for his lips to reach me, but he passes my mouth, moving right for my neck. "I like your hair," he says, his eyes a little hazy. His hot breath on my neck sends shivers down my arms and back.

"Thanks," I say. "Willow did it. It's for the dance."

He pulls away, but keeps his eyes fixed on me, on my bare neck.

"I'm visiting my grandpa after school," he says. "Wanna come? I'll bring you back before the game."

"I'd love to," I say, my heart thumping so heavy with hope. This is the first time Owen's done something different from the routine of his house, from checking on James, from being short with me. It's the first time in a week he's initiated the conversation, and it's made me feel happy enough to cry. I'm not sure why, but the sensation almost chokes me, suffocating my lungs quickly. I think it's because I've been afraid of losing him.

I'm saved by Mr. Chessman's entrance, and I turn to face the front, keeping my head down until the swell of emotion leaves my chest and I'm able not to act so desperate for his attention.

Owen's quiet for the rest of the day, holding my hand briefly in the hallway—sitting at our table for only part of the lunch period, kissing my cheek and telling me he'll see me after school before joining House outside. For a minute, I think I see him taking a drag from House's cigarette, but I can't tell for sure.

He skips science, and I notice the teacher put a packet to the side for him, his name scribbled on a sticky note slapped to the first page. It looks like notes for everything we've covered. This happens a lot. I wonder who delivers these to him, how his work gets done.

I'm already half expecting his truck to be gone when I walk out at the end of the day, so I move toward Willow's car, meeting up with her in the parking lot. "So what's the plan, chicka? Dinner with me, then the game tonight?" she asks, Jess coming up behind her and wrapping his arms around her body, pulling her close. Everything about them is so easy. I hate them for it right now.

"Uh, I don't know...I was gonna go with Owen somewhere, but..." I stand on my toes, looking around, but I don't see his truck anywhere. I pull my phone from my pocket, hoping there's a message. But there's nothing. "I don't see him, so he must have gotten busy."

I say these words, but what my gut feels is that he forgot. It hurts, but I can't get mad, because I've seen what life is like inside his house.

I follow Willow and Jess to Willow's car, and we all climb inside, me taking the small seat in the back. I pull my phone to my hand and watch the screen, waiting for a message from Owen, for anything.

"Burgers?" she says over her shoulder.

"Yeah...that's fine," I say, not hungry in the least. We head to Joe's Burgers, and as we pull into the parking lot, I swipe my screen and open a message to Owen. I want him to know where I am.

I probably want him to feel badly about it, too. It's selfish.

You weren't here, so I left with Willow. We're grabbing dinner.

I keep the phone clutched in my hand, waiting for it to buzz, and the instant I feel it, I step up out of the line for food.

"It's Owen. I'm not that hungry, so I'll wait for you guys out in the car," I say to Willow, her eyes focusing on me harshly for a few seconds before finally giving me her keys.

"I know. I'm not being careful," I roll my eyes. Willow knows a little about what happened with James, but I would never be able to give her the full picture. You can't understand unless you live through something like that—see it for yourself. I start reading Owen's message before I get to the car.

Shit, so sorry. Time got away from me. I came home to check on James. Mom had an appointment. Can I come get you? Where are you?

I text him back quickly.

I'm at Joe's. I'll wait out front.

I rush back inside and find Willow sitting at one of the window-counter tables, her feet swinging back and forth underneath—so carefree.

"Owen's coming to get me," I say to her, dropping the keys on her tray and moving my phone into the side pocket of my bag.

She grabs the keys and slides them in her jacket pocket, but she keeps her eyes on me the whole time. She hasn't actually said anything. In fact, she's been nothing but supportive. But that look she gives me makes my stomach feel sick, like I'm letting her down, letting myself down, breaking rules meant to be followed.

"What?" I sigh, unable to take it any longer. Willow's lips part, but she doesn't speak, instead her teeth catch the tip of her tongue and her lips roll into a soft smile, one that tries to erase every message her eyes have been giving me.

"Will, come on," I say, sliding into the seat next to her, my eyes shifting between the driveway out front and her. "Tell me now, before Owen gets here."

She breathes in long and slow, through her nose, filling her lungs. I know that breath—it's the one used for courage.

"Jess saw Owen buy drugs from a guy out in front of the movie theater last night," she says, letting her words fall out all in one breath, her body heaving forward with the loss of the weight of this secret. "Owen was with House. Jess said he couldn't tell what it was, but he could tell it wasn't something...well, something normal. It was really weird, and Owen didn't look right, and...he's been smoking. I see him smoking with House in the morning, behind the school. Did you know he smoked? I know...I know; it's not that big of a deal. It's just...I didn't know he smoked, and now I'm wondering what else he does. And his brother..."

She stops there, just short of accusing Owen of being an addict too.

I stare at her with my mouth a little open, my eyes wide, my brain working to find a place to put everything she just said—to file it and make sense out of it. I want to argue with her, tell her she's wrong, what Jess saw is wrong.

But I can't.

Then I see Owen's truck pull up outside behind her.

"I...I have to go," I shake my head, standing and trying to wake myself from the shock. "I...I don't know. I'll see you at the game. But I've gotta go."

She doesn't speak, and I leave before we even have a chance to look at one another again. I carry this new twisted feeling right into the truck cab with Owen, slamming the door closed, shivering from the outside air and the cold feeling still lingering inside his truck.

"I'm so sorry," he says, shifting into drive quickly and peeling out of the lot. I smile and buckle up, then I sniff for any sign of cigarettes, alcohol—*anything.*

"How's James?" I ask.

"Same," he says, his usual, one-word answer. He's chewing gum, and I can't help but overanalyze that now. I've never seen him chew gum—at least, I don't think I have? His mannerisms are nervous, almost jittery, and I find myself noting every single twitch. I'm staring at him, and he keeps glancing with his periphery, never fully giving me his eyes.

"Something wrong?" he asks finally, his arms working to turn his steering wheel onto the highway. The truck swerves with his jerk on the wheel as another car veers into our lane. Owen presses his hand hard on the horn, his fist pounding on the window as we fly by the other car. "Fucking asshole!" he screams.

My pulse is drumming throughout my entire body from adrenaline, and I keep my hands gripped around the material of my seatbelt, my palms sweaty now despite the quickly dropping temperature. Owen seems to have forgotten his question of me—or maybe he no longer cares. I don't dare bring it up, instead holding on for dear life and watching out the front windshield as we pass exit after exit, finally getting to ours.

His grandfather lives in a home that's been converted from one of the old farmhouses on the edge of town. The gravel drive is slushy from the rain and snow. There are two wheelchairs on the front porch as well as a plush seating set and a space heater. The home seems old, but it's painted nicely, and it looks like it's cared for. When we step from the truck, I scurry to the front and reach my hand forward, expecting Owen's to meet mine.

But it doesn't.

He stuffs his hands into his front pockets of his coat and walks up the path to the door, spitting his gum out into the rocks along the way.

My heart aches from his cold shoulder, and I feel the dark shadow overpowering us.

Owen rings a bell, and a woman answers, her hair pulled under a bright orange cloth. Her accent is thick, and it sounds Polish. She welcomes us inside, and hugs Owen, his rigid muscles softening under her touch. I'm grateful for whatever her embrace just did.

She welcomes us in; Owen takes my coat. There's a fire and a few people sitting in chairs watching TV. The room is warm and inviting, but the people in there feel lifeless, their faces lost somewhere in the past, their vision not quite focusing on the screen. Any activity happening around them isn't real to them at all. As homey as this place feels, it feels equally as sad.

I follow Owen to a room down the hall, and he knocks twice before turning the knob.

"Hey, Grandpa," he says, his body puffing up again with stress, his shoulders stiff and his breath held.

"Is that you, Relish?" An old man stands slowly from a sitting chair that's facing the window, leaning forward three times before finally getting enough strength to get to his feet. He reaches for the cane propped up against the table next to him then slides a pair of glasses on his face, his head covered in one of those plaid hats that snap in the front.

"It's me. I brought a friend. I'd like you to meet Kensi, Grandpa," Owen says, his voice no longer hard and angry, everything about him softening, as if his grandfather is a flame to his ice.

"Oh, yes...yes...Kensi. This is the one, the girl you...the metronome, right?" Owen's grandpa says, his feet shuffling forward, his weight being assisted by Owen's hold on him. I meet them in the middle of the room and look to Owen, whose eyes flit to me briefly with a smile. It disappears just as fast.

"Yes, Grandpa. That's the one," Owen says.

I reach my hand out, and Owen's grandpa squeezes it in between both of his. His skin is dry, and his hands are cold. His gray eyes are cloudy, and I wonder how old he is. "Well, aren't you lovely," he says, his smile so much like Owen's that I can't help but giggle a little seeing it.

"Thank you, sir," I say.

"Call me Gus. Tell me, Kensi...do you like Rosemary?" he asks, and I look to Owen for help. He shrugs and steps back as his grandfather hands over his cane and slides toward a small dresser against the far wall.

"I guess so..." I say, wondering what he means. Every step he takes is small and cautious, and his hands hover out in front of him, shaking a little. I slide closer, my hands ready to catch him, but when I look to Owen, he just winks and gives a small shake of his head. Gus pulls a record from a paper sleeve on top of his dresser, then lifts the lid on an old turntable sitting next to it, leaning forward, his hand shaking with the weight of the player's needle and arm. He drops it down with careful precision on the record's edge, and soon, soft music spills out into the room.

It's Rosemary Clooney. I recognize it immediately, and it makes me chuckle. "You know, not many people your age appreciate things like this. But I had a feeling you might. Owen says you're quite the musician," he says, reaching both hands out, his fingers twitching, calling me closer to him.

"*White Christmas* is my favorite," I smile, and Gus pauses, raising his plump chin toward me before turning to glance at his grandson.

"Did you hear that, Relish? This one's got good taste," he says, turning back and taking one of my hands and then the other. He holds my arms out to the sides and begins to sway me slowly from side to side, his chest humming along with the tune crackling from his record player.

"Why do you call him Relish?" I ask, catching a glance of Owen over his grandfather's shoulder. He's standing in the bedroom doorway, his head leaning against the frame, both of our coats draped over his arm while he watches his grandfather dance with me. His chest rises once with a short laugh when I ask about his nickname, his hand rubbing his face, then resting over his mouth, hiding what I think is a smile.

I wish he weren't hiding it. I'd give just about anything to see Owen smile.

"Shall I tell her?" Gus asks.

"I couldn't stop you, could I?" Owen says back.

"Ha...I guess not," he says, letting go of one of my hands and encouraging me to spin out and then back to his arms. "This one summer, when Owen was little, maybe four or five, before Bill died, we went to a lot of ballgames out in Kane County. Owen would beg us to take him. But then he'd get there, and the little bugger couldn't sit still. So...I started making a deal with this kid; I said that any time he could pick the winner in the hotdog, ketchup, and relish race, I'd give him a quarter. He picked *relish* every time. But what's weird, is relish *won*...every single time!"

I look back over my shoulder to Owen. With lips tight, he shrugs, his smile faint, maybe a little sad. Memories seem to do that to him.

"Well, this little son-of-a-gun, he found out that the announcers only had one video to show on the board, with *one* outcome. After about six dollars in quarters, I asked the ticket man about it and he told me. He's been *Relish* ever since," Gus says, a sense of fondness in his voice, despite the way his laugh taunts and teases.

"Yep, that's me. Relish," Owen says, his voice more distant. "Hey, I'll be back in just a minute. Take care of her, okay Gramps?"

Gus spins me away from him one more time, then brings me back, waving his hand to send his grandson off. Owen steps away from the door, back in the direction of the main room. Before he turns, I notice his brow pulled in, a deep wrinkle at the bridge of his nose.

"Have I told you about Grace yet?" Gus says, his gravelly voice so thick he has to pause our dance and reach into his front pocket for his handkerchief to cover his mouth as he coughs.

"I don't believe so," I say, wondering if this is going to spin into another interesting story about Owen's youth. I wish he enjoyed hearing them and sharing them more.

"Ah, Gracie. I met her at the Apple Festival, ya know," he says, and I can't help but smile when I realize he's talking about his wife. "She used to date one of the Wilson boys, the family that owned the orchard?"

I nod.

"Huh," he chuckles. "She would have made a mint in life if she just stayed with that fella. Those boys made millions off that land. Sold hundreds of acres to developers."

"I bet she was happy with her life just as it was," I say, spinning myself out for a turn during our dance now. I've only known him for five minutes, and already I think I would be willing to marry Owen's grandfather.

"Maybe so...maybe so," he says, a shadow of sorrow falling over his eyes, his posture sinking a little. "I spent ten cents on a kissing booth to kiss her. We were schoolmates, and I loved her my entire life. Let's just say when I kissed her, I didn't stop when the guy said time was up. He had to pull me away. But Gracie, she never kissed another man after that. We were married in the spring."

Gus steps back from me, reaching for the edge of his bed, so I move with him to make sure he finds his seat safely. He looks a little uneasy on his legs. "Are you sure you haven't heard this story before?" he asks, his eyes glossier than they were a moment ago. He's fumbling with his hands, his fingers working for his pocket, pulling out his handkerchief again, then reaching for the small glasses hanging from a chain around his neck.

"I'm sure," I say, my voice soft. I'm not positive how best to answer him.

"Oh, baby girl. I miss you," he says, and I can see actual tears forming at the edge of his eyes as he looks at me. Gus is confused. I recognize it. My grandfather had dementia, and often thought I was my mom. I can see what's coming; I am good at this terrible game of pretend. "Did I tell you Gracie died? Her funeral was so sad. Your mama was the prettiest girl in town."

I hear Owen slip in, and I turn to look at him, unable to mask my concern and sadness.

"This is Kensi, Gramps. You just met her," Owen says. He looks over the few books out on his grandfather's side table, surveying the room without making it look like he's snooping. Sadly, I recognize this too. My mom used to have to search my grandfather's room for stashes of untaken pills.

"Right, sorry. It's getting late. I get confused sometimes. I think maybe it's time for my medicine," he says, trying to stand. Owen puts his hand on his shoulder and smiles.

"I'll get Emma for you," he says, nodding to me to follow. We dip into the hall, and the woman who let us in is coming with a small box and a glass of water. She slips into the room with us and doles out a red pill, carefully handing Gus the glass of water and waiting while he drinks it down.

She smiles at us again, her lips never quite making the full curve though, then she whispers something to Owen, both of them looking at each other with a certain heaviness. When she leaves, Owen reaches for his grandpa's hand, giving it a squeeze. "I'll be back again in a day or two, Gramps. I promise," he says, leaning forward and kissing his grandfather on the forehead. I notice the nice leather shoes in the corner, the ones that used to belong to my father, and it makes me smile. They are in a far more deserving place, being worn by a far more deserving man.

Gus sits perched at the end of his bed, his gaze drifting off to the quiet happening outside his window, and Owen and I move to his door.

"You take care of my baby girl now, you hear Billy?" Gus says, his eyes never veering from the window.

"I promise," Owen says. What seems such a simple gesture, pretending to be someone he's not, is so far from that. Owen stepped into his nightmare just to let his grandfather live in a dream for a minute.

Another glance is exchanged between Emma and Owen as we leave, and when we reach the porch steps, I feel the darkness wrangle a hold of Owen even more. Everything about right now feels cold—more frozen than the ice beginning to frost the ground.

Owen walks to my door first, holding it open for me to climb inside, and he stays there long enough to close the door for me. It's gentlemanly, but it's also very robotic. When he gets to his side, his face is completely void of any emotion—he's wiped himself clean. He fires the engine and pulls away, his tires kicking up rocks as he pulls out of the long drive with too much speed. It makes me nervous, and I reach forward, gripping the dashboard's edge with one hand. Owen's eyes dart to my hand, and he sighs heavily, never really slowing down.

We drive in silence for a few minutes, the only sound the clicking repetition of the blinker while Owen waits to enter the highway.

"I'm sorry," I say softly, wanting to show him how much I understand, how bad I feel, how I know how much it hurts—those memories, his grandfather's illness, being called his *father*.

"Don't," he says quickly. Softly.

Cold.

Everything. Cold.

I keep my mouth shut for the rest of the trip, but my inner voice makes up for everything I don't say. I question it all. Question what Willow told me, what others said about Owen. I think about the warnings. I think about his brother, about his father, about his grandfather.

And I question everything I've felt. I still feel it though. And that's the problem. I want to scream at him, punch him, kick him and hurt him physically. I want him to feel the pain this frustration is causing me. But I love him too. And the only conclusion is that something must be wrong inside of me to feel this way. Loving Owen Harper is dangerous; yet I can't help myself.

"Why did you even ask me to go with you?" I ask finally, my voice shouting from the frustration of being stifled for so long. We're pulling into the school parking lot, and the sun is setting. Owen's mouth is in a hard line, his forearm muscles flexing. His head covered in his black beanie, hiding.

Always. Fucking. Hiding!

"You heard me!" I say, pulling my seatbelt from my chest before the truck comes to a stop near the bottom of the hill. He punches the brake to be cruel, and I fly forward, catching myself with my arms, bruising my elbow against the hard plastic of his dashboard. He never looks at me—not once.

"Why did you ask me to come if you didn't want me here?" I repeat my question, one hand braced on the seat, the other on the door handle. Owen is shaking his head, his eyes staring at the center of his steering wheel.

"I have no idea," he says, his voice an eerie calm, his head shaking with a breathy laugh. When his eyes move back to me, I see everything that's left inside him...and in a flash, it all falls away.

Owen. Is. Gone.

I slam his door shut, and turn, walking fast down the walkway to the band room, willing myself to look ahead. But I'm counting. I count every step I take that I don't hear Owen's truck shift—that I don't hear his engine rev, that I don't hear his tires squeal. I get to seventeen before I hear him disappear. I turn, only to see dust, his taillights faint as he whips around the corner.

"Goddamnit!" I yell, my stupid rebellion echoing off of the concrete walls around me. I yell because I'm alone. And I cry. I cry fast and hard, ducking into the shadows of the small outside stairwell. I hide there until the pressure of everything leaves—or at least until I'm able to hide it. All I'm left with is the sharp pain in my chest.

I avoid Willow and Jess during warm-ups, and I busy myself in a conversation with a freshman in the band, a girl I don't think I've ever talked to before. She's telling me about her dance class, and how she learned some sort of hip-hop move. She's excited to do it with her friends at the dance tonight.

She's so happy. Right now, right this second, I would trade places with her.

I didn't want to go to this dance before, *not really* at least. And now, I *really* don't want to go. But I don't want to go home either. I'm caught in hell.

It's the last game of the year, which means we don't have to wear uniforms. They're all being cleaned for competition next week, so I get to keep my hair up, to stay in my stupid flirty outfit—the one I wore hoping Owen would see me and change his mind, that he'd want to go with me.

Stupid girl. I'm such a stupid girl.

This is the same guy who put on a performance every day at lunch with a different girl, the same guy who provoked me with his flirtatious threats. This is the guy who cheats death, who actually seeks it out so he can laugh at that fine line—crossing it from time to time just to prove he can, other times, erasing it completely. My lips must be moving while I talk to myself, while I laugh silently about how crazy it is to think that Owen Harper wants to go to a school dance.

"You okay?" Jess asks, his voice low. He's trying to hide his question from Willow, and I'm glad.

"Nope," I say honestly, sucking in a deep breath to keep the tears where they belong, the sting coming back to the corners of my eyes.

"Owen?" he asks, tapping his drumsticks along his jean-covered leg.

"Yep," I say, watching him tap out a rhythm.

"Sorry," he says, moving his hands over to my lap and tapping the sticks on my shoes, my feet folded up as we sit on the floor. He plays out an entire song, and it makes me smile. He's distracting me, for a few seconds. I'll take this.

When Willow comes over to hold her hand out and lift me to a stand, I look at Jess, my eyes flashing a warning, and he closes his eyes with a quick smile. I know he won't say anything, and I'm going to pretend I'm fine.

I'm fine. I'm fine. I'm fine.

I walk with Willow to the field, a few of the band parents taking care of our equipment for us tonight, pushing my xylophone down the hill. I listen while she tells me about the dances at this school, how they usually go. I let her fill every second of empty air, and when I feel the conversation start to end, I ask her another question, and she begins again.

Our team is almost winning the game, which helps keep us all excited and invested. More blank space filled. If only I drove myself...I'd shove my hand down my throat right now to make myself throw up so I could go home, play *sick.* But Willow's so damned excited about this dance; I couldn't make her miss it just to take me home.

And again—home isn't much better.

The clock runs out, and our team actually wins. It's our first win, so students rush the field. You would think we just earned a play-off berth rather than a record of one and nine. I turn my attention to my things, to the long dark hill of the parking lot.

246

That's when I notice the souped-up, lifted pickup in the distance. I see the glow of his cigarette in the dark, and the glare is just enough to spotlight the two girls standing with him—one of them leaning into him, hanging on his arm.

I keep sneaking looks at him as we file down the bleachers, and I don't even hear Willow talking to me when she finally yanks on the sleeve of my sweater, jerking my body hard toward her.

"Where the hell are you?" she says, her eyes scrunched, her lips flat in a straight line. She follows my gaze to House in the distance, then turns to me again. "It's just House," she sighs.

"I know," I say back, my eyes still on him, my response barely a response at all. I watch as a few more people join him at the end of the parking lot. It's the regular crew. Everyone. Everyone but...

"Owen," she says, getting my full attention.

"Where?" I ask, looking around the lot, trying to find him.

"This...*you*. How you're acting," she says. "This is about Owen."

I keep my eyes on hers, unable to blink. I don't even know how to articulate what's wrong, but something is just...*wrong*. And it won't feel right again until I see him.

"I have to go," I say, my eyes still wide on hers. I'm begging her with them.

"This is what I meant," she says.

"I know," I say, looking back at the crowd of shadows, the faint sound of roaring laughter and House's voice in the distance. "But it's different, Will. I can't explain it, but I just know it's different."

"Whatever," she says, her eyes rolling as she turns to walk away from me.

"Willow, please..." I start, but she holds up a hand, her pace steady, toward Jess. I feel like a lousy friend. I feel selfish. I am selfish, because all I want is my Owen back, the sweet one—the guy who sat on the piano bench with me and forced me to remember things I loved.

The *Owen* I love.

I pull my arms around my body tightly, my hands nearly numb from the cold. My coat is in the band room. But I can't risk going to get it now. House—he might be gone by then.

He doesn't see me coming at first, and I pick up on hints of their conversation as I approach.

"Sasha is such a fucking skank," one girl says, pulling the cigarette from House's hands and putting it between her lips, dragging in slowly and letting a smooth trail of smoke stream from her lips as her chin tilts up to the sky.

"You're just jealous," says another girl.

"Whatev. I could be like her, totally hold some party so I could fuck Owen Harper," she says, handing the cigarette back to House, leaning forward toward her girlfriend. "But I don't need to...*been there, bitches!*"

The other girl laughs loudly in response. They saw me coming, and that conversation was for my benefit. This morning, it might have been enough. But tonight, my issues with Owen are so much bigger than some girl trying to make me jealous. I'm close enough now that House notices me coming, too.

"Ken Doll," he says loudly, an exaggerated laugh coming from the girl sharing his cigarette. "You ditching the punch bowl in the gym for some real shit?" He holds a bag out toward me, several rolled joints weighing it down. His eyes stay on mine with a heavy stare—he's trying to provoke me. But he has something I need, so I ignore his efforts.

"Where is he?" I ask. He pushes the bag back into the front of his sweatshirt, then drops his cigarette to the ground. The girl sitting next to him pouts, so he leans over and kisses her hard, his hand running up her leg and stomach until he's squeezing her tit in front of everyone.

That was for me, too.

"Get in the truck, baby," he says to the girl, and she slides from his hood, dragging her hand over his crotch while she walks by, her gaze on me the entire time. She thinks she's marking her territory. She can fucking have House.

He steps forward, his heavy black shoes stomping the glowing ash into the pavement, then he spits to the side before bringing his eyes to me.

"He'll be at Sasha's," he says, his smirk lingering. I wait for him to offer more, to say something more. But instead, he smiles—that stupid fucking obnoxious smile that's only halfway really there—his eyes barely slits, sleepy from whatever he's been drinking or smoking. I don't care how long he's known Owen—House is a dick.

"Give me your keys," I say, and he leans back, looking up to the sky, laughing hard once.

"If you wanna ride, get your ass in the truck. But I ain't giving you my fuckin' keys," he says, holding them on his thumb in front of me before clutching them. I stare at him, daring him. But House isn't Owen; he honestly doesn't have a line between right and wrong.

"Fine," I huff, brushing by him, giving his body a hard jab with my elbow as I pass. I climb in through the driver's side and slide to the middle, the girl waiting inside staring at me with a look as though I've just made her drink bleach.

"Who the fuck are you?" she says, her breath practically flammable. I look her right in the eyes, then turn to face the front, my mouth never once breaking its hard line. I just need to survive ten or fifteen miles.

House climbs into the truck and starts the engine quickly, my hands still feeling his seat for a belt as he rounds the corner and peels out of the parking lot.

"I don't have belts. Just hold on and keep your mouth shut," he says, rolling his window down at the stoplight and leaning out yelling something to another car pulling up next to us. The rest of the people that were with their group are packed into an old Bronco, and when one of the guys flips House off and speeds by, he punches the gas fast without even thinking, running the red light right behind his friend, swerving us into the middle lane to regain his lead.

The dodging and darting for position happens between every stoplight until we get to the edge of town, when House finally punches the gas hard, his engine growling as we speed away from his friend, toward Sasha's house, toward darkness. My hands are gripping the undersides of my legs hard, trying to keep my heart from bursting with fear, my stomach sour with

249

adrenaline. I hold my breath for minutes at a time, saying silent prayers to a god I've never talked to before—the pounding in my chest actually painful by the time we slide into the dirt driveway of Sasha's house.

Four or five other cars are out front, and the thumping of the music echoes around us. I don't hear any people, though, which only makes me feel less sure about the place I've stranded myself—about what I'll see when I get inside. House exits the truck first, then holds the door open and nods his head rigidly, urging me to hurry.

I slide out, my hand accidentally pressing on the horn as I pass the steering wheel, and House winces.

"Fuck," he says, pulling my arm, his squeeze on me rough. He slams the door closed once I clear it. He meets the other girl at the front of the truck, reaching his hand into the waistband at the top of her jeans, his hand on her actual ass.

I trail behind everyone, entering the house last. Everything is exactly as I remember it. The lights dim, the drone of music drowns almost everything else. People are gathered around the couch and floor, smoking something from a liter bottle. A few others are pouring drinks at the kitchen counter while others make out in dark corners around the house.

My turn is slow, my eyes careful to catch every face, every outline, weeding out each profile that's not Owen. But I don't have to find him. He finds me, his voice haunting, his words harsh—if not indifferent.

"What are you doing here?" he says, the sound barely audible over the loudness of the music. His tone isn't angry. It isn't curious.

It's nothing.

I step into the sitting room, toward the beanbag chair he's sunken into, the familiar clear glass propped between his fingers on his knee.

"Decided the dance sounded lame," I say, taking the seat across from him, leaning back into the softness, letting my arms fold across my chest, like a shield.

Owen keeps his eyes on me, and I let my mouth relax finally, but I don't smile—and I don't breathe. He pushes the plastic glass to his lips, the space between the vodka and his mouth paper-thin, then pulls it away, instead tossing it into the fire next to us—igniting a short burst within the flames.

"Have enough tonight?" I ask, the tightness in my chest relaxing with every second I'm here with Owen and he's quiet.

"Something like that," he says, his eyes lost somewhere off to the side. I want to get up; I want to move to him, to hold him and kiss him—to make him remember how he felt a week ago. But I'm so afraid of scaring him, of offending him—of the *other* Owen. So I wait, and I stare into the flames, catching glimpses of him from the side, waiting for him to move, to shift his eyes from whatever thought is holding him.

"My brother's gone," he says, his voice monotone, his gaze still on the blankness of the wall beyond me. "When I went home to check on him..." his head finally shifts, just enough, his eyes finding me—*finally.* "He. Was. Gone."

"I'm sorry," I say, still holding myself to my place, fearful of disrupting our connection, afraid he'll close this door right back up. Owen is in a cycle. His family is in a cycle, but Owen more so than anybody else. And it's killing him. I've watched it strip life from him in a matter of weeks.

"I wish he would just O.D. already," he says, his words flowing with a small laugh, one he quickly hides, ashamed of it. But I know that laughter, it's not the happy kind, it's the kind that tries to hide pain, hide the need to cry.

He keeps his eyes fixed on me, but not my face, almost as if he's not strong enough to look me in the eye. He watches my hands as I rub my arms, my body still cold from the ride here in House's truck.

"You're cold," he says, sliding his coat from the floor over to me. I lean forward and grab it, wrapping it around my body. I mouth the words *thank you*, and Owen nods.

"You drive yourself here?" he asks, his eyes coming to mine in fits, dropping away quickly.

I shake my head *no.* "I came with House," I say.

"You shouldn't have," he says, biting his tongue, his lips perched to say more, his mouth working to speak, but no sound coming out for several seconds. "I just meant it wasn't safe…not…not that you shouldn't have come," he says, his eyes coming to mine again, holding longer this time.

"Jess said he saw you smoking," I say, regretting it instantly, Owen's gaze quickly falling away. He shrugs. "You…you smoke?"

He shrugs again, and it feels empty. It makes *me* feel empty. I've never seen him smoke. I've never tasted it on him. He told me his only vice was drinking. Drinking…and death.

"Just a few times…" he says finally, his head to the side. His eyes lost again to the flames. "Only recently. It calms me."

I've seen Owen angry. He embraces it, lets it fuel him and carry him through anything. He's fearless. But this Owen is far from angry. He's beyond sadness.

"He says you bought drugs, too. Was that just about being angry, too?" I say, my hands squeezing my biceps, my arms hugging my chest tighter, my frustration building. This question, it seems to stir something, and Owen leans forward slowly, his eyes dark as his hands meet one another in front of him, his knuckles popping one at a time.

"Is this you trusting me? You get your friends to spy on me, spread rumors and come back to you with dirty little secrets?" he asks, the corner of his mouth twitching as his tongue wets the edges of his lip.

"Is it a lie?" I ask, looking at him with the same strength he's showing, not backing away from his challenge. I wait, and Owen waits to. Never answering.

After what feels like a minute, he leans back, his hands folded behind his neck. "James needed more of that shit your mom gave him. We don't have insurance, so I bought it off the street. House knows a guy," he says, his head leaning to the side again, but his eyes still fixed on me.

His answer stabs me in the heart, and I feel horrible for doubting him. The silence takes over again, choking me, and my chest burns. I don't know how to fix this, how to fix any of this.

"You get what you came for?" he asks finally, and I let the silence take over again, my mouth unable to work, and my mind unable to build words to say. The way Owen's looking at me— it's as though I fit into his collection of disappointments, and I don't know how this happened, and it's breaking me in front of him. The muscles in my legs are firing with the want to move, trying to help my heart escape this place before I show him what he's done, how easily he's destroyed me.

But I can't move.

As much as he's hurting me right now, he also owns me. And I let the tear slide down my face slowly without wiping it away. I let Owen see—I let him see inside.

"Why did you take me to see your grandpa today?" I ask, the same question I asked earlier, the one he never fully answered.

Our eyes lock, and I choke down the desire to blink away the water building in mine, giving Owen everything I have left. I wait. And I wait. The fire snapping, the sound of my breathing heavy in my own ears, the thumping of the music a room away, fading to a dull drumming pattern. I'm in a tunnel, Owen the only thing I see, and inside I'm screaming for him to give in, to feel something, to let himself *feel* anything other than wronged and cursed. Owen shrugs finally, his lip lifting the tiniest hint.

He's mocking me.

With one look, he breaks me, and the tears threatening to fall find the heat of my cheeks. My eyes flutter, almost feeling sleepy from the hammering of emotions tearing into me. I stand to my feet, listening to that voice inside that has been begging me to leave since the moment I slid into House's truck. My feet take three steps away from Owen, pausing while I shut my eyes. I ball my hands into fists and push them against my face. *Stop crying, stop crying, stop crying*... I can hear my own voice in my head, and even in my thoughts, I am torn and in pieces. I turn slowly, filling my lungs with one final inhale. I find Owen's eyes quickly, everything behind them empty—lost.

"And here I thought it was because you loved me," I confess, my chest caving in quickly, threatening to cut me off from saying the rest. I let it tumble out with my last breath. "Just as much as I love you."

I let my words hit him, my body still, my thumbnails digging into the palms of my hands—a subconscious effort to create pain anywhere else, to pull this feeling away from my heart. Owen never even moves.

Before the next wave crashes over me, I turn away, stepping over the sweaters and shoes thrown on the floor. I catch House's eyes on me from the kitchen, his mouth smirking, like he's satisfied at my failure to pull Owen back to the light. I pick up my pace, not wanting anyone else to notice me, to see how pathetic I am.

I barely open the door as I slip outside, and when I do, I'm hit with a wall of wind, air so cold it practically slices through me. I pull Owen's coat tightly around me, hating that it's his, that I need it, but thankful for it. I take lunging steps out into the driveway, through the gravel, past House's truck first, then Owen's, until my feet find the pavement of the small two-lane road that brought me here. I can see my breath, and the threat of more snow is very real. I know I can't walk home. It would very likely kill me. But I can't stay here.

I won't.

I pull my phone from my pocket, the few dollars I folded along with it coming out and falling to the ground. "Shit!" I say to myself, bending down and feeling for them, my hands stinging. I grip them clumsily, but stay low, squatting, while I scroll to Willow's number, knowing there's a really good chance she won't pick up. My thumb hovers over her number for a few seconds before my phone lights up, ringing with a call.

Owen.

I stare at the phone, not knowing what to do, then after three rings, his call disappears. Panic swallows me whole, and I drop my money again, my fingers fumbling to call him back when I look up and see him walking swiftly toward me. It takes him three steps more to reach me, his hands clutching my arms. At first I think he's angry, and I flinch at his touch. But he brings me to his chest, the weight of his body working to shelter me. His hand cradles my head against him, and he only holds me harder when I begin to cry, my body shaking hard with each shudder.

My core is starting to shiver from the cold, and Owen scoops me into his arms, holding me against him as he strides quickly to his truck, opening the passenger side and setting me inside, closing the door quickly, and running to the other side. He gets in fast, starting the engine and moving the heat to high, then slides

254

across the middle of the bench seat toward me, his hands cradling my face, his fingers rough, and cold.

"I brought you because I love you," he says, his words coming out in a rush, his eyes piercing mine, the darkness fighting with the light. "I wanted you to meet him because he's important to me...and so are you...because I love you. I hurt you...because I love you...because I'm fucked up, my family's fucked up, and my problems ruin everyone they touch. I don't know how to stop them, how to separate the good things from all the shit in my life. I ruin everyone I touch. People leave me...they leave me—" Owen's breath catches, stuttering, his eyes turning redder as he talks. "People in my life...they die, and if they aren't dead yet, they look for ways to kill themselves. And all I can do is watch."

"Owen," I whisper, my hands wrapping around his wrists. His head falls forward to mine.

"I love you, Kensi," he says, his lips grazing mine softly, before he pulls his mouth away again, leaving his head against mine. "I love you...but I will suffocate you. Drown you. Loving me...it will kill you."

"No, it won't," I say, my hands shaking his wrists. His fingers are still cupping my face, his thumbs trailing tiny circles along my jaw. He rolls his head side-to-side along mine, his breath coming out in a slow spill, his body full of nothing but fear and doubt.

I slide my hands up his wrists, to his fingers, threading mine through his along my cheeks then bringing them to my lips, kissing them, and letting my lips linger along his knuckles before resting my cheek against his palm. My touch finally opens his eyes, and I look into him, searching for my Owen, making him believe.

"I love you, and I'm not afraid to love you," I say. I can see the worry behind his eyes, the warnings working to remind him that he should run, that he shouldn't feel. I can tell I'm not winning the battle, but I'm fighting the war, and every piece of me I give weakens that fear a little more.

"I shouldn't let you," he says, his bottom lip held under his teeth, his breath a sharp intake. "But I don't care, Kensi. Because

I think I need you to survive. I think I need you to love me, because that's literally all I've got."

My hands wrap through his hair, grasping at the back of his head and neck, pulling him to me. Owen's hands are just as needy, our mouths crashing together hard and fast—this kiss, it's more than all others. We both hang onto it, neither one of us ending it.

I kiss Owen until the sun threatens to come up. And after he drives me home, I kiss him again, with the same sense of urgency. My father's car is gone; it's a concert night, so my world in my house is safe until tomorrow. I'd be content to stay here, though—in the driveway, in Owen's truck, kissing him. When my lips are on his, I know he's here.

When I finally steal myself away, the worry creeps in again, so I run up the stairs, into my room, collapsing by my window. Owen's truck is empty outside, and seconds later, his eyes are on me, his body where it should be, his smile finding its way.

Please, God, don't let me lose him again.

Chapter 18

I'm not sure whether or not Willow meant to text me the photo of her and Elise, smiling happily under the glow of a plastic disco ball. But I'm glad she did.

Her photo was waiting for me on my phone this morning as I woke up, and I texted back immediately, gushing about how cute they looked, how much fun I bet they had.

I wouldn't have traded my night for theirs for all of the disco balls in the world. I'd even live through the hurt and pain of the beginning again to end up with Owen telling me he loves me.

Yeah, well...the picture would have been cuter if there were three of us in it. Beeyatch.

Her attempt to call me a *bitch* makes me laugh.

You can't even spell it right, that's how I know you're not really mad at me. If you were, that bitch would be full of 'I'.

I hold my phone in my palms, my head under my covers, the morning light fading into afternoon. I slept hard and well, asleep at my window by three, then crawling up to my bed at six with a crick in my neck.

Bitch.

She sends the single word, and at first it shocks me, and I think she might actually be mad. But she writes again quickly.

You're right. That felt dirty. Lose the 'I'.

I laugh to myself, and smile, rolling to my side just enough to peer out the window to see if my mother's car is gone. It is. She has the long shift today, which means I'll be free of my father, too. No homework or projects are on my plate, the school semester winding down as Thanksgiving approaches, and James is gone. I know the worry of where he went is there, but the duty of caring for him isn't. I'm hoping—at least for the day—that Owen will be mine.

Everything...okay?

Willow's text is cautious. She's trying to be supportive, though I know that's not how she really feels.

He said he loves me.

I tell her because I'm happy. And because she's the only person in the world I would want to tell. I think, somehow, telling her this will make her see Owen differently. I know it does when my phone rings a second later.

"You're shitting me," she says. No *hello* or pause to wait for me to answer.

"I'm not really sure how to answer that," I say, "but *no*? I guess? Or *yes*, he loves me?"

There's a pop of her gum over the phone, and I hear her keys jingle in her hand. "I'm at the mall. This is serious, and I'm at the mall. Buying shoes. And there are all these people around talking, and I can't hear you very well," she's speaking a million words a minute. It's funny.

"I will give you a play-by-play later. I promise. Go buy your shoes," I laugh.

"Okay, but first...you said it back, right?" she says with a small pause in the middle. She's still worried about me.

"I did," I say. I said it *first*, not that the order matters.

There's silence on her end, and I can hear her moving through the door to another store, the faint noise of other conversations in the background.

"So listen," she starts, and I wait as the phone shuffles some more, and eventually the background noise fades, and her voice echoes. "I'm sorry I walked away from you. I was being overbearing and protective, and it's not really my place. But..."

"Are you in a bathroom?" I ask, really noticing the echo now.

"Yes, I had to pee. Now don't cut me off," she says, picking right up where she stopped. "Just promise you'll talk to him, about those things I said, what Jess saw."

My lips hover, barely parted, and ready to answer, but instead I close them, nodding. "I will," I say finally. I'm satisfied with the answers Owen gave me. But Willow, she'll be more satisfied if she thinks I had those conversations with him on her urging. She wants to be the *super* friend, and frankly, I've got an opening for one of those. I'd like to give her the job.

I hear the toilet auto flush in the background. "Okay, letting you go now," I say, holding the phone out from my ear.

"'Kay 'kay, call you later," she says, leaving her phone on as she stuffs it in her purse. I laugh to myself and hang up for her, but not after considering listening to her shoe shop for just a little while.

I've slept in, and I'm pretty sure Owen has too. His room looks dark, and his truck is out front. His mom is back on her regular work schedule, so I know the boys are home alone, which gives me an idea.

After a quick shower, I head to the kitchen and fry up the rest of the bacon left in our fridge. I scramble half a dozen eggs, then throw in some cheese and toss it all together in one of my mom's big spaghetti pots. I bundle myself, then bundle the pot in one of my mom's coats to keep it warm during the short walk across the yard. It takes Owen a few minutes to get to the door, and by the time he does, I'm shivering out front, the snow starting to fall with some strength now.

"You brought me...chili?" Owen asks, his eyes on the ridiculous pot I've bundled in a brown, fuzzy coat.

"It's bacon," I smile. "But if you don't want it, I could just..." I start to turn and Owen quickly snatches the pot from me. He teasingly tries to close the door after, but eventually pulls me inside quickly too.

Andrew stumbles down the stairs, his body long and awkward in nothing but a pair of pajama bottoms. He doesn't have his brother's build, and his youth is sweet, his chest a little boney and quite pale. He rubs his eyes, so much of him a little boy. Owen protects that part for him, so Andrew can savor it.

"Kensi brought bacon," Owen says, holding up the pot. The mere mention of the word wakes Andrew up completely, and we all move to the kitchen, where Owen pulls out three bowls and serves up my semi-omelet creation. I'm strangely satisfied watching them both eat.

"So now I owe you, what, like two meals?" Owen asks, his mouth full while he talks, one hand gripping the bowl, the other a spoon.

"You could just make it one *really* nice dinner," I say, folding my arms.

"Good," he smiles. "Done. Tonight, I make you a steak."

I laugh, but he steps to the side, reaching into his freezer and pulling out two frozen pieces of meat, tossing them in the sink to thaw.

"Oh, you were serious," I say, liking the idea of being here for dinner.

"Yep," he says, shoveling another giant forkful of egg and cheese into his mouth. "Andrew, you're going to Matt's house."

"Uh, I am?" Andrew says, and Owen drops his spoon in his bowl, holding both hands on the counter, looking at his brother, giving him *the* look. "Oh, yeah. That's right. I *totally* am. In fact, I'll call him right now, see if his sister can come pick me up. Oh, and in case you wondered, Kensi, yes, I do talk robotic like this sometimes. I'm not pretending at all for the sake of my brother getting you alone."

Owen flings a strip of bacon at his brother, and Andrew grabs it off the counter. "Do not...sacrifice bacon, O. You know better," he jokes, popping the bacon in his mouth before rinsing his bowl quickly and winking at me while he dashes around the corner and back up the stairs.

"I..." Owen starts, sliding his bowl into the sink too, along with mine. He moves closer to me, until he has me caged against the kitchen island, his lips starting at my neck and moving along my face, grazing my lips. "...want to spend the entire day doing nothing, but this."

"Oh...oh," I say, blushing. Owen doesn't stop kissing me, and within minutes, he has me slid up on the counter, his body positioned between my legs and his hands running up my back, under my shirt, pulling me closer to him.

"Ehem." We pause when we hear Andrew cough, and I duck my head into Owen's chest, embarrassed. "Matt's sister is on her way. Do you guys think maybe you could hold that shit off for like, oh, five minutes?"

Owen smirks at me, tipping my chin up to look at him, laughing at my shyness. "Nope," he says as his eyes meet mine. "We'll just take this shit upstairs. And you keep your mouth shut to Ma."

Owen scoops me up against him, carrying me backward piggyback style through the kitchen, past Andrew, and up the

260

stairs. I slap my hand to my face, hiding again as we pass his brother, but I'm glad we're alone the second Owen kicks his door closed.

I love the way his room smells. There's a faint leftover scent from his cologne, and there's a certain smell to his bed and clothes, something in the way he washes things. It's probably just fabric softener, but it's my favorite fabric softener in the world. I want to soak every bit of it up—and remember it forever.

Owen carries me right to his bed, kneeling and laying me down on my back, my head resting on his pillow and my body smothered in his messy blanket and sheets. I crawl underneath quickly, pushing my shoes from my feet and letting them drop off the side of the bed. Owen slips under the cover with me, pulling my body close, running his fingertips through my tangled, damp hair with an amused look on his face.

"I just showered," I smile, realizing I'm not very put together at all, even less than normal.

"I wish I was there when you did," Owen says, his lips finding my neck, teasing me. I cover my face with my hand, fighting against the redness taking over. "You blush so easily," he teases.

"I know," I admit.

Owen slides to his back, smoothing out the blanket over us and pulling me into him, letting me curl up onto his side. I can see the edge of my house through his window, and the thought that I was just sleeping over there, on the other side, strikes me. When Owen rubs along the back of my neck, massaging my sore muscles, I let out a small moan.

"Already, huh?" he teases.

"Nooooooo," I push at his side, but not enough to ruin the hold he has on my neck. It feels glorious. "My neck is killing me. I fell asleep at the window."

"I know," he says, his eyes grazing over my face, moving from my eyes to my mouth to my chin, then... "I watched you."

I love that he watches me.

"I'm so sorry, Kens...about yesterday," he starts, and I slide up his body and kiss him once, hard on the mouth, then press my fingers to his lips.

"Don't be," I say. We look into each other for several long seconds, our eyes skimming across each other's faces. How did I get so lucky? How did I get this boy to fall for me?

"I still love you, by the way," he says, his lip quirking on one side; his silly grin makes me melt. "For the record. Last night and today, still feel the same."

I nuzzle in close, letting my eyes concentrate on our tangled hands, the way they look together. I love watching his thumb run along my fingers, over the back of my hand.

"I really liked your grandpa," I say, wanting to focus on everything good from yesterday. Gus was good, and seeing Owen, his capacity to love—that felt good to see.

"Yeah, he's a lady killer. I was worried there for a minute when I left you alone with him. He's been known to steal a girl away from a guy," he says, his free hand finding my hair, drawing it out in long brushes of his fingers.

"Do you visit him often?" I ask. "I'd love to go again."

I feel Owen's breath let out, then his kiss presses lightly to the top of my head. "Not as often as I should," he says, his voice growing faint. "Might see him a whole lot more, though, real soon."

I pull back to look at him, not sure what he means.

"We're a little behind on our payments," he says, his mouth flat, dejected. Everything that sentence means is conveyed in the look on his face.

"Where will he go?" I ask.

Owen raises his brow high, his eyes get wide and he looks from side-to-side.

"But, who will take care of him?" My heart feels heavy even asking this, because I already know. Owen takes care of *everyone*.

"I let coach know. He said he'll keep me on the roster, but my season's pretty much done," he says, unable to mask the sadness in his eyes. For the first time, I can hear the disappointment in Owen's voice about basketball. We've talked about the unlikelihood of him playing in college, but I think he always counted on having his senior season to remember.

"Can't your mom...?" I stop without finishing, instead feeling the touch of Owen's lips back on the top of my head.

262

"Her job pays the mortgage. She kind of needs to keep it," he says, a breathy but somber laugh slipping out. "Besides, I think seeing my Gramps like he is makes her really sad. She doesn't visit much. We'll get help, from a home health nurse. His V.A. benefits will pay for that at least."

"I'm sorry," I say softly, wrapping one of my arms around him tightly.

We lie there quietly for several minutes, listening to the front door open and close, to Andrew drive away with his friend, and both of us think of how alone we are. I know he's thinking about it; the rhythmic tickle of his fingers along my arm is almost wearing a line in my skin, and the stare from his eyes on my mouth is making my skin twitch with want.

"You've been playing...piano. Willow said something about it the other day. You...thinking about it more?" Owen asks, his words coming out nervously, distracted. It makes me smile against his chest.

"I have...been playing, that is," I say.

"And college?" he asks, his fingers still trailing along my arm, their pace slowing, but his path moving higher, closer to my shoulder and breasts.

"I don't know. My dad's probably moving back in, so I definitely want to leave. But I just don't *love* the idea of studying music anymore. Besides, my showcase is Saturday. I'm not even ready, so I think I'll just bail," I say, my mind just now wrapping around the fact that Saturday is the day that's been circled on my calendar for nearly a year. Saturday. I'd nearly forgotten.

"You should still go," he says, his hand slowing down, his fingers flirting with the idea of moving more, of touching me intimately.

"I'll think about it," I say, not thinking about the piano now at all. Instead, thinking about where Owen's hand is going, what move it will make next, how alone we are, and how hot my skin feels.

I roll into him more, tilting my chin up slowly, hoping to find him waiting for me. His smile is tight and his eyes are trained on mine, the feel of his muscles beneath me, and around me, growing more rigid.

"Play something for me," he says, and I pull my brow in. "I mean, we don't have to go over to your house, just tap your fingers on me. I love watching your hands when you play."

I think about it for a few seconds, closing one eye and looking at him, judging whether on not he's serious. When I realize he is, his smile on me expectantly, I sit up, pushing off his stomach, and inducing a grunt as I knock the wind from him a little. "Sorry," I wince.

I straddle his upper legs, well aware of how close I am to the rest of him, then lean forward and place my palms on his chest. He's wearing a gray T-shirt that's thinning and has a hole in the center of the chest. The thin, smoothness of the fabric grips at him perfectly, and I force myself to pretend he's my keyboard when all I want to do is roam my hands along his curves in slow, smooth motions.

Closing my eyes, I rap my fingers a few times over his skin, feeling his stomach muscles tighten.

"Sorry," he chuckles. "Tickles."

Opening my eyes again, I smile, then stretch my fingers out, just as I would when presenting to the piano. "Okay, so *if* I were to go to my audition, I'd probably play this, along with one or two other songs. I'm a little rusty, but since you can't really hear the notes..." I stop mid phrase, lowering my gaze to my hands from his eyes, trying to concentrate on nothing but my tapping, the flexing of my fingers. I play Rachmaninoff, the same piece I played for Willow, and I let my fingers dance over Owen's chest, only glancing up once or twice to catch his grin as his eyes follow every movement I make. I swore I'd never play this song again, but this doesn't count—there's no sound.

When I finish, I press my palms flat, then smooth out the tiny dimples left behind in the cotton of his shirt. I feel a little foolish having just played air piano on Owen.

"That was fucking phenomenal," he says, and I laugh instantly.

"Shut up, you couldn't even hear anything," I say, and he reaches to grab my wrists, shaking them against him once or twice.

"Didn't have to. I felt it. How do your hands move that fast? That shit's crazy," he says, rolling his grip down to rub my fingers then back up my arms again, locking me to him.

"Thanks," I say, biting at the corner of my lip.

My breath exhales in a stutter, my palms growing hotter against Owen's chest the longer he holds me to him—the longer I look into his eyes. After a minute, he slides his hand from my arms to my thighs, running up my leggings until his hands cup my ass and he drags me forward.

I lean toward him as I move, coming to rest above him, feeling how hard he is through his flannel pajama bottoms, the heat searing from him and directly into me. His eyes never leave mine, and his hands move in fractions of an inch at a time, slow and calculated, until he pulls me down against him harder, making sure I feel everything he is feeling right now.

There is no mistake about what he wants. And his eyes, his smirk, his face…there is just the right amount of darkness in him. And I want it too.

"Remember when I asked you if you had a problem with sex, Kensi?" he asks, his voice gravely, deeper than normal. His tongue is resting at the edge of his teeth, like a serpent waiting to tempt me into sin, his lip curled just enough.

"Yes," I whisper back, my voice giving out, my breath stopping at the sensation of feeling him throb beneath me, my own body reacting, growing warmer…wetter. The first time we had this talk, it was confrontational. This time is different. This time, it's foreplay.

"You said you didn't care *who* had sex," he says, his tongue wetting his bottom lip before he holds it between his teeth, his eyes seducing me.

"Yes," I breathe again, relaxing into him, my thighs falling farther apart.

"I've had a lot of sex, Kensi," he says, his eyes blinking in slow draws as he peers up at me, his gaze growing more intense, his smirk honest. He owns his reputation, and as much as it bothered me, alone with those girls in the bathroom—right now, it's only making me crave him more. "But I have never wanted to feel what it's like to be inside someone more than I do right now. To feel someone I love. Fuck, Kensi, I want to touch all of you."

His fingers grip against my legs, squeezing my muscles, his hands barely able to contain themselves. I reach down for them, running my hands over his knuckles, then leading the way as I lift my sweatshirt up and over my head, quickly stripping my bra away next, leaving my breasts bare and cold, waiting for Owen.

His touch comes fast and hard as he sits up, his hands clutching at my back and his lips meeting my neck first. I arch as he pulls me into him, his tongue tasting its way down my neck to my nipple. Owen brings it into his teeth, looking up at me as he lets it slide from his grip slowly, his tongue circling the peak as his lips stretch into a satisfied smile.

I slide my hands up Owen, moving his shirt up his frame until he pulls it the rest of the way from his body. He reaches around me, lifting me and rolling me to my back, his mouth back to my breasts, which he sucks and kisses until they feel wonderfully raw.

He begins to kiss lower, hooking his thumbs at the waist of my leggings, dragging them down a few inches before stopping to let his kiss tease along my abdomen, kissing my bare hips as he slides the material further down my body, his fingers tugging at the small lace panties I wore with the hope he might see them.

Owen moves to his knees, pulling the rest of my clothing away completely before running his hands up my legs. He slides lower on the bed, kissing the inside of my knee, and I let my legs fall open, reaching for the pillow above my head to hide the redness building on my cheeks. Owen stops me, though, pulling on the corner of the pillow and moving it to the floor.

"Uh uh," he says, his tongue flicking against my thigh, dangerously close to my center. "I get to watch you. I want to see your face."

"But I'm embarrassed," I admit, squeezing my eyes shut, then letting one slip open. Owen slides up to my neck, kissing my ear.

"You're beautiful," he says. "And I want to watch you come apart for the very first time because of me."

266

"But you...I've...you made me, last time," I say, stretching my arm over my face, hiding. Owen lifts it and holds it over my head, kissing me lightly, his lips speaking against mine.

"Not like this I haven't," he says, brushing his lips down my body until he stops at my very center, his tongue taking long strokes against me, my legs spreading farther, wanting more with every pass of his mouth.

I grip the sheets and tug at the blankets, wanting to hide my face, but more because I feel like every touch of his tongue against my most sensitive parts is bringing me closer to losing control. Everything feels swollen, as if one more touch anywhere will send me over the edge, then Owen slides a finger into me, and the first wave crashes over me. My body shudders against his hand, and he holds on strong, pushing against me, his movements unrelenting until I feel every sensation stop, every pulse slow within me.

I. Am. Numb.

"That," he says, his mouth grazing against my ear, "was just the beginning."

Warmth rushes down my body, and a small whimper escapes my lips as Owen pulls away, standing in front of me. He removes his pants, and my eyes look, but quickly. There's so much of him—I don't know how it could possibly work. But I want it; my body is yearning for him to be inside of me.

Owen reaches for his dresser, taking a small packet from the top drawer, tearing the package with his teeth. I glance again as he holds himself, sliding the condom on with his other hand, and as nervous as I am about the pain, I'm more hungry to move past it, to feel him.

He kneels between my knees, his finger moving up and down my center, sliding in and out, relaxing me and exciting me all over again.

"I want you, Kensi. Please, I have to have you," he says, and I reach down, gripping his forearm, nodding at him, begging him.

"I want you too. Just...go slow," I say, my heart firing a billion beats per minute in my chest, my body clenching in anticipation of everything.

Owen positions himself between my legs, his forearms holding him above me, then he sweeps my hair to the side and kisses the corner of my mouth softly, letting me feel his smile against me. His hand drops lower so he can guide himself into me, and as the pressure of him pushes into me, his lips find my ear.

"Relax, Kens. I've got you," he says, coaxing my body to obey. He moves beyond the tip, pushing farther inside me, my muscles adjusting, my body stretching to take him—all of him—until Owen gives one final thrust, taking me from innocent to *his* in the flash of a second.

A single tear falls down my cheek, the pain stinging inside, and Owen notices quickly, sliding his thumb up to catch the drop as it falls toward his pillow.

"I've got you, Kens. I love you, and I've got you," he says, sliding back out from me almost completely, pausing to let my body relax again before moving into me slowly. The second time is easier—the stretching less, the sensation more—and soon, my body begins wanting Owen there, wanting to feel full from him, to take more of him, deeper.

"What feels good? Tell, me Kens. What do you want?" he asks, his voice sexier than it's ever been, the darkness there, but also a new kind of hunger. Owen may have the experience, but I have the control.

"Touch me," I pant, my eyes barely able to stay open as he moves slowly in and out from me. I feel his hand glide from my side, his thumb grazing my breast and traveling the length of my stomach until his fingers find my center and begin putting pressure on the rest of me, leaving nothing left untouched. Every bit of me is raw and open and on the verge, every push and stroke nearly ending me, until finally, I'm no longer able to hold on.

"Owen, I'm...I'm..." I say, arching my back and pushing my hips into him, feeling more of him against me with every pulse.

"You're so fucking beautiful," he growls, every push of his body harder, his eyes shutting, his breath stopping and his face growing tighter. Owen pushes into me two more times, his breath leaving his chest in one powerful burst before he pulls out from me and lies flat on his bed next to me, our bodies sweaty and tangled and happy.

We lie there for minutes, our hands linking, and our fingers teasing one another until finally Owen breaks our silence.

"That was easily the very best moment of my whole entire life," he says, his head falling to the side on his pillow, his hair tousled, and his eyes simply sweet.

I let my gaze fall to the side, too, meeting him. "I'm so glad Andrew went to Matt's," I smile, biting my lip and giggling.

"Me too," Owen says, standing and walking to his door, pulling his pajama pants from the floor. "He fucking hates that Matt kid, so he totally did that so his brother could *do it.*"

Owen flashes wide eyes, and he mouths "*oh*" as he laughs at me, backing away from his room. I reach to the floor and throw his pillow at him, which he catches at his chest.

"Not funny! Oh my god, I don't want your brother knowing about this, that we...*do it,*" I roll into the covers and pull them around my body and face. Owen leaps on me quickly, tugging the material away, pinning me to the bed and holding his mouth an inch away from mine.

"Everybody is going to know that you are mine, and that I am yours. And if I have to *do it* with you all weekend to make sure that look of bliss is permanent on your face—I will. My brother just already knows what everyone else will by the time I'm done with you," Owen says, his tongue teasing my upper lip before he moves away, standing to look down on me again, my body bare and ready to be touched again.

"Mine. All. Day," he says, his hands holding at the frame of the door, his body filling it completely. I watch him walk away, and listen as the shower water turns on. After a few minutes, I step from the bed and open the door Owen left cracked for me to begin with, hoping I'd follow. I step inside the hot water with him and let him tattoo happiness on my face just like he promised.

Chapter 19

I don't hear the sound of sirens or squad cars. I'm too caught up in my dream, asleep in Owen's arms, the hour late. We spent the day playing house, Owen burning our steaks on the grill, me burning the macaroni and cheese, melting away the water on his stove while I made out with him.

The entire day and most of the night, a dream—a delicious fantasy that is suddenly crashing down around us in a drowning wave of reality.

Owen wakes first, the sharp movement of his body as he lifts his head stirs me. He's to the window in seconds, then back to the bed, fumbling to put on his shirt and pants, sliding his feet into his shoes.

"What is it?" I ask, mimicking him, dressing myself quickly, my stomach sinking, sickness washing over me that something is wrong.

Something *is* wrong. Something is terribly, terribly wrong.

"Cops. My driveway, the street, it's filled with police. They have lights on my house. I'm not sure what's going on," Owen says, grabbing his phone in his hand, racing through his door, down the stairs.

I trail behind him, barefoot. There's no time for me to find my shoes. He slings the door open, ready to march out in protest, but he's met quickly with force, two large policemen standing guard at his door. One of them catches Owen, pushing him back into the house, knocking his feet off balance.

"What the fuck?" Owen yells, trying to push through the officer again. I reach to grab Owen's arm, to calm him.

"Stay in your house!" the officer yells, his finger pointed at both of us, his voice stern and loud.

"What the hell is going on?" Owen asks, pushing to see outside again.

"Sir, I'm warning you, get inside right now. Close this door, and find a safe place in your house and lie low, on the ground, hands over your head," the officer says, pulling the door closed and barricading it. Owen pulls the door a few times, turning the knob with no luck.

"Owen, what's happening?" I ask, my body tingling with nerves. Owen's pacing, moving through the kitchen to his back door, looking through the window to see more SWAT officers positioned there. He rushes to the living room, to the windows that face the backyard, and spots another pair of officers, weapons drawn.

"What the fuck landed in my front yard?" he says, running his hand through his messy hair, walking quickly from window to window, trying to get a glimpse of something, anything that will give him a clue what's happening outside.

"Drop your weapon!" We both hear a voice yell from outside over a megaphone, this warning followed by an eerie silence. Owen turns to look at me, his face frightened, a look I'm not used to seeing him wear. He rushes toward me, grabbing me by the arm and pulling me with him up the stairs, back to the safety of his room, and he pushes me to the far side, the other side of his bed.

"Kens, please! Get on the floor, under the bed if you have to," he says, pushing me down, pulling blankets and pillows to cover me, as if the cloth could stop anything from harming me.

"Owen, stay with me!" I scream, my hands gripping at his floor, my legs kicking to push my body under his bed, my face flat against the roughness, eyes searching for Owen's feet, to find out where he is. He sits low near me on the other side of the bed, so he can look out his window, out over the driveway.

And all at once, I see it—I see everything that is happening outside reflected in the absolute horror that suddenly paints Owen's face.

"James," he lets out in weak breath, his hand losing its hold on his phone, dropping it to the floor near me, his body growing weak in an instant. His knees fall from under him, and he grasps at the windowsill as he collapses, his arms just strong enough to hold his body to the window, his face pressed against the cold glass. His breath frosts it quickly, and he pulls a fist up, tucking the sleeve of his sweatshirt over it, wiping away the moisture in a manic circle.

"What is it? Owen, what's happening?" I scream, my body working to move closer to him, to hold him, to see what he sees.

"No! James, no!" Owen yells, his fist pounding at his window so hard he breaks it, slicing his hand, blood rushing down the length of his arm instantly. The sound of the glass, of Owen's screams and pounding, is so loud it's all I hear. It's the only sound.

Until it isn't.

The shot fires, but only once. Owen falls to the floor, his body nearly lifeless with pain, with sorrow, with grief, with guilt. Everything hits him all at once. I pull myself the rest of the way out from under his bed, rushing to hold him. I pull him to my lap, wrapping his sheet around his hand, doing my best to slow the bleeding from cuts I know are deep.

Owen lets me, his body weak in my arms, his heart—broken.

"Somebody! I need help, please! He's hurt. Help me!" I scream as loudly as my lungs will let me, my voice growing hoarse, raspier with every shout, until finally two officers and a medic come rushing through Owen's door.

"Please, help him. Please, he hurt himself, on the window. There's glass in his arm; I think some of it's still in there," I plead, my arms not wanting to let go of their hold on Owen. His face is strewn with tears, his gaze lost out the window, to the scene below.

I'm afraid to look.

The medic works to stabilize Owen's bleeding, tearing cloth and rewrapping his arm, removing what glass he can. He speaks into a radio strapped to his shoulder, asking for help transporting Owen, and soon two more firefighters arrive, carefully placing Owen's arm in a splint, urging Owen to lie on his back, on the stretcher, so they can carry him down the stairs.

Owen fights them, unable to say actual words other than "no" and "leave me alone." He eventually walks with assistance down the steps, to his living room, his mom rushing in the door, meeting him with her own tears.

Horror. Both of their faces...horror.

And I can't help.

James was high. He was high, and he was scared. He stole a car from a mall parking lot three towns over, then led police on a chase along the highway, hitting several cars, leaving a trail of injuries and damaged vehicles along the roadway as he exited the wrong way up a ramp. He raced down the two-lane roadway to his home, down the dark stretch of country road Owen had once raced on carelessly with me, down the strip of roadway James had taught Owen to drive fast on as a kid.

He swerved through his mother's front yard, clipping the bumper of Owen's truck, and spinning the stolen car to the side, stopping near the end of the driveway—sideways, the hood bent open and the wheel crushing the brick of the house.

Police had him then. He was circled, the three cars that had followed him collapsed on him, six officers opening their doors quickly, drawing their weapons and ordering James to just. Stay. Put.

But James was high.

And he was scared.

And that gun, the one Owen once held to his own head in a dare, the one that I saw James threaten Owen with only a few weeks ago—it was in James's hand.

The police called for back up, and SWAT came quickly. That's when Owen woke up. James held the gun to his side, his other hand behind his head, scratching at his hair, rubbing his neck vigorously, his brain trying to think under a fog of impairment, his heart desperate for a solution, for a way out of *this* hell.

More guns were drawn. James became agitated, holding the gun up over his head. This is when officers began to order him to drop his weapon, when Owen and I ran up the stairs.

It all happened in seconds, slices of time that felt as though they took hours to pass. Owen saw his brother out that window, he saw how frightened he was, how cornered he was, and he knew there was no way out.

Owen knew.

He saw it coming before James lowered his arm just enough, tilting the gun just right, the barrel pointed to his head. He knew a millisecond before his brother drew his finger back, pulling on the trigger with the right amount of pressure.

Owen knew his brother was dead the minute he came home from school two days ago and saw James was gone. He didn't know how it would happen. But he knew it would.

And he knew he'd feel like it was his fault in the end.

Chapter 20

My father hasn't been back to the house, and I haven't asked my mother when or if he's coming. I don't care any more. He can move in here, and my mom can give in, live in her self-made prison. I hope she doesn't, but either way, in six more months, I won't be here to see it.

I haven't resolved myself to college or the road, but whatever it is, it will be my choice—of *my* doing. The only person I care about disappointing is myself.

And Owen.

Owen hasn't been to school, and I've noticed the piles of homework left in Mr. Chessman's class for him. Every day, the pile is gone, so someone is taking Owen his work.

There wasn't a funeral. Funerals are expensive, and no one would show up for James, Owen said. I go over to his house every night, and we sit in his room, perched on the edge of his bed, holding hands, but not talking.

We never look out the window.

His mom is home—time to grieve. But even she doesn't seem broken. They just seem as if they're going through motions, carbon copies of themselves—the same tired and exhausted bodies, but spirits and hopes completely washed away. Owen's taking care of the "paperwork" and filing death certificates; investigating old credit accounts in James's name and calling relatives. His mom began cleaning out his room within a few days.

Neither of them has cried again like they did the night James put the gun to his head. I just don't think they can anymore. They're...empty.

Willow and Jess don't know what to say. Even now, days later, they walk along with me out to the parking lot, making plans, talking in half sentences, afraid everything they say might offend me. Everyone's heard the story. Things like this, they spread quickly in Woodstock.

The Harper boys—they're wild. What James did has only cast more eyes on them; I see them look at Andrew when he comes to our school in the morning, before he takes the bus to his school. I bet they look at him there, too.

I bet they'd look at Owen like this. That's why he doesn't come.

"Are you...still in for the competition Saturday? I think Mr. Brody would understand. You know, if...if you can't perform?" Willow asks. Eggshells—everyone is walking on eggshells.

"I'll be there," I say, smiling, eyes wide.

"Okay, but, if you can't..." she says.

"Ohhhhh my god!" I yell, tossing my bag into my passenger seat. "Please. Not you. Please, Will...just be normal. I need you, *you* out of everyone, to act normal. I'm begging."

She's standing before me, her arms folded in front of her, her fingers picking at her elbows nervously, her eyes searching mine. I know this is awkward for her. It's awkward for me, but I'm not Owen. When she sees him, *then* she can get all uncomfortable and formal and careful. But now, when it's just her and me and Jess and our friends—now is the time to be blunt, to pop her gum, to pretend I don't have other shit happening in my life.

"So I'll pick you up at six?" she asks, a shrug of her shoulder to punctuate her question.

I smile and nod. "Yeah, six. And bring snacks for the road trip," I add. I get in my car and watch as she and Jess get into hers from my rearview mirror. Driving away, I don't look at her again, because that small exchange was normal, and I don't want to ruin it. I hold onto it for the few miles to my house, and then I pull into the driveway and see Owen's truck and forget all about normal.

His house is first, and I leave my backpack in my car and don't bother going to my own home. My mom is home today, but she'll see my car out front. She knows where I am—where I've been *every* day. She's been trying to help with paperwork, answering Owen's questions about where to file things, how to handle closing accounts, who he needs to notify.

James didn't leave a very big mark on this world electronically, and erasing what there was of him wasn't very hard.

276

I don't bother to knock, instead just stepping inside Owen's home. His mom is labeling boxes at the table, taping things closed, and moving them to the front porch one at a time. She marks FOR DONATION on the last box, and I pull it from her arms and take it to the porch for her. When I come back inside, she's still standing at the table, her hands pressed flat against the now-clear surface, her eyes intent on the center.

When I move closer, she flinches, snapping awake again, and runs her hand once over the smooth tabletop before pushing the chair underneath. "Thank you for helping with things this week, Kensi. O and I...we appreciate everything you and your mom have done," she says, her eyes never able to meet mine completely. "Can I get you something to drink? I think we have..."

She opens her fridge, pausing when she sees it's empty. She starts to laugh lightly, closing it, and backing away until the backs of her legs hit the table. She stumbles a little and catches her balance, then turns to me, a full smile on her face, her laugh coming out harder.

"We have nothing," she says, her lips squeezing tight, trying to hold onto normal. Her body begins to shake with laughter again. "Oh my god, we have...*nothing!*"

As if a switch flips, her laughter shifts into tears and her breath escapes her, her knees buckling again, sending her to the floor.

"Are you okay?" I rush to her, helping her to one of the chairs. "Wait here, I'll get Owen."

"No, it's...it's fine. It just, it gets to me sometimes—all of it. It's all just...so much," she says, her red eyes peering at me, her face pale, her hair thin and tangled.

"I know," I speak, not sure what else there is to say. I don't *really* know, but I know enough.

Owen's mom takes a full breath, closing her eyes just long enough to clear them of tears and hide the redness, then she stands and pulls a hair tie from her wrist, pulling her hair back into a ponytail. "I'm going to run to the store. Owen's upstairs; he'd love to see you," she says, grabbing her coat from the hook by the door and leaving in a rush.

Everything has to happen fast, and there always has to be something to do. If there isn't, she'll fall apart. That much I understand.

I pull my own coat from my body and leave it on the table, then I climb the stairs, catching the soft sound of Owen's stereo. He's listening to the Black Keys, the same album he's listened to for five days straight. There will come a time, I fear, that he will never be able to hear these songs again.

Knocking softly, I push his door open enough to slip through. He's lying on his side, his arm propped up on an elbow, a pile of homework in front of him. "What's this...Owen Harper studying?" I tease. I've actually never seen him do homework, so the sight of it strikes me.

Owen smiles, the curves never quite making it fully up his cheeks, then tosses his pencil in the crease of his book, closing it, and pushing the papers to the side to make room for me. I crawl into his arms obediently.

"I'm a little behind. Just trying to catch up," he says, his nose cold as he nuzzles against my cheek.

"That's nice that the school got this for you. Nobody's really saying anything. You know, about what happened?" I say. Owen lifts his hand, running it through my hair and stopping at the back of my head to pull me to him for a kiss. He backs away a little after and sighs, his chest rising and falling in a pattern that he's kept up for days. Every breath he takes is heavy, an attempt to cleanse himself from how he feels inside.

"Mr. Chessman brings things over for me every couple days. He lives a block or two away. He's cool like that," Owen says, his eyes sculpting my face, looking at me endearingly. His affection for me has never waned, not once, through this tragedy. I think he's clinging to it. And I'm clinging to him.

"How's my boyfriend, Gus?" I ask. I've been wondering about Owen's grandfather, how his role in their house fits now.

"He's good. He misses you," he smirks.

"Well, he and I...we sort of had a fling. He's a really good dancer," I say, sucking my top lip in. Owen leans forward and gives me a chaste kiss, his lips grazing over mine until I let my lip free.

Owen pushes himself up to sit, and I join him, my hands spreading out a few of the assignments stacked on his bed. I notice Owen's math homework, and I pull it out from a folder, looking at the problems that he's already completed. His homework, it's different from mine. It's more advanced.

"Just one of many," he says quickly, taking the folder from my hand and pushing it back into the pile with everything else. He flips his English book open again, pulling the pencil out and tucking it behind his ear.

"I've gotta stop in at home, check in with Mom. I'll let you get to some of this. Maybe next week, you'll be at school with me?" I ask, standing from his bed. Owen smiles quickly, his eyes full of a fake kind of hope, pretending for my benefit.

"Maybe," he says. "I'll text you later, 'kay?"

"'Kay," I say, my eyes on his for a few extra seconds. Every look feels like he's drowning, and I'm trying to pull him back ashore.

I grab my coat and stop by my car for my backpack on my way back to my house, rushing up to my room before my mom has a chance to stop me. She's on the phone and nods with her finger up as I fly by her on the stairs. She'll come find me soon, but maybe I'll have a few minutes to log onto my computer, to be alone first.

My computer isn't where it should be when I get to my room, which sends me back downstairs, back to my mom, who ends her phone call and turns my computer screen around for me to see when I enter the kitchen.

"Why do you have my computer?" I ask, reaching for it. She snaps the screen shut and slides it back a few inches with her fingertips, just out of my reach.

"Why do you have a listing posted on Craigslist for the piano?" she asks.

Shit! How did she find that?

"It's my piano; I can sell it if I want to," I say, reaching again for my computer. This time she picks it up with both hands and hugs it to her chest. "Mom..."

"That's enough, Kensington. You have been stomping around here, acting like the adult of this house, for weeks. You may be eighteen, but this attitude needs to stop right here. Now tell me, without your new brand of sarcasm, if you don't mind, why the piano is on Craigslist?" She's doing that thing where her eyes blink at me slowly. She's pissed. And I still don't know how she found out about the piano listing.

"How did you find it?" I ask.

"Doesn't matter," she says. Her answer is fast. Too fast.

"Uh, no...I kind of think it matters. I put my phone number on there, and my personal email. So..." I wait for her, my head leaned to the side, my brow pulled in tight. And then it hits me.

Dad.

"He saw it, didn't he? That's what this is about," I say, shaking my hand, my feet shifting and beginning to trail back to my room. Fuck it. She can keep the computer.

"Yes, your father saw it. You know he's always looking for good buys on instruments for the program. He recognized this immediately and called me. Kensington, you cannot sell something that's your father's," she says, and I stop in my tracks, spinning on my heels, my blood boiling.

"His?" I shout. "*His* piano? Mom...are you...are you joking?"

"Kensington, you need to take this down...now," she says, opening the computer and spinning it around for me.

"No," I say, folding my arms. I'm throwing a fit. A staunch, standoff kind of fit—like I did when I was four and didn't want to eat my green beans—but a fit nonetheless. This is ridiculous.

"Yes," she says, the word coming out slowly, her eyes scrunched, wrinkling at the corners. We stare at each other like this for several minutes, and the longer I look at her, the longer I think about what she said, the angrier I get.

"You said it was mine. *Mine!* You said that was my piano. You told me when I was ten, after I won my first competition. Grandma died and left that piano to you—*your* mother, not his! And then *you* said it was mine. You told me that it was always meant for my hands, and you loved the joy it gave me. You don't get to take it back. And if I want to sell it, because it doesn't give me joy any more, then I'm going to! And he doesn't get any say in things! You can sweep those awful things he's done under the rug if you want to, but I will never forget. And I will never forgive him!"

I turn around the second my last word is uttered. With a calm but quick pace, I climb my stairs, turning back only after I've made it up the first few. My mother is frozen in her place, her hand just where it was on the computer, her mouth slightly parted, her eyes wide and on me...almost. I may as well have slapped her.

I get to my room and slam the door, like a child, and move to my window, putting my headphones on and pulling my knees up to my chest while I unzip my backpack and pull out my pile of homework. I look up every few minutes, waiting for Owen to look back, and after an hour, I can't take the waiting any longer, so I send him a text and ask him to come over.

My mom must have let him in, because I never hear the doorbell or knock, just the sound of him slipping through my door moments later.

"Homework done?" I ask, everything inside me still churning, still fuming.

"Uh huh," he says, his head tilted to the side as he moves toward me a little apprehensively. "You're pissed about something. Your dad coming over? Cuz I'm not so sure I'm up for wrestling him again."

"Ha," I let out a short laugh, then let my head fall forward into my hands, rubbing my eyes. "No, you're safe. Just doing that thing where I yell at my mom, but I feel bad about it. Even if I'm right...I feel bad."

Owen slides down on the floor next to me, both of our backs against my bed. He flips through a few of the things I've let fall out of my backpack, looking at the back of one of the books I picked up from the library. "This looks like a chick book," he says, tossing the copy of *Emma* I picked up from the library back onto my stack of notebooks.

"It is. It's one of my favorites," I say, looking at the cover. It's an image of the movie version, a carefree Gwyneth Paltrow holding her bow and arrow. "How come you have advanced calculus homework?" I ask the question quickly, keeping my eyes on the book, not wanting to make a big deal out of it. I sense

Owen's pause though. I don't know why this makes him uncomfortable.

"I tested out of freshman algebra. I've always been a year ahead in math. Brain just sort of likes numbers, I guess," he says, his voice trailing off at the end. He reaches his arm to my leg, grabbing my hand and pulling it into his lap, cupping it with both of his and playing with my fingers. "What was this fight about? You know your mom gives me bacon; I hope you didn't mess up my supply," he says, leaning into me.

I smile, my gaze into my lap. Owen's joke is sweet.

"She's letting my dad rule things. She always has, and it just...it makes me so mad," I say, the frown taking over again.

"What's he trying to rule?" Owen asks.

"Her," I say quickly, looking up at him. "And me, by extension."

Owen lifts his hand and tucks a loose strand of hair behind my ear, leaving his hand on my cheek when he's done. "So don't let him," he says. Simple, plain. "Is this about your playing again? Because I thought we had that figured out—you do that for *you*, wasn't that the deal?"

"I thought so," I say, standing up to move to my doorway, checking to see if my mom is still downstairs or up. "But apparently it's not *my* piano."

When I turn back to Owen, his eyebrows are pulled in, one eye closed. "Last I checked, it's not the piano that makes that kick-ass music. It's you," Owen says.

"Exactly, so there's no reason I can't sell it," I say quickly, regretting my words just as fast.

Owen's standing now, his body moving behind me. I turn into him, reaching my arms out to hug him, embrace him, move away from talking—but he greets my hands with his, holding his arms out stiffly, keeping me at a small distance so he can watch my face. "Why would you sell it?" he asks.

He knows.

I shrug, nodding ambivalently, as if I haven't thought this through.

"Kens," he says, his eyes looking over my shoulder, out my door, then back to me. "You're not selling your piano."

I let go of his fingers and lean back against my wall, my arms folded—pouting. Pouting and pissed. Why is everyone insistent that I can't do what I want with *my* piano?

"Kens," he chuckles, moving closer to me, pulling on my arms, which I'm holding together tightly against my body. My stubbornness makes him laugh harder, until he pulls his hat from his head, tosses it on my bed and rubs his eyes. He sits down next to it and calls me over to him. I scoot my feet closer reluctantly, and when I get to him, he loops his fingers into the pocket of my jeans and drags me onto his lap, wrapping his arms around me tightly, his lips at my ear.

"It is so sweet that you want to help my family. But that would pay for what? Another couple months of my Grandpa's expenses? I can't let you do that. The cost is too high," he says. "But I *love* that you're willing to do something like that for me."

"I don't want the piano anymore. And it would help," I say, my eyes growing heavy with tears.

"Yes you do. You don't think you want it...but you do," he says, swaying me side to side in his lap, his cheek against mine. I let my head fall on his arm, running my hands along his, holding his caged arms around me tightly.

I don't want the piano. All I want...is Owen.

Six in the morning arrives way too quickly. Owen stayed late, my mom never coming up to my room and telling him he needed to go home. I left my door open, knowing she would feel more comfortable with him here if I did, and I heard her move to her bedroom hours after our fight downstairs.

I feel worse about it today. She's still asleep when I sneak downstairs to brew a cup of coffee and grab a packet of Pop Tarts from the pantry. Willow texted me when she was leaving her house, which gave me precisely seven minutes to shower and get dressed. I lock our front door behind me and pull my coat around my body, shielding the hot coffee mug from the freezing air.

I'm bundled from head to toe, the only things exposed are my lips and nose and the tips of my fingers through my gloves. Jess leaps from the front seat and holds the door open for me, then moves to the back.

"Thanks for letting me ride shotgun," I say, unwrapping my neck from my scarf, letting the heat from Willow's car penetrate my body.

"Thanks for giving me a sip of your coffee," Jess says, reaching through the center to the cup holder where my mug is steaming.

"Go ahead," I roll my eyes.

"You're too nice. I would have spilled it on him," Willow says, backing out of the driveway with enough speed to make the bump jerk Jess's hand a little, splattering coffee on his chin and cheeks.

"Your such a bitch in the morning," he says, slurping the coffee once more before putting my mug back.

"See, now when he says *bitch* it sounds authentic," Willow says to me.

"That's cuz you are one!" Jess says from the back seat. Willow raises her middle finger and smiles at him in the rearview mirror.

"Are you two going to fight all the way to Champagne? I'm just saying, that's like...three hours of bickering. So if I have a chance to bail out now and drive myself, I'd like to take it," I say, looking to Willow. She smirks at me.

"No, we're just going to bicker for the first ten minutes," Jess says from behind me. "The rest of the time we'll be all shmoopy, making kissy faces at each other, and I'll keep feeling her up from the back seat."

"Uh, that's not happening," Willow says, pointing at him in the mirror.

"Worth a shot," Jess says, settling back in his seat, pulling his coat up over his lap.

It's still dark out when we hit the highway, but by the time we make it to the University of Illinois, three hours later, the sun is shining. It's one of those rare days where there's a tiny bit of leftover snow on the ground, too, so everything feels especially bright. I know it will all melt by the time we take the field for

284

competition, but the early morning sun makes the ground look as if it's covered in jewels.

"We're going to tune in ten minutes, then we go to photos and pre-staging before we compete. You're going to love this, Kensi," Willow says. She's wired on a few energy drinks. I counted three empty cans in her car. I'm pretty sure that isn't safe, but I'm also fairly certain that there's little difference in her personality—wired or not.

Willow walks around each section, listening and adjusting instruments as everyone warms up, her whistle perched at the edge of her lips.

"Just one more reason why drum line is the best," Jess says, rapping out a drumroll on the rim of his snare. "We don't tune."

I laugh and wait at the back of the moving truck for a few of the booster parents to help unload the xylophone, smirking when one of the wheels falls off into my hand as they pull it from the truck. I bend down and lift the leg up so I can work the wheel back in place, and suddenly the weight is lighter.

"I hope you know this is butt-crack early, and I would only show up to something like this for you," Owen says, his head buried in its usual black hoodie.

"You're here!" I squeal, rushing into his arms. He catches me and holds me under the sides of his coat, shielding the cold breeze from my skin. We changed into our uniforms the second we got to the campus, and I haven't been warm since.

Owen rubs his hand on the giant feather on the top of my hat. "You guys look like birds. Why do you have to wear these?" he asks.

"It's so the judges can see us on the field. Willow says it makes the formations *pop* more," I roll my eyes.

"But you don't march..." he says, fluffing my feather once again. I slap his hand away and straighten my hat.

"Yeah, I tried that argument, but here I am, all plumed," I say.

"Well, you're adorable. Go win something. You do get to win something, right?" he says, taking a few steps away, moving backward toward the stadium.

"That's what Willow says. This is like her Super Bowl, you know?" I say, wide eyes.

"Yeah, so I've heard." Owen shields his mouth as he passes Willow, but she hears him anyhow and punches him on the arm. "Owwww!"

I smile as he turns, my heart feeling warm inside. Everything feels right—at least for right now.

Most of the morning is spent standing around, rolling my xylophone from patch of grass to patch of grass, until we're in the tunnel. It's kind of cool being in here, and I look around at the motivational words painted on the wall, the most amusing the threat that any opponent will feel the *Orange Krush.*

Before today, there was no reason I would ever find myself in a sports tunnel at a major university. The whole scene feels silly, and maybe a little pointless, but it also feels...*good.*

As we get ready to take the field, Willow calls us all in for one final huddle, and Jess leads everyone in a chant of *hoorahs,* as if we're actually the university's football team—about to scream through the tunnel to take on Ohio State or Kansas. The longer everyone cheers, the more it makes me giggle, and the louder I'm cheering too.

Once we hit the field, it's just like any other Friday—Willow atop a small ladder, her arms keeping a steady beat that we all seem to be perpetually a hint behind. What's different about today though is how everyone in the stands is paying attention. People are actually cheering—people from other schools, either already having gone or waiting to perform. They're supportive, appreciative, and when they whisper to one another between songs, I can tell they're competitive.

Willow was right—this...feels...*awesome!*

It seems like it takes us only minutes to pack up after the performance, and soon we're in the stands, waiting for the final two schools to perform. Owen stays, sitting behind me, his legs on either side of me, his arms wrapped around my body, keeping me warm. We were allowed to change out of our uniforms after the performance, but most of us left our shirts on, wanting to feel like a team.

The award ceremony drags on, with awards for dozens of categories. Willow is beaming because she received a medal of distinction for drum major.

"She does wave her arms with excellent precision," Owen jokes in my ear. I elbow him because Jess is close, but when I hear Jess laugh, I ease up on Owen.

We're all amused because every time our school is called for an award, Willow has to step forward, saluting, then she walks over to the master of ceremonies to shake his hand and take our trophy. We end up winning six, including Willow's and a third-place overall finish. Jess rushes down to the field to help her carry them all.

"I have to admit, that was kind of cool," Owen says during our walk from the stadium to the parking lot. We stop at Willow's car, and Owen pulls out the bag holding my uniform. "Is it cool if I drive you home? It'll be four or so by the time we get home. I'd like to take you to dinner."

"Dinner's good. I never did get my steak," I tease, standing on the tips of my toes to kiss him.

"I'm pretty sure you made out all right," he says, rolling his hands down my back, to my ass and pulling me to him closely. I blush and look to see who's watching, but the moment his lips hit my neck, I care a whole lot less.

"I don't know, I really wanted a steak," I joke, and Owen spanks me once, squeezing his hand hard on my cheek.

"You sure about that?" he winks. I nod *no,* because…no, I'm not. In fact I might forgo eating for days for more nights with Owen. If only I could erase everything that happened the day after.

Willow packs the trophies in the backseat of her car, promising Mr. Brody that she'll bring them to school on Monday. Owen and I wait for them to drive away before walking to his truck.

"Hey," he says, tugging on my arm, taking a step back before letting me climb inside. "Can I take you somewhere in the city? Like, on a real date? Would that be okay?"

"You sure?" I ask, knowing how expensive places in the city are. Owen doesn't have the money to do something like this, but he's looking at me with such excitement, I can't just outright say no.

"Positive. I have a place in mind," he says, his eyes lowered, giving me that look that would make me follow him anywhere. I nod okay, and Owen opens my door, waiting while I climb in and buckle the seatbelt before closing it for me.

I haven't driven in southern Illinois since I was a kid, so most of the things we pass aren't familiar to me. Most of the state looks the same—lush and green in the summer, and thick of dead leaves and stickily trees in the winter. But there's something beautiful about the usual today, and I let my eyes glaze over as I watch the rays of sunshine flash in and out of the thick branches as we rush by.

The constant hum of his engine draws me in, and somewhere along the way, I slip into a short slumber, not waking up until I feel Owen push the gearshift into park then reach behind his seat, pulling out a heavy plastic bag.

I stretch my arms and look around, doing my best to adjust my body's clock, to recognize my surroundings. The gothic buildings orient me immediately, and I flash to Owen, the look on my face panicked.

It's panic punching me from the inside out right now; I know it is. Why did he bring me here? Why are we here? This isn't a date!

"Owen!" I start unclicking my buckle, even though I have no intention of leaving this truck.

"Hold on! Before you get all...*Kensi* on me. Listen to me. Please, just listen to me. And if I don't make any sense, I promise we will drive right out of this parking lot and I will take you to the best steakhouse in the city," he says, crossing a finger over his chest, his other palm flat toward me, as if warning he comes in peace.

Crap—he's coming in peace!

My body deflates in retaliation, but I lift my chin enough to look at him, to stare him in the eyes while he pleads his case.

"I know you think you don't want this. And...and," he raises his hand to stop me from interrupting, my rebuttal stammering at the tip of my tongue. I let it simmer longer. I owe Owen a listen; he's right. "In the end, you might be right. Maybe...*maybe*...you won't want this. But I kinda think you do,

Kensi. And if you don't try, if you don't at least just see this through, look inside that door, you will regret it. You are so gifted, and unlike me, you have options."

"Owen, you have options, too," I start, but he grabs my hand quickly and holds it, shaking it lightly and smiling.

"That's not what I meant," he says, his lips curve into a smile against my wrist as he holds it to him. "I'm good with where I am, Kens. I'm all right with not being able to have everything. When I play ball, it's purely recreation for me. It's not a dream. It's not this thing that I always thought about doing for a living. It's an escape. It's the way I lose myself, take control, be someone else, for just a few hours," he smiles.

His head falls to the side, against his headrest, his leg propped up along the seat. He lowers my hand in his and presses it flat against my leg, resting his palm over mine. "I've seen you. No...not just that...I've heard you, Kensi. I've *felt* you when you play, when you lose yourself so completely to that piano. For you, it's different. And for you, this is something that could mean the rest of your life. And you might not think you want it now, but Kens, believe me, when something's gone—" he swallows hard, his jaw flexing, his eyes struggling. "When something's gone that you love, and you start thinking about how much you didn't appreciate it when it was here...that shit will poison you. And I'll be damned if I'm not going to try to save you from that."

To my left, out the window, is the main music hall for the University of Chicago. I know those steps. I've climbed them for years. There's a small hallway to the right, as soon as you enter, and it dips down, below ground, to a long line of offices and practice rooms. It's where I play with Chen. It's a place I haven't been in months.

And Owen's right about one thing; not going, missing it—my time with Chen—it gnaws at my insides when I let it in.

I draw in a deep breath, the heat from Owen's truck mixing with the coolness of the glass window by my face. I look back at him, his eyes hopeful. I want to do this, maybe more for him than me. And maybe for me, too.

"I don't have anything to wear," I say, looking down at the silly band shirt and jeans I have on. Owen pulls the plastic bag up to his lap, sliding it over to me, inside a plain black dress and a simple pair of black ballet flats. It's exactly what I would have picked on my own.

"I scoped out your closet before I left your room last night. And yes, I had to tell your mom what I was up to when I stopped by your house this morning to get this. But don't worry; she's not coming. I told her I had to trick you into coming, and her being here would probably scare you away," he says.

He's right. It would have.

"My time's at four o'clock," I say, looking at my watch. It's a little after three thirty.

"I know," he says, his head now resting along his arm, against the back of his seat. His jaw is rough, his beard showing more than it usually does.

"Will you come in with me?" I ask, the bag of clothes held close to my chest.

"Wouldn't miss it," he says, a smile so soft, so honest, it makes me believe that maybe I can do anything.

I lead Owen through the corridor, to the hallway bathroom I'm familiar with, and I change quickly. I'm glad Owen brought what he did. Anything...*more* and I would feel uncomfortable. The only thing I need to work past now is the growing nerves threatening to derail the strength and control in my hands. Owen notices them trembling, reaches down, and threads his fingers slowly through mine as we stand along a sparse hallway, the applicant before me staring at the crack in the auditorium door, waiting for it to open, for someone to welcome her inside.

Once she enters, I squeeze Owen's hand harder, looking to my right, to the long wooden bench, and the two boys who have sat down, each of them dressed in a suit.

I pull my hand from Owen's briefly, blowing on my palms, trying to make the sweat stop. Please, for five minutes, just stop!

"Miss Worth?" There's a young woman standing in front of me now, clipboard in her hand, the list of names on it—long.

I smile and let go of Owen, wiping my hands along the skirt of my dress and passing through the doors with him, watching to see just where he sits. I notice Chen at the main table in the center of the auditorium as I pass through the rows of seats. He doesn't smile at first, but when nobody else is looking, he raises his thumb and winks.

I needed that—more than he'll ever know.

"Miss Worth, what will you be playing today?" a man with a graying beard and glasses pushed to the tip of his nose asks.

Clearing my throat, I flex my fingers, searching for the memory of everything I know. I know this. I *know* I know this.

"*Rachmaninoff Piano Concerto No. 2*," I say, my voice losing its confidence the moment the sound of it hits the airy stage, the vastness around me swallowing me whole.

"Very well. Begin," the main man says. I move to the piano, possibly the nicest one I've ever seen, and smooth the wrinkles on my dress. Looking down, I search for the pedals, placing my feet in familiar positions, finding my comfort. I close my eyes and run my hands once in opposite directions, just as I do every time, until I come back to center, and my hands find their natural groove.

It's there; that sensation, the one that tells my fingers they are home. I don't open my eyes at first, instead just letting my mind take me back to my room in the city, the practice room that used to feel like home. The sound from my hands—it *feels* like that home, like my old life, and the longer I play, the more of the Concerto I complete, the more my mouth tastes funny. I'm hitting the right notes, everything coming out just as it should. But what's missing is the passion.

My stop is abrupt, my fingers recoiling into my fists, my eyes flashing open—thoughts of Owen, of Willow, of my life *now*, the good and the bad, surrounding me.

"Miss Worth?" There's a throat-clearing sound. They aren't happy. I'm pretty sure this is how someone blows an audition. But I can't continue to play something that I just don't feel.

"I...I'm sorry. I've changed my mind," I say, my eyes searching for Owen. He's leaning forward in a far seat, his elbows propped on his legs, his head tilted to the side. He's afraid—worried that I'm quitting, giving up. But I'm not. I'm just doing this on my terms.

"If it's all right, I'd like to begin again?" I ask, my fingers finding one another, fretting...maybe hoping a little too that they will get the chance to show everyone exactly what they can do.

"You may," the speaker says, his tone growing more tired with me.

Deep breath.

"Thank you," I say, retaking my seat and looking at the expanse of keys before me, the pattern, the way the black and white lines dance. I'm going to make them dance. I rest my hands loosely, nothing like this room full of professors would wish me to, but...I. Don't. Care. "This is *C Jam Blues*, written by the great Duke Ellington. I'm going to be playing it as inspired by Oscar Peterson. I hope you enjoy."

When I turn to face the keys again, I smirk, my stomach settling, and my heart soaring. I don't even remember hearing the sounds my hands make. This moment, the five minutes I play and pound, smiling the entire time—it's like recess. I'm on one big life recess, and I never want to come back.

I never bother to look, just playing on, dragging out a few of the jazz riffs, some of the repetitions, a few more times than necessary. I do it because I can tell everyone is hanging on every single note I'm playing. They won't admit it—but I have them. I have them because this...*this* is what my hands were meant to do. What *I'm* meant to do.

When I'm done, I feel euphoric, and I stand, the bench screeching along the floor as I move it out of my way. "Thank you," I say, stepping to the side exit, down the steps to the end of the hallway where Owen is now waiting for me.

I'm worried he's going to be mad, maybe disappointed, but he rushes to me, sweeping me into his arms and twirling me around the tiny hallway, his kiss proof that what I did in there—Owen liked it too.

"That was fucking fantastic. I mean, holy shit, Kens! Did you see those guys? They had no idea what to do with you. I mean, I don't know how they work these things, or how they score that shit, but damn, girl!" His celebration is enough, and I tuck myself along his side, the plastic bag with my jeans and band clothes dangling from Owen's other hand.

292

We climb the small steps up the narrow hallway, my hand on the door I've pushed through so many times. Chen bursts through the opposite side of the hallway, his eyes finding mine right away, his face proud and beaming.

"Ohhhhhh Kensington," he's nearly weeping, and I can see the surprise in Owen's face as this man, probably in his sixties, brushes Owen aside, hugging me as if I'm his own daughter. "So proud. You make me...so proud," he says, his hands on my cheeks, pushing in tightly. I can see in his eyes that he's genuinely happy for me, and I can also see that I blew any chance I might have of joining their program.

And Chen and I couldn't care less.

I introduce him to Owen quickly, and their handshake is fast and awkward before Chen rushes back inside. I breathe easy for the two hours it takes to drive through the city, to Owen's driveway. Owen asks me questions about Chen along the way, about my lessons with him, about my underground lessons—the times we knew my father wasn't around, wouldn't hear. I talk about how Chen made me love jazz, my chest alive and full and anxious for more.

I want to run through the streets of our neighborhood when I skip from Owen's truck, making noises in celebration just to hear them echo off of the dark houses around us. The moon is out, and still the stars are bright—a pairing that shouldn't happen. And I want to dance, for hours, out here in the freezing cold in Owen's arms. The way he's looking at me, the wonder in his face, it spurs me on, drawing me to him.

And then there's a crack in his façade. My feet stop before him, his arms catching me, his fingers fumbling for mine, teasing the ends, never quite holding on completely.

"What?" I ask, every drop of elation in my body from before now exchanged for dread.

"I'm moving to Iowa," he says, and all I hear is the humming of the blood passing along my eardrum. The color is gone from my body, and the strength is failing my legs. "I know. God, Kens, I'm so sorry. To tell you now...this way...after your night—"

"Why?" I cry, holding my fist to my mouth. I hold it there for several seconds, my lip quivering underneath, until the tingling in my lip is so strong that I know I won't be able to hide how this is all making me feel.

"Kens...it's all been too much. It's just...it's too much for me, for my mom. And Andrew. We're underwater with the house, but if we sell it, the bank has agreed to wipe the slate clean. My mom is going to look for something cheaper, maybe an apartment. And then the extra money from her check will pay for my grandpa," he's speaking so fast; his words don't even make sense.

"What happens in Iowa? Why can't you stay here?" I take a step back, my feet pounding the pavement like a child. I'm embarrassed how it looks, but I'm so afraid of what this means. I'm losing Owen. I just got him, and already...he's gone.

"My uncle lives there. My dad's brother? He owns a print shop, and I'm going to work for him. I'll be able to send some money to Mom, and I'll be able to save for college. The shop isn't much right now, but he says in a few years, he'll leave it to me, retire. I...I could make that place into something maybe. There's a great school there for Andrew, and he'll be away from this...at least for a little while. When my mom gets settled, maybe if she's able to find a place big enough, he'll move back," Owen says.

He'll move back.

I keep my head to the side, my eyes piercing him, my nostrils flaring. Owen can't say anything to take this feeling away, and the longer he stands there, his arms to his sides, his expression just as broken as my heart, the more I want to cry.

"I have a few weeks," he says. "Tonight, let's celebrate you. I don't want to think about the other stuff anymore." He steps to me in small movements, treating me like a deer caught in the sights of his gun. Owen...he's the hunter. And I am dead, my heart broken and time no longer relevant.

294

Chapter 21

We haven't talked about Iowa again. It's coming. I can tell. Owen's mom had a realtor to the house on Monday after school. I walked by them at the table on my way up to Owen's room. Owen and me—we never mentioned it.

On Tuesday they told Andrew their plan. He's about as happy about it as I am. I came over when they were sitting in the living room, after dinner. Andrew walked out in the middle of their talk saying, "I fucking hate Iowa!"

We passed each other through the doorway; Andrew never looked at me.

I understand. I fucking hate Iowa too.

Today, he's packing his room. He's been working on it a little at a time. Owen stayed late at school for a test, still catching up from the days he didn't go. I've been here at his house...waiting for him. I've been stuck to him like glue, not wanting to miss a single second of the time we have left.

"Hey," I say, leaning on Andrew's doorway. He drops a book in a box and puts a lid on top, sliding it into a corner. "Seems like a waste of space. You should probably pack more in that box than just a book." I'm trying to be light, but neither of us is feeling it.

"I shouldn't be packing at all," Andrew says, his mouth twists into a reluctant smile, his shoulders shrugging. I move into his room and sit down on his bed next to him.

"At least you'll have family there. Owen says the school is really good," I say, picking up one of his sweatshirts and folding it over my lap. I don't believe a word that's coming from my mouth.

"You're such a bad liar," Andrew teases, leaning into me. I put my arm around him and lay my head on his shoulder. "I've never even had a girlfriend. I want one of those...here...in Woodstock. I want to get my license, then pick a girl up and take her to the Miller Movie House. I want to go to the Apple Fest with her, and win one of those big, stupid stuffed bears."

"We love those big, stupid stuffed bears," I sigh. Andrew's shoulder rises with a small laugh. "You'll have all that in Iowa too," I say.

"Yeah…" he says through a heavy sigh. "But it won't be here."

"Owen says you'll get to move back; when your mom finds a place," I say. Andrew leaves his eyes on mine, doubt all over his face.

When I hear the door downstairs, I squeeze Andrew once more and step out of his room. Owen meets me at the top of the stairs, his hand finding its comfortable place on my cheek, his lips finding home on mine.

"How'd you do?" I ask about his science test.

"Good, I think. Seemed easy," he says. "Hey, I have to run up to the home. You want to come with me? I know how you love Grampa."

I do love Gus. But more than that, I'm doing *everything* with Owen, up until the very last second. I don't even care if it's a trip to the grocery store for toothpaste—I'm making it.

I nod *yes* and thread my arm through Owen's as we move back down the stairs. I watch Owen as we drive. I've been watching him a lot, watching how he looks at things. He's been living his life, day-to-day, ever since he told me about his family's plans. His eyes never pause or seem sad when he looks out at stuff; every day passes, just as it always did, as if these days aren't coming to an end. The only times he gets sentimental are at night, when we're alone. For a couple of evenings, he sat in his window, on the phone with me, and we listened to each other breathe. But for the last two nights, he's come over around midnight, letting me sneak him upstairs before my mom gets home. I lock my door, not that she ever checks on me anyway, and he holds me while we both lie awake…not talking about Iowa.

Emma remembers me when we enter the home this time, and she nods toward Gus's room, urging me to go on while she and Owen talk.

"He's expecting you," she says as I pass. We exchange smiles, and I think to myself how much she reminds me of my favorite book by the same name.

296

Gus is facing the door, his cane in his hand, ready to help him stand as I enter. I can't help but smile at the sight of him, and I get to him quickly, giving him a hand to his feet. He hugs me as if I'm his own, his hardened hands squeezing my shoulder then wrapping around my back, patting.

"How's the metronome, young lady?" he asks. I feel guilty, because I haven't used it yet. But I will.

"It's keeping time," I say, walking with him toward his door.

"Let's bust out of this joint," he teases, winking at me. His heavy eyebrows dip down then up when he winks, like caterpillars exercising. I wonder if Owen will look like this one day?

I hold Gus's arm as we make our way out to the main room, to a small table with a checkerboard on it. Once he's sitting, I take the other chair. Gus begins to put the pieces in place, his hands shaking a little as he drops the checkers onto their squares with careful precision.

"So, what's this business about the boys and Iowa?" I'm surprised when he asks. I wasn't sure how much Owen had shared with him, or how much he'd remember.

"I guess Iowa is the land of opportunity," I jest, my answer laced with sarcasm.

"Horseshit," Gus says, tapping his finger on the board between us, then moving his first piece. "That uncle of his ain't worth a damn, and neither is his business. Now Billy...I always liked Billy. Owen's dad? But Richard, Owen's uncle? Well, let's just say I have a hard time trusting a fella named *Dick* for short."

Gus keeps his eyes trained on the pieces on our game board. I'm glad, because I'm blushing from his bluntness. I'm also feeling more uneasy about Owen leaving.

"I want him to stay." My honesty surprises me. Gus, he has a way of filling me with comfort, and I have to talk to someone about how I feel. I think he might be my only outlet.

He looks up at me before reaching forward to grab a checker, his heavy brow cocked on one end. "You need to convince him it's safe to stay," he says, letting his hand go from the board. Gus leans back in his chair, folding his hands over his chest. He looks around the room, and when he sees Owen and Emma far away, sitting at her desk, he looks back at me.

"Owen's always craved security," he says. I can't help the way I react, flinching in surprise.

"Owen laughs in the face of danger," I say, my mind easily counting a dozen things I know about Owen that defy the very idea of feeling comfortable.

"I didn't say *safe*. I said *secure*," Gus says, patting his hands once on his belly. "That boy has a nose for danger. He likes thrills. But he also needs to know that when he comes back, after he's done playing stuntman with all of his antics, that there will be something there waiting for him—a *home.*"

"I kind of thought I was his home," I answer, my chest hurting.

"You are," Gus says. "But Owen's used to people leaving. And he's never prepared for it. Billy's death did a number on him. He needs to know he has a place. Right now, he's looking at Iowa, at that numbskull uncle of his, as a security blanket for his future. He'll have somewhere to go, something to do...someone to be."

I'm starting to understand more, and I'm starting to feel more hopeless. I lean forward as Gus does, and I watch him move one of his checkers. He puts it in a place where it's vulnerable, where I have no choice but to jump it and keep it as mine. So I do. He makes the same move again, and I jump again. We play without talking for a few minutes, and I grow a small stack of Gus's checkers, feeling bad that I'm winning, and wondering if I should start making different moves to let him catch up. And then, he moves one more into place, and I see it. He's been baiting me. As I sit back and look at the board, only a few of his red checkers left, the rest of the board covered in my black, I see the trail he's left behind. My mind does the math, and I know instantly there's no way I can win.

"Give him a place," Gus says, picking up one of my pieces and handing it to me before working his way out of the chair to stand. He holds his hand on my shoulder, his eyes penetrating mine, his smirk full of confidence and assurance.

A place.

I think about Gus's words the entire way home, about how nice it feels to know your future, to have a plan before you. I think about the way I felt on that stage, when I quit playing for everyone else—and I played something for me. I found my place that very instant. I don't know where it will take me, what college, if a college at all, where I'll be able to play that kind of music. But I know that I need to be able to do that in life if I want to feel that feeling again, to feel alive.

The thoughts and ideas linger in my head the rest of the day, into the late hours. My mom is home tonight, so Owen stays at his house. We text a few times, and I promise to let him know when my mom heads to bed so he can come over, but by midnight, she's still awake. I hear her on the phone with someone, and she shuffles into the small spare room downstairs for privacy. I think she's talking to my dad. She's been hiding their conversations from me.

Eventually, Owen gives up on our plan, texting me goodnight, looking at me once more through the window before turning out his light. I turn mine out as well, but my conversation with Gus keeps rolling through my head.

There's no way I'm sleeping, so I pull my laptop up from the floor and flip it open. I look at pictures of DePaul. I click through their basketball program until I find the picture of the man I saw with Owen, the one who gave him his card. He's on the coaching staff. Then I type the words: BILL HARPER WOODSTOCK DEATH.

The obituary is the first thing to come up. It's a scan of an old, yellowed clipping from the Woodstock News. I read the list of survivors over and over again—James, Owen, and Andrew. That word...*survivors*...it catches me. Surviving someone—I don't know that there's a better way to describe Owen.

I flip through a few more pages, some of them not the right Bill Harper, some of them stories about the warehouse Bill worked at, condolences from longtime co-workers and friends. I'm about to flip the computer closed when a small photo catches my eye.

Owen's dad is standing in front of a big forklift, his hair hanging heavy over his eyes, his face so much like his son's. But it's the face next to him that stops me. It's familiar, and the name with it can't be a coincidence.

I don't sleep at all, too anxious to get to the next day. I greet Owen in the driveway in the morning, and he's a little surprised to see me up so early. He's leaving with Andrew, his brother's school bag slumped over his back, his body wearing sadness like a suit.

"Don't you get to sleep in later now?" Owen asks. His hair is still wet, and it smells like his shampoo. I kiss him on the lips quickly, breathing the scent in through my nose to remember it, then run back to my own car.

"I do, but I have to do something for English. It's an extra-credit thing, and I have to get it in this morning," I say. I can tell Owen doesn't believe me, but I keep moving forward, waving at him, closing my door, and driving off without glancing back. I know I'll have a good half-hour at school before he shows up. I just need Mr. Chessman to be there, too.

I'm hopeful when the teachers' lot is halfway full, and when the light is spilling out from Mr. Chessman's classroom, I pick up my step into a light jog. I startle him when I stumble through his door.

"Kensi, good morning! To what do I owe the pleasure?" he says. I notice the stack of homework on his desktop, Owen's name scribbled at the top of a few papers. He pushes them into a pile, moving them to the side, trying to get my attention away from them. But it's the only thing my eyes see. I leave my gaze there as I speak.

"How did you know Bill Harper?" I ask.

I take the silence that greets me as confirmation. I move closer to Mr. Chessman's desk, sliding the printout of the picture I found online in front of him. He picks it up, holding it in both hands, his eyes spending long seconds on every detail. It's more than recognition that shadows his face; it's memories.

"How did you find this?" he asks, his eyes still on the black-and-white page. The photo is a bit fuzzy, but the faces are distinct. It's the eyes. I saw *him* in those eyes.

300

"At first I wasn't sure why the guy standing with Bill looked so familiar. I thought maybe it was a relative, or that I was remembering a picture I saw at Owen's house. I'm not sure how you flashed into my head. But I'm glad you did," I say.

Mr. Chessman puts the picture down on his desk, the caption below labeling Bill Harper and Dwayne Chessman. His palms are flat along either side of the paper, and he peers up at me slowly.

"How did you know him?" I ask again. I know it isn't a happy memory. Mr. Chessman's eyes are distant. His breathing is slow, and it takes a few seconds before he resolves himself to answering my question.

"Bill and I worked at the warehouse together. For about a year," he says, leaning back in his chair. He folds his arms in front of him, his eyes moving lower, to the space under his desk. "I had just gotten out of the Navy, and I was back home, trying to put myself through school. I took the job at the warehouse because the hours fit my classes. They paired me up with Billy because he'd been there the longest," he says, his eyes coming up to mine briefly before he stands and begins pacing his classroom.

"Bill trained me on the machines, and I liked working with him so much, they let me stay on his team permanently. His wife, Shannon, would bring him lunch every day, and after a few months on the job, she started bringing a lunch for me, too. I spent a year on Bill's team, and for a year I sat outside on the picnic table, next to him and across from his wife, eating sandwiches and talking about my college classes and learning about their kids. Shannon wanted to go to college too, but they never had enough money."

Mr. Chessman's gaze drifts away again, his eyes fixed outside, to the sidewalk along the street. More students are arriving, and I know my time with him alone is growing short.

"Is that why you help Owen? Because you knew Bill?" I say. He turns to me quickly, his brow pinched. I move to his desk and lift the stack of papers, all Owen's. "His homework. His grades. I know you've been collecting things and turning things in for him when he misses other classes."

Mr. Chessman's mouth slides into a smile as he chuckles, moving over to his desk and taking the stack from my hand, spreading it out between us.

"I don't do anything *for* him. I collect his work, check in with his teachers, sure. But Owen...he always does the work himself. He finds a way, finds time. He's always been that way, ahead of the rest of the class," Mr. Chessman says, a proud and satisfied grin showing as he pushes the papers back together before moving them to a wire basket on his back table.

"Ahead?" I question. Mr. Chessman leans against the table, crossing his legs and folding his arms. He's told me so much, more than he probably should. His quiet worries me, and I start to think I've gotten everything I'm going to from him. It's not enough. I need more; I need to find out if there's enough there for him to help me, for him to convince Owen to stay.

"We don't offer classes here for college credit like they do at some other schools," he says, and my lungs fill with relief that he's still sharing. "But we were able to work with the district and the university board so Owen could test at the end of the year, but stay here for basketball. It's basically the same program his brother's in, without going to that school. Hopefully he'll leave here with six or nine credits under his belt already."

I nod, thinking back to how Owen answered me, how he said math is easy for him. I don't know why he didn't tell me he was trying to earn credit, unless he just believed it would never happen. That thought...it doesn't surprise me. Owen doesn't expect anything good in the end.

"Why do you help him?" I ask, and I leave my eyes on Mr. Chessman's. My look, it's pleading with him, begging him to give me an answer. His expression drops before he turns to look out his window again, his hands wrapped around the corners of his table, his forearms flexing and letting go. Of every teacher at this school, Mr. Chessman was always the one to stand up for Owen. He was Owen's advocate, and I need to know why. "Please..." I say, leaning forward, my hands pressed together.

"Bill had these quirks," he begins, his back to me while he speaks. "His face would sometimes tick, and he'd talk to himself. I asked Shannon about it one day when we were eating alone;

Bill got called back to repair something. She told me he was bipolar, had hallucinations. His medication took care of it most of the time, but sometimes he'd go a few weeks without taking something. Our insurance at the job was crap, and the pills— they were expensive. The hallucinations would get really bad when he'd go a few weeks."

Mr. Chessman turns to look at me again, his face washed in grief, a look I've only seen one other time—on Owen, the day James killed himself.

"They were laying people off at the warehouse," he says, his lips parted, a small breath escaping, his jaw working side-to-side. The anger from the memory he's sharing is still fresh for him after all theses years. His eyes snap to mine. "It was between Billy and me, and I was a couple years younger...a couple years *cheaper.* So he got the pink slip, sent home early."

Mr. Chessman sucks his top lip in, his eyes squarely on mine as they grow with redness. His jaw muscles are working, still trying to understand the rest. His head slowly starts to nod, and my breath shakes when the rest of the story becomes apparent to me, too.

Bill Harper came home early—fired from a job that didn't pay enough to begin with, his brain already confused from his illness, his pockets too empty to afford the medicine he needs.

And then he took his son to a festival...and stepped away from life.

We sit there in silence, and the sounds of students milling outside grows louder, feet scuffling along the sidewalks just beyond the door, lockers slamming against the nearby walls. I entered this room twenty minutes ago, proof in my hands that there was more to Owen's story, hope in my heart that Mr. Chessman was the key—that he would help me find Owen's *place.* Yet all I feel now is crushed, hopeless and heartsick.

"He's going to leave," I say, my eyes looking to the few minutes I have left, my mind able to draw enough gumption to search for a miracle. "Owen's moving to Iowa, and he's going to turn down an offer from DePaul. He's going to quit school, go work in some print shop with his uncle, so he can send money to his mom to help pay for his grandpa. Mr. Chessman...please. I need your help. He needs to see that none of these things are because of him, that he isn't cursed. He needs to stay."

"Kensi, I don't have a lot of money. Not the kind *they* need. If I did, believe me, I'd find a way to give it to that family," he says.

The door opens behind me, and the sound of students filing in drowns what's left of my hope. I stand my ground, not leaving the desk I'm in and leaving my eyes on Mr. Chessman's for as long as I can, until a girl asks me to get out of her seat. I look at him when I stand, and we continue a silent conversation until I back up to the door—my eyes begging him to find a way, his telling me there isn't one.

Chapter 22

The way the sky looks outside—bleak and gray, like a giant blanket over the sun—that's how I feel inside.

Two days go by. Two more days that Owen and I don't talk about Iowa. Two more nights that I sneak Owen into my house at night, that I cling to his arm, forcing myself to keep my eyes open so I can look at his skin, smell him—know he's here.

Mr. Chessman never says anything to me, but there are glances. I stare at him during English class, daring him to break away before me. I always win. There is no prize, though.

The FOR SALE sign shows up while I'm at school, and when I get home, it's standing there in Owen's lawn, the red-and-blue stripe, the bold white letters—a wake-up call that we can't live in pretend much longer. Reality is going to smack us both in the face. Owen sits in his truck, staring at it when I pull into my driveway. I kill the engine and walk over, sliding into the passenger side and into his open arm.

"Well, that sort of makes shit real, doesn't it?" Owen says. I chuckle against him.

"Yep," I say, my eyes on the same letters as his.

This is when I should beg. I could ask him to stay, tell him that we'll come up with a plan, find a way for his family to make money, to pay for his grandfather, to keep Andrew safe. But each time I breathe deep, daring myself to speak, to say something that will make a difference—I can't think of anything at all. Truth of the matter is I can't promise Andrew will be safe, or that Owen's mom will be able to earn enough on her own, without Owen working too.

I think I'm giving up. And it makes me sick to my stomach.

Owen and I sit together, his hand running slowly up and down my arm, our eyes trained out his window, for almost half an hour. Neither of us speaks. And when the cars pull up behind us, we don't notice until there's a loud rap on the passenger window behind me. We both jump, and when my mind realizes who I'm looking at, that sick feeling in my stomach starts to get replaced with something else.

Hope.

"What's Mr. Chessman doing here?" Owen says, moving his arm from around me and opening his door. "What's up?" I hear him ask as I sit in the cab, waiting a few seconds to climb out and join them. Just as I'm pushing my door open, I realize Mr. Chessman isn't alone.

"Owen, I think you've met Mr. Mathison. He's from DePaul?" I hear Mr. Chessman say. My lungs open wider.

"I have," Owen says, shaking the man's hand, just as he did the last time they met, after Owen's game.

"Good to see you, Owen. Sorry for this impromptu visit, but I was hoping maybe we could chat. Just for a few minutes. Your mom home?" Mathison asks. He's carrying the same briefcase he was when we saw him at the game, and I kind of think he's wearing the same DePaul shirt and jacket, too. Owen nods to him and leads him and Mr. Chessman inside.

"I haven't been inside yet, but I think she's here," Owen says, glancing toward his mother's car in the driveway.

I smile at Mr. Chessman as they turn to walk up Owen's driveway. He raises a brow in return, just a small symbol that he's feeling as anxious as I am, that he has the same sliver of hope. I follow them inside, making myself part of whatever conversation is about to occur. I should probably give them privacy, but I'm too invested in the outcome.

Owen's mom is walking from the kitchen, a dishtowel drying her hands, as we walk in, and when she realizes Owen and I aren't alone, her footing stumbles. "Oh, I'm sorry. I...I didn't know we were going to have company. Dwayne...hello..." she says, her face flushed as she looks around the house, a few boxes scattered. "I'm sorry, the place is a bit...out of sorts. We're...we're moving."

She steps nervously over to Mr. Chessman, her hands wringing the towel repeatedly before she stretches a hand out to his. At the same time, he reaches for a hug, and she opens her arms quickly, just as he puts his down, offering a hand instead. "Oh, uh...sorry..." he laughs lightly. There's a quiet between them, it lasts a few seconds, and no one really notices. But I notice. They finally hug, and I watch carefully, Mr. Chessman's hand sliding with a tender touch around Owen's mother's back, his eyes closing when they embrace.

He loves her. I see it.

I stick to Owen's side, our fingers linked under the table as we all gather around. Mr. Mathison pulls his briefcase to the table, flipping the gold latches open quickly, pulling out a thick envelope and sliding it over to Owen. He has a few envelopes in there—at quick glance, I count six.

"Full ride. DePaul. And we won't redshirt you. You might not start...at first. But, I think you'll be a pivotal part of the rotation within the first season. By your sophomore year, you'll be the reason people show up to watch the game," Mr. Mathison says.

Owen's eyes are forward on the envelope, and his mother's mouth is open wide. "I heard you're thinking of going to Iowa," Mr. Mathison continues, and my heartbeat picks up, my eyes looking to Mr. Chessman's. He won't look back at me; he's working too hard to stay in character. "Iowa, they won't treat you right. You'll redshirt, and you won't succeed on their court. They don't play your kind of game. We do."

Holy shit, he thinks Owen's going to college in Iowa. My mouth hurts from the pressure of not laughing. I know if I let it slip, I wouldn't be able to stop. It would be that maniacal kind of laugh, the type filled with nerves and wheezing hiccups and such. And I think it would start a chain—one that moves to Mr. Chessman next, and then Owen. Shannon is looking at everyone around the table, her eyes in shock, not following anything that's happening, but knowing enough to realize that she should play along with this charade as well.

"I've got one more meeting, tomorrow morning. It's in Elgin, and I'll swing back by your school on my way out. I'd love to shake your hand and make it official, but you look these papers over, let me know what you think," he says. As Mathison leaves, he shakes everyone's hands, and Mr. Chessman walks him back outside, both of their cars parked in the road behind Owen's truck.

"What was that all about?" Owen's mom finally says, her voice coming out wavering, a sort of whisper, nervous laughter blending with her words. "That man is offering to give you a scholarship? So you can play basketball? Honey…"

"He's not the only one making offers," Mr. Chessman says, closing the front door behind him, holding his hands together and rubbing them as if to say *jackpot*. He's grinning widely, his feet practically skipping as he joins us at the table. "Can you believe he bought the Iowa thing though?"

We all look at him when he says it.

"Look, I never lied. Someone had to call him to report your grades, send in transcripts. I volunteered, and all I said was that I thought he should know Owen was thinking of going to Iowa. Not a lie," he smirks. I slap his shoulder, then apologize quickly, realizing he's my teacher and I've just punched him in the arm.

"Why did you do that?" Owen asks. His eyes are still on the envelope, and he doesn't seem to be sharing the same thrill of opportunity the rest of us are. "Did you put him up to this?" Owen turns to me, and suddenly I can't breathe.

"O…" I start, not sure how I'm going to defend myself, but desperate for the right words, the ones that will make him understand, and say *yes* to this chance.

"It wasn't her. *I* did this. The school knows you're moving, and I merely asked Kensi if everything was all right. She was honest and said she was worried about you. That's all," Mr. Chessman says. The way he covers for me, the ease with which he spins the story—he's practiced this, thought through everything. He cares…he cares about Owen, and he cares about Owen's mom. His eyes never stay on her long, but they search her out every other minute. A constant system of checks and balances to make sure she's there, in her chair, listening, engaged, happy, safe.

Owen sighs heavily, leaning back in his chair, his hands holding the edge of the table, his thumbs pinning the envelope down. He slides his palms flat toward it, then he picks it up and unfolds the top. He tilts it sideways, sliding out brochures and booklets and a letter, signed by Lon Mathison and another name.

"Owen, if this man is offering you a chance to go to college…you have to take it," his mother says, sliding one of the brochures closer, her fingers running over the glossy photos. There's a certain sense of longing in the way she looks at them.

His head shaking, Owen drops the letter from his hands, then leans forward, rubbing his hands over his eyes before pulling them down over his mouth. He looks to me next, his face every bit of lost and unsure. His eyes stay on mine; they're asking me a question. He's torn by duty. And he doesn't know what to do. His mom and Mr. Chessman are exchanging brochures, each pointing out things for the other to look at—both excited about this opportunity. All Owen sees is how he'll be abandoning his mom, his family, when they need him most.

"How are we going to afford Grampa? You know how much money I'm going to make in Iowa, Mom. That paycheck—it's guaranteed. And it will *save* us. What happens with Andrew? Are you going to send him down to Iowa alone? Or does he stay here, where he has to live under Dad's shadow? And I'm sorry I'm bringing it up, Mom, but you know it's there. Iowa is a chance for him to get away from all those things that—" Owen stops suddenly, swallowing as his eyes close.

"Those things that you think killed James," she finishes for him. Owen's mother's voice is soft, her heart broken for both the son she lost and the one who feels responsible for his death. "You can't spend your life protecting Andrew, Owen. And you deserve things too. Good things. And we'll find a way to make it work."

"I don't know," Owen says, pulling his hat from his head, laying it on the table over the documents that are now overwhelming him, his hands rubbing his head. "I don't know, I don't know, I don't..." His voice dissipates, until it's nothing.

Owen stands and stares at me, then turns to his mom. He reaches forward again, grabbing the letter, carrying it with him as he leaves the room. He pauses at the bottom of the stairs, looking at us all. "Let me think about it, okay? And I will...I promise, tonight."

I stand from the table, too, walking over to Owen, his body leaning heavily on the banister. He looks like he's been in a fight rather than just had a major university drop a pot of gold on his table. I don't know why I thought this would be so easy. I was so sure Mr. Chessman would find a way to tip the scales away from Iowa. What I hadn't counted on was Owen's sense of duty.

"Hey...this..." I say, tapping my finger on the edge of the paper in his hand, "is a good thing. I know you have to think about it, but options...they're always good, right?"

It sounds pathetic. My reasoning, it's flawed. It's hard to see something you want as attainable when so many things need you on the other side.

"It's good," Owen says, his lip pulling up enough to press a small dimple in his cheek. He holds it there as he gazes at me, his eyes holding mine while Mr. Chessman comes over to where we're standing.

"Owen, I know you need to think this over, but it's really a once-in-a-lifetime chance. There's always a way," he says, his hand moving to pat Owen once on the back.

Owen's mom joins us then she walks Mr. Chessman to the door, their farewell exchange just as awkward and brief as their greeting.

"I have to get home. My mom hasn't seen me yet," I say, the voice in my head asking him what he's thinking, what his plans are and begging for an answer—the answer I want. Inside my head—there's a lot of begging.

Owen tips my chin up, kissing my lips lightly at first, then moves his hands to my head, pulling me closer and moving his kiss above my brow. I love when he does this, the sweetness of it all, the affection in every touch. I love it, and I'll miss it if he leaves. He *has* to stay.

I wait while he steps backward a few times, moving up to his room, and I turn after he does and leave his house to enter mine. My mom is sitting in the middle of the floor, right next to my piano, with rolls of holiday paper around her and stacks of framed pictures on my piano.

"Hi, honey," she says, her fingers holding small strips of tape, and a curled ribbon dangling from her teeth.

While I kick away my shoes and dump my coat on the floor, I watch her tape down the edges of bright red paper then tie her ribbon around one of the wrapped pictures, holding it up to show me when she's done.

310

"That's...awesome. You're wrapping crap we already own," I say, sliding closer to her in my socks, peering over her to the various large paintings and décor still waiting to be wrapped, I presume.

"My mom used to do this, every Thanksgiving. She'd wrap the things hanging in our house like presents, and then we'd have Christmas joy around us all season long," she says, turning her first package to face her. She straightens the ribbon then proudly sets the picture down to the side once she's satisfied with it.

"Yeah...that's not weird at all," I say, counting at least sixteen more things she needs to wrap.

"There's some mail for you in the kitchen," she says as she begins cutting and measuring paper for the next package.

I head to the kitchen and grab a Diet Coke from the fridge before turning to the island counter and sifting through the stack of papers and envelopes, discarding the various advertisements and coupons I know we'll never use. Caught in between two of the bigger mailers is a heavy envelope, with no address. I look over my shoulder, and my mom's still in manic-wrapping mode, a nearly empty glass of wine next to her on the floor, so I pull the papers from inside.

The top of the packet is labeled with an embossed masthead for Walt, Kendall, and Katz law firm, and just below that I catch the word *divorce.* I read on quickly, taking in enough to realize what I'm looking at, then I step into the wrapping fray, dropping the packet in front of my mom—right on top of the package she's taping.

She sighs when it lands in front of her, but instead of speaking right away, she reaches for her drink, taking a long sip until she's tipping the glass upside down.

"I'm sorry, Kens. I didn't mean for you to see that," she says, moving it to the side and continuing to tape gold paper on top of green.

I drop to the floor, sitting next to her, and pick the packet back up, flipping it between my hands a few times, waiting for her to give me more. She pretends I'm invisible.

"Does this mean..." I wait for her to finish my statement for me, but she only nods her head toward the tape, a silent request

311

for me to help with this insane craft project. I rip two pieces off and push them onto the paper where she asks. She turns it over to face me when she's done. It's my baby portrait, wrapped and bowed. I don't know how to respond to seeing it, so I just lift my brow high and smile.

"Well, I like it. I think they look pretty. And your father never let me do campy holiday décor. He said it was junky," she says, moving right along to the next picture in the pile, this one a larger framed painting. "And yes, *this,*" she says, nodding to the packet from the law firm, "means I am filing for divorce."

Wow. I wasn't expecting this, and I'm so overcome with pride for my mom that I rush her, leaping on her lap and tearing the paper she's cutting. I kiss her cheek as I hug her, and she laughs with me, but only for a second or two, her focus quickly going back to her task—her eyes never staying on mine for long. "I'm not quite to celebrating status yet. I'm still sort of in acceptance...if that's okay," she says, curling ribbon.

"Acceptance is good," I say, pulling on one of the curly cues on her completed present, letting it spring back into place. "What made you change your mind...if...that's okay to ask?"

There's a harsh ripping sound as she presses with the scissors firmly, her hand striking against the ribbon grain with more force, each pass growing a little rougher until she finally snares one of the ribbons against the blade, ripping it from the cluster. She sets the scissors down, untangling her legs as she stands, her gait wobbly as she makes her way back to the kitchen, reaching for a half-empty wine bottle. When she comes back to the living room, she pauses before sitting back in her spot, her lips forming a tight line, her smile like the Mona Lisa— only there if you look for it.

"I was cleaning out old boxes a couple days ago from your room, the empties from the move. I thought I found one under your bed, and when I dragged it into view, I saw it had a *pretty* expensive-looking dress in it," she says. I wince knowing what she saw, and I'm angry at myself for being so careless with it and not hiding it better or simply throwing it in the trash like I had planned.

"Curious, I opened the letter that was tucked inside the box," she says, her eyes on mine, her smirk somehow growing more wicked. "She wrote you a lovely letter, full of naïve apologies and half-baked excuses. She explained how broken she was over losing him, how he was re-promising himself to me, and how she let him...ha ha! She *let* him go, because she knew that's what was right. You needed to have a father at home, she said. And that's the statement that made me stop. You need a father? Kens, I look at you and have no idea how you've come out as normal as you have. And when I read that, it hit me...you don't need *that* father. And I don't need that man."

Well, damn. I don't think I've ever been more proud of my mother, and all I want to do is celebrate with her. But she's put a ban on celebrating, so instead, I sit with her on the floor and wrap three more pictures from the collection from our walls, not prying any more, and only taking in the extra information she offers.

"And I hope you didn't want that dress," she says finally, mid-tape.

"Why?" I ask, holding the paper flat for her to fasten.

"Because I threw that damn thing, and her letter, in the fire," she says, her teeth tearing at the ribbon in her mouth, her eyes intent on the project at hand. I smile, and I let it beam, because she's not looking.

"Did you get the rest of your mail?" she asks, clearly done on the subject of my father.

"Oh, no. I'll grab it before I head upstairs. I need to call Owen. He might not be moving after all," I say, my mom smiling softly and glancing my direction, but her thoughts still clearly rooted in her own drama. I look forward to the day this chapter is done, because it would be nice to have my mom guide me through some of this.

I sweep the rest of the pile of mail into my arms and race up the stairs, positioning myself in front of the window. Owen's waiting on the other side; I can see the top of his hat, his back resting against the window's wall. I drop the mail in my lap in front of me and reach for my phone to text him, but before I dial I catch a glimpse of one letter—the address on it familiar, the seal exactly as it always appeared in my dreams.

The envelope is thin, and I'm not sure how to take that, so I slide my finger along the edge, tearing one end carefully, pulling the typed letter from the University of Chicago out and unfolding it slowly.

The first sentence stops my breath.

We are pleased to inform you that you have been selected...

I drop it instantly, exchanging it for my phone, dialing Owen, who picks up in the middle of my first ring.

"Hey," he says, turning to face me, the sight of his eyes on mine like coming home.

"Hey, you're never going to guess what I just opened," I say, waiting for him to actually guess. He starts to laugh after a few long seconds.

"I really have no idea how to answer that...a bank account. You opened a bank account," he says, scratching his head.

I hold the letter up, waggling it.

"I can't read that," he teases.

"I got in," I say, and there's silence for a few seconds until it settles in and he realizes what I mean.

"You're kidding," he says, a small laugh growing into a more powerful one. "Holy shit! You got in...doing it your way! Wow, that's...Kens, that's amazing. I'm so proud of you."

"I'm proud of you too, you know," I say, my compliment greeted quickly by silence on the other end. Owen is struggling, and I'm daft for thinking he's ready to make a decision on this so quickly. Like my mom, he's not in celebration mode either—I just hope he's moving toward acceptance.

"What are you going to do?" Owen asks, focusing on his happiness for me.

"I don't know. I was kind of done with the idea of going there, ya know? But then I got this envelope, and it feels real, and now..." I say, looking back to my lap, to the stamp from the school I've dreamed of for so long.

"You should go, Kens. It's what your heart wants," Owen says.

I slide down against the window, letting my head rest along my hand so I can look at him. Maybe once that is what my heart wanted, but now, all it craves is the boy looking back at me.

We don't talk about my letter any more, and we don't talk at all for long. But we never hang up, keeping our phones next to us until our eyes can no longer stay open, so we can listen to each other dream.

Chapter 23

I must have heard him. There must have been some sound, something familiar that stirred my mind just enough to force it to remember that I had something to do in the morning. That's the only explanation for the feeling that sinks my heart into oblivion the very moment my eyes open.

I don't remember leaving my room. I don't remember how I traveled down the stairs. And I don't recall how freezing the air was outside when it blasted its way inside my lungs. All I remember is my heart, how it ripped in half the second I saw the small piece of paper tucked in my car window, Owen's truck...gone.

Even now, two hours later, it's like reading it for the very first time.

I had to leave this way. If I didn't, I would never do the right thing. I will love you...for always.
~ Owen

My eyes are raw from crying, and my mom has given up on trying to help. We've been sitting here in the kitchen, sipping strong coffee and sniffling into tissues from the moment I woke her up with my heavy sobs. I couldn't make it back to my room, collapsing on the door when I stepped back inside the house.

The sun wasn't up yet, the clock reading only four in the morning. And I just knew. What I keep playing over and over in my mind is how close I was to stopping him. He only could have been gone for minutes.

I want to stay home from school, but I also want to talk to Mr. Chessman. I need clues, and I need him to stall Mr. Mathison. I've dialed Owen's number at least sixty times, every single time my call going right to voicemail. I've only left a handful of messages, each time my words come out broken, my sentences only halves.

When it's time for school to begin, I drag my bag along the driveway with me, my eyes on the ground most of the way until I reach my car door. Andrew is standing in his driveway, a heavy coat pulled around his body, his backpack by his feet.

"He's coming back, Kens. He has to," Andrew says, rubbing his hands together and blowing into them for warmth. Andrew's been crying; Owen must not have said goodbye to him either. I wonder if he got a note, too.

"Come on. I'll give you a ride," I say. He tosses his bag in my back seat and slides into my passenger side. Seeing him there hurts. It hurts because he looks like his brother, dresses like him…smells like him. But he *isn't* him.

I take Andrew to his school, then drive the few miles back to my own, pulling in next to Willow's car. I can't bear the thought of seeing my friends right now, talking to Will, so I hide low in my seat until the morning bell rings, then make my way from my car to Mr. Chessman's classroom. He has a class, but when he see's me peering through the small window slit in his door, he excuses himself and meets me in the hall.

He knows the moment he sees my face.

"He's gone," I say, my lip shaking just saying the words. "I can't get him to pick up his phone. He's going to miss that meeting. I…I don't know what to do."

Mr. Chessman pushes his hands into his pockets, looking down at his feet. He kicks at a crack in the hallway floor, his shoe scuffing against the roughness a few times before he nods his head and purses his lips. When he brings his eyes back up to mine, he's resolved in the fact that Owen isn't coming. I wait for him to slip back into his classroom before retreating to the girls' bathroom.

Instead of the one near the band room, I climb the stairs to one on the third floor, where I'm more confident I'll be alone. Once inside, I pull my feet up, hiding them from view while I sit in the stall. I bring my phone to my lap and type a few more texts—I type them because he'll see them, and maybe if I say it enough, he'll come home.

I love you.
I love you.
I love you.

I look at my history and count. I've sent the same message to Owen seventy-four times.

When the bell rings, I wait for everyone to rush by, holding my breath when a few students enter then leave my small restroom. When the bell rings again, I exit my hiding place, opening the band door and putting on my game face just long enough to fool Mr. Brody.

"Sorry, I was sick to my stomach. I feel better now," I say as I pass his office quickly. He nods and holds up a hand before going back to his computer. I continue down the hallway to my practice room, my hands reaching for the surface of the piano and my face collapsing against my arms, the tears coming out in another rush against the raw skin around my eyes.

I give in, and I let myself cry hard for a solid five minutes, and then I cut it off, rubbing my nose along my sleeve, forcing myself to breathe in long, steady inhales and exhales. This is the same way I deal with anxiety over getting shots, and the longer I control my breathing, the funnier the comparison seems to me, and eventually I'm laughing to myself.

With my head slung forward, my fingers travel lightly along the keys, walking a finger at a time and somehow finding all of the sharps and flats. I'm setting the sad notes free.

"It's probably good you didn't audition with that."

My stomach drops the moment the sound of Owen's voice hits my ears. Everything in me falls apart in an instant, the tears running down my cheeks and my body losing strength as I turn and reach for him, clinging around his waist until he's sitting next to me, holding me in his arms, his lips kissing the top of my head.

"I couldn't go. I couldn't do it. I'll find a way to make it work. For my mom, and Gramps. I'll find a way, get a job here," he hums in my ear. "I couldn't go."

I pull away just enough to look at him, and his smile is tight, his eyes on mine, his hand stroking the skin just under my eyes.

"These are puffy," he says, bending down and pressing his lips to my tender skin. "I'm so sorry, Kens. I did that. I was trying to do what was right, but I don't know."

318

My lips form a sloppy grin and my body shakes with happy tears, and every time I shudder, Owen holds me tighter.

"I made it all the way to the border. Do you know how far the border is? I kept trying to make the hard choice, thinking I had to. But all I wanted to choose was you. And then it hit me," he says, his hands finding my shoulders. He turns to the side, forcing me to face him, my legs lying across his, my fingers gripping the fabric of his shirt, wrapping it tightly within my hands, not wanting him to disappear. "I was running scared, Kens. I've never run scared in my life, even when I should. But I did. I was afraid I would fail, that I would be selfish, and then it would cost those I love."

He leans forward, his forehead on mine, his hands finding mine, which have now become fists stuffed with his shirt. He chuckles when he pries them loose, bringing them into his lap, holding them tightly.

"Losing you, the thought that I could love you and lose you too—that scared me—so I figured what was the point if it was all going to just end up hurting me in the end. And then I realized how much it hurt to give you up," he says, stopping to watch the reaction in my eyes. I suck my bottom lip into my mouth, taking quick shallow breaths through my nose, telling my brain, my body—my heart—that this moment is real. "And those texts...you kept sending those texts," he laughs. "What were there, like...sixty?"

He pulls his phone out and holds it in front of me, his hand on my neck as he leans forward and presses his lips to mine, his smile against my mouth warming my chest, numbing the pain and healing the brokenness.

"I got a ticket. Two hundred and eighty dollars, you believe that shit?" he says, pulling a folded, pink paper from his other pocket, a court appearance date stapled to the top. "I drove so fast. I didn't even see the cop on the side of the road. And I picked right back up after he wrote me this, because I had to get back here...back to you!"

The relief continues to wash over me, every minute a wave crashing and pulling away more of the fear and worry and pain that consumed me when I woke this morning. Owen and I stay here, me in his arms, for the entire period, ignoring the bell when it sounds, and passing on the next one too.

A few students come and go from the band room, the lunch hour now, and some people open the door to our tiny haven, hoping to squeeze in some practice. Everyone leaves us alone, though. They don't know our story, or understand how long it took for us to get here, but they let us have our moment anyway. No comments because it's Owen Harper, no questions over my tears, and no lame jokes about needing to get a room. Our affection is chaste, more of a never-ending embrace, and our love for each other the realest damn thing I've ever known.

We stay here, hidden from Owen's past, for as long as we can, finally slipping back into the masses as the lunch hour ends. Owen walks with me to our algebra class, passing Mr. Chessman's classroom along the way, and he sees us. His chest fills slowly with air, and his hand rubs at his neck as I pause at the doorway to our next class, holding my hands together in front of me, praying a *thank you* to him. He closes his eyes, and I know he's saying it back.

Owen's feet slide into their rightful place, his heavy shoes leaving chunks of dirt and debris next to my leg on my seat. When he threatens to pull his foot away, I cling to it, and he laughs.

"All right. I'll leave it," he says.

After the first few minutes of class, the door opens and one of the student aids passes a note to our teacher, both of them looking to Owen. I'm not surprised when they call him to the office. I look at him as he stands, tugging quickly on his arm before he leaves.

"What are you going to tell him?" I ask, knowing Mr. Mathison is waiting for his answer, wanting Owen's commitment just as much as I do. Owen doesn't answer me, but he bites his lip and lets his smile slide up one side of his mouth, winking as he backs away, turning to take the slip from our teacher then make his way out the door.

He's gone for the rest of the class period, and I waver between believing this time is a good sign and a bad one. I practically race from the classroom when the bell rings, and my

320

eyes begin searching for him as soon as I step into the hallway. He pulls me back against him, his body leaning along the wall just outside the door.

I turn into him, and his hands find their place along my face quickly, his lips on mine within seconds, his mouth consuming me until his smile forces itself to break free. I love the way his smile feels against me.

"Well, does this mean you're going? Did you commit? Everything's...good?" I ask, pressing myself closer to him, students bumping into me as they leave the class and hurry through the halls.

"Everything's...*very* good," Owen says. His eyes look up to the ceiling as his grin takes over again, the smile somehow growing bigger than him. He looks back at me, his tongue caught between his teeth, something important waiting to spill from his lips. He's staying. Owen is staying, and he's going to DePaul and life is going to be amazing. It's in his face. I know it—just looking in his eyes.

"How do you feel about orange?" he asks finally, and the only reaction I have is a firm shake of my head, my eyes closing with confusion. But my heart—it still feels happy.

"Orange. Orange is good...I guess," I say, my eyes on him with playful suspicion.

"I've got an idea to run by you," he says, his hand sliding down my arm until he finds my fingers, threading his with mine and tugging me toward the door. "We should go home to discuss."

My legs follow willingly. But my heart follows first. It can't help itself. Owen—he *owns* it. I gave it to him.

And I will follow him anywhere.

Chapter 24

One Year Later

"Leave her drum alone," Willow says, slapping Jess's hand away from the harness and snare drum on my floor at the end of my bed.

My roommate this year has been very tolerant. I knew the second I was accepted to the University of Illinois's jazz program that I would also join the marching band. Turns out, though, that playing the snare drum is harder than it looks. I've had to practice, and my roommate Shay invested in some seriously awesome headphones to block out my constant noise. I think she was excited to meet Willow, mostly because she knows I'll be rooming with her instead next year.

Jess pulls my drum over his head and raps out a quick rhythm. Seconds later, Shay stuffs her books into her backpack leaving us for the library.

"Bye. Nice meeting you!" Willow yells over the loud sounds popping off of the drumhead in front of Jess. As soon as the door closes, she grabs the sticks from Jess's hands and passes them to me. "You ran her off; what's wrong with you?"

Jess shrugs, pulling the harness back over his head and resting it on the floor. "Some chicks don't dig drummers. Not my problem," he says, jumping backward to lie on my bed. Willow tosses his feet to the side when he does.

"You're getting shit all over her bed," she says, rolling her eyes.

"Great to know you two are still getting along so well," I joke, straddling my chair and sitting as Willow moves to sit next to Jess. She pulls her legs up and sticks her tongue out at him. He reacts, grabbing her quickly and pulling her on top of him, tickling her until eventually they're kissing. "Wow. That's my bed you're on," I say, standing and closing the clasps on the sleeves of my uniform.

"I can't believe you're marching. I can't wait to see this," Willow says, beaming with pride, as if she is responsible for me being able to walk and pound a plastic surface at the same time. Actually, that took practice too, but thankfully the instructor and I get along really well. Both of us play the piano and love jazz, which has made him more tolerant of the two left feet I seem to walk on.

My phone buzzes in my pocket, and I pull it out to read a text from Owen.

I'm at the stairs.

"He's here," I say, picking up my drum and ushering my friends out the door. I lock up just in time to see Owen step through the stairwell door and walk toward my room. College has been good to him. I swear he's an inch taller, if that's possible, and his face and body—all of him—more of a man than he was a year before.

More than the physical, though, is the peace that seems to have come to him. It didn't happen all at once, and there were times when I thought this idea—this plan he concocted during a two-hour drive from the Iowa-Illinois state border back to Woodstock—was going to explode and ruin us both forever. But Owen stuck with it. Something changed during that drive, an idea found its way into his head, and it invaded his heart, and he wasn't going to let it go.

I was happy with the thought of him going to DePaul. I would have been happy in the city, studying with Chen. Not *my* music, but music still. And I would have seen Owen, our schools only an hour or so away from each other.

But Owen had a flash during that drive, his mind catching on something Mr. Chessman said the day before. DePaul—it wasn't the only school interested. Owen's always been bold. The only thing that intimidated him was the idea of forgiving himself for not being able to save his father and James. Calling his coach at seven in the morning, asking for names, schools, the list of people who have asked to see his highlight tapes and stats—that was easy. And when his coach mentioned that the University of Illinois had been calling a lot lately, that was all he needed to hear.

He stopped at a diner in Rockford, made a few calls, and mentioned to a certain scout that he was getting some serious offers from DePaul. Then he looked up the University's music program, more specifically the jazz division, and saved it. Thirty minutes—and one speeding ticket—later, he found me.

"I still think the uniform's sexy," he says, making the few final steps to me, pulling both ends of my bright orange jacket into him until I'm fully in his arms. He kisses my neck and tries to work my jacket from my body, but I push him away.

"So, I'm late for warm-ups, and Jess and Will are here," I say, tilting my head toward the end of the hall where my friends both raise a hand to say hello. Owen pulls his hat low on his head, feigning he's embarrassed at being caught. I know he's not— Owen still loves to kiss in public.

He leans forward and whispers in my ear, "Okay, but we're ditching them after the game, just for a little while."

"Bright orange jacket just does it for you, huh?" I joke, spinning in my obnoxiously florescent uniform. He stops me mid-spin, wrapping his arms around me and pulling my back into his chest.

"You do it for me," he says, his words always perfect.

We walk to the game, and I join the band while Owen guides Will and Jess over to the student section. He sits with the other guys on the basketball team, and they usually get shown on TV once or twice. I mentioned this to Willow, and I noticed she was wearing a lot more makeup tonight than she normally does.

We've performed for six home games, and every time, the thrill of being out here, of being a part of something like this, gets to me. I think I fell in love with this school the moment I stepped through the tunnel with Will and Jess—and Owen remembered. His season started a few weeks ago. I volunteered to play in the rally band for basketball games too, just so I could watch him. Last week, the crowd started chanting *Harper*. Owen says he didn't hear it, but I know he did. I know because I saw it in his smile—the cocky smirk I fell in love with a year ago.

Much like in high school, our football team is only average, and Owen texts me that Willow and Jess are bored by the third quarter. They only wanted to stay for the band's half-time performance anyhow. Willow's never really been in it for the sports. I text Owen back and tell him to leave with them and head to the pub. I'll meet up with them after. I want to change and clean up anyhow.

The game lasts another hour, and Owen sends me a few texts of pictures of Willow and Jess dancing. Owen snuck them in, like he usually does with me, and I can tell he's also helped them get beer, Willow's craziness amplifying a little more in every picture he sends. By the time I finally get to the bar, my friends are cuddling in a booth looking at stunt videos on YouTube that they for some reason find hilariously funny.

"I left you in charge of them for like, what? An hour?" I say, sliding up behind Owen, my hands moving around his sides over his stomach and up his chest.

"That better be Kensi feelin' me up, otherwise my girlfriend's going to kick your ass," he jokes, pulling me around to face him, his trademark dark jeans and long-sleeved black shirt calling for me to touch him. I move in close, resting my cheek on his chest, his heart beating underneath. I put on his favorite outfit, too—a red shirtdress with black leggings and a pair of brown leather boots. Even now, a year later, I still want to be the only girl he notices.

"Come on," he says, his hand sliding down my arm until his fingers find mine, his eyes drawing a line down my body. He walks toward the dance floor, a small wood-planked square crowded with pretty girls and guys on the prowl, and pulls me into the very middle, holding me against his body. He cups my face, stretching me up to my toes, and dusts his lips over mine, speaking against my mouth. "I want to dance with you," he says, his hands reaching into my hair as he kisses me harder, with enough heat to draw a few whistles from the couples standing next to us. He can feel me blush and start to pull away to hide, so his hands only get firmer, his mouth curving into a smile against mine.

"Don't you go run and hide. They're just whistling at a guy kissing the prettiest girl in the room, wear that crown proudly, princess," he says, his hands growing more bold, sliding over my hips, his thumbs flirting with the waist of my leggings, reminding my body of how quickly he can own me completely.

"I thought you didn't dance," I say, my face tilted up to look at him, his eyes peering down on me, both of us hiding under the shadow of his hat.

"Mmmmm," he hums, pulling me close to him, his chin resting on my head. "This isn't really dancing. It's more like foreplay."

Oh.

"Hey, have you heard from your mom? Did your grandpa get moved in yet?" I ask, and Owen's body slumps in reaction.

"I say foreplay, and you ask about my grandpa," Owen chuckles.

"Well, you always knew he'd steal me away from you. It's kind of your fault when you think about it—you put us together," I laugh. Owen shakes his head, then kisses the top of mine as he holds me against his chest.

"Grampa's good. I still can't believe your mom got him into that program near her hospital. Really, that was amazing of her," he says, everything about his body so different from the stress and worry that always lived inside of him before. My mom started working on Gus's case the day his mom sold their house. The Harpers moved into an apartment down the road until school let out, and by the time Owen graduated and the money had run out to pay for his grandfather's current home, my mom had worked him into the program for veteran's through her hospital downtown. Emma agreed to let Gus stay for a fraction of the cost until my mom could finalize his move.

"My mom has good connections, and I think she's finally getting used to the fact that she can make demands for things, and people will listen. Besides, I think she's a little smitten for Gus, too," I say.

Owen squints at me, his lips pursed.

"I'm not sure I'm comfortable with all this obsession with my hot grandpa," he says, unable to contain his smile, a laugh breaking through and ruining his character. I nestle back into his embrace.

"My mom has a date," he says, his chin once again resting on my head, his thumbs caressing small circles along the small of my back.

326

"Oh yeah?" I say, having a hard time seeing Owen's mom do anything other than work. In the year I lived next to her, I think I saw her ten times, her eyes always heavy, her body always thin and fatigued.

"You'll never guess who with," he says, his tone all I need to know. I can't help but grin against his chest. I told Owen about what I had learned, about how Mr. Chessman knew his family. I wanted him to know how much he loved working with his father, and how much he respected them all. He needed to know that there were people out there that saw past the wild—people who saw the good. I didn't mention my suspicions about how Mr. Chessman felt, the way I saw him look at Owen's mom. But I think that will all work itself out without me.

"You're kidding?" I say, stepping back and looking up at him again. I love how he towers over me.

"Not kidding. I just feel really bad for Andrew. His teacher is dating his mom, I mean...wow, right?" Owen says, his chest raspy with laughter.

"He's only his teacher part of the time," I say, as if that somehow makes it better.

"Yeah, *okay*," he says, brushing his thumb over my cheek, his eyes doing that thing where they zero in on me and me alone, the rest of the world fading away. We've quit swaying an entire song ago, the pretense of dancing long gone. We're standing in the middle of the crowded dance floor holding each other, and looking at each other wanting more. I can tell by the way Owen's breathing, by the way everything about him, about us, slows. Owen draws his finger down my chin to my neck, looping it under the small key charm resting at the bottom of my necklace between my breasts. He pulls the key up to his mouth, biting it in his teeth, his brow lowering and his lips curling.

"You think those two will notice if we ditch them, head back to my room?" Owen finally says, my body reacting as it always does.

"Willow has a key; I think they'll be fine," I say, glancing over at my friends, who are settled even lower in their booth, content to stay there until the sun rises I'm sure. My response is enough for him, and he sweeps his arm around me, tucking me against his side, guiding me through the crowd of football fans still pouring into the bar.

We walk the few blocks to his dorm, the same chill in the air that was there the first night I kissed him, the night he gave me the bracelet I still wear every day. I love it when he sees me in it, and I love how he kisses my wrist, like he is right now, as he slips it from my skin.

I love how he watches me, how he watches *over* me, fights for me, and makes me a better version of myself.

I love him.

Truth is, Owen Harper shot me through the heart that day he pointed his finger at me and pulled the trigger. I fell for him then, and I've been falling every day since. All I wanted was for him to catch me.

And he did.

THE END

Acknowledgements

This book. This book!

It was something that grabbed a hold of me, out of nowhere, and wouldn't let me go until I finished. It had me, from the very beginning, and, while a mother shouldn't choose her favorites, for me, this is it. This one; it's my favorite. If I didn't own up to it being my favorite, I would be cheating it. I love this book and am unbelievably proud of it, and I cannot thank you enough for the time you've given it.

This book scratches the surface of some extremely heavy topics—suicide, addiction and the struggles of living with mental illness. I want you to know that these topics, they matter to me. I put a lot of care in how I handled them, and above all, I wanted to be honest in the portrait I painted. And to those of you who work in a field that supports those suffering, I commend you with the absolute highest honor. You are angels—remarkable humans.

This is my seventh novel. That number astonishes me, and now I'm eager to watch it grow. I would not be here if it weren't for the amazing readers out there who support me and champion me to continue, who lend their time and give me the ultimate gift—reading my stories. I thank you, from the depths of my heart.

I also must thank my amazing support team, starting with my husband and son, who only think it's slightly weird that I carry my laptop around to baseball practice and make manic plot point notes on my phone in the middle of the Target electronics section. Thank you also to the amazing *Wild Reckless* beta readers: Jennifer, Shelley, Ashley, Debbie and Brigitte. You field my crazy questions when I'm not sure about something, and you push me when I'm afraid to go somewhere I really should— THANK YOU for making me take Owen to such challenging places. He wouldn't be the man he is if I hadn't, and you helped me accept that.

They say your words are only as good as your editors—Tina Scott and Billi Joy Carson, you are the A-Team of editors, so I always feel prepared going into battle. Also, Wordsmith Publicity—a million thanks for helping stretch the spotlight, encouraging it to shine on my stories whenever you can. Your team is mighty, and my thanks to you enormous.

While this book is my favorite work, I'm also quite in love with its cover, and I owe much of that to the talents of photographer Annabel Williams and models Jessica Slemmons and Jamie Connell. Thank you for helping bring Kensi and Owen to life.

If you enjoyed this book, please consider leaving a review. Your reviews are often the only way small stories like this can be seen, and I for one know the power readers have. I'm so grateful for every post, mention, recommendation, book club, Tweet, pin and more that readers have given to my books. I hope to give you lots to talk about in the future.

Books By Ginger Scott

The Falling Series
This Is Falling
You and Everything After
(Coming Soon - 2015) The Girl I Was Before

The Waiting Series
Waiting on the Sidelines
Going Long

Standalones

Blindness
How We Deal With Gravity
Wild Reckless

About Ginger Scott

Ginger Scott is an Amazon-bestselling author of seven young and new adult romances, including *Waiting on the Sidelines, Going Long, Blindness, How We Deal With Gravity, This Is Falling, You and Everything After* and *Wild Reckless.*

A sucker for a good romance, Ginger's other passion is sports, and she often blends the two in her stories. (She's also a sucker for a hot quarterback, catcher, pitcher, point guard...the list goes on.) Ginger has been writing and editing for newspapers, magazines and blogs for more than 15 years. She has told the stories of Olympians, politicians, actors, scientists, cowboys, criminals and towns. For more on her and her work, visit her website at http://www.littlemisswrite.com.

When she's not writing, the odds are high that she's somewhere near a baseball diamond, either watching her son field pop flies like Bryce Harper or cheering on her favorite baseball team, the Arizona Diamondbacks. Ginger lives in Arizona and is married to her college sweetheart whom she met at ASU (fork 'em, Devils).

Ginger Scott Online

www.littlemisswrite.com
www.facebook.com/GingerScottAuthor
Twitter @TheGingerScott

Made in the USA
Columbia, SC
30 October 2018